I0817904

The Rhise of Truth

Book Three of the Darkness Overcome Series

By Max B. Sternberg

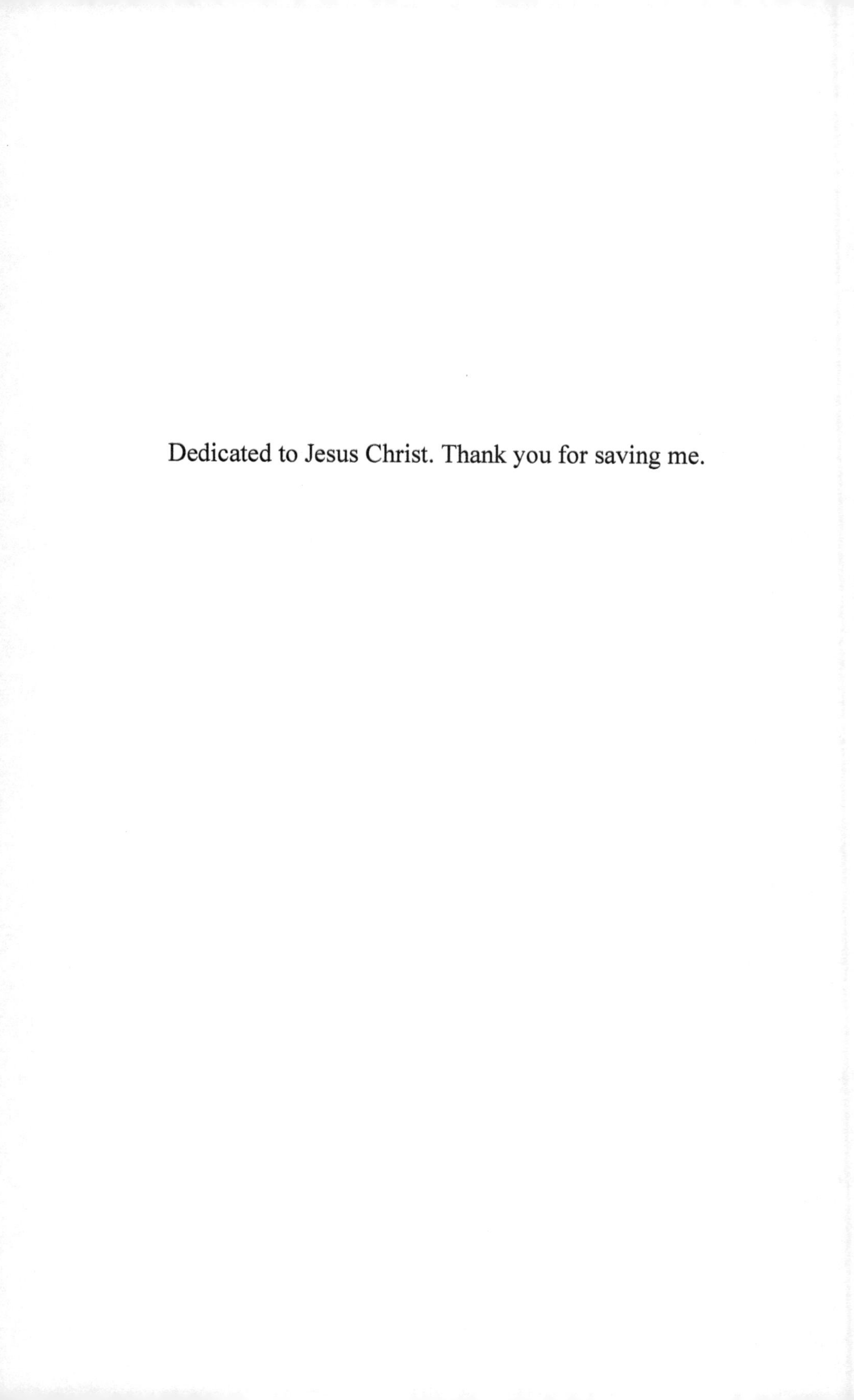

Dedicated to Jesus Christ. Thank you for saving me.

E-book ISBN: 978-1-7369989-6-0
Paperback ISBN: 978-1-7369989-7-7
Hardcover ISBN: 978-1-7369989-8-4

Front Cover Design by Laura Hollingsworth
Map created using Inkarnate

You can find more about the Darkness Overcome series and the author at:
www.maxbsternberg.com
https://www.facebook.com/maxbsternberg

Map of the Kingdom

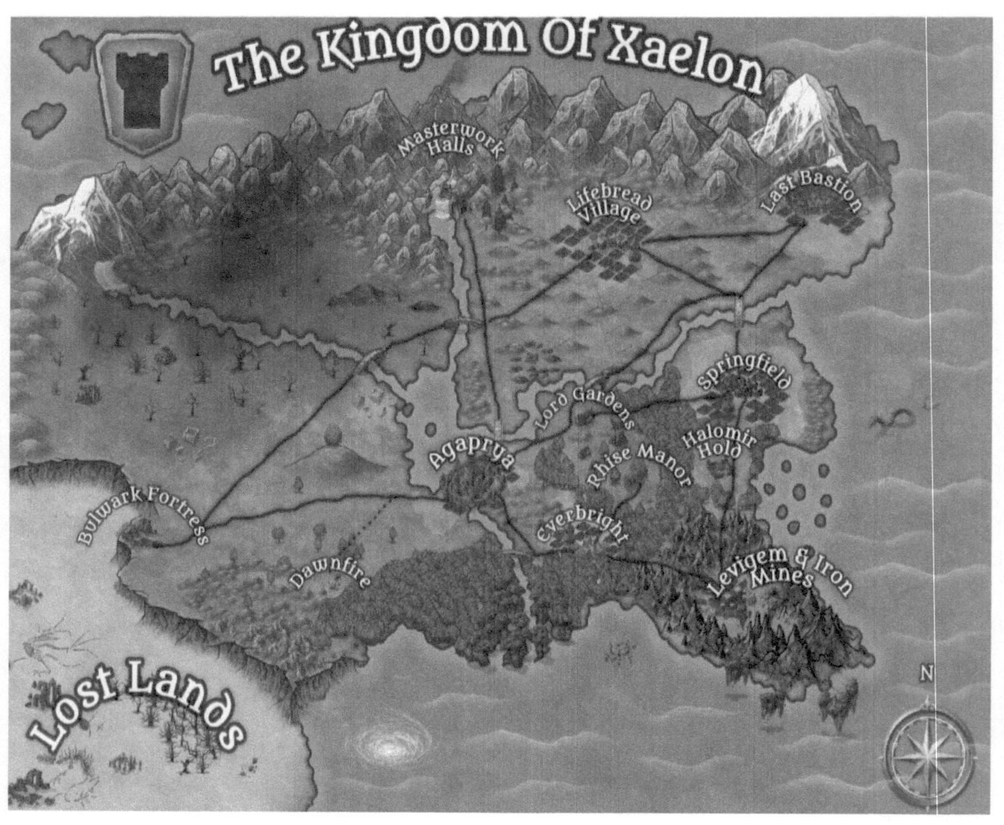

Table of Contents

Contents

Part One: The Overwhelmed

He reveals the deep things of darkness and brings utter darkness into the light.
- Job 12:22 NIV

Prologue: The Delve

Twenty years ago...

"What do you have to lose?" Lucien asked, excited by the prospect of discovery.

"Me position on tha council. Me reputation. Our lives, if something be down there." Phonz Jasperfoot responded. A hooded lantern swung from his hand as he crossed his arms. The dwarf would have appeared imposing to Lucien had he stood at the same height. Phonz's shorter frame was filled with corded muscle that had been shaped from years spent mining and honing his craft. A well-worn pick hung from his side, ready for use. The consequences would be dire if they were caught, but Lucien thought the risk was well worth it should they succeed.

Lucien patted an old gladius that was slung at his side. It was one of the heirlooms left to him by his father, Liam. The simple double-edged weapon had cut down many undead in its day. After all, Liam Rhise had been an exceptional general for Xaelon's army before he built his mining empire. Lucien's own experience with the blade was quite different though. He recalled the feeling of the flat of the blade as it landed against his backside as a youth.

His father had been a staunch disciplinarian all throughout his childhood. While the discipline had been effective, it had also created quite a distaste for the old gladius. Yet, from the multitudes of both functional and ceremonial weapons that hung at Rhise manor, Lucien chose to carry his late father's sword most often. The respect his father earned had now passed to himself, along with the hated sword. "If anything is down there, I have this, and you have your pickaxe. Besides, this was your idea. You said you sensed iron down there with tha–"

"Oi! Keep yer voice down!" Phonz hissed, as he looked around. Nobody was nearby, as they had already slipped through a roped-off area, and slunk up to the base of one of the strange, monolithic stone towers that stood within the Halls. It had been a relatively easy feat due to the lack of guards on duty in the late hours of the night. No other dwarves wandered close to the structures; exploration within them was forbidden due to the belief that they were haunted. Since the dwarven occupation of the Halls had begun, they found numerous traps that the giants who once inhabited the towers had left behind. Traps that Lucien believed led to their centuries long superstition.

The boarded-up doorway of the tower reached higher than Lucien's head, and was certainly much taller than any of the dwarves. Phonz deftly pried a few of the boards free with his pick, and squeezed through the opening. He shone his lantern down an interior corridor. Lucien stealthily followed behind, and they both crept down the long dusty hallway. The sound of their steps echoed softly against the stone floor. They each emitted a small gasp when they reached the tower's inner chamber and saw all its grandeur. Phonz opened the shuttered slats of his lantern, and the room became fully illuminated. Long shadows were cast from the enormous oversized furniture as the light filtered through the cobwebs and dust that hung in the air.

"Well?" Lucien asked, "Feel anything?"

Phonz lifted his free hand, and the ring he wore reflected in the light. Lucien was still skeptical of its power, and found himself doubting Phonz's claim of what it could do. *Still, how much easier would it be for the Rhise family if we had the Diviner ring at our disposal?* He thought.

Phonz's arm dropped sharply down to his side, and Lucien noticed that the dwarf's arm muscles were straining. After a moment Phonz's arm relaxed, and he looked up at Lucien. "Below. There's definitely iron below."

Lucien grunted and walked to the edge of the circular room. The light from the lantern followed him as Phonz stayed close behind. A giant-sized stairway, that led into the unknown depths below, was revealed in the lantern's light. They clambered down the enormous curving steps until they reached another landing in the subterranean tower. With every step taken, the excitement of their foray further masked the internal pain that Lucien felt.

He knew that his journey here had just been an excuse to get away from home. To get some space from Erika and the newborn baby, Leon. Luckily the childbirth had gone well, with no ill effects on mother or child. Their other children had been impacted by the new arrival as well. Liara was just starting to toddle around the manor and was curious about Leon. Laric, however, was clearly not enthused by his brother's arrival. With the knowledge that Erika and their household would be okay for a week, Lucien leapt at the opportunity to meet with his counterparts in the mining business.

His excuse to leave had been a flimsy one, he knew. Truthfully, Lucien had a hard time with everything that was happening at home. The loud noises. The constant short-temperedness. At a mere five years old, Laric seemed to have developed a predisposition for back-talking – which Lucien was beyond fed up with. Yet, Lucien refused to be like his father. Refused to go down the ugly road of abuse.

Lucien shook himself from his ruminations, and followed Phonz down a wide and tall corridor of enormous and irregularly interlocked stones. Their footsteps continued to echo in the passage, and soon they came to two boarded-up doors that stood on either side of the hallway. Phonz held his hand with the ring out and pointed further down the hall. A sudden pounding noise came from their right causing them to both jump.

"Is somebody else down here?" Lucien asked in a whisper, as he drew his deceased father's blade. He hoped that whomever, or whatever, it was, was not also an undead.

Phonz whispered loudly back, "How should I know ya daft–"

The pounding noise sounded again, this time accompanied by a muffled voice.

They crept close to the boarded-up doorway nearest them, which held the source of the noise. The muffled voice grew just loud enough for Lucien to make out someone asking for help! Thinking fast, Lucien hacked at the wooden barrier into the room as Phonz hissed, "Wot are ya doing? We don't know who that is, an' we ain't supposed ta be here!"

"It sounds like someone in trouble! If nothing else, it could be a dwarf in need!" Lucien reasoned.

After reducing the dry old wood to kindling, Lucien stepped through with his sword in hand. The room's interior was spacious, and had a ceiling that sloped downward, making it triangular in shape. Phonz grumbled as he entered with his pick held in one hand and lantern in the other. The shadows in the room peeled away to reveal strange writing all over the walls. Spiderweb-like symbols were splayed in irregular patterns that oddly retained the shadows as the lantern light passed over them. The light also fell upon the center of the room where Lucien and Phonz saw a thin stone slab that sat atop a stone coffin. It cracked and split as the thumping from inside of it continued, until a fist slammed upward through the rock.

Phonz yelled and ran toward the emerging figure, causing the lantern to swing in his grip as he crossed the short distance. The dwarf brought his pickaxe back to strike when a movement flashed so quickly that Lucien couldn't register what it had been. A yelp sounded from the dwarf as the lantern flew to one side of the room. As it landed, its slats clapped over it, leaving them in total darkness.

Few sounds could be heard through Lucien's panicked gasps. He held his sword out defensively in the black nothingness as he heard the clink of metal and swoosh of fabric sound against the stone floor. A grunt was emitted from a timbre that did not belong to Phonz. He heard the rustle of movement and of hands smoothing over cloth. Lucien swiped his sword a couple times in the darkness, hoping to hit whatever had escaped from the coffin. His blade met no resistance, merely slicing through the stale air. As Lucien edged back, he stumbled and hit the floor hard. Pain, which he tried to ignore, lanced through him as he continued to focus on pointing his sword towards the room.

"Hmm. Interesting."

The masculine voice was monotonous, as if the individual held no actual interest in what he commented on. The unknown voice sounded as though it came from across the room. A sliver of light escaped from the shuttered lantern that lay on the floor, helping Lucien's eyes begin to adjust to the darkness. The light fell across a tall shadow, and Lucien stuttered, "Ph-Phonz?"

"The dwarf is unconscious, but otherwise fine. Tell me, what is a human doing in the Halls? Times must have changed."

Confusion rampaged through Lucien's mind as he asked, "You're… not a dwarf?"

The laughter that came from the individual was hollow, almost bored sounding. "I would be offended if I were not thankful for you. Your pain, your desire for… revenge… it seems. It woke me. It was quite loud, you see."

Lucien's fear grew to a lump that lodged in his throat, making it hard to speak. "My pain? Revenge?" Recent memories plagued him. Ones centered around those he had thought loyal to him. Friends. Family. His father, Liam. A storm of infractions and betrayals of trust, which justified his rage and pain.

The figure sighed from across the room in what sounded like satisfaction. Thoughts raced through Lucien's mind as he tried to think logically and remain in the present, "What– what are you? Some sort of lich? Reading my thoughts like a page in a book?"

"My eyes are not red or glowing, what does that tell you?" The voice responded, now tinged with the barest hint of amusement.

Lucien strained to see through the darkness. The shadowy figure stayed in its place across the room, and while Lucien appreciated this entity's desire to talk, he had no patience for riddles in the dark. A brashness overcame his fear as he retorted, "It tells me nothing. Only that you are amused by my lack of knowledge about you. What are you? Who are you?"

The tiny light in the room illuminated the figure as it bent over to pick up the lantern. It hovered over the unconscious form of Phonz for a moment, and Lucien could swear he saw a shadow seep into his dwarven friend. The individual stood upright as he lifted the lantern and opened a slat to reveal himself.

He was normal. Slightly tall for a human, but he bore no red eyes or rotting skin. Indeed his skin was pale, probably due to being locked down here for who knew how long. He was thin but otherwise looked healthy. The man wore an outfit of dark thick leather, which matched his long dark hair that was pulled into a ponytail. A thin, wide smile adorned his face as he strolled up to Lucien with his palms upward to show he held no weapon.

I am so confused. Lucien thought, his sword dropping slightly.

"I mean you and your kin no harm. In fact, I thank you for waking me. I am merely a man trying to make my way in the world. As are you Mister…"

In an effort to overcome the fear that had risen again, or at least try to regain control of the situation, Lucien accepted the man's proffered hand and allowed himself to be hoisted to his feet. *He's thin, but his grip is strong.*

"Lucien. Lucien Rhise."

"A pleasure to meet you, my good friend." The man shook Lucien's hand which he still gripped. The gesture was firm, and almost reminded Lucien of a shake that sealed a business deal. The man's broad smile grew even wider as his monotonous voice continued.

"My name… is Silas Anakim."

Chapter 1: The Flight

Twenty years later...

"Duamé, I am about to leave without you!" Leon yelled at his friend.

"It's jus' one more barrel o' java!" The dwarf reasoned, as he hustled up the gangplank with a large container that sloshed over his shoulder.

Everyone else who was traveling with them had already boarded. After so many defenders from Masterwork Halls volunteered, lots had been drawn to see who would be permitted to join on the maiden voyage of the first dwarven airship, *Esperella*. Over a hundred people would journey with Leon to defeat Xhormas' horde, and they crammed every weapon, scrap of armor, and crumb of food on board that they could.

Thus, Duamé had to shoulder past Gezado when he reached the top deck. Duamé stood almost to the troll's waist. The dreadlocked dwarf ducked under the former troll leader's four arms as he made his way past and below decks. Gezado was busy bellowing to his newly crowned wife and leader Thur in trollish. She, along with many other well-wishers, would remain behind. To Leon their foreign dialect caused everything to sound as though they were hurling insults at each other, but such was the speech of the entyrnet trolls.

Those on board of the *Esperella* were a mix of the finest warriors that the dwarves and elves had to spare, as well as several mancers and shapers from both races. Racial peculiarities ensured that the dwarven race only produced geomancers while elves produced hortimancers. The mental toll of manipulating earth and plants was intense on those who could do it. Still, many of them volunteered to join the hardy crew of the *Esperella.* After all, the wand-like turrets that Gionna designed to stand along the top deck railing required a mancer's touch to work.

Thoughts of mancer powers caused Leon to look around at those who bustled about in an effort to secure crates and equipment to the top deck, until he found the one person he was looking for. Miala's eyes locked on Leon's, and she graced him with a faint smile. She nodded to him in acknowledgment of his presence, which caused Leon's pulse to quicken. At the peak of the battle for Masterwork Halls, both had confessed their love for one another when they feared they were about to die. Whether the feeling had been brought about due to their shared experiences, being the only two humans around in their recent past, or because the entyrnet trolls and dwarves already thought they were married, remained to be seen.

Kelleren woofed by her side and bounded around in his excitement at their anticipated airship ride. Leon's heart continued to thud in his chest as he gazed at her fair features.

"Oi! Loverboy! I thought it was time fer us ta leave!" Duamé hollered, as he returned above deck. Leon's face grew red, and he had no way to hide it as his helm was buried underneath the rubble near the former gates of Masterwork Halls.

"Aye, captain. It's time." Kérik Silverspine affirmed as he grasped *Esperella*'s wheel. The older dwarf nodded solemnly to Verne who stood at the top of the gangplank. "Granitehands! Try not ta let tha Halls fall apart any more while we're gone."

"Yer jokin' right? With ya gone, I can finally get some improvements done!" Verne chortled. "Jus' come back when yer done."

"We will all care for the Halls. This is our temporary home now, after all." Queen Chlorae chimed in, as she adjusted her dress which was made of thick, interwoven vines. The matronly queen of the elves had initially insisted on accompanying her daughter on the airship, but Princess Schalae pointed out that one of the two of them needed to remain behind in case of the worst. After much discussion, the queen relented.

Leon looked around at his companions who had chosen to follow him into war. The survivors of the battle of Masterwork Halls brought whatever they could onto the ship in preparation for the coming clash. Dwarves were armed to the teeth. Elves had multiple quivers full of arrows. Each of the inaugural crew of the ship knew their chances of survival against the apocalyptic undead horde were unlikely. Even so, they intended to bring the fury of retribution with every crossbow bolt, arrow, cannonball, and projectile that they could launch against Xhormas' forces. With the horde numbering in the several tens of thousands it would take all their efforts, and all of the munitions on the *Esperella,* for them to see this through.

That and Adonai. His power had been heavily displayed when he blew the fallen dragon Nachash Seraph apart. The lightning bolt also scored a prominent Judge's mark onto the aft side of the airship. It was the same symbol that adorned Leon's armor and spear, and it symbolized hope for those who needed it. The symbol made it clear that Adonai was with them, no matter how bleak their situation. It also reminded everyone that the fallen god, Xhormas, and his undead horde, could never overcome Adonai's infinite power.

Yet, in the back of Leon's mind, though he wanted to charge in to save Agaprya and defeat the undead horde, his thoughts repetitively strayed to his family. For twenty years, almost as long as he had been alive, Leon's father Lucien had kept company with someone that could very well be aligned with the enemy. So many of his private questions had been answered when Phonz Jasperfoot described his family's long-time Senechal. However, even with so many of his questions answered, more questions continued to sprout in their place.

How did Silas end up here at the Halls?

Has he been in cahoots with my former father the whole time?

Are my mother and sister safe? For that matter, is Laric?

Can I save them?

Adonai, please help me save them!

After letting out a sigh, Leon refocused. First, he would attack the undead army. Lives were at risk. The last living kingdom in the world hung in the balance. *What were a few lives in comparison to that?*

Leon stepped over to the ship's wheel, where Kérik and Gionna stood together, ready to take off. He smiled at them as he clambered up and stood on the assemblage of pipes near the wheel. Gionna said they were intended to make shouting messages throughout the entire ship easier. Right now, he needed to send a message to everyone assembled.

From this vantage point, he could see those on the top deck more clearly. There were a few mancers, the numerous crew members who would attend to the twenty deadly cannons below decks, and a sea of people who stood nearby to see the *Esperella* and her crew off. Verne, Phonz, Jaq, Thur, and Qas all stood at the foot of the ship, and shushed the crowd. Leon felt everyone's eyes as they looked to him, the Judge of Xaelon. The captain of the first airship to be crafted within Masterwork Halls.

After thinking of what to say, Leon's voice echoed throughout the large cavern. "All of us are fighting in this war whether we want to or not. This ship, this crew, we go to fight for our very survival."

"But survival is not the goal. Our goal is nothing less than the destruction of the undead! So we can rebuild. So we can be safe. So we can do more than just scrape by and survive! We go to fight so that we can not just live, but be fully alive! So that we can thrive!"

"Adonai is with us, so we cannot fail! He routed the horde from the Halls. He destroyed the serpent Nachash Seraph! With Adonai on our side, whom shall we fear? So we go with expectation! Knowing the battle is already won! Because in the end, nothing can stand against Him!" Leon shouted as he thrust Revelator into the air.

All who were assembled enthusiastically cheered in agreement, and the shell of aeonyte that encased the *Esperella* glowed brightly in response. The mysterious metal which adorned Leon's spear, his new shield, and the airship tangibly reacted to faith. Whether it shone a faint light or turned undead and evil creatures to salt or ash, aeonyte had certainly proven to be a unique metal.

Leon stepped from the speaking pipe assembly, turned to his pilot Kérik, and issued his first order, "Let's head out."

"Right!" The elder dwarf responded, his voice brimming with excitement as his grey mane of hair trembled. He snapped a pair of goggles over his eyes and stepped up to the ship's wheel. A red control levigem adorned its center. It was similar to the one attached to the glove of Leon's shield hand. Gionna stood nearby and rubbed her hands together while she cackled.

"Now dearie, the ship has four levigems… So it might be a little sensitive." She cautioned Kérik.

“We haven't even taken off yet an' yer already tellin' me how ta drive!” Kérik complained, as he grasped the wheel. “Everyone strap in!” He yelled.

Those aboard the airship reached for the leather harnesses they wore and clapped them to the nearest metal eyelet hoops, which were spread along the ship. This was followed by almost everyone on board, except the elves, stumbling when the *Esperella* shot straight up towards the cavern ceiling. Cries of alarm echoed throughout the area as the *Esperella* stopped a hairsbreadth short of being skewered by stalactites.

“Don't say it.” Leon overheard Kérik mutter.

“Say what, dearie? I told you so? Or that you’re lucky you didn't break my ship?” Gionna replied without humor.

“Why’d we bring her along anyhow?” Kérik complained to Leon.

“Because she wanted to see her design in action, and I didn't want her to blow me up if I said no.” Leon replied, as he eyed the gnomish inventor with a wary gaze.

The ship slowly glided down to hover in front of the entrance as Kérik leveled off the wheel. Gionna emphasized each word with a tap of her metallic cane against the wooden deck. “Gently. On. The. Steering. Dearie.”

“Do ya jus’ want ta drive this thing?” Kérik quipped.

“I can’t see over the wheel, puffball! Though I can explain to you how to not kill us all before we even–”

“An’ we're off!” Kérik Silverspine interrupted, as he pushed the wheel forward.

The *Esperella* shot through the cavern opening and waterfall. Leon felt the press of their acceleration against his body as the curtain of water at the cavern entrance was pierced by the enormous aeonyte fist that had become the figurehead of the vessel after the battle at Masterwork Halls. Leon found the brief immersion in the waterfall’s deluge refreshing, as the first metal airship rapidly flew south towards the undead horde. They were ready to join the fight.

The wind whipped over Leon and the others as the *Esperella* sliced through the air. The vessel, which had been built to defy the undead horde, was headed to fulfill its purpose.

To end the Dead Wars.

✦✦✦✦✦

That night, Leon took a shift at the helm while Kérik slept. The fast-moving airship was indeed sensitive to the touch. The naval wheel had a small control levigem, which Gionna had tuned into the larger levigems that skewered the vessel's sides. She explained the process to him before she went off to bed.

"It requires a physical application of the control gem to each tip of the levigems. You simply contact one to the other, and that is it. The larger gravitational levigem movement will mirror the movement of the smaller control gem, along with the runic inscriptions on the control mechanism that the wheel is attached to."

Leon grew confused, "But how did someone put runes on the *Esperella*?"

"One of my late husbands was a runemancer, remember? Taught me a thing or two." She replied sleepily, before her cane steadied her walk down below decks. Most of the others had already headed to the hammocks below decks, to rest up before the next day. Leon was left with only a few crew members above decks. Some manned the mancer and crossbow turrets, keeping a watchful eye, while a few elven scouts kept keen eyes on the night sky.

Leon's thoughts again turned to his family, and his 'former' father. While they rushed to defeat the undead, to end the Dead Wars once and for all, Lucien Rhise plotted his own moves. Leon suppressed the slight urge to shout in frustration at the mental reminder that his older brother, Laric, was about to marry princess Giselle and ascend the throne. Anyone could see how obvious Lucien's plays for power were. Yet, with the exception of the dwarven race, he held the respect and support of most at court.

Thoughts of his estranged father made Leon involuntarily arch and stretch his back. Under his armor, which had been made by Duamé and his friend's recently deceased father Ignys, lay a nasty scar across his lower back. A scar from a wound that would have, and should have, killed him. The healing power of Adonai and Revelator were the reason he still drew breath. The elven princess, Schalae, and Miala had used the spear and its light to heal him. Still, the assassin sent by Lucien was a stark reminder that while the undead needed to be dealt with, another threat still remained. One that would soon control the Kingdom of Xaelon.

What drives a man to try to kill his own son? Leon asked himself as he flew the airship.

Why does he feel that I am such a danger to him?

For that matter, why didn't he just kill me when he kicked me out of the manor?

Too many questions plagued Leon's mind. Questions about his family, about Revelator, about Silas, the war, and how it all tied together.

Maybe Rohiel and Lochemetel will provide some answers. If they're not too busy being cryptic with their responses.

Uneventful hours passed, and Kérik came to take his promised early morning shift along with fresh scouts. Leon thanked them with tired handshakes and clambered down below decks. Regularly interspaced glowing crystals lined the top edges of the interior. They illuminated the cannons, the armaments stacked near them, as well as two ballistae in the bow of the ship. A few of the crew who hadn't fit in the sleeping area of the deck below had settled themselves on this level.

As he made his way to the bottom deck of the *Esperella*, Leon was greeted by snores from dwarves in gently rocking hammocks. While the elven royalty, Gionna, Miala, and other females occupied the two rooms near the ship's bow, the menfolk had good enough sense to take the hammocks. All rested as much as they could during what could be their last night alive. Leon walked through the ranks of slumbering warriors, and found an unoccupied space next to the loudly snoring Duamé. Leon smiled as he noticed that his dwarven friend cradled a well-crafted doll in his sleep. A reminder of his daughter.

Leon quietly set his spear and shield down next to the hanging fabric of the hammock before he clambered in. A heaviness in his heart matched the weight of his eyelids as he shut them to rest. A whispered mumble escaped Leon's lips as he drifted to sleep, "If you are both there, we need to talk." Moments later, sleep overtook him.

Like the times before, a flat grey horizon awaited Leon. Warmth and light bathed him from the incandescently bright sphere that shone from high above. With a sigh of satisfaction, Leon got straight to business.

"I need to learn." He announced to the vast emptiness.

"Adonai's people are destroyed for a lack of knowledge." Came the echoing reply.

Leon turned and found Rohiel standing behind him. The angel's head was radiant as the sun, causing Leon to cast his eyes down to the advisor's aeonyte and gold-trimmed armor. The peace he felt within the expanse was countered by the unease he felt due to his questions. The need for answers drove Leon to pointedly question Rohiel.

"Lochemetel once told me that she was keeping things from me. That it was to make sure I didn't make the wrong choices. Were those secrets about Silas and my father? Is that what you kept from me?"

When the angel remained silent, Leon became further angered. Indignation arose within him about the whole blasted journey he had been on over the past two months. Over all of the nightmarish scenarios that he had gone through. With his family. With his friends. The injustice of it all roiled inside of him like a storm.

"Did you know?" He yelled.

A heavy sigh echoed within the featureless expanse before Rohiel responded, ***"Yes."***

Before Leon could ask anything further, the armored arm of Rohiel rose and conjured a change in the landscape around them. Leon felt a loss of balance as he stepped into the recent past.

A picture of himself in the branches of a tree formed. Tear tracks were evident on his face. This was the first night after Leon had been cast from Rhise manor. His first night cradling the spear in his arms as he slept. This was the night he had been told he could be a Judge.

"You've shown me this once before." Leon spoke through gritted teeth.

"You have eyes, but do not see." Rohiel responded, as Leon felt an itching sensation begin in his eyes. After he rubbed them and opened them again, he gasped in surprise.

Flitting around his sobbing form in the tree were dozens of Mazzikin. Their dark leathery wings carried them in tight concentric circles around him. Occasionally, one or more would hover close to his ears and whisper in them before rejoining the pack of dark creatures. That night Leon had contemplated dark things. Thoughts about ending his own life on the blade of the spear he held. Thoughts about ending all of his pain. He had been brought to the brink by the enemy.

"But what does that have to do with Silas? With my father?" Leon asked with vitriol. He was tired of being kept in the dark.

"The Mazzikin were under directions. Orders from a superior."

Connections bridged in Leon's mind as he applied what he knew about the unseen spiritual realm with those who opposed him. "Silas?"

"Indeed." Rohiel replied. ***"If you had moved against him earlier, if you attempted to go back to the manor before now, you would have been killed. You would have failed, and all that you could have accomplished would be brought to ruin."***

The finality of the angel's words allowed no room for rebuttal. It was a statement of fact, as accurate as if Rohiel said that levigems float. Leon took a moment to calm the storm of emotions that raged through him. When he was ready, he asked, "And now?"

A wave of light pulsed from above and washed away the scene of that fateful night. It dissolved and returned them both to the grey expanse. The light wave also passed through Leon and brought a calmness as Rohiel spoke.

"Now, you are armed with friends who love you. Truth that guides you. Faith that shines brighter than the stars."

The angel stepped close and clapped Leon's shoulders with his gauntleted hands.

"Now, Leon, fulfill your purpose, and bring judgement."

Chapter 2: The Reinforcements

A day later…

"We're comin' up on Agaprya shortly! Everybody get up an' ready!" Kérik Silverspine's voice broadcasted through an opening in a metal pipe near Leon.

His eyes snapped open as warriors all around him burst from their hammocks. Dwarves donned their chainmail and exceptionally crafted armor. Then they filed up the stairs, where their footsteps clomped on the wooden decking. Elves secured their bows, quivers, and swords over their black bark armor. Leon knew from prior battle experience that theirs was an incredibly dense armor that could turn blades away and absorb impact very well.

Leon buckled on his own armor, and after picking up and securing his shield, he secured Revelator to his back. He clambered up the stairs alongside the other warriors and stood in a hastily moving line. Amidst the preparation, Duamé poured and handed out cups of java for people to gulp down as they passed. The energizing liquid was a welcome addition on this trip, as Leon felt himself perk up.

"Thanks Duamé." He said.

"We're gonna need a whole lot more o' it before we're done!" His friend replied, sipping from his own cup.

The cannon crews took their positions alongside Gionna. She ensured that the dwarf in charge of them knew his job. Based on the way his head nodded vigorously at her instructions, he appeared to be intimidated by the genius gnome, and rightly so. After she had finished speaking with him, she looked Leon up and down and exclaimed, "What are you staring at me for, dearie? You need to get up there!"

Leon obligingly walked onto the top deck and saw more dwarves and elves taking their assigned positions. Mancers were stationed at their turrets.

Dwarves at their crossbows. A contingent of elves stood with their comrades at the ship's center, ready to let their arrows loose. Finally, Gezado stood at the very bow of the vessel, armed with his axes. All had their leather harnesses strapped in, and all were ready for war.

Leon walked over to stand near Kérik at the wheel of the ship, where the old dwarf repeated, "Tha city is just up ahead according ta tha scouts. Well, that an' all tha smoke. Take a look."

The old dwarf nodded to a spyglass that hung near the wheel. Leon extended it and looked out over the raised deck towards the aft of the *Esperella*. Beside the lake was a veritable sea of undead. Tens of thousands of bodies were massed against the capital of Xaelon, ready to exterminate all life. The vast horde's numbers were staggering. They swarmed near the city's walls, as catapults from inside of Agaprya lobbed boulder after boulder out towards them. Leon saw that there were a few giants among the horde who picked up and threw some of the boulders back into the city with deadly accuracy.

A few mechanical clicks from nearby told Leon that someone else had begun to look through their own spyglass. Gionna's voice piped, "Would you look at that! Those dreadnought airships seem to be pulling their weight… so to speak."

The aerial combat seemed to be just as ferocious as the war on the ground. Three massive behemoths of ships circled the air above the city. The dreadnoughts that Lucien Rhise had manufactured made mincemeat out of the undead they encountered. Salvo after salvo of cannon fire sailed toward both the undead army, and the flying monsters that winged their way toward them. Dragons and gryphons did not only attack the dreadnoughts, but also any other vessels that weaved their way through the airspace. The attack craft flew around the northern portion of the city as cannons, crossbow bolts, and entropic blasts from mancers were launched from the airships.

A line of transport airships, and a few mail carriers, flew eastward out of the city and away from the battle. A dreadnought floated between the smaller vessels and the undead army in order to try and keep the dragons and gryphons at bay while they escaped. Leon surmised the escaping vessels would swing northward towards Last Bastion after putting a bit of distance between themselves and the horde.

They must still be evacuating the city. He thought.

Leon watched as one airship exploded mid-flight, likely due to dragon fire igniting a powder magazine for its cannons. It careened down into the city and wrecked in the wharf area. Smoke rose from its point of impact to join the other plumes that dotted the besieged northern part of the city. As the two forces clashed, Leon knew that every ship and person lost meant Xhormas was one step closer to his goal of total annihilation.

"The watchtower! Captain! They are signaling us!" Came a shout from an elven scout located near the bow of the ship.

Leon redirected his spyglass to the large tower on a man-made island just outside of the city. Crossbow and ballista bolts arced from it towards the flying beasts that assailed its peak. Through the battle that was being waged at the top, Leon saw a soldier waving signal flags toward the *Esperella.*

It took a moment for Leon to understand the message.

"Help… Defense." His response was laced with sarcasm, "Well, since they asked so nicely."

The other elven scout then reported, "It looks like the undead are summoning dragons! Look to the rear of the army, next to the lake!"

Leon redirected his gaze to verify the scout's report, and saw what they had spoken of. While the undead's frontal ground forces continued to attack the city walls, Leon watched as a dragon flew up from the ground at the rear of the horde. Just a moment before that area had been occupied by a circle of liches and black swirling clouds. The dragon immediately joined in the aerial warfare. Next to that summoning circle he observed several other liches who were in the middle of their own rituals. Dark clouds spiraled just above them as a few powerful undead mancers exchanged ritual sacrifices for their own flying lizards. When they had encountered a dragon while in a transport vessel once before, they barely managed to defeat it.

Now, Leon felt better equipped to deal with the problem.

He pointed as he shouted through the copper pipes to the top deck before him. "We need to stop their summoners! That should be our first target!

Cannon crews, prepare your canister shot! Port side. Kérik, take us in! Everyone, get ready to engage the enemy! For Adonai!"

The responding chorus of 'For Adonai' was matched by a bright pulse of light from the aeonyte hull. Kérik Silverspine's own shout of excitement unnerved Leon just the slightest bit. Nevertheless, the *Esperella* dipped forward and accelerated toward the rear of the horde.

Projectiles, both magical and not, started to fly towards the *Esperella* as it careened down toward the water. Three circles of liches were in the middle of their ritual summonings next to Lake Xael. They appeared to be guarded by a few giants and wretches. Arrows and large rocks began to arc toward the aeonyte hull of their ship. Had it been made entirely of wood, like all other airships, Leon would have heard the crunch and splintering of its planks under the assault of the projectiles. However, thanks to its aeonyte reinforcement, the occasional missile that made contact merely clanged against it, causing minimal damage. Once they were close to the ground, the airship rocketed towards the grouped-together summoning sites. As the circles of liches neared, Kérik slowed ever so slightly.

"Cannon crews ready… FIRE!"

Loud successive explosions propelled the canister shot from the *Esperella*. Mid-flight, the canisters opened, and multiple smaller iron balls peppered the undead sites. Skeletons broke apart where they stood, their bones shattered from the impact. A Nephilim giant doubled over after taking a direct hit to his legs. A few shots missed the circles entirely, and went into the undead horde. Still, Leon reveled at the abject failure of all three summoning circles due to their liches being broken apart.

While the crew cheered, Leon watched as the dark swirling clouds that had hovered over the circles also dissipated. Behind them, several dragons and gryphons also took notice, and broke off from the battle. They flew directly toward the *Esperella* in what Leon was sure to be a retaliatory strike.

"Kérik! We need to move! Cannons, reload with round shot! Turrets, get ready!"

The dwarven pilot laughed as he pushed the wheel forward. The *Esperella* flew up and away from the winged undead who were mid-dive toward the space their ship had just occupied. As they took chase, the turrets in the ship's aft turned to engage.

"Turret crews! Fire away!"

Brown and green spheres of energy, tinged with white, leapt from the large wands of the mancer turrets. Leon clearly saw joints break and wings crumple upon the energy's impact, causing gryphons and dragons to fall into the water below.

With the winged forces of the undead horde still in pursuit, Kérik angled the *Esperella* upward and over the horde, towards the other fighting airships. Just as they were breaking through the enemy lines, a scout leaned back from the railing and shouted, "Dragon under us! It's about to breathe!"

Gionna cackled madly as she yelled, "Bring it on!"

Leon raced to the railing and confirmed that the beast was winging its way up from the ground forces, flames spewing from its mouth. The beast was too close for them to react as it breathed out against the underside of the aeonyte hull. The gnomish inventor's improvement over completely wooden airships appeared to work! The hull's integrity remained intact, and the dragon angled sharply away, beating its wings furiously. Then, instead of launching another futile attack on the underside of the ship, it flew up and in front of the ship's bow a short distance ahead.

Amid the cries of concern, Leon shouted, "Kérik!" The elderly former admiral hollered back in response, "I see it! I see it!"

While most others would have broken off and turned away, Kérik Silverspine angled the *Esperella* straight towards the flying beast while he pushed forward on the wheel. They accelerated towards the dragon, and Duamé began to cry out from a crossbow turret, "What are ya do–," before a sudden jolt of impact rocked the ship.

Leon watched with awe as Kérik's skilled steering caused the aeonyte gauntleted fist figurehead to angle upward, which resulted in a direct blow to the dragon's horned head. Upon impact, all Leon could see was a bright burst of light against scales. Then salt and shards of bone and horn began to skitter across the top deck of the ship as the rest of the dead dragon fell toward the army below.

Kérik laughed just as manically as Gionna had moments before, which proved to be infectious enough for the rest of the crew to join in. The shine of the hull briefly grew brighter in the unbelievable joy of the moment.

"You… You just punched a dragon!" Leon said to Kérik.

"Yeah I did!" The dwarf nodded with an exuberant smile.

"It beats Leon punchin' alukahs." Duamé commented from his turret.

"YES!" Gionna shouted from nearby, "Do it again, puffball!"

Meanwhile...

"WHAT DO YOU MEAN 'IT'S NOT ONE OF OURS'?" Mancer Clybourne roared at Admiral Schlymyal. The mancer's nearby bear grunted and huffed, but luckily it didn't participate in the tirade against the admiral whom Lorog had been assigned to defend.

Lorog was thankful that his wife and children had made it onto the transports. He would gladly exchange his life for their protection. So much had happened to him and his family over the past several weeks. After having been evacuated from the Lost Lands, they migrated to Agaprya searching for a better life and a fresh start. Fortunately, he had found a job in the War College quickly, and was then conscripted into the military. His imposing orcish musculature filled the tabard and chain mail that he had been hastily given, and he did the best he could to support his family with his newfound career.

The weeks had sped by as his family adjusted to their new life in the city, when suddenly the herald's news shifted from optimistic to very dire. Bulwark Fortress had fallen. From that moment on Lorog's training increased at a rapid pace, and the populace of Agaprya suffered from ever-growing anxiety about the incoming horde. Upon his rapid graduation from the War College, Lorog had been hastily assigned to a post with the instruction to defend the city, and to act as a guard to the orcish admiral during the battle. Whether that had come about because they were both orcs, or due to random happenstance, Lorog couldn't guess. He did observe that Admiral Schlymyal's behaviors stood in stark contrast to all of his previous encounters with other orcs. Under different circumstances, had Schlymyal been a member of his own clan, Lorog would have killed the dishonorable creature.

Given everything he knew about their enemy, he wished he was able to engage in the fighting at the outer walls of the city. His orc blood craved the battle, but he tempered those impulses with the glimmer of hope that he would be allowed to accompany the admiral on a transport to Last Bastion. Once there, he could reunite with his family.

For now, he fulfilled his duty to guard the admiral. Being assigned this post also had a few undeniable perks. Lorog was able to view the battle from high in the northern tower of the citadel, which was located in the center of the city. He was also able to be an unobtrusive fly on the wall during the planning and strategies meetings between the admiral and the Head Mancer. Occasionally, they would send a pilot on a fast mail carrier to convey instructions to the flying airships or the northern walls, where the fighting was heaviest.

As the battle progressed their discussions had grown terser, until finally a mystery ship had appeared. At first, everyone in the tower was awestruck by its effectiveness against the horde. However, after receiving a compliment on it, Admiral Schlymyal admitted that he had never seen it before. The tension in the tower climbed even higher when Clybourne's brown mancer robe, with all of its lavish embellishments, swished as he whirled on the orcish admiral.

"What is that ship? Where did it come from?" The mancer demanded of Schlymyal.

The orcish admiral sputtered his response, "I–I–I have n–no idea! It doesn't look like it's Agapryan!"

Clybourne bit back at the orc with a scathing retort, "Well thank you, Admiral Obvious! Look at its ability to chew through those airborne undead! Can we get a message to it? Flag it down?"

They directed their gazes to another soldier who stood in the room. A flag officer who communicated when mail carriers weren't able to do the job. The officer looked through his spyglass and said, "Beg your pardon, sirs, but I don't see a flag officer on their ship. It looks like a bunch of elves and dwarves!"

“What? Give that to me!” Admiral Schlymyal roared, as he ripped the spyglass from the flag officer’s grip. Lorog noted that the admiral had been growing increasingly brash with the others in the room. A few moments passed as everyone watched the shining ship in the distance. It pulled up and away from the rear line of the undead horde with a cloud of gryphons and dragons in pursuit. As it darted through the air, pulses of light and cannon fire shot from it, colliding with the undead that gave chase close behind.

“Well?” Asked the geomancer.

Schlymyal growled as he shoved the spyglass back to the flag officer. He was silent for a few moments before he uttered, “It’s elves and dwarves on there all right. Maybe from Masterwork Halls, given the direction they came here from. But that doesn’t make any sense. The horde just came from there! How could anyone still be alive?”

The jingle of steel on stone sounded from behind them. Lorog looked backward and saw his commanding general, Xiphos, approach from the stairwell. She approached Admiral Schlymyel with hurried steps while Mancer Clybourne turned to acknowledge her presence. When she reached them, she wiped some of the battle grime from her face with one hand, while she deposited a squirming elderly gnome next to them with the other.

“Well, really!” The gnome declared, as he smoothed his white beard and dusted off his clothes.

“How nice of you to join us, General Xiphos, Master Magnus. Welcome to the end of the world.” Mancer Clybourne stated theatrically. The nearby bear growled almost mournfully.

“How are the evacuations coming?” Xiphos asked. She wiped her sweat-soaked face with the least dirty part of her tabard. Lorog listened intently as he watched for any potential threats around the trio. The general had more than a few white hairs that had come loose from a tight bun. The exertion of battle did not seem to weigh on her though, and the few rents in her plate mail armor did not appear to cause her issue.

Here is a warrior who is worth following. She comports herself with honor. Lorog thought. She was much easier to respect than the orcish admiral who growled out his response, “We should have about all the population on their way to Last Bastion. Soon we can start evacuating the troops. How are the walls?"

"We are currently holding them. It is only a matter of time until they get through though. I caught this one trying to jump the line onto the transports." Xiphos replied, as she lightly shoved the gnome she had brought with her.

"The rest of my people are already evacuated! I was just trying to join them!" The gnome named Magnus reasoned.

General Xiphos admonished the old gnome sternly, "You can wait your turn like the rest of… What is that?"

She pointed towards the glowing ship that the mancer and admiral had been discussing prior to her arrival. It was still being pursued by numerous gryphons and dragons. The ship careened this way and that above the undead army, while pulses of light continued to shoot from behind it towards the undead creatures who gave chase.

"A very welcome sight against the unexpected aerial undead and dragons. I believe that it is reinforcements." Mancer Clybourne offered.

The small gnome named Magnus pointed at the ship and shouted, "That–that symbol on the side of it! That's the Judge's Mark! It's the Judge!"

Everyone present stared at the ship Magnus pointed to, which continued to weave through the battle. The crack of cannons came from a nearby dreadnought ship, startling the orcish admiral.

"I thought the heralds said the Judge was a hoax." Admiral Schlymyal commented. Lorog bit back the urge to speak out of turn. He thought he had heard about the Judge earlier than almost anyone else. Several weeks ago, while still traveling to Agaprya, he had befriended a dwarf who talked about the Judge to a herald. It certainly hadn't seemed like a hoax to Lorog, and he felt as though his belief in the Judge was vindicated while he watched the glowing ship.

"That hoax just killed another dragon, and it is still flying," Xiphos replied. "Bring it here so we can talk to the captain."

The command was given to the flag officer, who repeatedly waved two signal flags at a mail carrier that hovered nearby. The pilot angled up to the tower, where admiral Schlymyal relayed the instructions. The pilot nodded and then zoomed off towards the Judge's ship. The rest of those assembled at the tower's parapet watched as the battle continued to unfold in front of them.

"You said that we will evacuate the military forces soon?" Mancer Clybourne asked.

Admiral Schlymyal nodded, "Yes. We may need a couple of hours at the most, but we need to pull back to Last Bastion for the coronation, and for the best defensible position. We can defeat the horde from there, then return and rebuild."

After a moment, Clybourne snapped his fingers at his black bear companion and stepped towards the exit. "I need to take care of a few things at the Academy. I'll be back soon."

The orcish admiral gave a tusked smile as he needled the mancer, "Are you sure you wouldn't like to take a mail carrier? It would be faster."

Lorog heard the mancer growl similarly to his bear as he replied over his shoulder. "You know how I feel about flying. You're lucky that Grym and I are boarding an airship to evacuate. We will return in time for that, I just have a quick errand."

With that, the mancer and bear descended the tower stairs and left. Lorog saw the gnome, Magnus, shift and fidget amidst those who remained. "Do, uh, do we think that it is wise to call over that airship? Don't you see all those beasts following them?"

Xiphos was looking through the spyglass at the ship as it turned closer to them. "Master Magnus. Weren't you married to Gionna Gærheart?"

The gnome's huff of frustration was quite evident, "More than once. Odd time to bring up my love life, Xiphos. We are in the middle of a war. Why?"

"Because I believe she is on that ship, Magnus."

Magnus's loud voice belied his tiny stature, "What? Where?"

"On the ship. She's next to the wheel." The general clarified, as she passed the spyglass to the old gnome.

It took but a moment for Magnus to lose almost all of his remaining composure. "What does she think she's DOING? Get her over here!" He shouted.

Lorog winced at the tiny gnome's volume.

Chapter 3: The Briefing

"Would ya stop tellin' me how ta drive?" Kérik roared at Gionna as they made a sharp turn and rocketed forward. The screech of a nearby undead gryphon was cut short when Leon speared it before their momentum carried them away. A swarm of other flying creatures followed close behind the *Esperella* as they flew over the battle.

The rear turrets on the ship hammered the cloud of undead beasts. Leon, and any other defenders not manning mancer or crossbow turrets in the aft area, were left to defend Kérik as he flew their ship about the battle. Leon stabbed at any aerial enemies who got too close, and salt frequently scattered across the top deck before the wind wafted it off in their wake.

The fierce fighting continued all around him. Everywhere he looked, the living battled the dead. Arcs of white fire lanced through the air from Miala's braided wand, and consumed a couple of attacking gryphons. Arrows shot from the center of the top deck, where a group of elves encircled Princess Schalae. She looked for, and pointed out, any incoming undead who tried to come at the ship from different sides.

The flying undead creatures chased the airship as it wove through several of Xaelon's flying vessels. Kérik flew this way and that, taking them over towers and below other defending airships. The senseless fury of the flying undead beasts drove them to pursue the *Esperella* alone, and other aerial defenders soon began to exploit this fact.

As the *Esperella* wove through the battle, the other airships began to fire their own salvos at the flying horde as they chased them. Cannonballs from different vessels all whistled through the air toward the airborne undead. A few ships came too close, and Leon watched as a couple of gryphons and a dragon split off from the central mass to consume them. Leon kept his eye on a nearby mail carrier that flew towards the *Esperella* on what appeared to be an intercept mission. He yelled to Kérik in the wind, “Mail carrier! Port side!”

“I see it, lad!” The dwarf hollered back, as he angled toward the small ship. The mail carrier pivoted and zipped alongside *Esperella's* top deck.

“Protect that mail carrier!” Leon shouted to the mancers and dwarves on that side of the ship. He stepped toward the tiny vessel and its pilot, who flew just in front of the aft. The young looking woman who controlled the mail carrier was dressed in blue and black Agapryan leathers. No stray hair escaped the simple leather cap she wore, and her wind protection goggles masked any other distinguishing features. Her body language indicated that she was distracted by both the flying undead and the strange metallic airship. Her shout sounded frantic as she called, “Where's the captain?”

“That's me!” Leon replied from the railing.

“You're needed at the inner tower!” The pilot yelled back, as she pointed toward the inner stronghold walls of Agaprya. They surrounded the royal structures of the city, and he could see a couple of the smaller airships hovering around the prominent tower she indicated.

Leon gestured toward the cloud of undead that chased them with his shield hand, “Um, we're kinda busy at the moment!”

“The fleet admiral insisted!” The pilot clarified.

Remembering his last encounter with a mail carrier pilot, Leon was hesitant to trust this woman. Thoughts of the assassination attempt that led to his recent brush with death clouded his mind as he scrambled to think of a way to solve the immediate issues of both her presence, and request. Truthfully, he did want to get more information, but he had no idea what to expect if he went with her. This was further complicated by the fact that his face was on every ‘wanted dead or alive’ poster that his father had commissioned the Herald Guild to make. If this woman did recognize him, she didn't say so.

After another moment of thought, Leon turned back to the aft. “Kérik?”

“Ya?”

“You're taking command. I'll be back.” Leon thought for a moment, and then added, “I have to go get briefed…”

“We're a little busy right now, lad!” Kérik interrupted.

"...by the new fleet admiral."

The ex-admiral of the fleet grew wide-eyed as he yelled, "Wot? Ya find out who it is an' grind their granite!"

"Take some people with you dearie! For protection. Once they find out who you are..." Gionna cautioned.

"Right!" Leon replied. Gionna had given voice to his own concerns about their plan to rescue Agaprya. With Lucien and Laric vying for the throne, and their underhanded schemes, there weren't many individuals Leon could trust outside of those aboard this ship.

Duamé manned a nearby turret with Miala and Kelleren, and Leon clambered over to where they were. "I have to go with the mail carrier. Think you can make sure I don't get stabbed in the back this time?"

Duamé steadied himself on the deck with his maul, and motioned for another dwarven warrior to take over his post. "Yeah, alright."

Miala simply pocketed her wand and nodded.

Leon then turned to Gionna and asked, "Are you coming?"

The gnomish inventor looked over the *Esperella* before she yelled at Kérik Silverspine, "Try not to break my ship!"

They made their way back to where the mail carrier waited on the other side of the ship, and Leon called over, "Four people and a companion coming over!"

The pilot wordlessly brought her vessel as close as possible, lining it up slightly below the railing. Duamé jumped in first, then caught Kelleren when Miala hoisted him over the side. They made room for Miala who jumped in next, followed by Gionna, and finally Leon.

As they peeled away from the *Esperella*, Leon hoped that Kérik and the rest of their crew would be alright. The speed of the mail carrier was slowed by the weight of the additional people crowded onto its small frame. They angled downward from the skies, and headed closer to the northern walls of Agaprya where the ground forces were engaged.

Lines of arrows and bolts flew back and forth from the ramparts and the outskirts of the city. The shantytowns on the exterior of Agaprya were gone. Their debris was being used by the undead to scale the high walls. Leon hoped that the sick and infirm who hadn't been permitted to enter the city before had not become fodder for the horde to consume when they arrived. He also saw that there were giants interspersed throughout the front ranks of the undead army. They hefted and lobbed boulders, along with any other large debris they could find, towards the city walls and low-flying airships.

"Uh, we have company!" Miala yelled from the front of the mail carrier, as she whipped out her wand and pointed it behind the pilot. Leon twisted and saw that three gryphons were angling towards their vessel as it struggled to speed away from the battle and into the city. Their wings flapped furiously as Miala shot a small beam of fire towards them. They flew away from it, dodging the blast, before converging again to continue their chase.

When one grew close enough to reach out with its talons, Miala fired once more and successfully bisected its wing. The gryphon squawked and tumbled out of the mail carrier's range. The two remaining beasts flew serpentine patterns in the air, still doggedly pursuing them past the outer city walls.

A few tense minutes of narrow misses and close calls dragged on as they passed over the deserted streets of the capital city. Debris and discarded possessions littered the empty cobblestone roads. The once pristine streets were now visibly marred by the panic and fear of its inhabitants. While Leon could see squads of people rushing about near the walls in tabards and armor signifying Xaelon's armed forces, there were no civilians to be found. Ahead, towards the eastern part of the city, Leon watched several airships of various sizes land where the chariot races were usually held. If people were still being evacuated away from the northern wall, he figured that would be the most sensible area to do so.

As they approached the inner citadel fortress walls an occasional crossbow bolt flew from the ramparts at the pursuing gryphons. They screeched and squawked as Miala coordinated her attacks with those of the rampart soldiers, until their combined efforts finally brought down the second beast. The last remaining creature kept swerving out of the projectiles' arc, and pursued them all the way to the tower where they were supposed to meet the admiral.

Leon saw more than a few figures at the top of the tower, and the mail carrier swung wide before the pilot jerked at her control wheel and caused the small airship to fly parallel to the walls. This allowed for plenty of the guards stationed along them to shoot at the undead half-lion, half-bird. Soon fur and feathers came crashing down upon the wall.

"Nice flying!" Leon complimented the pilot, who breathed a sigh of apparent relief once their chase was over.

"Thank you. Nice shooting!" She replied and said to Miala. The pyromancer nodded back at her, but Leon noticed she did not holster her wand in her robes. Their eyes met in an unspoken agreement. They knew that depending on what reception they received, things could become violent rather quickly.

After giving it a moment's thought, Leon leaned towards his friends and said, "Everyone get ready. Things could go sideways quickly."

Duamé slapped Leon on his shield arm as he said, "If yer planning' on tellin' tha truth, an' nothin' but, then I–"

"Will be supportive… and aggressive only when necessary." Miala finished.

The dreadlocked dwarf rolled his eyes and tightened his grip on his elegantly crafted maul.

The mail carrier slowed and stopped at a high tower on the north side of the citadel. Several figures watched them, and Leon internally thanked Adonai that he saw at least one friendly face. He pointed Magnus out to the others before they landed, and saw Gionna tap her multi-lensed glasses to see her former husband more clearly.

Duamé and Leon jumped down first, then they helped Miala, Gionna, and Kelleren from the mail carrier onto the tower. Leon turned and saw quite a few people staring at them. The person dressed most like an admiral wore black and blue naval leathers paired with a sour expression on his orcish face. Next to him was another orc, dressed in chainmail and a tabard, that Leon swore looked familiar. The group watched him intently with their weapons at their sides, as they cast guarded looks between themselves. Magnus stood between their two groups in his archivist robes, and broke the tension in the tower.

"Gia! What do you think– how did you– why–" He spluttered.

"When I asked to speak to the captain of that airship I didn't expect the whole crew to show up!" The admiral interrupted, as he approached Leon with an outstretched hand. "Admiral Schlymyal."

Leon walked forward and firmly shook hands with the orc. "I'm the captain of the *Esperella,* and the Judge of Xaelon."

There was an expectant pause, making it evident that they were waiting for his actual name. This became more apparent when an armored woman also stepped forward to shake his hand and said, "General Alexandra Xiphos. And you are?"

Duamé's voice was a wary whisper behind Leon, "Boyo, whatever ya think yer gonna say–"

But Leon knew the price of lies. He knew the cost of running from his father and his influence. He refused to hide anymore, no matter what the wanted posters said.

Who would care when the kingdom was under attack anyway?

With a smile, Leon shook her hand and started to explain, "Leon. Formerly Le–"

The whisper of steel being drawn from sheathes accompanied the immediate panicked backpedaling of the admiral and general. They both, along with the soldier who guarded them, pointed weapons towards Leon and his friends.

"–don't say that." Duamé finished.

"Wait. So the man 'wanted dead or alive' is the Judge?" General Xiphos asked aloud to everyone.

"This… this is impossible!" Raged the orcish admiral. Leon was not overly concerned with the short sword he held in one hand, however the small crossbow in his other caused him to pause. Schlymyel snarled viciously as he continued. "Guard, arrest him!"

Leon saw movement at his side, but instead of the orcish guard, he saw Miala step next to him. Her braided wand with its ball of aeonyte at the end was raised, but no fire came from it yet. Duamé also drew close to his other side, raised maul in hand. Nobody else moved toward them while Leon tried to reason with those in authority. "Really? Why would I willingly come to aid Agaprya if I was a threat to it? I can assure you that I am not the outlaw that the heralds make me out to be."

"Mags, can you help us here?" Gionna asked through gritted teeth.

The head archivist squeaked, "Yes! Please everyone, lower your weapons and let's talk this out."

When nobody moved, Gionna sighed, "This is ridiculous." She tapped her glasses frame, rotating the lenses in front of her eyes, until the one that held a small suspended discerner cube rested in front of them. She gestured to it grandly, so that everyone present could see what it was before she turned to Leon.

"Judge, do you wish harm to any of these people?" She asked.

"Of course not!" Leon replied. The cube's telltale flash of green told everyone that he was telling the truth.

"Well then, I imagine there is an explanation as to why you're here." General Xiphos stated.

Here we go. In for a copper crow, in for a golden eagle. Leon thought.

"I am here to stop the undead horde and the forces behind it. Which may or may not include Lucien Rhise."

The silence that followed his response was tense. Leon stood there, hands raised, gauging their reactions. His pronouncement made all the sense in the world to him, given what he knew. Looks of shock and revulsion splayed across the many faces of those who heard him. The female general broke the silence. "While we welcome your addition to our defenses, that is a very serious accusation. Defenses, I might add, which include ships manufactured by Lucien himself."

"I know it sounds crazy, but it is true." Leon replied. The green flash from the discerner cube made the armored woman lower her sword slightly.

One of those gathered, the orc soldier, cleared his throat before he spoke, "General Xiphos. Permission to speak, ma'am?"

The general replied, "What is it, soldier?"

The orc lowered his sword to the stone floor as he spoke. "This man. I recognize him. Before he was a wanted criminal, he helped my family and I on our way to Agaprya. Much to the detriment of himself. My experience with him shows he comports himself with honor."

“Flint an’ feldspar! Lorog, isn’t it?” Duamé exclaimed.

“Indeed.” The orc replied.

Leon silently thanked Adonai for the fortuitous turn of events before he explained further. “His family needed the last room at a waystation near Agaprya more than we did. How are they, Lorog?”

The armored orc rumbled, “Evacuated towards Last Bastion. I hope to join them soon.”

A few tense moments persisted before the general sheathed her sword. The orcish admiral looked at her frantically and seethed, “You don’t believe him do you? What are you doing?”

“Admiral Schymyel, we should hear him out. He did come to help. If he is associated with Gionna Gærheart he can’t be all bad, right? Conspiracy theories aside, of course.”

The wide-eyed admiral seemed to calm slightly, as he also lowered his weapons. His deception was exposed when he suddenly lunged, grabbed Magnus, and pulled the elderly gnome close to him. The admiral held his short sword to the gnome’s throat amidst exclaimed protests from everyone present.

“What are you doing?” Xiphos cried out, as she drew her longsword from her sheath once again.

“How dare you! Unhand me!” Magnus shouted.

“I knew you had no honor!” Lorog exclaimed.

“Everyone back! Get back!” Admiral Schlymyel roared as he shook the gnome in front of him. He slowly edged along the parapet towards the mail carrier that was parked near the stairs that led down. Due to the admiral’s behavior, Leon was able to hazard a few guesses. He figured that one of his father’s henchmen now held Magnus hostage. Leon unlatched Revelator from the strap on his back and asked, “How long have you been in Lucien’s pocket, admiral?”

“I have no idea what you are talking about!” Schlymyel exclaimed, as he slowly moved closer to the airship.

Gionna’s discerner cube flashed a bright red as she hissed, “He’s lying! Mags, stay calm. Everything will be okay.”

"Easy for you to say! You don't have a sword to your throat! Let me go, Schlymyel!" Mags squirmed and struggled until the orcish admiral pressed the blade tighter against his skin. "Everyone drop your weapons, now!"

The clang of metal hitting stone all around Leon signified everyone's obedience to his demand. Gionna stepped closer, her cane tapping against the stone of the tower. The orcish admiral snarled, "Stop right there!" She did, her hands resting on her cane, unmoving.

Schlymyel continued, "Magnus and I are taking a trip in the mail carrier." He leaned down and lifted Magnus with a growl in his ear, "Looks like you get your wish of escaping the battle early after all."

The orcish admiral glanced toward the mail carrier behind him a few times and gestured for the female pilot to exit the airship. Her hands were raised as she slowly climbed from the small vessel. The tusked grin of the admiral as he stepped into the airship infuriated Leon, who felt that there was nothing he could do to save the small gnome.

As Admiral Schlymyel looked to the wheel, instead of those arrayed against him, Leon heard a few mechanical clicks and whirs. With a single gesture Gionna Gærheart pointed her metallic cane at the hostage-taker, and within a mere second it had converted into her makeshift crossbow. She lined it up, pulled the trigger on the handle, and the string twanged loudly – which caused the orcish admiral to turn back and see what was going on. Thus, a crossbow bolt flew from the bottom of her cane and embedded itself right between the admiral's shocked eyes.

Leon lunged forward and used the aeonyte shield on his arm to wedge between the orc's short sword and Magnus. He pulled the gnome away from the blade and shoved the admiral's limp body away. Shouts and exclamations abounded from others as they registered what had just happened.

A sigh escaped General Xiphos' lips, "I never liked Schlymyel. Even less now that he seems to have shown his true colors."

"Yellow." Lorog grumbled.

"Are you alright Mags?" Gionna asked.

"Perfectly fine, Gia. Perfectly fine. Thank you." Magnus said as he dusted off his robes. The gnome then picked up the fallen admiral's shortsword, which appeared quite heavy for him, and went to the other side of the mail carrier. A tiny yell came from him as he raised the shortsword overhead before bringing it down. A few thuds and cuts could be heard as Magnus ensured that the admiral would not rise again. As he came back around the airship, with a few bloodstains dotted on his robe, he announced, "Okay, now I truly am fine."

"What… What do we do now? The admiral is dead. Our withdrawal is completely compromised." Xiphos stammered.

"Good thing we brought another one." Duamé commented.

"What?" Xiphos asked.

"Kérik Silverspine." Leon explained. "He's piloting the *Esperella* at the moment, but if you need an admiral of the non-corrupt variety, we brought one with us."

"Non-corrupt as in, one not beholden to the Rhises you mean?" Xiphos asked, as she looked through the spyglass towards the *Esperella*.

"Definitely not." Leon confirmed. Considering the shocking turn of events, he figured now was the best time to reveal more truths. "My former father had his influence in many places. The heralds, Schlymyel, Baron Halomir as well."

Xiphos pounced on what Leon had said, "Wait, wait, wait! Your 'former father'? You're a Rhise?"

"Leon Rhise. Disowned about two months ago."

Xiphos looked to be exasperated at having to ask questions over and over again. "Wh–why?"

Leon tried to think of the most straightforward answer. "For having a conscience."

"It's true. He is a former Rhise, and the Judge of Xaelon." Magnus piped in as he tried to wipe the short sword clean, "I met him shortly before our emergency council meeting."

Alexandria Xiphos whirled on Magnus, clearly frazzled by the unfolding events, "Why didn't you say anything before?"

Magnus held his head up high as he pronounced, "I was asked not to before, and as he is here before you now, I felt it was no longer necessary. Besides, my life was just in danger! Let the Judge explain it all to you!"

Amidst the battle that raged outside, Leon bared his soul to the general and the soldiers posted there. At this point, he was unafraid of others knowing his beliefs and his past. He gave a short summary of Adonai and how he learned that belief in Him could prevent undeath. He explained the tenets that he lived by, and about the lesser god of undeath Xhormas. Lastly, he disclosed the connection between Lucian and the mysterious Silas. How they met twenty years ago when he was but a newborn in the Rhise house.

To General Xiphos' credit, she seemed to take the news well. It also helped that Magnus and some of the others chimed in at times. Leon at least felt that he was getting better at spreading the news about Adonai. The truth was becoming easier for him to stand on. *After everything I have seen and experienced, how could Adonai not be the answer?* He thought.

"So there you have it. Who I am, and what I am fighting against. Now, what is the situation here?" Leon pointed with his spear to the line of airships that headed east. "How are the evacuations coming along?"

"They are moving. Slower than I would like, but moving." Xiphos complained. "We have almost all of the general populace gone as of a few hours ago, but we still need to evacuate the rest of our forces when we withdraw. Meanwhile, for now we are holding the walls, but eventually we will need to pull back and evacuate our own without being overrun. That way, we can protect the transports on the way to Last Bastion and the coronat–," She sighed in evident frustration, "I–I'm still trying to work my way through this. I knew he was ambitious, but I… I didn't know how far Lord Rhise would go."

Leon understood her frustration. While the initial shock of his father's duplicitousness was unsurprising, the total weight of Lucien's actions was something that he was still coming to grips with as well. "One thing at a time. We can stop my father and brother once we are done here. Hopefully."

Thoughts of his family brought both the pangs of regret, and the remembrance of family members he still cared about. His invalid mother and older sister were in danger around Lucien and Silas. While he may not have been able to do anything about their situation when he returned to Rhise Manor the first time, he knew that something must be done now. He must protect the family members who were innocent.

General Xiphos nodded, "First we've got to deal with all those undead out there, I just wish–"

A commotion came from the stairwell as raised voices trailed behind a figure that ran up them. A whistle of steel sounded as the General and Lorog's swords were drawn and pointed toward the threat. As everyone else readied their weapons, Leon shouted, "Wait!" He recognized the dark green-robed man who revealed himself at the top of the landing.

A sheen of sweat donned the bald head of Calvin's thin figure. Panting, he approached Leon and clasped both of his arms before bringing him in for a short hug. Leon's confusion abounded as the last time he had seen Calvin was when the chronomancer knocked him out and made Leon forget about their conversation. It was only recently, on the way to Masterwork Halls, that Leon remembered Calvin and the strange compulsion the mancer put on him to return home to Rhise Manor in the first place.

Calvin, between gasped breaths after his exertion to get to them, wheezed, "You're doing great, laddie! Everything is coming together! Right now, though, we need to go!"

"Wait, who is this?" Miala asked warily.

"Miala, it's the chronomancer! The one I was telling you about!" Leon exclaimed.

Calvin almost comically tried to pull Leon in the direction of the parked mail carrier. "We haven't a moment to lose! We must go, now! Before he gets there on foot!"

Duamé cackled, "Ha. That's a good one. Chronomancer. 'Time' guy."

Leon, however, caught the seriousness of the man's tone, "Calvin. What–what are you doing here?"

General Xiphos piped in sarcastically, "Yes. By all means. Barge in here and say something ominous to capture our interest. It's not like there is a war going on."

Calvin cleared his throat before he responded vehemently, "I'm trying to save us! Now quickly, Judge! You, Miss Miala, and I must go to the Mancer Academy this instant!"

"Are we forgetting introductions?" General Xiphos asked icily.

Calvin cocked his head to the side, blinked rapidly, and pointed at each of them in turn as he pronounced, "Xiphos, Magnus, Gionna, Lorog, Duamé, Miala, and Leon formerly Rhise. My name is Calvin. Satisfied?"

Shocked silence met them all as the pilot in the mail carrier cleared her throat and started to speak before Calvin interrupted. "And her name is Ophelia."

Among the amazed faces and reactions, General Xiphos stammered, "W–w–where did you come from?"

"Mancer Academy. To which I must return immediately with Miss Mytheriyn and Mister Leon or even if we win against the horde, the future is lost!"

The future?

Baffled, Leon was about to ask why before Miala jumped into the conversation with concern, with wringing hands and eyes that constantly darted towards the General. "I can't go back there! I'll be–"

"Perfectly fine, the likelihood of which decreases the longer that we wait!" Calvin interrupted.

Leon had his concerns. He remembered that she had left the Academy after incinerating her former abusive teacher and was branded a deserter. Since then, she led as quiet a life as a pyromancer on the run could. In the process, she had found Kelleren and settled in Everbright village. That was before she accompanied him and Duamé on their adventure.

"Why are you so desperate for the two of us to leave with you? What about Duamé and Gionna? What about the battle? Why should we even go with you?" Miala railed at Calvin.

After a sigh, Calvin raised his hands non-threateningly and approached Miala slowly. When close, he leaned over and whispered in her ear. Whatever he said brought tears to Miala's eyes as she looked at the old man sharply. He nodded at her solemnly before turning to the mail carrier pilot and speaking to her. "Can you take us to the Mancer Academy, young lady?"

The pilot started to protest, "Um, I don't know you, and don't take orders from you."

"Please." Miala stated as she whirled on the pilot, "Please, take us."

It took several moments for Miala and Calvin to convince everyone else present that they did actually need to go. After some discussion, it was agreed that Duamé, Gionna, and Magnus would fly back to the *Esperella* to coordinate the defense with Silverspine. At the same time, Leon, Miala, Kelleren, and Calvin would head to the Academy.

Leon was concerned by her sudden change of heart and their insistence that he come to the Mancer Academy; but if it was vital for them to go, then so be it. After Gionna and Duamé agreed to head back to the *Esperella*, Leon and Miala climbed into the mail carrier with Kelleren and Calvin. At the urgings of Calvin, they zoomed off and accelerated at an immense speed.

Leon noticed Miala trembling as they headed away from the battle to the north. The ship's bow pointed to the southeast and the varying-sized towers that dotted the compound of the exclusive Mancer Academy. Kelleren's tongue lolled while he peeked out the side of the airship. The wind whipped at his tan furry face, while both Calvin and Miala's faces bore somber expressions. Leon hated the unknown that he was heading towards. Seeking more information, he tried to open the conversation gently.

"Why the change of heart?" He asked Miala, "What did he whisper to you?"

Miala looked at Calvin, who nodded an unspoken agreement to her. She reached across the small vessel and made an effort to allow close contact. Leon felt her warm hand clasp his, and her piercing green eyes spoke volumes to him.

"He told me that it is time to destroy the Dark Room."

Chapter 4: The Academy

"I'm sorry, the what?" Leon asked in confusion. He had never heard of it before.

"The Dark Room." Calvin repeated for Miala, "It's a wholly detestable place. But now, we have a chance to destroy it. Minimally defended, you see!"

The wind whipped at Leon's face, which caused locks of Miala's hair to dance in the flowing air in front of him. She sat facing him at the bow of the airship, looking highly stressed. Leon figured it was due to her lack of desire to ever return to the Mancer Academy. *Maybe it was this 'Dark Room' she never wanted to go to instead.*

Calvin and Kelleren sat midship on the small mail carrier, and Calvin cackled in glee at Kelleren who was occupied lolling his tongue in the wind. Once he regained his composure, he continued speaking, "I do apologize for assaulting you, my dear boy, but it was necessary, you see? Now we are here, and capable of dealing with this problem once and for all!"

Confusion was becoming a regular companion to Leon. Irritation from being kept in the dark boiled over into his voice. "Except you still haven't told me what the 'Dark Room' is exactly. Or why you need us. Or why you told me to go home in the first place. Do you even know what happened to me there? What has happened since then?"

"I know some from visions. Dreams. Oh, hang it all Leon. I'm a chronomancer. Not Adonai! Stop looking at me like that!"

Leon was awestruck by the fact that the old mancer knew of Adonai without having been told. Before he could even ask, the man who could see through time spoke. "Yes. I believe. It's hard to not believe when enough events converge before your eyes. I've known about Adonai for a long time. Before you were even born! I've not been the best of followers, but now that you are here…"

The old mancer trailed off and stared off into the space in front of him. Leon grew concerned and leaned in, only to see the man's eyes were glassy with pupils that had turned grey. Leon waved a hand in front of Calvin's face, but received no response in return. He was breathing and clearly still alive, but whatever void he had peered into at that moment robbed Calvin of the present. Leon hoped and prayed that the intriguing man would be okay.

"Interesting fellow." Miala commented.

"Very." Leon replied. After a thought, Leon asked, "What can I expect at Mancer Academy? What's it like?"

Miala shuddered slightly. Leon didn't know whether it was from the chill of the airflow or her memories. "It will… not be what you expect. It certainly isn't a happy place."

"Isn't it a school?" Leon replied incredulously.

"Except that what they teach there is power. The power to destroy and defend. To take orders and comply." Miala shuddered again, "Everyone there is locked in a constant battle. One where they must gain favor for instruction, but also keep to themselves enough that they won't be too noticed by the wrong people."

"Wrong… people?" Leon asked.

"We are coming up on the Academy!" The pilot Ophelia hollered. Which seemed to stir Calvin out of his stupor. "-ave faith!" He almost shouted, only to realize his predicament and sigh heavily to himself. Leon looked past the strange chronomancer and gazed at the rapidly approaching Academy.

Multiple spires of varying sizes dotted the walled-off space allotted to the Mancer Academy. Some towers were triple the size of others in height, while even more could barely be called such, as they were wide and only slightly taller than the outer walls. All were made of stone and mortar, with curved tiles that served as their sloping roofs. A strange oddity was the scarcity of windows. Leon searched, but could only find a single one among all the structures. Old threadbare banners, bleached from decades in the sun, flapped from poles that dotted the enclosure. Even faded, Leon could tell each stone monolith had its own colors congregated around it. A decent-sized stone and wooden building sat against the crenelated southwestern wall of the capital. As he looked around, Leon couldn't find anywhere that could be described as a dark place, much less a dark room.

Though he did notice a feeling; there was a heaviness that Leon encountered as he entered the airspace directly above the Academy. It was an indescribable weight that settled in his chest, like a stain upon the air that he inhaled. He could feel that there was something not right about the Academy, but he couldn't pinpoint what it was.

No one could be seen on the well-manicured lawns as the mail carrier descended. When it landed, Leon hopped out of the airship and turned to help Miala and Kelleren out, taking full advantage of the eerie quiet to get his bearings. Calvin's gangly legs clambered out of the vessel onto the soft grass without issue. He then turned to the pilot and spoke to her in a low voice as Leon took in the sight of the Academy. Whatever was said must have been urgent, as she immediately zipped off once he released his grip on the mail carrier's railing.

They hurriedly followed Calvin across the quiet grounds of the Academy, and Leon became increasingly unnerved by the emptiness of the place. Miala once told him that a few hundred people had been in attendance at the Academy with her. While Leon knew that many must be off fighting the undead horde, he would have expected at least a scant remainder to be here. Instead, they crossed the extensive grounds to the building at the rear of the Academy unchallenged. It was significantly larger up close. Stone pillars and flying buttresses adorned the entrance, making the entire structure look grandiose. Heavy double doors with large pull handles were framed by thick rune-etched wooden beams. Again, Leon noticed the lack of windows. Instead, blank stone walls with wood trim extended from the edges of the doors.

Miala's hand reached for one of the large handles but she hesitated as she turned to look at Leon, "The Dark Room… is where mancers are made."

Leon took a second to process the simple information that Miala had given him. It was gravely important, of that there was no doubt. *But why would she be so bothered by it?*

"How?" Leon asked, confused.

Her eyes were red-rimmed and brimming with tears as she whispered, "Torture. Abuse. Trauma."

Leon felt his heart nearly drop to his stomach as his mind bridged connections from their past conversations. He remembered how she said that her parent's home was burnt down when she was such a young child. She had blamed herself because she was a pyromancer. He knew that traumatic life event was followed by Miala's trusted uncle violating her in the most heinous of ways. Then a former teacher also attempted to commit unspeakable acts against her while she was a student at the Academy. She had burned her uncle's house down with him inside of it, and later had burned her Academy teacher alive.

She was just a child then... a child whose trauma induced power had grown stronger over the years. Leon thought.

Through Leon's service in the military, he had met a few mancers. Whenever questions about the origin of their powers were brought up, mancers kept their answers mysterious. One time an aquamancer even abruptly left the room, with their platypus in tow, and never opened up to the crew again. *Could this truly be such a devastating secret for them? The reasons mancers come into their powers are torture, abuse, and trauma? They're not always actively born with it, or had it imbued by some artifact, but something much more sinister brought it about?*

He thought back to earlier stories he had heard. Ones about the king's mancer bodyguard Emirah. How lightning had struck her multiple times. Questions multiplied rapidly within Leon's mind, as if he himself had been struck by lightning. *Did the elves receive their hortimancy the same way? Anissa from the Archives? Was that how they all received their power? Is this the aftereffects of the underlying cause?*

Calvin closed his eyes for a moment, and when they opened, his pupils were grey. His body stood rigidly upright and twitched ever so slightly on occasion. Before Leon could process what he had been told any further, the old chronomancer's eyes blinked back to their original brown as he shouted, 'Get that door open! We've run out of time!"

Miala and Leon pulled on both doors, causing them to grind against their frames. A brightly lit interior room awaited them as they all rushed inside.

Glowing crystals shone down upon the space from a vaulted ceiling. Kelleren's hackles were raised as his nails clacked against the smooth stone floor they walked upon. The entryway was short, with a few stone steps that led down to a table-lined eating area. The tables had no place settings on them, but had instead been pushed and arranged to act as obstacles for anyone who might walk in. A large open kitchen was off to the right, while a rather sizable shelving system to store robes and books was to the left.

Leon was about to follow Calvin and Miala through it all, towards the even larger room that lay straight ahead, when he saw a dart of movement within the kitchen area. He tapped Miala's arm, who gave a slight jump, and looked at him. He silently pointed, mouthing that someone was over there, and before either he or Calvin could object, Miala communicated silently with Kelleren. The companion issued a quiet woof and shot towards the kitchen area.

A small yelp of surprise, followed by a loud bark, was all they heard before Miala hissed, "Come on!" and ran towards her dog.

Calvin whispered loudly, "We don't have time for – wait, wait, alright it could work." before he followed.

When they entered the kitchen they came upon a short woman in a cook's frock, who, upon closer inspection, Leon saw was a stout female dwarf. Her shoulder-length, braided blonde hair shook as she clutched a long wooden kitchen utensil with a large, flat, rectangular section on one end. She hefted it up with another yelp and threatened in a shrill voice, "Don'cha come any closer, or I'll wallop ya!"

Miala held one hand up toward Leon and Calvin and her other toward the woman as she spoke softly, "We don't mean you any harm Gérda, just put the giant bread peel down."

This response seemed to only make the dwarven woman raise the wooden peel higher as she said, "How d'ya know my name? I don't kno–" before she stopped and peered closer at Miala. Her long, unconventional weapon lowered slightly as she sputtered, "Mi-Miala? Miss Mytheriyn?"

Miala smiled as she stated, "Two apples in the morning with porridge."

The dwarven woman crooned as she leaped over and embraced Miala. It seemed welcome, which shocked Leon to his core. He thought Miala had incinerated her only attachment here at the Academy. Yet here was a middle-aged looking dwarf who looked like an old acquaintance. After several pats on the back, they broke from their hug, and Miala explained to Leon, "Gérda has been the cook here for as long as I can remember. She is one of the kindest people that I know, and I was heartbroken to leave without saying goodbye."

"Well, ya had ta leave, missy!" The woman jerked a thumb at Miala, "After she toasted tha bad egg Psiente, I gave her as many apples as I could before she hightailed it outta here. What are ya doing here?"

Miala stiffened as she stated, "We are here to destroy the Dark Room."

Gérda's eyes widened as she clutched Miala's brown robes, "Don'cha try to do it, missy! Malloch an' Clybourne has killed everyone who ever tried! Jus' get outta here!"

"We have a chance now, and we should take it." Calvin said with a tone of finality before he turned to Miala. "If you don't want your companion to die, you should leave him here with her."

After calming the dwarven woman down, whom, Leon learned in the middle of their short conversation, was not a mancer, Kelleren agreed to stay with her. Miala, Calvin, and Leon would proceed onward. The worried dog seemed to distract himself with the smells and food that lingered in the ransacked kitchen. Gérda had been instructed to stay and keep feeding the mancers, but with all of them at the battle, she had found herself entirely alone.

The trio continued beyond the mess hall and into a stone corridor that sloped downward without Gérda and Kelleren. Empty lecture rooms branched off on either side of it, and they passed by a few before Leon whispered, "Who is Malloch?"

Calvin's own quiet reply provided no encouragement. "A thoroughly evil man. The guardian of the Dark Room and an aeromancer of considerable power. We will not be able to destroy the Dark Room without defeating him first."

The hallway ended, opening up to an ornate, stone room with lofty vaulted ceilings. Large stone pillars were arranged in two concentric circles along the outer edge of the immense square room. Many were beautifully and painstakingly carved to display a mancer using an element. Leon could easily determine earth, air, fire, and water, but then saw several other pillars with more distinctive features.

One scene depicted a mancer with lightning coursing up their body. Another showed runes being carved over surfaces. The gravimancer lich they faced in the Archive was brought to Leon's mind when he saw a pillar that highlighted a mancer, along with various other objects, floating in the air. That same encounter helped Leon figure out the imagery carved into the pillar for kinetomancy. The eerie face of that pillar showed a carved woman manipulating a smaller carved man with strings that came from her fingers, almost like a puppet. The kinetomancer pillar stood adjacent to another that seemed odd and unfamiliar. It showed a man who was surrounded by the carved faces of different emotions– happiness, rage, fear, and others. Lines flowed from the faces to the man and then back to the carved faces again.

More pillars dotted the room with other various themes. Uncut, plain pillars could also be seen in the grand room, which indicated to Leon that the different branches of mancey may not have all been discovered yet. Though it seemed as if there was already more than enough power on display throughout the room. Power that, to an innocent onlooker, might be highly sought after. Yet, now that he knew the secret of how mancer powers were obtained, they didn't seem worth it. Looking around, Leon saw that Calvin and Miala had stopped in the center of the room.

They stood still, staring at a hooded man in a mancer robe. He leaned against a wooden door on the farthest wall from the building's entrance. His yellow robe bulged in odd places, and metallic clanking could be heard as he shifted at the sight of the newcomers. His smile was welcoming, almost infectious, as a slight breeze began to waft in the air and gently circle around them.

Malloch? Leon guessed.

A slight accent, foreign to Agaprya, escaped the smiling man's lips as his pleasant voice echoed around the room. "Miala. You have returned. Here I thought that you had left for good. Mancer Psiente would be so pleased. Had you not reduced him to ashes, that is."

Miala tensed at the sound of his voice. She grit her teeth and clenched her fists. "Well he certainly didn't incinerate himself, Malloch. Now, get out of my way."

"He's not going to do that." Calvin opined.

Malloch's warm, friendly eyes darted towards Calvin as he spoke, "That is correct. Otherwise, I would be quite the terrible guardian. Unless, of course, you would like to use the Dark Room?"

The runes across the hem of Miala's robe glowed as heat shimmers came off of her person. After a few calming breaths, the temperature in the room lowered once again, and she spoke in an even tone. "You know that I won't."

Malloch's smile became deeper. He shrugged, and more clanking sounded from the interior of his robe as he asked, "Then why are you here?"

"We are here to destroy it." Miala announced.

Leon expected the Mancer to attack. He expected some sort of visceral, angry response. He did not expect laughter.

Metallic clinking accompanied Malloch's belly laugh as he leaned back against the door into the Dark Room. The wind in the room began to gust with more strength, and a low whistle accompanied his next words. "You seek your death then? Few have tried over the years. All have failed."

He stepped forward from the stout-looking wooden door, and Leon saw that its edges were sealed shut with barbed chain. was The jingle of metal accentuated Malloch's steps as he strode toward them unafraid. Calvin and Miala stepped backward, trying to keep their distance from the aeromancer, while Leon stood his ground.

"Keep away from him, Leon!" Calvin hissed.

Malloch smiled at the Judge as he jovially scolded, "You are not even dressed like a mancer. I do not see any robes to indicate you as such. You are not allowed here."

Leon had enough of this smarmy, creepily joyous individual. This Malloch stood mere feet away, and while the aeromancer's wind was funneling through the room in a blatant display of power, this could all be resolved quickly. Leon grasped the spear that was strapped to his back and pulled it free just as multiple strands of small chains snaked their way from

Malloch's robes. Just as Leon reared back to deliver a strike from Revelator, the chains rattled as they shot through the air towards him.

Leon noticed barbs and hooks along the lengths of chain as they wrapped around the shaft of his spear and the edges of his shield. The wind picked up even more and whipped at Leon's face, causing him to squint as its force lifted him off the ground. Barbs and blades hung from a length of chain that snaked upward and stopped just in front of Leon's face. Sharp pain lanced along Leon's cheek as a blade on the chain ran across it.

Above the tumultuous wind that buffeted him, Malloch's voice echoed. "So be it. You shall be the first to die."

Chapter 5: The Room

Leon watched as the deadly chain flicked towards him, before a bright white line of fire cut across its midsection. The fire continued to burn through all of the chains that held Leon aloft, until he was finally freed and collapsed awkwardly to the ground. Pointed metallic thorns dug painfully into the flesh on his arms, and he tried to pick off the barbs while he scrambled to put distance between himself and Malloch.

As he backed away, Leon watched Miala fence with a whip of pure white fire that emanated from her wand. It batted at every length of chain that danced toward her. Wherever it made contact molten metal would drip, and small sections of chain would drop uselessly to the floor. Those severed sections were then caught up by the whirlwind Malloch continued to feed in the center of the room.

Malloch appeared unconcerned about the continuous severing of chains that shot from his robe. Instead, a wry smile crossed his face before he gestured towards Miala with an outstretched hand. The torrential winds suddenly increased in her direction, which flipped her fiery whip back at her. She quickly extinguished it, and dove behind a pillar with a yell. Multiple sharp chains flew through the space she had just occupied, only to screech back across the empty stone floor as they recoiled within Malloch's robe. Having been unsuccessful at capturing Miala, the incredibly powerful aeromancer once again shifted his attention towards Leon. As Malloch began to stroll towards him, Leon scrambled to place a barrier between them.

Leon quickly edged around the far side of one of the pillars and spotted Calvin. He was crouched out of Malloch's sight, near the far corner of the room. Calvin motioned for Leon to join him, and Leon was quick to heed the chronomancer's summons. Clenching his jaw tight with determination, Leon ran. His black steel-toed boots slammed against the floor as he sprinted, and while mid-dash he chanced one backward glance across the open area. Malloch had stopped in the center of the room, and simply watched Leon dart between the pillars wearing an infuriating smile.

Miala's voice sounded from the other side of the room as she hollered over the winds, "Why defend the Dark Room, Malloch? You know what happens there! You should know how wrong it is!"

Once again, the aeromancer laughed as he stood in the midst of his growing cyclone. His echoed reply sounded all around them, "It serves an important purpose. War requires warriors. The Dead Wars would have been lost long ago had it not been for our work here. All victories come at a cost, and I gladly help pay whatever I can to see Xaelon survive."

"What cost have you paid? What have you sacrificed?" Miala continued to rage.

Another bout of laughter, his voice more faint this time, "I know what I do is wrong, and I may one day suffer for it. But it is done for the right reasons."

A few moments passed by, and the increasing howl of the strengthening wind was the only audible sound all around them. Calvin suddenly dropped down to the stone floor. Though Leon knew he should follow suit, he was prevented from doing so by a long-bladed chain that was flung around the stone pillar they had been hiding behind. While he had not been able to duck beneath the chain like Calvin, he had at least kept Revelator in front of his face – which prevented the bladed chain from tightening onto his neck. Instead, the chain continued to wrap around Revelator. Then Leon felt the air shift around him, and a sharp tug on the spear pulled him back around the stone pillar.

Rather than struggle against the pull, Leon willingly took a few steps before tapping Revelator against the Rhise family levigem embedded in his glove. The intended weightlessness immediately occured. As soon as Leon rounded the pillar and saw Malloch, he leapt towards the aeromancer. The mancer's smiling expression morphed into one of shock as Leon careened towards him and bashed into the side of his head before ricocheting off. Due to his weightlessness, Leon found himself swirling through the windstorm above, anchored only by the chain that was still tightly wrapped around

Revelator. As Malloch recovered from the blow, his infuriated gaze once again focused on Leon, and he sent chains whipping towards him. Calvin chose that exact moment to run out from the other side of the pillar with a frenzied scream, causing a momentary distraction.

Leon had once seen the elderly chronomancer take on a gang of heavily armed youths with only his fists and feet. Calvin had dodged every strike with ease, and knocked them all unconscious with an effortlessness that was truly imposing. Now, Leon watched Calvin jump, twist, and duck under every hooked and barbed chain that swung at him. With every dodge, the chronomancer drew closer and closer to Malloch, causing the aeromancer to grow more and more agitated. The echoing growl of frustration that accompanied each missed chain swipe grew louder and louder, until finally two chains caught the green fabric of Calvin's robes. Malloch's growl of frustration turned to a cry of exaltation as Calvin was also hoisted into the air, and then suspended upside down.

"Your luck has run out, old man!" Malloch chortled.

"What luck? You did exactly what I wanted!" Calvin replied.

Miala then reappeared on the other side of the room, and ran towards Malloch while releasing white-hot orbs of fire in rapid succession from the aeonyte end of her braided wooden wand. The orbs were shifted off course of their intended target as they were swept up into the ever growing whirlwind. Between the chains that flew from Malloch's robes, the ferocity of the wind itself, and the orbs of fire that swirled within the cyclone, there were almost too many life threatening hazards to keep track of. A few spheres of fire whizzed past Leon's head as he watched several barbed chains shoot from Malloch's sleeve. Miala promptly intercepted them with a flaming shield that extended from her outstretched hand. As she drew closer, Leon's heart leaped into his throat. The weightlessness he felt from the levigem's contact with Revelator dissipated when he saw a chain swing low and wrap around Miala's foot. With a yelp, she was promptly turned upside down, and hoisted up to join Calvin and himself in the cyclone.

Malloch's manic grin once again spread across his face as he eyed each of the captives who hung from his chains. Another smaller chain snaked up and plucked Miala's wand from her grasp while she attempted to aim it at him upside down. During his inspection of it, he drawled, "I told you. All have failed. Your death is assu-ACK!"

Leon had let go of Revelator, as it was the only thing that held him in the air, and tackled Malloch. His knee connected solidly with Malloch's head as they collapsed on the ground. The wind abated slightly, causing Calvin and Miala to dip from their anchored heights, and Leon wasted no time. He punched with his shield hand, then followed up with a hook from his right, as he and the aeromancer started to clamber to their feet. With each successive blow the wind lessened more and more. Until finally, Malloch's concentration was broken. Chains, Leon's friends, and Revelator all clattered to the ground after Leon landed a solid blow to Malloch's gut. The aeromancer collapsed to his knees, coughing, and trying to suck air back into himself.

The irony of an aeromancer with the wind knocked out of him was not overlooked. Leon grabbed hold of the back of Malloch's head, only to immediately feel the mancer's heavy chain-laden hands scrape and scratch against his own. Barbs and blades dug into his skin, and he flinched from the pain before he simultaneously brought his knee up and hand down. A few repeated strikes to Malloch's face was all it took to reduce the powerful aeromancer to a senseless heap on the floor.

Tired, in pain, and breathing heavily, Leon cradled his bleeding hand as he went to Miala, and carefully unwrapped her limbs from the barbed chains. Her robe seemed to protect her, and after being freed she gave Leon a brief hug before scrambling toward the still form of Malloch with a snarl. Calvin had already separated himself from his bindings, and held a hand up to stop her. The older man stood over the unconscious form of their foe. "Not by your hand Miss Mytheriyn. Besides…" Calvin pointed towards the chained wooden door, "You must go in there."

The feral look of rage that Miala had leveled at Malloch was redirected by Calvin's pointed finger to the stout wooden door. She walked gingerly toward it, a couple of steps at a time, while her fingers grew brighter and brighter. Heat-resistant runes began to glow across the seams of her robe as she ran her fingers through the metal chain links that crisscrossed the door's surface. Once they were melted she paused to take a few deep breaths. Leon watched as she swayed in place, and thought that she might pass out. Instead, she grasped the door handle with a hand that was once again at normal temperatures, and pushed. Hinges on the inside of the door creaked loudly as it opened into a dark hallway that lay beyond. Turning slightly, Miala met Calvin's eyes, and he gave her a slight nod of encouragement. She then shifted to look at Leon, and spoke in a quiet voice, "Don't... Don't come in here. You... No one should have to see this. To be subjected to what I... What we have been through."

"I won't." Leon promised.

Miala's eyes became red-rimmed as she gave him the barest hint of a smile, "Hey, you don't have to ask me this time."

Leon felt a lump form in his throat, "Ask you what?"

A tear began to trail down her face before it dried from the heat that had begun to distort the air around her.

"To burn something down." She replied, before she turned and walked into the dark hallway and out of sight.

The scrape of metal against stone caused Leon to turn around. Calvin was attempting to drag Malloch's unconscious form to one of the carved pillars. Stepping over, Leon helped the chronomancer prop their foe into a seated position before binding him. They gingerly took some of the long chains that came from his sleeves and wrapped them tightly around his robes, careful to avoid any of the small hooks and barbs that adorned them. After a few minutes, Calvin punched Malloch's already bruised and swollen face. "He was about to wake up. We are fine for now... It's stressful."

Leon was puzzled by the odd man's demeanor, "What is it like seeing the future?"

Calvin met Leon's eyes with a meaningful glare, and Leon realized he had just answered his question before it had been asked. Moments later, the old man elaborated, "I've told you before. Causality. Certain events in time are fixed. What is not as fixed is how you get there. You'll see soon enough." The older man sighed heavily as he gestured around to the intricately worked pillars. "Do you see chronomancy shown here among the pillars?"

Leon looked around, but try as he might, nothing depicted being able to peer through time the way Calvin could. "No."

"That is because as tantalizing as it may sound at first, people do not like to be told their futures. Especially when the future is so grim for most. Will things get better for me? Will the Dead Wars ever end? When will I die? What do I need to do to win so-and-so's heart? My predecessor and I were constantly asked the same questions over and over again, but when the truth is given, and the answer isn't liked…" Calvin's voice trailed off as he stared off into the distance.

"You stayed in your tower?" Leon asked.

Calvin nodded. "For years. I grew tired, Leon. Weary. I knew my mission, my purpose. Yet, I ignored it. Squandered it. When Adonai gives you a gift, He expects it to be used for His will. It took me a while to be fully reminded of that."

Calvin stared at the open doorway to the Dark Room, and smiled. "She is coming back."

Leon could see tendrils of smoke as they wafted up from the corners of the doorway. Soon, a light could be seen in the dark hallway – generated by Miala's glowing red hand. Held high, she used it to light the way for the three gaunt figures who accompanied her.

The oldest appeared to be no more than thirteen years. The child had orcish features, with a pronounced jawline, and small tusks that protruded from it. He had long auburn hair that obscured most of his face. His hair appeared to continue to grow down his neck and onto his shoulders. He was dressed in a tan robe, and distanced himself from Miala and the two other children as soon as he reached the doorway. For a brief moment Leon thought he might attack either himself or Calvin, based on the feral look he gave upon seeing them. Once he understood that Leon and Calvin would not move to harm him, he relaxed – even if ever so slightly.

Another boy who emerged was tiny. For a moment Leon thought he was a toddler, until he noticed his angular features and yellowish hair that were typical to the gnomish population. He wore a brown robe, similar to Miala's, and tears streamed down his tiny face. He visibly trembled with emotion while he walked into the cavernous hall.

The last child walked hand in hand with Miala. She was a small girl, in a deep blue mancer robe. Her expressionless face was framed by straight black hair that fell to her shoulders. She was small enough that Leon guessed she had not yet reached her tenth year, although her eyes looked years older. They told a story of having seen things beyond what her years dictated, things that Leon knew she never should have seen, and were hollow and sunken because of it.

As they all exited the passageway more smoke began to pour from its opening. The smell of burning wood reached Leon's nose at the same moment that Miala reached him. Her hand returned to normal, and she hugged him fiercely. Leon felt her tears on his neck, and he just stood still while he held her. Whatever pain, and whatever past, she confronted while destroying the Dark Room had brought the full weight of her battered emotions to the surface, causing silent sobs to wrack her body. Calvin spoke softly to each of the children, while Leon supported Miala. She spoke against his armor in a muffled voice, "It's going to be okay, right?"

"Yes. Yes it will." Leon replied.

"Not to be a downer, but we need to leave. Now." Calvin stressed.

"Wh-why?" Leon asked.

Calvin wrung his hands, "Time is short. Come on, kids! This way!"

Calvin prodded the group towards the kitchen and mess hall, until he suddenly dove and tackled Leon to the floor. Leon felt a sharp gust of wind, as a short length of barbed chain flew through the air where he had just stood. He landed with a crash, scraping the back of his scale-mail, and immediately craned his neck to see where the children were in regard to the new danger. Malloch was still propped against the stone pillar and bound in his own chains, but was awake and looking at them all with murder in his eyes.

"You will not take them away from us! I'll kill you all before I let you leave!" He shouted as he sent more shards of chain flying in their direction. Leon felt helpless as he lay splayed out on the floor, with his shield hand on the wrong side to do any good. Moreover, he knew that from his location he could only protect himself and Calvin. Miala and the children were exposed. Unprotected. For a moment, Leon thought he had failed.

The girl in the deep blue robe held up a hand, and a blue light flashed in front of her. Even from his location on the cold stone floor, Leon felt the young girl's incredible display of raw power. A power that should never have been given to her. Power that stemmed from the evils done to a child was now being reflected back upon the one who hurt her. It was a power that made the air around them grow colder, while a giant wall of ice coalesced in front of them all, offering a solid shield of protection. The block of ice had grown rapidly from the cold air that surrounded it, and the outermost layer was covered by frosted shards and spikes. The tinks of metal chain clashing against the far side of the block were barely discernible over Malloch's wailing tantrum, "No. No! NOOOO!"

The little girl still held her hand up in the air. With cold determination in her tiny voice, she squeaked a small, "No," before the wall of ice began to move. It inched away from their huddled group, gathering momentum, until it slid faster and faster towards Malloch's chained form. His yells were abruptly cut off when the ice wall impacted the spot where he lay. Still sliding, the wall bounced off the pillar and continued until it slammed against the far wall, and the Dark Room's entryway, with tremendous force.

Malloch and the Dark Room were no more.

The little girl fainted to the floor.

It took another minute for Leon to scramble to his feet, shocked over what had just occurred. He holstered Revelator across the strap on his back, and lifted the small unconscious girl into his arms. Her exposed neck and legs were cold to the touch, but she was light and easy to carry. Small puffs of cold air escaped her lips, telling Leon she still breathed.

They made their way towards the building's mess hall, where Kelleren and the dwarven cook anxiously waited. Gérda let out an explosive breath in relief, while Kelleren's tail wagged so hard it slapped against his tan flanks. Miala started to make introductions for her companion, but the childlike smiles were cut short when Calvin stated, "We've run out of time. We have to go!"

Sensing the urgency, Leon stated, "We can do this on the way back." He hurried to open the large entryway door and usher everyone outside.

The setting sun painted the various mancer towers in hues of oranges and reds. They matched the oranges and reds of several airships that were partially on fire above the city. It seemed that the battle outside had moved within. The fighting was no longer contained to the northern walls. Distant cannon fire constantly sounded in the air, as dragons, gryphons, and airships all appeared to swarm in a giant mass.

One particularly low flying mail carrier, just outside the gates of the Academy, was intercepted by a fast moving gryphon. They collided, and both the undead gryphon and rowboat-sized carrier tumbled to a crash landing within the grounds. Next to their remains, turning a corner at the gate, came a large lumbering shape with a figure astride it. Calvin, who watched the scene unfold from next to Leon, blanched at the sight of the figure. He slapped Leon's pauldron and pointed to a small tower that stood off to their right, which looked separated and secluded from its neighboring structures, "To my tower! Run! As fast as you can! Go!"

They all ran. The athletic orcish child was in front, next to Miala, who carried the small gnomish child. Calvin and Gérda ran in the middle, and Leon lagged behind – slowed by his armor and the young girl he carried. Kelleren barked once on the way to the tower, and Miala hollered over her shoulder, "He's coming!"

"Who's coming?" Leon asked.

"Clybourne! The head of the Academy! Run faster!" Calvin yelled.

Leon faintly remembered walking past the headmaster of the Academy on their way to the Archive, and recalled the large bear that accompanied the man. He knew he could go no faster with his current encumbrances, and a prickle of dread ran down his back as the stress of the situation increased.

When they were halfway to the tower, Calvin yelled in apparent anger. Then the ground ahead of Miala and the orcish child rose like a grassy wave. As everyone tried to stop and go around it, the wave just grew and spread, until grass and brown earth came crashing down in their midst. The shouts of panic and fear that came from the conscious children, and Gérda, were accompanied by the rumble of soil as it built up around them. Dirt and earth converged to form an impenetrable barrier on all sides, save a singular small opening.

Just as quickly as it had started the falling dirt halted, as if frozen in place by some invisible shield. They huddled together within the small earthen cave that had formed in mere moments, and watched as geomancer Clybourne dismounted from his huge bear right outside of its opening. The bear growled at them, as the middle-aged man with shoulder-length brown hair, and a suntanned, weathered face patted its flank in a calming motion. He then tugged at a glove he wore – a glove that looked as though it had three wooden wands that poked out from between his knuckles. The claw-like glove was pointed in their direction while the geomancer stared at them wordlessly.

The tension grew as each moment passed. The headmaster looked at each of them in turn before his eyes settled on one individual in particular. "What have you done, Calvin?"

"Wait, he knows who you are?" Leon blurted out.

Calvin took a step forward, towards the small entrance. "I'm finally righting some wrongs, Dyre. I told you countless times to stop what you were doing. I finally had the opportunity to take action."

Clyborne's eyes flitted to the children among them, and his stance didn't waver as he asked, "Malloch?"

Miala spoke before anyone else, "Dead."

"An impressive feat. Wait, I know you," Clybourne said as he peered at her, "You are the deserter. Mytheryin. The pyromancer who burned Psiente."

Miala lifted her head and stuck out her chin in defiance, "I do not deny it."

"She destroyed the Dark Room at my direction." Calvin added. "The things done there, Clybourne, should never have been done. It needed to end. It all does."

"Welcome to the end!" Clybourne gestured behind himself with his other hand. "The city is lost. While evacuating our forces, after the populace of course, the undead broke through. They are now ravaging the city. The remaining undead air forces have been systematically destroying every ship that we have. Pretty soon the only things left will be the unstoppable ones.

That shining ship, and the dreadnoughts. Everyone else is headed to Last Bastion – where the living world will end."

The geomancer snarled at the chronomancer as he continued, "Face it Calvin. We've lost. We're doomed."

"You're wrong, Dyre. There is still hope. Hope here. Hope in Adonai. These people, they are–" Calvin retorted.

"You can't chase me out of your tower with your fairy tales anymore." Clybourne interrupted as he pointed behind him with his non-wand hand again. "This is reality! We cannot stop the tide of undead! We have tried and failed!"

Calvin responded in a calm voice, but his words dripped with fervor, "Then by all means Dyre, tell us what you came here to do."

The tension of the moment built, and Leon thought they would all be buried with a simple wave of Headmaster Clybourne's hand. It certainly seemed as though there was no love lost between the two powerful mancers. The geomancer finally blurted, "I came here to make sure that the undead horde had no liches to make."

Calvin scoffed, "You came back to kill everyone here because you thought the battle was lost? You came here to cover up your failures and hide what you have done from anyone who might yet survive. You came here because you are a coward to the end, Dyre!"

As the geomancer raised his wands to close the opening and trap everyone inside, a large explosion sounded behind him, causing them all to look. One of the massive dreadnought airships, commissioned by Lucien, had careened into one of the large mancer towers in what appeared to be an attempt to land. The ship's wooden hull had splintered as it knocked the tower down. Both stone and ship were sent crashing to the earth below, causing the terrifying sound. The vessel slid toward them, across the open lawn, before it came to a stop only a few yards away.

Calvin jumped toward the headmaster while he was distracted, and twisted his arms around Clybourne's neck. Positioning himself behind the geomancer, and on the opposite side of the bear, Calvin screamed, "Go everyone! Head to my tower! It is the only way to escape!"

The bear roared ferociously as Leon led the children, Gérda, and Miala, out of the makeshift cave. They ran at a sprint towards the tower, and Leon turned around to check on Calvin. The chronomancer still held the geomancer in a headlock while they looked to see who would disembark from the large vessel's several gangplanks. Naval soldiers of all races rushed off the ship, as well as a few well-armored but gaunt civilians. They ran down in twos and threes, then they began to swarm by the dozens, as they all made a beeline for Calvin, Clybourne, and the bear.

Every last one of them bore the glowing red eyes of undeath.

Chapter 6: The Tower

The shock of seeing the undead pour out from one of his father's airships was tempered by Leon's concern for Calvin.

"Go, Leon! Go, now! Have faith!" Calvin shouted, before he released Clybourne and spoke a few separate hushed words to him. The two mancers had only a few moments before the rush of undead would overtake them. Leon was torn by a yearning to help defend them, and the knowledge that he had to help the others up the tower. On top of that, his arms were starting to ache from the unconscious little girl he still held.

Reaching his decision, with an understanding of the sacrifice Calvin made for them to escape, Leon once again raced toward the chronomancer's squat tower, securely holding the child in his arms. The rumble of churning earth came from behind him, and the roar of the headmaster's bear chilled Leon's blood. Not daring to slow down or look back, Leon continued to hustle towards the circular tower that rose a meager three stories in the air. When he reached the old, simple, wooden door he barrelled inside and found Miala waiting for him.

"The others have started to go up already. Calvin…" Miala trailed off as she looked behind Leon. Her face grew pale as she closed her eyes, and hurriedly shut the door. A small coat rack stood to one side of the tower entrance, while many wooden barrels filled with supplies were stacked and crammed against the stone block center of the structure straight ahead. To their left, a wide staircase with an accompanying handrail began to spiral up along the outer wall of the tower. Overall, the base of the tower was simplistic in its design.

"He's not coming." Leon stated.

"He must have known this was going to happen, right?" Miala asked, as she started to climb the staircase. She held a steadying hand on the railing that ran alongside it, and looked numb from the whole experience. Leon couldn't blame her. The Academy, Calvin, and a crashing dreadnought airship full of undead had not been what he anticipated when they came to defend Agaprya. Let alone to then be told to run to a tower, and that it would be their way of escape? Leon had noticed how far away the tower was from the outer walls of the Academy, and he couldn't see a way out of their current predicament.

The circular stairwell that wound its way up the tower soon transitioned from stone to wooden planking. The flimsy thump and creak of the dry wooden steps caused Leon to worry that he might fall through each one he placed his weight on. After cautiously climbing up a few more, Leon ran smack into Miala. While he had been looking down at each spot he placed his feet, she had come to a standstill. She stood and stared at a scrap piece of parchment, with prominent flowing letters, that had been attached to the wall.

It was addressed to them, which would have been impossible had Calvin not been the owner of the tower.

Miala: Everything will be fine, don't worry.
Leon: Don't forget to break enough steps behind you so
that if the undead do come in, they cannot go up.

"This is…incredible." Miala breathed. "I was just starting to worry about how we will get out of here when…"

Leon's arms were burning by this point. "Can you take her? I guess I have to destroy the steps."

He gingerly handed the unconscious little girl to Miala, who then continued up the stairs in a daze. Meanwhile, Leon turned around and began to stomp on each wooden stair. The old wood was rotted in places, and more often than not, gave way easily under the extra force. His limbs were tired, and he was drained both emotionally and physically, but the desperation of their situation brought a fresh, needed vigor to his task.

After ascending a quarter turn up the tower, and destroying enough steps that not even an ogre could jump the distance, another parchment awaited Leon on the wall.

That should be enough, Leon. You're not going out that way.

Wondering just how many notes the mancer had left them, Leon turned and continued to climb the stairwell. A short distance later, he reached a platform where Miala was gently handing the unconscious girl up a small ladder to Gérda and the orcish boy. Leon scrambled to help them carefully pull her up, and soon they all found themselves in a dimly lit room. The only source of fading light came from a window that faced outwards from the Academy, towards the city's center. The sun had almost set, but the chaos of the battle was still told of by the cannon blasts and distant roars of beasts. Gérda, now taking a turn holding the little girl, muttered, "Dreadful noise outside that is. Still, how are we gonna get outta here?"

"Let's see." Miala responded, as she held a hand up and lit it with her internal heat. As it transitioned from a dull red to a bright yellow, it illuminated more of the tower's interior, which caused everyone to gasp.

Some things were expected to be seen in the illumination of the dim light: a bed along the wall, a wardrobe next to it, even a small writing desk with notes and sheets of paper on it. Crumpled bits of parchment were littered around the desk, some of them with half scrawled messages that ended mid-sentence. A small barrel near the window was half full of water. There was even a circular rug in the center of the tower chamber, and a small ladder off to the side.

What hadn't been expected, were the strings and cord suspended above it all. Different colored strings, marked with small pieces of parchment at various points, were tied from different points of the room and interwoven together before they all connected onto one central piece of rope. It was like looking at a gigantic fraying rope that was being repaired at several different areas. Occasionally, two or more strings would twine together in different places, and a note would hang from that point. Other times strings would end abruptly, or be tied upon the central rope, which appeared to be the crux of the structure.

While they all gazed upon it in soundless wonder, Leon's eye caught one particular note that hung where one string ended and connected to another.

Leon's mind reeled as he saw the familiar name of his deceased captain. The prince who had been dying, and to whom Leon had delivered the final killing blow, ensuring he would not rise again as undead. The act had mutilated Leon emotionally, as he had been eaten alive by guilt for months. After Leon confessed all of his wrongdoings to Adonai, and requested forgiveness for them, the matter had become something that he struggled less with. Yet here was a note in a strange man's tower that brought all of the emotions flooding back. Leon fought back tears, realizing it had been days since he had last thought about Gelan, and his failure to successfully fulfill his duty to keep the prince alive. Bitterness and guilt threatened to rise up again, but Leon tamped it down by recalling the lessons he had learned from his teachers Rohiel and Lochemetel.

Filled with a desire to know more about the intricate tangle before him, Leon started to track the prince's string to others. Distantly, he heard Gérda state that the young girl he had carried was coming around after a drink of water. The girl coughed and sputtered before she weakly croaked, "That's pretty," as she pointed to the strings Leon was investigating.

Kelleren woofed quietly, padded over to the girl, and licked her face. Where a typical child might laugh, she remained silent and made no motion to pet the animal. Gérda broke the silence again by saying, "There there, missy. We are safe fer now. Me name is Gérda Brasstoe. What's yer name?"

The girl remained silent but started to pet Kelleren, who wagged his tail in response. After a few moments, she muttered, "Brigid."

"Oh, that's a nice name, missy!" The dwarven cook was obviously trying to stay bright and cheerful for the child. She looked up from her current charge and asked the others, "What about ya lads?"

"Sam." The older orc child stated, his short tusks adding breathiness to his name, "The gnome is called Tyne. You got her to talk. She rarely does."

"Well, a quenched thirst helps loosen tha lips!" Gérda responded, as Leon found where the prince's string connected with the central rope. He followed some of the other lines that wound along the rope, and read several other notes that were attached with names or events. Leon recognized some names of lords and ladies from the Xaelon court as he followed along the strands. Other obscure names trailed off the rope or ended abruptly. He felt as though he was making no progress, until he got to one end of one rope that was on the wall, and saw two names on two separate strings. King Garinth's father, King Gaermik, was labeled for one string. The other string had another name that was familiar to Leon:

Liam Rhise

Leon's hands started to tremble as the realization of what the strings and rope actually were dawned on him. They were lives. Lives that Calvin must have known or observed through his mancey.

This could give me more answers! He thought.

His fatigue gave way to excitement as he looked over the entire structure with renewed interest. Leon quickly saw the two strings of Liam and Gaermik twining and traveling together next to the rope. After a few uninteresting notes, those strings gave way to newer ones, those of Lucien and Garinth. The strings of his siblings, Laric and Liara, appeared, as well as the two royals, Gelan and Giselle. Even the late Queen Dionne and Leon's mother, Lady Erika, became involved in the intricate tangle of lives that Leon was tracking. A feverish desire to know more about these strings arose within him, as he continued to follow them to where they culminated in a massive knot. Many of the strings branched away from it, while new ones were added. Leon saw the queen's string break off just before the massive knot – a sign, he surmised, of her passing. A hanging note confirmed his assumption.

But there was no note for the giant knot itself! It was bigger than any of the others that he saw, so logically, it must be an important event! Frustrated, Leon was about to give up on the whole endeavor when he saw that a light blue string, which started from within the knot itself, was labeled with a small note not too far away:

Leon

Was the knot... my birth? Leon guessed.

He started to follow his string until his task was interrupted by Revelator suddenly turning on. The bright white light illuminated the room much better than Miala's hand, which prompted her to speak as she ceased using her mancey, "I was wondering when sunset would happen."

The others in the tower looked at the light in wonder, and Gérda asked Leon, "Who exactly are y'all?" Leon didn't respond.

He was too busy staring at the envelope Revelator's light had revealed. It was addressed to him, and hung from the center of the strings in the room. In big letters that covered both sides of the packet, the envelope lazily twirled 'Leon' over and over until he cut it down with Revelator's tip.

The action had a cascading effect of undoing a large part of the string structure. Several strings twanged, and then others fell apart. A few voices, along with his own, groaned their disappointment and frustration. What events were lost? *What did I miss?* Leon lamented to himself as he grasped the envelope and finally responded.

"Besides being a bumbling fool, I am Leon. Judge of Xaelon."

"The bandit?" Gérda recoiled.

Leon gestured at the pile of string on the floor. "Right now it seems more like a destroyer of precious clues."

"What's that?" Miala asked, as she came over to him.

Leon opened the envelope to see a few folded pieces of parchment. "I think... It's another note Calvin left. For me."

Miala looked between Leon, the note, Gérda, and the children huddled around Kelleren before she stated, "I'll go fill them in, and give you some privacy."

Leon mouthed 'Thank you' before he opened the letter with nervous hands and began to read.

I can't tell you how many times I have wondered if events would unfold as I had foreseen or not. Adonai granted me this power, of that I fully believe. It's not like one of the dark powers, forced upon those who would not have wanted them to begin with, had they known what they would be subjected to in order to receive them. They did not have any choice in their powers. However, we know that for those of us who love Adonai, and are called to His purposes, He will use what was once malignant in our lives for the betterment of ourselves and others. Of that, I am thankful.

Indeed, I have had the time to look back and reflect on my own wrongdoings. My lackadaisicalness. My hesitancy to deal with the issues that persisted here at Mancer Academy. I tried to take a gentle approach, by reminding the headmaster that what we were doing was wrong every time he visited me. It took using the mancey I had, and looking into possible futures, to realize my error. When we are called to His purposes, but we remain inactive, He will call someone else. I remained relatively silent for years, even though I was entrusted with such a gift as this. Because of my inaction, Adonai called you to His purposes. Being able to see ahead is something that I am thankful for. But this gift of foresight also comes with its own curses.

One such curse was seeing my own death. It was a reoccurring dream, like many others. I came to realize that the more times I dreamt of something, the more likely it was that the event would happen. Only some events are fixed, you see. Pre-determined. How we get there, and who is there with us, is up to us. We are time-based beings, after all. Adonai is not. But, if memory also serves, you've already had that lesson.

I would ask you not to grieve for me, since, to you, we are mere acquaintances. We have, or will have (using the correct tense is absolutely infuriating when peering through time) only met two times. A small part of me wishes that you would grieve, though. Because, for me, well, I've watched you practically my entire life! I've had to watch you, to ensure that things unfolded the way they needed to, to guarantee the best possible outcome for you. That is why I must impart certain truths to you.

First and foremost the knowledge that I should impart to you is this: the spear that allows you to read this was deposited in Rhise manor as a housewarming gift. It wasn't always rusted, and my predecessor saw the need for it to be there, so I followed orders. It was me, Leon. I placed the spear there after Lord Liam Rhise built the manor. I'll pause here to allow the weight of this revelation to crash about your shoulders.

Another insight you should have is that there were three possible choices for who could take up the spear. I am thankful that you did, as the other possibilities would have brought about a much darker result, but the same eventual outcome. I am sure your advisors could fill you in, if they choose to. We all have our choices to make, you see. I have made mine, and I am thankful you have made yours. It led you here with the children, which is my next major revelation.

These children that we rescued are essential to the future. Should you succeed, should Xhormas be stopped, they are vital to the survival of everyone afterward. Protect them. Guide them. Nurture them. I can tell you that while one of them has revealed (or perhaps will reveal) their powers to you by the time you read this, the others soon will also. I won't spoil that surprise, as much as it may infuriate you. Causality, you see?

I pray you succeed. I can't see it all, unfortunately. I started to pray to Adonai again after having stopped for so long. Keep doing it yourself, as He always listens when you do. He answered (or will answer) my prayers when I saw (will see) you again at the tower. Blasted tenses again!

Remember what Prince Gelan told you: lead with love, because love conquers all. Remember your tenets: Love. Joy. Peace. Patience. Kindness. Goodness. Faithfulness. Gentleness. Self-Control. Make them a part of you. It is one thing to know them in your head. It is another to know them in your heart. But what a heart it is already. I am as proud of you as any father, or at my age, grandfather, could possibly be. You have grown strong, kind, and exhibit the tenets that were taught to you just as they were taught to me.

Glad to have known you,
Calvin Caerx

P.S. - Stick Revelator out the window. The Esperella is about to pass over.

Leon stumbled to the window as he wiped the tears that flowed freely from his eyes. Stuffing the letter under his chest armor, his eyes continued to well up as he held the shining spearhead out of the window, and into the darkening night. Waving it for the *Esperella* to see, he spoke over his shoulder in response to the quizzical locks that came from Miala and the others, "The *Esperella* is coming."

Sure enough, a few moments later, the similar bright glow of the sizeable aeonyte airship lit the night sky. Its bright hull caused Leon to squint his eyes as it glided near, and descended below the window. Miala whispered to the children and Gérda about the airship, and they gathered next to Leon as the upper deck appeared. Princess Schalae and General Xiphos stood at the railing. Duamé, Gionna, and Magnus were gathered near them as well, showing they had made it back safely. Lorog stood near General Xiphos with his sword held out, as he watched for flying foes.

"How did you know we would be here? To look for Revelator?" Leon asked.

"The old man, Calvin, gave instructions to us." Hollered Xiphos.

"Hurry! We don't have much time!" Princess Schalae yelled, as Leon half climbed out the wide window. The glowing ship gave off enough light for Leon to easily help each child, and Kelleren, up and over the side of the main deck. As Gérda made her way on board, a warning shout from near the bow caused some of the turrets and fighters on the top deck to reposition. A few shadows flitted nearby as Miala hopped over. The nearby crossbow and mancer turrets began to fire just as Leon grabbed ahold of the railing.

Lorog bellowed, "Look out!" before a shudder and crash jarred Leon, causing his weight to shift unexpectedly. A scream came from nearby, and someone shouted, "Wilhelm! No!" Leon looked and saw the remains of a gryphon, dwarf, and a crossbow turret tumble to the nearby ground. His hands were slick with sweat, and arm muscles worn out from exhaustion, but Leon held onto the railing as the *Esperella* jolted and started to move forward.

"I'm slipping!" Leon yelled, right as he felt hands grab onto his forearms. Looking downward in the darkness, he could see that the tower base was ringed with the red eyes of the undead. Heads, weapons, and arms were all stretched upward, bent on mindless destruction. A few projectiles were lobbed at the ship, and clinked against the hull as Leon began to be pulled upward. A stray bolt scraped against Leon's armored elbow before a sudden yank quickly hauled him up.

It hadn't been the combined efforts of several people pulling on him that had brought him sprawling onto the deck. It was the teenaged orcish boy, Sam. Smaller than Leon, with a frame that was wiry from malnourishment, the miraculous feat of strength still hadn't seemed to tax him. As Sam continued to pull him to his feet, Leon noticed that the exertion didn't even cause the boy to breathe hard. While some crew members simply looked at the boy with the strength of a giant in awe, others, like Duamé, moved forward to help steady Leon.

"Thank you," Leon said, as he clasped the boy's shoulder in a gesture of friendship.

"Don't mention it." Sam rumbled. The orcish boy's face was a mixture of emotions that Leon couldn't decipher.

Duamé clapped Sam on the back, "How in the hematite did'ya do–"

The screech of a nearby undead gryphon caused Leon to jerk as the *Esperella* picked up speed. Leon looked in the direction the sound had come from, and saw a mass of fur and feathers engaged in a fight with the entyrnet troll, Gezado, near the bow of the ship. His four arms and three axes whirled at the beak and talons that the gryphon wielded. As the sharp beak snapped too close, Gezado brought down one of his smaller axes on the chimera. It crunched to the deck as the entyrnet troll finished the undead beast off with his other weapons. Rather than pitch the mostly whole corpse of the half-lion, half-bird over the side, Gezado wordlessly met everyone's eyes as he pushed the beast down the bow's stairwell.

"That's tha third one! Ya don't need anymore!" Duamé yelled at the troll.

"I hungry! Fight make Gezado hungry!" The troll bellowed back.

A few chuckles trickled across the deck. He saw a few familiar faces that had been added to their ship's crew. Magnus stayed close to Gionna, and fiddled with the small airship straps on his harness. The guards from the tower were present as well. Surprisingly, the airship pilot Ophelia was on board. Her mail carrier was tucked near the bow of the ship, as she was at the wheel of the *Esperella* under Kérik's watchful eye. Leon's attention was then drawn to the scene behind them.

In the growing dark of night the battle could be seen beyond the ship's aft. The undead army had invaded the city, evidenced by the sea of glowing red eyes spread throughout its streets. The skies above looked just as menacing. Dark shapes flitted menacingly around the few remaining ships that were escaping to the northeast. Many of the other ships had been reduced to piles of burning wreckage in the city. Those heaps of rubble were stark reminders of the *Dawnfire* crash, which had sparked his journey.

The flying gryphons and dragons that attacked the remaining ships were becoming further away, as were the undead who had chased the *Esperella*. Leon noticed the recognizable shape of the Agapryan amphitheater in the city lights below. The enormous structure, once used for chariot races, now sat empty. Their airship flew east, alone. Behind them, what remained of the city was consumed by the horde.

They were retreating, which made sense to Leon, due to the darkness of night. The flying undead would be very difficult to see against the black sky. It looked as though the airships in the battle had suffered significant losses. While he could understand their forces taking some casualties, confusion over the turn of events roiled within him. "What happened during the battle? The air forces had been doing so well! Why were… There were wretches and shamblers coming out of the dreadnought that crashed at the Academy! Did we get all of the military forces out? Where are we going?"

Nervous glances passed between those in Leon's immediate vicinity. Kérik Silverspine's rough timbre finally sounded through the pipe assemblage originating at the wheel, cutting through the whistle of the wind on the top deck. "Anyone too exhausted after tha battle better head below. We got a small reprieve fer now. I'll sound off when we switch shifts."

The older dwarf gently placed a hand on Ophelia's shoulder, before he and Duamé headed towards Leon. From the glow of the airship's hull, as well as Revelator's projected light, Leon could see the grave expressions on their faces.

"What happened?" Leon demanded again.

"We'd better go below. Things just took a turn fer tha worse." Kérik replied.

Chapter 7: The War

It turned out that the nailed-down benches and tables in the *Esperella*'s galley were extremely useful for holding meetings. Leon sat next to Duamé and Miala, while the general and admiral sat opposite them. Princess Schalae, Gionna, and Magnus all sat at nearby tables. They were all tired, and the air was saturated with the smell of oiled armor and sweat. Gérda, giant paddle in hand, quickly took over the kitchen area of the ship with the mancer children. She took stock of what provisions they had, and soon the pleasant aroma of baking bread and sizzling meat accompanied the sound of her whispered instructions on how to cook this or that in the meeting's background.

"At some point after you left for the Academy the aerial tactics of the undead changed." General Xiphos started. "They stopped attacking this ship and started going after the others."

"An' by goin' after, she means tryin' ta take 'em over!" Kérik added.

"What? How?" Miala asked.

Kérik spoke grave words, "Tha dragons an' gryphons started ta bring shamblers an' wretches up on ta tha airships. Many on our side were caught totally unprepared. As tha undead started ta slay those on tha ships, they would turn. Then tha wretches an' liches aboard would turn those airships against tha others, an' tha walls themselves."

Leon felt like his heart dropped into his stomach. The undead army figured out a way to combat the aerial forces that had kept them out of Xaelon for so many years. No wonder there were so many piles of wreckage throughout the capital.

"Were our forces able to evacuate?" Leon asked.

General Xiphos shook her head. "Not nearly enough. When they started taking over our ships, it was like a fast spreading poison to our forces. Ship turned against ship, targeting both the crew members on board, and the levigems that held them aloft. When the undead vessels became too damaged, they deliberately crashed where they could do the most damage. They careened into other airships, or against our troops at the northern walls who were trying to hold off the horde's ground forces."

"It was a slaughter." Kérik agreed. "On the *Esperella,* we lost a few excellent warriors on tha top deck, an' a couple o' mancers too. Plus, we're down a crossbow turret. On tha bright side, we're all set fer ammunition, since we were able ta raid Miss Gærheart's house before we left tha battle."

A few of those present cast wary glances at the inventor gnome as she smiled brightly. "All too happy to help, my dearies."

Leon remembered the shack located on his friend's property with the large supply of black powder inside, as well as the half-built inventions that were strewn about her home workshop. Several of those scraps were now splayed around the airship's cargo hold. Miala informed him that with Duamé and Gionna's help, they could recycle some of them into workable materials to repair and resupply some of their stores.

"What of the dreadnoughts? The vessels my father committed?" Leon asked.

"One dreadnought was overtaken by the undead, which you saw." The general ticked off weathered, but strong, fingers as she spoke, "The other two I saw heading for Last Bastion before the fracas worsened. Perhaps a few more intact ships followed them after that."

Leon sighed in relief. At least those two ships were spared from the undead threat. "Then I imagine they are acting as the rear guard of the airship convoy headed to Last Bastion. So then, where are we headed now? Is the mail carrier pilot, Ophelia, still at the helm?"

"Aye, she's a smart lass. I thought I recognized her at first in tha battle, but admittedly, me attention was elsewhere. She was a decent recruit a few years back, an' a superb pilot. So I took her on as our Lieutenant an' third pilot. We need more than just tha two o' us flyin' this ol' girl!"

"As fer our destination, Ophelia told us where we needed ta go from that there Calvin fella." Duamé commented. The somber mood grew worse before Duamé continued, "Calvin told her that after tha battle, we needed ta head ta tha Lord Gardens. We need ta go ta Rhise Manor."

The temporary relief Leon felt turned to ice in his veins. "But everyone is heading towards Last Bastion! We need to stop Lucien, and halt Laric's coronation!" Leon protested.

"Not everyone is there." General Xiphos clarified. "Lucien and Laric Rhise were waiting for your mother and sister to meet them in Agaprya, but they never arrived. They were forced to leave with King Garinth's retinue, without them. Your mother and sister never showed up afterward. So either they went to Last Bastion by themselves, or…"

"Or they are still at the manor. With Silas." Leon finished. The concern he already carried for his mother and sister festered inside him.

Leon's mention of the Senechal was greeted with looks of confusion. The danger his family faced couldn't be sufficiently understood by those who didn't believe in Adonai, but he felt the need to make sure everyone was on the same parchment. For the next several minutes, Leon outlined the discovery of Silas by Lucien and Phonz, as well as the threat he posed. Then he recapped how the dwarven ring, the Diviner, had fit into Lucien Rhise's business plans to expand his mining empire from just levigems to iron as well. It all fit together, but there were still crucial puzzle pieces missing.

With one hand entwined with Gionna's, Magnus raised his other to ask a question, "Weren't there any menacing indications, or clues, as to the true intentions of this Silas fellow? He lived with you in the manor for years, yes?"

Leon thought about the question, as memories surfaced from his childhood.

Ten years ago…

"Leon!" A sharp voice hissed from down the hallway.

Guilt wracked through him as Leon turned to face his mother. She stalked toward him with a stern expression on her face, her light, golden blonde hair wafting behind her with each step. Once she was within arm's reach, she grabbed Leon's hand and pried it open. Try as he might, Leon couldn't hide the hairpin he had been using to unlock Senechal Silas' room.

His mother's slight frame was only a couple of heads taller than his, but her implacable will might as well have made her a giant.

She plucked the hairpin from his hand and looked around. No house servants were in the hallway, though, the portraits of stern-faced ancestors looked at Leon in silent judgement. This wasn't fair. Liara had not even finished counting to one hundred during her turn to search for Leon. *It was such a good idea!* He thought to himself, lamenting at being caught. Alone together in the hallway, Lady Erika herded Leon away from the Seneschal's room before whirling around on him.

"What were you thinking?" She demanded.

"Sis and I were playing hide and seek, mother! She never would have looked for me there! I thought I could just–"

"Break into a room? Violate our hospitality? Dishonor your family and father?" Lady Erika finished for him.

More guilt bubbled up inside Leon as the fun of the game dwindled into shame. "I–I did not think of that."

Hands on her hips, Lady Erika arched an elegant eyebrow, "Clearly."

A scuffle of shoes from further down the hallway made Leon turn. Suddenly, he was thankful for his mother's intervention as there stood Senechal Silas. His formal outfit was immaculately cut, and his long, dark hair was brought back into a tight ponytail. He held his white-gloved hands clasped together behind him, as his monotonous voice queried, "Is there something I can help with?"

The man must have a gift for almost always appearing at the exact worst moment, Leon thought. He felt his mother's gentle embrace from behind, as she rested her hand on his shoulder. "We are well, Senechal. How are you?" She inquired politely.

Silas' pale face remained impassive as he replied, "Fine, Lady Rhise. I hope I–"

Liara rounded the far corner of the second-story railing, her brown ringlets bouncing behind her. She cried out, "Found you, Leon!" before she skidded to a halt. Her bright young eyes widened slightly at the scene before her. Leon immediately saw a way out of the awkward situation, and rushed over to his older sister.

“I didn’t find a hiding spot in time, sis. But now it’s my turn to find you!”

“Leon!” Lady Erika hissed. Leon heard her admonishment but didn’t feel disappointed in his manner of speech the way his mother did. Abbreviating his words was something that grated on the Senechal. His father, Lucien, also didn’t like it. Their reasoning for abhorring it was that it sounded like commoner speech, but Leon had heard dwarves speak before and thought their cadence was delightful. However, whatever fallout had occurred when Leon was a mere babe caused Lucien to detest anything that reminded him of the dwarven population.

Senechal Silas’ wide lips tightened. “Mind your tongue, young Rhise.” He reprimanded, in a bored tone.

“No more hide and seek for today, children.” Lady Erika chided. Her tone was firm, but there was something else in her voice that Leon couldn’t figure out.

“But mother–” Leon and Liara protested together.

“Run along now, children. It is best that you do what your mother says.” Silas said. He ran a white-gloved finger across the top of the wainscotting and inspected it, clearly disinterested in their presence.

At the silent urgings of their mother’s gestures, Liara took Leon’s hand and whispered, “Come on!” They left the hallway, walking towards the grand staircase and entryway. A pale light shone from the glowing crystal chandelier on the ceiling. Various paintings and ancient artifacts that the Rhises had collected and hung on the walls over the years were illuminated under it. The housecleaning service was bustling through the halls, and gave Leon and his older sister warm smiles as they passed. Leon’s nose crinkled as he caught a whiff of an ogre, who stood at attention on the lower level. Liara’s nostrils flared as she looked at him, and they stifled their laughter while they quickened their steps toward the other wing of the home.

Out of the household staff’s earshot, Liara whispered, “What were you doing back there? Why did mother look upset?”

Leon huffed, “She caught me trying to get into the Seneschal’s room.”

Liara knocked Leon in the stomach with the back of her hand. It didn't hurt. She may have been older, but she was still smaller than him. "What were you thinking? No one goes in there!"

"Which is why it would have been perfect!" Leon wailed.

"Or dumb!" Liara retorted. "He gives me the creeps."

Leon saw his sister shiver and felt the need to reassure her. "Ah, he is just a glorified butler. C'mon, we can go read that book about heroes that father has in his library."

"Ugh. Again?"

Present day…

As he tried to convey every detail that he could about Silas, Leon wondered if he had ever really known anything real about the man. Obviously, there was a lot of missing information about him. Information that was crucial. If Rohiel claimed Silas directed the Mazzikin to attack him, what else was Silas capable of? Why hadn't he made any moves earlier?

"Living with him for twenty years, you would think you knew more about him." General Xiphos complained, "Still, what we do know is… disturbing."

A silent pall fell over the room until Duamé blurted, "Ya know, ya could just take a nap an' ask tha others."

That sparked a whole new discussion and explanation about Revelator, and the angelic dreams, for the newcomers. What first was met with resistance and doubt gave way to curious speculation by those who hadn't heard about their prior experiences. The angels had provided answers before. They could do so again if they chose to. The more Leon thought about it, the more he liked the idea. "Duamé, you're a genius!" Leon replied.

"Took ya long enough to admit it." He retorted.

There were still several hours until they would arrive at Rhise manor, which would provide plenty of time for a rest. Before Leon headed to the hammocks below, he sketched the layout of the manor and its grounds. General Xiphos had requested it so she could work up a plan of attack and rescue. If Silas was there with his sister and invalid mother, then Leon planned to rescue them no matter the cost.

Other members of their group also decided to get some rest, as fatigue from the battle of Agaprya overtook them. The mancer children, tired from their ordeal at the Academy, were given one of *Esperella*'s official rooms to rest in. The other room was given to the ladies of the ship, though it was becoming a bit cramped. Leon could faintly hear the teenage orc, Sam, protesting to Gérda below decks at being treated like a child, and insisting on guarding the children's room himself.

Leon dragged his own tired feet to the hammocks, and noticed a few vacant spots. Casualties were inevitable in war, yet the deaths of the *Esperella*'s crew members still stung Leon. Each person had a face, a life, and a purpose that had been cut short.

How many lives have been lost?

How many souls had been consigned to death because of Xhormas and his ungodly ambition?

The gentle rocking of the hammock helped Leon drift off to sleep, fully expecting that Rohiel or Lochemetel would greet him and answer some more of his questions.

Leon's dream began shrouded in fog. It wasn't numbing or desensitizing, as it had been before, but he felt confused by its presence. Shapes and flashes of light swirled all around Leon, and a cacophony of muffled sounds surrounded him. It sounded vaguely familiar, yet warbled. Discordant cracks of light and sound pierced through the fog. Leon willed himself to see through it, and tried to summon Revelator, as he had in prior dreams. He remembered an earlier lesson, one about walking by faith and not by sight. He stepped blindly forward into the fog, trusting that Adonai would keep him from harm. As he stepped through, his eyes itched furiously, and he found himself midair, above the city of Agaprya.

There before him were dragons, gryphons, and airships assaulting each other. Tooth, claw, and fire fought against cannons and projectiles. The crash of undead against airships reverberated around Leon, and the visceral intensity of the battle rocked him to his core. It was one thing to be a part of the battle, intent on survival and defeating the enemy. It was another to witness it, and see just how violent the war was. Yet, for all the plumes of dragon fire, all the cannon blasts, all the groans of splintering wood, they were still muffled and pale in comparison to the other battle that raged amid the chaos.

Thousands and thousands of Mazzikin filled the air. Like clouds of birds, they flew in waves and violently clashed against the equally aggressive malakim forces that stood against them. Bigger shapes, the winged and shadowy Nephilim, also peppered the sky. They spearheaded the attacks of the Mazzikin, to great effect. Those ghostly spirits of giants rallied all of the dark forces against the malakim. Leon thought that the battle they had just endured was intense enough. This otherworldly battle was almost maddening in its ferocity.

Unfamiliar shapes and creatures crashed against each other. He noticed spherical creatures made of golden, concentric, rings within rings that constantly turned. Every one of the creature's rings was covered with eyes, and while Leon first thought they might be nefarious, he saw that they were guarded by familiar-looking angelic beings. Their angelic guardians glowed from their faces and were armored in radiant aeonyte.

Some of the angelic hosts flew on giant pale wings in organized formations against the shadowy Mazzikin. Their bright flaming swords cut through shadowy weapons and tendrils, while the hairs on Leon's neck and arms raised in gooseflesh. Fervent war cries of rage or anguish filled the air, and were sometimes louder than the cannon fire from the oblivious airships that weaved through the battle.

Leon stood midair and surveyed Agaprya, while a war older than time itself raged around him. An unearthly groan of metal caused him to turn to the southeast – towards where he assaulted the Academy with Calvin and Miala. The entire space where the Mancer Academy should have been was shrouded by a dark cloud. Large black chains, like Malloch's tendrils, wrapped and undulated around the space, and the groan of metal resulted from those chains rasping against each other. That sound seemed to influence the battle itself. Every time a chain screeched, the dark forces would surge against the angelic ones. He watched as it sounded and an airship was rent asunder in midair by a dragon; which caused the angelic forces who had protected it to fly away and reposition.

Leon's eyes kept darting every which way, as he saw the battle through a new lens. In the back of his mind, he knew it was replaying for him to gain understanding. While this was not what he wanted to talk about with Rohiel or Lochemetel, it was a spectacle to behold.

"Rohiel?" Leon asked aloud.

"Have no fear." Rohiel's voice stated. Leon saw the angel step forward next to him, his head blazing bright like a torch. A warmth exuded from the light, and Leon saw that his bulky aeonyte plate armor also gave off a faint glow.

"You keep saying that." Leon stated.

"Minds can rarely comprehend the gravity of what they see. Many times when ones such as we appear to you, fear is the initial response. Fear, or worship, which is even worse."

They watched the battle rage on, as the forces of light and creation struggled against the forces of darkness and rebellion. A low hum built upon the edges of Leon's hearing. Pleasant to the ears, it reminded him of the sound that Revelator made when he and a friend grasped it together.

Then he saw the source of the humming sound: the *Esperella.*

A beacon of light soared across the sky, with a multitude of winged angels who bore flaming swords following closely behind it. To Leon, the *Esperella's* glow was reminiscent of the glowing ball of light that normally appeared in Leon's dreams. Spheres of rainbow hues fired from the ship's top deck, and cannon fire barked intermittently from its gun deck. While the undead's aerial forces couldn't prevail against it, more noteworthy was that all the forces of darkness couldn't even touch it. The Mazzikin and Nephilim forces seemed to slow or stop when they came within the light's reach, making them easy to dispatch for the angelic hosts.

"Why did the tactics of the enemy change?" Leon asked.

"Because of your efforts." Rohiel replied. A gauntleted hand rose, and for a moment, everything froze in place. With Rohiel's other hand, he guided Leon's eyes, and they turned to face the dark space that encompassed Mancer Academy. Time sped up as Rohiel rolled his hand, until he stopped, and the battle resumed at normal speed.

The metallic rasp screeched so loudly that it made Leon try to cover his ears, to no avail. As he watched, the dark spot quivered like a gelatin mold, and the dark chains that undulated from it exploded. Link by link, they faded into nothingness. Cracks of light appeared within the darkness, generated by a white fire that spread and burned it away until only the normal architecture of the academy was left.

"The Dark Room being destroyed held that much influence over the battle?" Leon asked, confused.

"Yes. Like so many sacrificial altars, or false idols that are worshiped, that place needed to be destroyed. Purged. All false altars must be brought low, for Adonai is the one true God. No b'nei ha'elohim, no fallen one, can take His place. In the altar's destruction, the enemy became weaker. More desperate."

The dark clouds of Mazzikin and Nephilim, who were no longer trying to destroy or pierce the glowing shell of the *Esperella*, shrieked in a demonic chorus. As one, they shifted their attention from the shining ship. The evil creatures, instead, accompanied the aerial undead and turned against the airship fleet. Leon watched as their newfound efforts, coupled with the dragon's tactics to deposit undead onboard by the clawful, shifted the tide of their battle.

The Mazzikin whispered their influence amongst the living, distracting them from their tasks at hand. Wretches, liches, and shamblers would slay those on board the ships, and then take over the ship itself. They would use those ships to ram others, or crash into the defenses on the northern wall. The wall of Agaprya soon broke, and the undead horde that had been held outside the gates poured in over the wreckage and through openings that were made.

Clouds of dark Mazzikin and Nephilim descended on the city streets. The very air around Leon felt oppressive, as Agaprya was overtaken and consumed. While the city fell, the heavenly defenders rallied around the last of the evacuating ships that fled to the northeast. A wave of Rohiel's hand dissolved the war back into the blank grey landscape, bathed in light from the glowing sphere above.

Leon was still processing the gravity of what he had seen, and the multitudes of beings that had been all around them as the battle raged. Not wanting to be deterred from his original purpose of the dream, Leon asked, "I… I must learn. About Silas. Who is he?"

Rohiel's glowing face dimmed slightly before he replied, ***"An abomination."***

"That doesn't really tell me anything." Leon quipped.

The grey landscape shifted to another familiar scene. The frozen images of Leon's friends, and Phonz Jasperfoot, surrounded the broken coffin in the abandoned giant tower. All of them, save Phonz, had a pale glow around them. The shadowed script along the walls of the oddly shaped room seemed ominous, almost sinister. As Leon tried to decipher what they meant, whether they were letters, or pictures, or even just art, his vision swam. Whatever it was, it was evil. This was confirmed by the faint sound of Rohiel's voice.

"Haughtiness, lies, hands that shed innocent blood, wickedness, evil, betrayal, warmongering."

Leon could feel the revulsion Rohiel felt from even just saying the words. The words evoked a slew of questions, but one stood out amongst the others. "His tenets?"

"Yes. Just as you follow Adonai with yours, so does he follow another with his. His lineage is a perversion. A mixing of kinds. Of Xhormas and humans."

Looking back on what he had learned in the Sanctuary, Leon made a few mental leaps and connections. "He's descended from Xhormas? Giants? A–A Nephilim?"

The scene from the tower dissolved away as a wave of light burst forth from above. The worry and concern that Leon had regarding the Seneschal dissipated as it crashed over and through him. Leon felt himself starting to wake up from the vision, but heard Rohiel speak once more.

"You must be ready."

Chapter 8: The Return

Upon waking up, Leon thought he should relieve Ophelia at the helm, as she must have flown through most of the night. She tiredly accepted his taking charge, and though it was still in the early hours of the morning, he tiredly tried to process everything he had learned. So much of his world had changed in the past couple of months. It had been easy to respect the chain of command, and simply follow orders when undead hordes were all he had to worry about. Life, as hard as it had been while growing up, had been simple back then. Ever since his eyes were opened to the truths of the world, to the evils both seen and unseen, Leon couldn't ignore the feelings that roiled inside himself. Maybe it was the 'Judge' part of him, but his rage toward Silas, Xhormas, and all that plagued the living festered inside.

Those feelings caused Leon to be a bit terse as he responded to the General and their other group members, who briefly met with him as they flew above the Lord Gardens. Over their cups of java, they discussed their plan of attack for the manor, and how to best deal with Silas. He answered questions about his childhood home as best as he could, but his one or two word answers quickly became telling. Leon's tiredness dissipated with every sip he took of the bitter liquid, but the bitterness inside of him grew.

When their meeting concluded, crew members peeled off below decks to either rest, or share what they had overheard in relation to their next mission. Leon had almost forgotten how news and rumors were as deeply embedded in a ship as the people who manned it. Within a few hours, both their meeting, and their plan of attack, would be repeatedly regurgitated by individuals who hadn't even been a part of it.

Duamé stayed behind in the predawn darkness, and kept Leon company. Silence stretched between them as the airship sped on. While many of the crew members slept the pale glow of the airship dimmed, causing its light to blend with the stars. As they continued their flight through the sky, the silence became almost unbearable to Leon. His emotions had reached a boiling point, and even in the dimmed light of the airship hull, his face clearly betrayed his inner feelings. Duamé finally broke the silence. "Ya alright, lad?"

"Does everything look alright?" Leon railed. "We are heading to face someone who is a danger to not just us, but the entire world! I grew up around said person for fifteen years with no idea, and now it just feels like we are headed to my house to clean up my mess. I should have known, Duamé! Adonai knows I had plenty of clues growing up."

His friend grunted, and reached up to pat him on the back. "Did ya ever hear tha legend o' Jairus Jadeeye?"

"Jairus?" Leon questioned. *What does this have to do with anything?*

"He's a dwarven legend. First dwarf ta figure out tha process ta make steel."

With Leon's seething silence at the helm, Duamé continued, "He figured it out late in life, and he had passed the knowledge down to his twin sons. Both o' his sons were alright in their own way, but when they got together, they would constantly bicker an' argue. Especially when it came ta who would run Jairus' forge when he was gone. Bein' tha first ta make steel, they were gonna be profitable right enough. An everybody knew that if Jairus chose one, tha other would be ruined. Tha secret ta forgin' steel would break his family if he told it to 'em."

Curiosity over the tale's outcome won out, and Leon asked, "So, what did he do?"

Duamé explained, "On his deathbed, he told one o' his sons half tha process. Tha other son got told tha other half. Told em both ta keep his secret from tha other brother until it was tha proper time. That way, they could only make tha steel if they worked together. They acted so nice ta each other, tryin' ta learn wot tha other knew, that they ended up becomin' good friends as well as brothers. An' so, later on, their relationship was restored."

Leon tried, and failed, to puzzle through Duamé's underlying message as he held the airship wheel. "So, what are you saying?"

The dwarf barked a laugh. "Flint an' feldspar! Yer as daft as dolomite sometimes, boyo! Tha point o' tha tale is when ya know something, ya have a responsibility ta use that knowledge wisely. Ya can't fault yerself fer when ya didn't know about this Silas fella. If ya know now, an' ya choose ta do nothing about it… Well, that's when I get ta knock me hammer upside yer Rhise head!"

The anger that burned inside Leon lessened as he continued to ponder his friend's words.

"...Thanks, Duamé. I appreciate the lesson."

"No problem! In exchange, I want first pick o' tha loot."

Confusion blossomed in Leon once again, "The what?"

"Tha loot! Ya said durin' our meetin' that yer home has a slew o' stuff, an' art, hangin' on tha wall. Tha last weapon ya took off there turned out ta be yer saltshaker! Since I had ta give away me ring we found in that alukah cave, I get first pick o' tha loot! Some o' tha stuff there might be useful!"

Duamé's logical reasoning caused Leon to think he was completely serious.

"So, just to be clear, you want to raid my childhood home, and the home of the soon-to-be king, for loot that may, or may not, be magical?"

"That's wot I said, ain't it?" Duamé bantered. "I got first dibs. I'll let ya ruminate on how fair that is while I go get some breakfast. Ya want anything?"

"Sure. Thanks, Duamé."

Breakfast came and went, along with the last few predawn hours. As the eastern sky brightened, just before sunrise, their airship began to pass over the last few manor houses and estates bordering the Rhise family lands. The Lord Gardens area was dotted with homes owned by various dukes and duchesses, and all of them were as extravagant as possible given the current circumstances in Xaelon. Dark outlines of grand mansions passed by on both the port and starboard sides of the *Esperella*. If any signs of life existed among the shadowy buildings below, Leon and the evening shift of elven scouts were unable to see them.

The landscape quickly became more familiar, and Leon knew that his childhood home was drawing near. With every second that passed, his muscles coiled tighter in anxious anticipation of what he would encounter. A shudder visibly passed through him, and once again he prayed aloud to Adonai for the safety of his mother and sister. He prayed that they would be able to defeat Silas, and that whatever plot he had would be foiled. As the words tumbled from Leon's lips, the glow of the airship and Revelator grew slightly brighter.

Afterward, Leon leaned over and spoke into the pipe assemblage near the ship's wheel. "We are approaching Rhise manor. Everyone who had been selected for the assault team should get ready."

Crew members climbed up the stairs to the top deck. Some made beelines toward the turrets with crossbow bolt cartridges in hand. Others, Leon saw, received a static shock as the mancer turret wands bonded to whichever elf or dwarf grabbed hold of them. Miala and Kelleren ascended a nearby stairwell and immediately made their way to Leon. Miala gave him a warm smile, and Kelleren padded over to briefly lean against his legs before dutifully returning to Miala's side.

Soon Leon began to see the other members of their inner circle make their way up. Gezado climbed the stairs crunching on a gryphon's leg and wiping his dirty hands on his leather armor. Gionna and Magnus also approached, still holding hands. Princess Schalae was the next to step up the stairs, giving a silent nod to Leon. Her Broken Bough was in its bow configuration, a few full quivers were strapped to her back and legs, and she appeared ready for whatever would come.

Kérik Silverspine was the last of their group to arrive, and he tapped Leon gently on the shoulder. Relieving him of the helm, the dwarf suggested Leon inspect and speak with the crew before reaching their destination. "A commander is only as good as his communication." Kérik rumbled the adage he had repeated several times before.

Leon walked among the crew while everyone not scouting the pre-dawn landscape watched him. Elven and dwarven eyes followed his every step as he addressed the ship. He reviewed the situation, and their plan of attack, while watching as their nods of assent and conviction were bolstered. Confidence blossomed within Leon. The more he talked about Adonai, about having faith in Him, the brighter the hull of the *Esperella* glowed. The ship now clashed against the gradually decreasing darkness and Leon made his way to the bow of the ship where he finished his speech. With Revelator held high, and pointed toward the giant aeonyte fist that adorned the front of the ship, the *Esperella* crested the final hill that led to the manor grounds.

The walls and the grounds surrounding the Rhise lands were completely empty. Leon couldn't see anyone as they passed over. No patrols of guards, no workers in the fields, there weren't even any grazing animals. Crop fields next to the stone border walls and fence lines were overgrown with produce, long since ready for harvest. Cornstalks and hayfields lay nearly untouched. Whatever defenses or resistance Silas might have in place, Leon hadn't expected to find this – nor had their plan accounted for it. It looked quite like what the scouts reported to Kérik at the helm: abandoned.

Yet, as they approached the manor, Leon felt a heaviness in his spirit. It was similar to the feeling he had at the Academy, and caused him to wonder what the manor looked like in the unseen spiritual realm. He knew, deep in his heart, that darkness still lay inside the structure. A shout from Kérik communicated that he was going to circle the manor before landing in the front courtyard. As they circled, Leon looked down and saw the abominably ugly fountain that sat just beyond the front steps. He cringed at its multi-tiered sculpture that represented Lucien Rhise's levigem mines. It was then, staring at the fountain, that he caught the first hint of movement from the corner of his eye.

Leon shifted his focus and looked up. He could faintly see wings and shapes flitting about the edge of the *Esperella*'s glow. At first he thought they were night birds, or bats. It was when the first sliver of the dawning sunlight pierced the horizon that the truth was revealed. Leon saw translucent wings and faint, dark reptilian skin as it winged away from the *Esperella* to join the other Mazzikin. A large vortex of them flew in a circle above the manor, and Leon recalled the time when he saw them fleeing the battle of Masterwork Halls. Hundreds of the spectral beasts flew above his childhood home, and he stood amazed at the sight.

He turned to Miala, who was only a few paces away, "Will you look at that?"

"At what?" she replied, confused.

Leon turned back and pointed to… nothing. There were no swirling Mazzikin, no vortex above the manor spinning like a tornado of darkness. The first rays of sunlight had touched the sky, ship, and manor, banishing the supernatural vision. Leon was convinced of what he had seen though, and even Miala's skeptical looks couldn't sway him. Leon waved her concern off with a hand and shouted for the ship to land. As the ship slowed he and Miala made their way across the top deck to the aft. The *Esperella* gracefully glided one last circle around the manor before it scraped across the gravel road on the far side of the fountain.

"Easy… EASY PUFFBALL!" Gionna shouted as the stone drive grated against the aeonyte.

Kérik gestured wildly at the ship as soon as he released its wheel. "Do ya want me ta get a crate from below decks? Ya can stand on it an' drive! If ya even ask nicely, I'll secure it ta tha deck fer ya!"

Those closest to them chuckled at his antics, and broke the tension of the moment. The gangplank was promptly extended down, where it rested at the swell of a hill Leon had climbed a couple of months before. Turrets swiveled and pivoted to ensure every structure, such as the horse stables and the fence-line, was covered.

Memories flooded through Leon as Gezado sauntered by him. Memories of the physical abuse from his older brother and father during his childhood. Memories of escaping every chance he could on horseback rides, or of playing games with Liara outside. The nights he spent crying into his mother's lap.

As he stood there, Miala, Duamé, Gionna, Kelleren, Schalae, and a few more dwarves and elves followed the entyrnet troll down the gangplank. The warriors were armed to the teeth with heavy axes, leaf-thin swords, and crossbows and arrows. Metal clinked, leather creaked, and the dark bark armor became more and more noticeable as the light of the morning shone brighter. Leon pulled both Revelator and his shield from the harness at his back. Securing the aeonyte shield to his forearm, Leon couldn't help but trace the small red levigem embedded in the glove with his finger as he descended from the ship. His last time here, he had been forcibly kicked out of his home.

Now, Leon wanted nothing more than to kick the front doors in.

Leon joined the meager twenty people at the base of the plank. Their initial plan had called for a small entry force. Granted, that was also when they planned on having to eliminate any resistance outside. Though that plan hadn't been necessary, no loss of life or munitions was a boon to their situation. Leon nodded to General Xiphos and Kérik on the top deck, and watched as the *Esperella* raised the gangplank and lifted off. The four large levigems that adorned its sides brought the airship up quickly, and unlike at Masterwork Halls, there were no stalactites to stop its vertical climb this time.

On the ground, their bows strung with arrows and crossbows cocked, the large group swept the interior of the stables to confirm no undead were inside. There were no undead horses, no feed, nor even any muck on the ground. If it weren't for the stray straw and rushes on the ground, Leon would have thought the place unused. The men and women present were all trained warriors though, and moved with purpose and determination to check every last corner in their tactical groups of two or more. They made quick work of clearing the building, but the sense of purpose began to weigh even heavier on Leon. Their group hurried from the stables toward the manor proper; the gravel crunching under his boots sounding as loud as exploding canister shot to Leon's ears.

Leon looked through the windows, but could see no movement inside. Doubt crept into his mind about their presence. From the exterior, the manor appeared abandoned. The interior could be a completely different story, but so far there had been no sign of life, or for that matter, unlife, either. Calvin had apparently insisted on them coming here instead of traveling to Last Bastion with the other survivors. General Xiphos had also told him that his mother and sister hadn't joined Lucien and Laric, much to their distress. Leon was determined to understand what happened with Silas, and where his missing family members were. Even if the manor was abandoned, even if he had to tear it apart to find clues, Leon would find his answers.

Duamé, silent until this point, sidled up next to Leon as they walked around the fountain. "Yer family's home is larger than I thought it was."

"Sorry. I know my grandfather, Lord Liam Rhise built it. But it flourished with stolen dwarven money."

After a moment, Duamé barked a laugh. "True. In a manner o' speakin', yer dad funded his manor in a terrible manner."

"Ugh, Duamé, even for you that was pretty bad." Miala groaned.

"Indeed. There are several armed people surrounding you, should you try a pun like that again." Schalae pointed out, with a slight lift of her bow.

"You're all puny, with just two arms. Four better." Gezado commented, not grasping the gist of the conversation.

"Is stealth any part of this mission?" Hissed Gionna, after which they all fell silent.

Their silence stretched until they reached the steps leading to the oaken front doors of the manor. No servants were present to pull the doors outward, and Leon gestured to their team that they were to stand with weapons ready for a fight. Confusion registered on Gezado's face, and though Leon tried to clarify, the entyrnet troll seemed unable to understand. Leon slowly pointed at the doors then motioned that they might take cover on either side of them. The troll holstered his axes as he immediately misconstrued Leon's meaning. Instead, Gezado leapt up the stairs and grasped the handles to both front doors.

"No! No! Wait!" Leon called in a frantic whisper.

But it was too late. Gezado forcefully yanked both doors open, then with a grunt and straining muscles, he ripped them clear off their ornate hinges. Leon saw that the main interior hall was lit, but not much else. Gezado's body suddenly shook from several crossbow bolts that were fired and embedded themselves in his torso. The large troll staggered backward and fell down the stairs, as Leon and the others cried out in alarm, and ran for cover against the manor walls. A familiar voice shouted, "Reload!" while Leon and a few others scrambled to drag Gezado's limp form away from the front doorway. The troll had a dozen heavy bolts sticking out of his chest that had easily punctured his leather armor. Eyes rolling wildly, the troll yanked the projectiles out of himself with his four hands. Halfway through the act, the troll's limbs fell limp over his massive chest.

Vengeful anger boiled inside Leon as he chanced a glance inside, protecting himself with his shield. The image of the grand entrance was burned into his mind. Red, glowing, undead eyes of the people who had once guarded the estate. Household staff who had succumbed to undeath. All of them faced the front doors in anticipation of their arrival. Leon's eyes fixed on a few particular people for the briefest moment before he withdrew. Retreating before more bolts could be fired, he relayed what he saw to his group with haste.

"Shamblers and wretches with weapons on the first floor. Two undead ogres! A dozen wretches with crossbows at the second floor railing! Two hostages with Silas among them!"

"By all means, come in! Let my eyes rest upon the Judge of Xaelon." Silas' menacing voice shouted from his position at the second floor banister. The brief glimpse Leon had gotten of him was overwhelmed by images of the knife and sword that were held to his mother's and sister's throats. The thin frame of Lady Erika sat unmoving in her wheelchair beside the Seneschal, her pale blonde hair framing her worried face. Liara was being held against Silas – her neck in the crook of his elbow. Leon didn't know what to do. As soon as he revealed himself, he could be shot down. Glances at his friends revealed shaking heads and silent pleas for him to not do it. Leon's gaze fell to rest upon the dead troll, Gezado, at his feet.

How many more will die today because of me?

"Silas! Release them!" Leon roared from next to the door.

"But we have so much to discuss. Besides, the fear from this one is absolutely delicious." Silas replied. Leon heard a slight struggle, and a yelp from his sister, before the Senechal continued, "If you care at all for them, you will drop your weapon and come in. Once you are dead, I might even let them go."

Leon's insides twisted at his predicament. Gionna leaned in next to him and whispered, "Buy time." Then she hurried from the side of the doorway and waved her hands and cane at the hovering *Esperella*. Leon numbly watched the small mail carrier depart from the main ship and glide down – presumably to meet her.

Giving his attention back to the grand entrance, Leon racked his brain over the situation. Silas had some sort of unfathomable command over the undead. They made no move to attack him and remained within the manor's entrance, safe from the airship's line of fire. Leon scrambled to think of something, anything, that he could say to Silas to get him to let them go. "Let them go first, then I will give myself up!"

"Leon! Don't!" Liara screamed.

Silas hissed, "Silence your tongue, woman. I would hate for his naval sword to kill his sister as well."

Rage built within Leon as he realized Silas threatened his family with his own naval sword. Realizing that Mazzikin were probably flitting about unseen, stoking the flame of his negative emotions, Leon took a few deep breaths and fought to clear his head. He noticed that the mail carrier had returned to the *Esperella*, and Gionna had transformed her cane into a crossbow as she hobbled back toward him. The red monocle fell over one of her eyes as she crept closer to the mansion.

"Come on, Silas! They aren't part of this. Let them go." Leon reasoned.

"Oh, but they are a part of this! For twenty long years, I have waited for this time. I've watched you all tear yourselves apart. Delighted in your torment of each other. But now the curtain can fall, and the living will die. Now my ultimate father will cleanse this world, and I will ascend to my rightful place."

The Seneschal's monologue gave Leon a revelation that made him feel as though he had been struck by a hammer. In the end, just like Lucien, it always came back to power. Because the Seneschal descended from Xhormas, and Leon followed Adonai, Silas would forever be diametrically opposed to him in every way. "It's too late. Adonai worship has returned to the world. You and Xhormas have lost, Silas!"

Silas erupted in a malicious laugh that felt wholly unnatural. Leon couldn't recall a time when he had ever heard the Seneschal laugh before. "Not if we simply kill everyone who still lives! Just like your sister and mother if you do not come out here this instant!"

Panic for their lives made Leon rush into the doorway, despite the protests of those around him. The shocked look on Liara's face was accompanied by a worried crease in her brow, and a wicked looking knife at her throat. The blade that pressed against her pale neck was crafted with several vicious hooks and curves. What struck Leon the most though, was truly seeing his mother for the first time in five years. She sat unmoving, in a basic looking wheelchair, but her piercing eyes held Leon more captive than anything Silas could do. Silas cast a predatory smile at him, his mouth stretching wider than what should be normal. The sword the Seneschal held against his mother, Leon's old naval sword, glinted in the light of the glowing crystal chandelier overhead.

Flanking them on either side were six undead guards. All of whom were armed with crossbows that poked out between the balusters. With their bolts aimed directly at him, it was hard for Leon to pull his eyes to the dozens of undead that stood in front of him. Weapons that had once adorned the manor's walls were now held in the grasp of his family's servants and soldiers. Humans, a few orcs, and two familiar looking ogres with large cleaver-like swords, all stood in silence. Their red glowing eyes never shifted from Leon, but that appeared to be the only evidence of their death. These individuals were recently slain, and only a few of the bodies showed any outward signs of small wounds.

If Leon had to suffer at their hands, then he would take as many of them down with him as possible. He just needed his sister and mother to be released. "Here I am, Silas. Now let my family go!"

As Liara struggled against the Seneschal, her dark hair and lithe limbs began to shake against his taller frame. The distorted smile on his face began to morph into a snarl as he said, "I would rather just make them watch you die, and then kil–"

The shaft of a crossbow bolt buried itself in the Seneschal's shoulder, and Liara elbowed Silas in the stomach a moment later. While he doubled over, his sister wrenched herself from Silas' grasp, and Leon heard Gionna shout from behind him, "Leon! MOVE!"

Noting the urgency in her voice, Leon grasped Revelator in his shield hand and immediately felt the weightlessness that stemmed from the levigem in his glove. As he launched himself up to the second floor landing, Leon saw the fast moving mail carrier pass directly underneath his feet. It flew where he had stood mere seconds before, and collided with one of the ogres in the horde on the ground floor. The flying rowboat splintered apart causing wooden shards to fly everywhere. Battle cries sounded from behind Leon, and crossbow bolts that were fired by the undead pinged off his shield and armor.

Focused on the scene that played out before him, Leon watched as Liara dodged a knife thrust from Silas and protectively threw herself toward her mother. Full of visible rage, Silas raised the naval sword to end the lives of Leon's family with one clean slice. Before he could complete his stroke, his head turned and his eyes grew wide. The Judge of Xaelon flew over the railing and straight for him – intending to end his existence once and for all.

Part Two: The Reckoning

"Rejoice with him, O heavens; bow down to him, all gods, for he avenges the blood of his children and takes vengeance on his adversaries. He repays those who hate him and cleanses his people's land." Deuteronomy 32:43 (ESV)

Chapter 9: The Unexpected

Silas ducked out of Revelator's path just before it pierced the oil painting of an aloof Lord Liam behind him. The tall man snarled in rage and struck out with Leon's naval sword, but it clanged off of Leon's upraised shield. Silas stepped closer and stabbed with his knife, but Leon countered by shoving against him with his shield, and immediately slicing with his spear.

The edge of the spear caught on the oil painting's frame, causing the whole thing to crash over Silas' head. As the man struggled to free himself from the confines of the canvas and wood, Leon stabbed at one of the crossbow wielding undead nearest to them, reducing him to a pile of salt. Chancing a glance over the railing, Leon saw that the undead horde was clambering over the mail carrier's splintered remains. They rushed to engage his assault team, who had run into the manor to defeat them. He watched Princess Schalae, Gionna, and a few archers open fire on the undead with their bows and crossbows, before he had to refocus his attention back on Silas.

The Seneschal untangled himself from the painting and launched himself toward Leon, swinging his sword and knife with swift precision. He roared in anger as Leon blocked or dodged each slice. Leon knew he and his family were in a bad tactical position for this battle. At any point the undead that lined the balcony railing could turn and shoot him in the back. Worse still, they could shoot his mother and sister. He also knew that he couldn't allow Silas to gain any ground; he was a quick and strong adversary. Using the spear's extended reach to his advantage, Leon stabbed and swung whenever he could to prevent Silas from advancing. Leon shouted over the din of the battle, "Liara, stay behind me! Protect our mother!"

"Focus on Silas, Leon!" That response had not come from Liara.

The voice those words belonged to was Lady Erika.

Confusion filled Leon as Silas recoiled from a few of his rapid-fire stabs. Glancing back, he saw that Lady Erika had pulled a decorative short sword from the wall and was currently fending off undead on the far side of the landing. Liara stood between them, and was reaching for a fallen undead's crossbow when Leon forced his gaze back to Silas.

How was she moving and talking? I was told that she was mute and paralyzed by...

The malicious grin Silas wore was quite unbecoming on his typically expressionless face. He let loose another fearsome snarl, and deflected one of Leon's stabs with the naval sword. The Seneschal then closed in on Leon with a fierce swipe of his wickedly hooked knife. It produced a hair raising screech as it scraped across the aeonyte shield, before catching its edge. Silas gave it a sudden, sharp yank. His attempt to wrest it or unbalance Leon failed, and his sword's follow-up slash was knocked away by the spear's wooden shaft.

The quick bladework and swordsmanship that Silas displayed was hard for Leon to keep up with. Between the battle that raged downstairs, his mother and sister's well being, and the overarching sinister plan he was trying to thwart, too much pulled at his concentration. Arrows and bolts that flew through the air, or the roar of an undead ogre, caused Leon's reaction times to be slower than normal. Worry for his family and friends also fought against his focus in the midst of Silas' attacks. Throughout all of his mental distractions sword and knife continued to clank relentlessly against his defenses, desperate to find an opening.

At the very last moment, while ducking under a crossbow bolt, Leon saw Silas slide his knife down Revelator's shaft towards his hand. He was forced to let go of the spear to avoid the blade's perilous proximity. As the spear fell to the ground Leon punched out with his shield hand, solidly hammering against the bolt that still protruded from the Seneschal. It bit deeper into his shoulder, and Silas was brought low for a brief moment. Before Leon could strike again, or retrieve Revelator, Silas managed to roll out of his reach.

Leon was too slow. He was unable to pick Revelator up before Silas stomped on one end of it. His upraised shield was his only defense as Silas launched blow after blow with the stolen naval sword. Words of frenzied frustration escaped from the Seneschal's lips, and he screamed, "Just die already!"

Leon didn't have time to respond. With surprising speed, the hooked knife arced at a diagonal angle towards his face. He grabbed Silas' wrist with one hand, deflected another sword swing with his shield, then slammed the Seneschal's knife hand repeatedly against the railing. On the third blow, the knife tumbled down to the first floor, and was lost in the chaos below. Not even a moment later, the price for disarming Silas was paid.

A sharp sting blossomed into harsh pain as Silas cut low and sliced into Leon's thigh. A shrill laugh at having caused injury escaped his lips – even as Leon shoved him away in response. Thankfully Leon's armor absorbed some of the impact, not allowing the cut to dig deep. Though pain still pulsed through it nonetheless. "It will not be long now!" Silas crooned, as he renewed his assault. He was determined to not give Leon any quarter, or a chance to retrieve Revelator.

Leon deflected every one of Silas' blows with his shield, and Silas was smart enough to stay out of Leon's reach after each attack. Both scrambled to find and take advantage of any opening while the battle raged around them. Leon was dimly aware that a fire had begun below, probably a result of Miala's pyromancy. It had crept up a wall, and blocked off the base of the nearest stairwell, preventing anyone from coming to his aid against Silas. The undead guards with crossbows had all been felled by arrows, which still protruded from their heads. Leon didn't have time to look behind him again, to gauge how his mother and sister fared against the other six guards. He hoped that they could successfully handle them together.

Silas found a sick pleasure in commenting throughout their struggle. Taunts that outlined what he would do to Leon's friends or family made his blood boil. It wasn't until Silas almost removed Leon's head with a rapid swing of his blade that Leon realized what was occuring. Silas was trying to get in his head, and succeeding. This was a man who could influence and control Mazzikin. He could certainly engage in mental warfare as well. Silas suddenly grew more frustrated when Leon deflected another blow.

"Ready to die, Judge?" Silas needled.

"Only after you!" Leon quipped.

The nearby fire had spread up the curving stairs as the battle continued below. Leon focused on Silas, unable to worry about his friends. He had to trust in their ability to defend themselves and dispatch the undead below. As he made the conscious effort to trust in his friends, and Adonai's protection over them, his faith was rekindled. Leon enjoyed how the tables then began to turn on Silas. A fresh wave of anger distorted Silas' features as he stabbed at Leon, overextending ever so slightly. Leon dodged, brought his shield hand down, and trapped the sword in its opening. Silas shouldered Leon in an attempt to jostle and disengage the sword, but only succeeded in causing them both to drop it.

Now without any weapons, the two resorted to a battle of fists and feet. Silas punched, but his blow glanced off Leon's head as he dodged. In turn, Leon launched his fist into Silas' gut, eliciting a groan as they grappled with each other. Neither wanted to give in, or let the other grab a weapon from the floor. Leon felt he was at a distinct disadvantage, due to his heavy scale and plate armor and bulky shield. Silas was far less encumbered by his leathery black suit. The Seneschal was also slightly taller in stature, and had a longer reach. Silas and Leon stumbled in the direction of the stairwell; its roaring flames licked towards them with more intensity than a heated oven.

While Silas threw his knee up, trying to land blows when and where he could, Leon grit his teeth against the pain that radiated from his thigh and head. He grasped the fletching end of the bolt still embedded in Silas' shoulder, and bent it around. Silas cried out in pain as he tried to turn away, wrenching Leon off balance. They pulled each other down the hall toward Lucien's office and away from the balcony over the grand foyer. Leon's back slammed into a wall just before Silas threw another punch at his head. Leon protected himself with his shield as he counterpunched, and his fist made a solid connection with Silas' face.

On and on they struggled, until Silas landed a punch squarely into the wounded flesh on Leon's thigh. Pain exploded from the site, causing Leon to roar as he fell to his knee. Silas kicked out and connected with Leon's shoulder, which knocked him to the floor. Leon struggled against the weight of his heavy armor to get up, but Silas planted a boot firmly against his neck. Pinned to the ground, Leon tried to awkwardly punch against the

Seneschal's foot. The pressure on his neck increased as Silas leaned down and used his hands to pin Leon's to the ground. The weight of his foot caused a pain so intense that Leon thought his neck would snap.

"If I want something done right," Silas growled into Leon's ear, "then I must do it myself."

Leon didn't think the pain in his neck could become any more severe as the unbearable pressure forced his windpipe shut. Leon's vision dimmed as Silas commented, "To think that I get the pleasure of dispatching you myself after the dragon I sent to attack the *Dawnfire* failed."

Leon glared at Silas with what little vision he had left, and squirmed in an attempt to free himself and exact revenge on the man. The pain of the past, the guilt that he had borne, everything he had blamed himself for was due to *this* man. Leon tried, without success, to bring a leg or a knee up and knock Silas off him. The Seneschal proved to be implacable and unmovable. As the last of Leon's vision faded, and he was succumbing to unconsciousness, the boot slipped from his neck allowing his sight to snap back into focus.

There stood his mother. Lady Erika was behind Silas, with the hilt of Leon's naval sword in her hand. Its blade protruded through Silas's chest, where it had passed clear through from behind.

"Do not touch my son!" Her frigid voice spoke, as she pulled back on the blade. Silas' back spasmed and was forced rigidly upright from the motion. He coughed, eyes blinking as he stared from Leon to the blade leaving his chest. Then, just before Lady Erika fully withdrew the blade, the man stretched his face into a repulsive, too-wide grin. Without a second's hesitation, his mother proceeded to make Silas a head shorter.

Disbelief filled Leon as he shoved the lifeless body of the strife-causing man off of himself. He groaned and pushed himself up from the floor, then stared at his mother with a slack-jawed expression. For so long his perception of her had been shaped by what he knew of her relationship with Lord Rhise. Meek, subservient, and a co-recipient of Lord Lucien's volatile anger. Now she stood before him thinner, shorter, and in an embroidered dress that completely contradicted the naval sword held at her side. A strength and stubbornness that Leon had never seen before exuded from her.

Something about her had changed. Something more than just her ability to walk and talk – which she supposedly couldn't do before.

"M-mother… I… How are you?" Leon stammered.

"All will be explained, Leon." She said patiently. She looked at Silas' lifeless form once more before her resolute composure crumbled. Sobbing, she hugged Leon fiercely as they stood there. They were finally reunited.

The heartfelt moment couldn't linger amidst the crackle of flames and crash of wood that sounded from down the hallway. They made their way back to the entrance hall, and found the undead horde below had been quelled. Miala and Duamé were hurrying the other fighters out through the manor's doors. Leon could swear that Duamé was picking up every weapon he could find as he walked throughout the ground floor. Some he tossed back to the floor, but others he cradled in a small pile in his arms as if they were a bundle of firewood. Princess Schalae was talking animatedly with Liara at the top of the remaining stairwell, near the family bedrooms. Flames licked close to Leon as he and Lady Erika ran towards them. The mother and daughter embraced while Leon paused his sprint to pick up Revelator. Once Leon caught up with them Liara hugged him just as fiercely, seemingly unable to stop her uncontrollable sobs.

As they stood there, arms wrapped around each other, smoke began to curl along the ceiling. Princess Schalae was forced to state the obvious, "We need to get out of here!"

Lady Erika quickly readjusted her grip on Leon's naval sword. Though smallest in stature among the four of them, her tone was the most commanding as she spoke, "Everyone else go. There is something I need to do."

Still hugging Liara, Leon looked over her dark hair at the area around them. One of the two curving staircases had been consumed by the fire; its flames had spread to block the hallway, and a fourth of the entryway itself also burned. There was no discernable way to douse the blaze. The rich oil paintings added fuel to the inferno, and Leon realized the manor would likely be lost within the hour.

"The Princess is right. We must leave now." Leon agreed.

Lady Erika didn't say anything further. She just walked down the hallway towards the family's living quarters. Leon gently handed Liara's sobbing, traumatized form to Schalae and said, "I'll be along shortly."

"Don't dally." The Princess responded, as she began to help Liara down the stairs.

Leon charged after his mother only to find that she hadn't gone far. She used his old sword to assault a door that had always been locked during his childhood. She had succeeded only in making a few rents in the wood before he arrived. Without protestation, Leon took the sword from her and finished the job with a few forceful swings. The sword's weight felt different to him as he had become so used to carrying Revelator over the past couple months. Once the door to Silas' room had crunched and splintered enough to allow Leon to reach in through the hole, he unlatched the lock from the inside. He was eager to discover whatever it was that his mother wanted. He wrested the door open and stepped into the anteroom preceding the decent sized bedroom, unsure of what to expect.

Lady Erika slid past him and stepped purposefully into the room. She ignored the sigils and scrawlings that covered the walls. Leon noted that they were reminiscent of the writing in the room Phonz had led them to at Masterwork Halls. The shadows within the room were also larger than what was normal – more pronounced than they should be. While Lady Erika moved straight to a small table beside a simple unadorned bed, Leon's eyes snapped to the only other thing that occupied the room.

Across from the bed, on a small bench against the wall, was what Leon could only describe as an altar. Small random items lay scattered over its surface. Jewels, bundles of hair, and small bones all rested either singularly or in piles around the bench's central feature: a clay statue roughly the size of Leon's shield.

The statue was significantly larger than the one that had been concealed within the mancer robe of the lich at the Archive. A headache began to build within Leon's skull as he looked at the statue with its black tendrils and ruby eyes. In the room's darkness, shadows appeared to combine with the statue's tendrils, granting them the illusion of movement. As his headache increased, Leon felt the malevolence that radiated from the statue of Xhormas.

Sword in one hand, and spear in the other, Leon knew which one needed to be used. A single stab from Revelator caused a bright flash within the room, and a high pitched screech of rage filled the air. The clay idol turned white and granulated into a pile of salt before Leon's eyes. With that one simple act, the statue was gone, shadows receded, and the headache disappeared just as quickly as it had begun. A yelp sounded from Leon's mother as the statue disintegrated. He turned to her and saw that she stared at the pile that had once been a statue with a small tied up bundle in her hand.

"Is… is that salt?"

Leon couldn't resist dishing her own words right back at her. "All will be explained, Mother."

She closed her eyes and took a deep breath. With a nod, she opened them once again, and pushed her hair back. "I deserved that, I suppose. We can go now."

Curious, Leon pointed to the bundle she held. "What's that?"

"Our letters to each other over the last five years."

So much pain and heartache had stemmed from the lack of communication from his family during his naval service. The heartbreak, the desolation and isolation he felt at having never received anything from any mail carrier over the years, all made sense to Leon now. Of course Silas had taken every letter. Of course they had been intercepted every time. Tears threatened to fall from Leon's eyes, and they weren't entirely due to the smoke that was filling the house. So much of what had happened grated on Leon's mind. He had wanted to make sense of it all, and now he would finally have a chance to.

"We'll have time to read them when we get to safety."

She nodded again, and grasped the letters tightly against herself. "Yes. We must go."

The heat within the entrance hall was almost unbearable. The fire and smoke that came from the far side of the space was intense and suffocating. They fled down the stairwell and to the front doors, where Duamé waited.

“What are you doing, Duamé?” Leon asked, gesturing to the multitude of weapons in his hands.

“Waitin’ fer ya! An’ makin’ sure I get me own saltshaker… If ya know wot I mean! This yer ma?”

Leon helped Lady Erika through the doors and away from the piles of undead that were starting to burn. “Yes, introductions later! Let’s get out of here!”

Leon turned to bid a silent goodbye to Gezado. The large troll still lay in repose, but a tapestry from inside the manor had been respectfully draped over him. The brave entyrnet troll had made the ultimate sacrifice for them, and while Leon grieved his loss, he could only hope that none of his other friends had also lost their lives in the assault. He sheathed Revelator and his shield in the harness on his back, then hurried around the fountain towards the *Esperella*. Lady Erika gasped at the sight of the aeonyte airship. With a smile, Leon shooed Duamé forward, then helped her up the gangplank and onto the deck. Shouts of, “Captain on deck!” greeted them, and Leon smiled at Lady Erika’s bemused expression.

Duamé reported that they had lost six of their warriors in the fight at the manor. None of them were Leon’s close friends, but the sting of losing any crew members still hurt. These were individuals that Leon had fought alongside in more than one battle. A camaraderie had formed with those he entrusted his life to. Every life taken by the undead was unacceptable, but the loss of crew on board the *Esperella* wrenched at Leon’s heart. The destruction of the mail carrier was also unfortunate, but Kérik’s quick thinking paired with Gionna’s crossbow bolt in Silas’s shoulder, had saved Leon from imminent death.

Overall, their mission at the manor had been a success. Silas was dead, and Ladies Erika and Liara had been rescued. Liara stood close by, staring at Leon and the transformation that had occurred in him. An even more wondrous change had occurred in Leon’s mother – who seemed to not only be mobile, but in constant motion. Her eyes darted about, every which way, as she took in the sights of the ship and her rescuers.

Solemn faces nodded to him, waiting for instruction. Leon cleared his throat and announced, “We mourn the lost, but are thankful that we did not have to strike them down once more. We just landed a major blow to the undead forces with the defeat of Silas. Now, let's finish the job! Set course due north for Last Bastion!"

Several affirmations were given, and Kérik nodded to him from the helm. The dwarf began issuing directions to prepare the *Esperella* for launch, but Leon couldn't hear what was said. His orders were drowned out by Liara's astonished exclamation, "Leon… How did you know we were here? How are YOU the Judge we've been hearing about? What in the world is going on?"

The gangplank behind him was noisily set into its resting place before Leon replied. "I imagine we all have tales to catch each other up on. If you would like, we can head below to discuss what comes next."

"Leon. Liara. Look."

Lady Erika had turned and pointed at the manor. The roar of the fire and the stench of smoke could be easily heard and smelled from where they stood. The waves of heat distorted the air and made the manor seem to quiver. A groan escaped the house, as wood bent and part of the roof collapsed inward. The shattering of glass and clay tiles joined the cracking wood. A cloud of smoke and embers puffed up into the air as if the building had taken one last fatal gasp. The mansion was nothing more than a pile of burning rubble. Leon felt his sister's hand slide into his and squeeze tightly. As the *Esperella* lifted off the ground, Leon felt as though a foundation block of his life had also been taken away. His home was gone.

After helping his mother and sister into simple airship belt harnesses, Leon escorted them to a nearby stairwell. There they were met by Kelleren, who ran in between Leon's legs. Pain throbbed through Leon's thigh with every step, but he smiled inwardly at the dog's antics – Kelleren reveled in cheering others up. The animal had proven to be a source of comfort and support, which was further confirmed by Liara happily ruffling his tan fur. She gushed over the canine as they descended to a landing and headed to the nailed down tables near the kitchen.

As they sat down, Miala, Duamé, Gionna, and Schalae also came down the stairwell. Liara and Lady Erika looked confused until Leon patiently introduced his friends to them. Feeling it would be best to first fill his family in on their adventures, Leon wasted no time launching into his accounts. He shared how he had become a Judge, about Adonai, and how belief in Him prevents people from turning undead. He recounted how he pretended to be Laric to gain entry into Agaprya, and that the wanted posters were the repercussions of his lie.

Liara and his mother took it all in. Liara asked a few questions, while Lady Erika remained silent as she listened. They seemed understandably surprised when Leon shared the more fantastical parts of their journey. They had heard that the Northern Elvenwood burned, and that the horde had attacked Masterwork Halls, but presumed that none had survived either event. Some accounts were clarified, and everyone had a good laugh over some of the vague descriptions that had been given to Liara about the supposed Judge of Xaelon.

"I was told the Judge had a white horse, slayed countless scores of undead, and carried a massive sword that only he could wield." Liara chortled.

Leon used the humorous interlude to start talking about Revelator and its mysterious powers. He told them everything from how it turned undead flesh, giants, and dragons to salt, to how it hummed when multiple believers held it, and everything in between. They were then treated to a visual example of his description when Princess Schalae and Leon used Revelator together, to tend to the cut on his thigh. His family marveled over the way he was wounded one moment, and the next he stretched his leg out, completely healed. His dreams and visions fascinated Liara, who engaged in the conversation much more than their mother. She already had a passing familiarity with Princess Schalae, and they both knew the famous inventor Gionna.

"At least these two had the presence of mind to not ask me for an autograph!" Gionna glared at Leon and Duamé.

"They did not!" Liara chuckled.

A few tears were shed when they recounted Anissa's reconciliation with Miala, and her subsequent passing. Then tears of laughter came from Liara when Duamé told of how he explained to the Entyrnet trolls that Leon and Miala were married to avoid an uncomfortable misunderstanding. Liara certainly looked delighted by the story, but Leon couldn't gauge his mother's reaction. She simply watched. Emotionless. Expressionless.

Soon enough, Leon found himself recapping their experiences during the defense of Agaprya, and their assault on Mancer Academy. During that retelling, Miala reached over and grasped Leon's hand for support. Her hand was abnormally warm, and Leon smiled at her before catching the amused look on Liara's face as she watched them. The subsequent story of how they rescued the children from the Dark Room, was punctuated by their arrival with Gérda. The dwarven woman ushered the children hurriedly past while they all nodded a friendly greeting. Gérda gathered them in the galley kitchen, apparently intent on cooking lunch.

Leon's throat felt dry by the time he finished catching his family up on all the notable adventures and experiences that had occurred since he left Rhise manor. An awkward silence trailed his story, which needed to be filled with another explanation. Both Leon and Liara turned to their mother, waiting to hear what she had to say. As the smells from the galley began to waft in their direction, Lady Erika's tight lipped expression cracked. Her aloof demeanor broke as the tears welled up in her tired eyes. Stress lines and crow's feet, that Leon hadn't noticed before, decorated her face.

"Mother, what happened?" Leon asked.

"Yes! How long have you been able to walk and talk?" Liara joined in.

Leon turned to his sister in confusion, "Wait, you didn't know?"

"Of course not!" Liara cried. "I had no idea that she could move until today."

Miala looked at them with concern in her eyes as she got up to leave. "Maybe we should let this be just between family."

Everyone looked to the teary eyed Lady Erika as she held her head in her hands. Her long, light hair cascaded over her fingers, and her voice was muffled as she spoke into her hands. It sounded as though she was saying the same thing over and over. Finally, she slammed her hands down on the table. The sudden action caused a few of them to jump. Scoffing, and shaking her head, she fixed her sight on the aeonyte hull instead of making eye contact with anyone in the room. Leon's mother repeated herself once more.

"I had to pretend. Otherwise everyone would have died."

Chapter 10: The Plot

Lady Erika breathed deeply before she continued, "Please. Everyone, sit. Your adventures have filled many of the gaps in my knowledge. I–I would not deny you the same courtesy."

Once everyone settled back down, Leon's mother spoke again, "It began about twenty years ago when Lucien returned from his trip to Masterwork Halls. When he left, he had wanted to be alone. But when he returned, he brought a strange person with him. He stood taller than most, and at first seemed nice. The man was willing to help around the manor, and proved to be extremely intelligent. Lucien taught him the mining business quickly, and made sure that Silas had a secure position at the house."

"So, they never told you how they met?" Leon asked. He had just told her about his experience in the crypt-like room of the giant tower minutes before.

"No. Lucien just brought him home and expected him to be listened to and obeyed." Lady Erika replied hotly. She sighed again before continuing, "I had you, your brother, and your sister to raise. I was busy. But more importantly, I was blind. Blind to how Lucien was changing. Blind to how his temper was growing. It was just little things at first. An outburst that was slightly too loud, or a punishment for one of you that was a little too severe."

"The years went by as Lucien's temper grew worse… and–"

Duamé raised his hand as he interrupted, "Wait. Wait. Wait! I'm all fer a good trash talk o' Lucien Rhise, but I thought we were talking about that Silas feller."

Leon's mother held up her own hand in a placating gesture. "The two men are linked. I know not how. I did start noticing though, that Lucien's temper would flare more often and more severely. Others around the house noticed as well. I even succumbed to anger outbursts a few times, until I started to suspect the cause."

Leon guessed, "Silas?"

"The man could somehow… influence emotions. When he was present, it would be easier to lose control. Not just anger, but stress, and anxiety too. He could manipulate the emotions of others, but I did not know how until later on."

"An empamancer!" Gionna exclaimed, as she pushed her multi-lensed glasses up on her face. "Thought to be the least useful of mancer abilities. No fireballs or lightning, and useless against the undead."

"But not useless against the living it seems." Leon finished.

"Indeed." Lady Erika affirmed. "Silas would enjoy it. He toyed with people quite often."

"How do ya know all this?" Duamé asked.

Lady Erika held up a hand again, "I am getting ahead of myself. But for years, I observed. I stayed silent and watched Lucien consolidate power both before and after you were born." She reached out and grasped Leon and Liara's hands firmly, "By the time you both reached your teenage years, Lucien had already become more influential than any of the other lords or ladies at court. Behind him, helping him along every step of the way, was Silas."

Leon remembered when his father had been noticeably absent from the manor during his teenage years. When Lucien was gone the studies Leon had with Liara and Laric ruled his life. Then his father would come home. Lucien's need for control, backed up not by Silas, but by repeated physical abuse from his own hand, would then rule. Leon never saw Laric receive such torment, only himself. The years of mistreatment had certainly built a wall of resentment and animosity towards his father, but Leon had already made the decision to forgive him from afar. Holding on to those feelings interfered with his effectiveness as a Judge, and opposed the tenets that he was supposed to follow. It had been one of the hardest lessons he received from Rohiel – who said that Leon should hope for Lucien to come to know Adonai, instead of dwelling on the past hurts.

Hate the sin. Leon reminded himself. He willed his anger to dissipate as Lady Erika continued her explanation of life in the manor over the years. "I watched how Silas covertly played his game. I began making a few suggestions to Lucien, and tried to help him listen to reason. He… would not. He was too far gone. Then you left for naval service."

A faint smile grew on her lips as she continued, "I thought the idea was brilliant. You would become your own man. Safely separated from Lucien and his rage, and away from Silas and his intrigue. With your presence gone, Lucien might be able to change back into the man I remembered."

Leon's heart trembled as he asked, "Why… does he hate me so?"

It was a short while before she answered in a quiet voice, "Oh my sweet boy. I think Silas helped influence that a great deal. I know you both have always been at odds with one another, but I think his anger has always been displaced." She grew silent for a few moments as she composed herself. Then she graciously accepted a mug of water from Gérda, who had begun handing out trays of cubed cheese and crackers. Liara cast Leon a knowing look as she took a few pieces of cheese for herself.

"As Liara and I wrote to you, we were increasingly convinced something was wrong. We heard nothing from you Leon. We knew your animosity was not aimed towards us, but we could not understand the silence. Then, three years ago, everything changed."

"Your accident. Father threw you down the stairs." Leon growled.

"No. No!" Lady Erika shook her head vigorously. "It was not Lucien that did it. It was Silas."

Grunts of disgust and hisses of disapproval abounded as Duamé muttered, "Good riddance."

Lady Erika nodded to him as she explained, "I bumped into him quite by accident, and one of your letters, that he must have just received, dropped from his coat. I was about to storm off and find Lucien to tell him what Silas was doing. Unfortunately, we were alone in the main entrance way at the time. Before I knew what was happening, he grabbed me and tossed me down the stairs."

Leon's insides squirmed as he remembered accusing his former father of the act during Liara's engagement party. He had declared that Lucien must have hurt her during one of his tirades. As damaged as their relationship had already been due to Lucien's past actions, Leon realized that he had allowed his anger and resentment to make him falsely accuse Lord Lucien of that heinous deed.

His mother's story tumbled forth, "My yells of pain attracted the attention of both Lucien and the staff. I–I think Lucien was just as shocked as I was from falling down the stairs. But the first person to reach me on the floor was Silas."

"He whispered threats to me. Told me that if I said anything, he would torture and kill my children, and then me." Fresh tears began to flow down Leon's mother's face, as she spoke, "So I did the only thing I could do to protect them. I had broken a few bones in the fall, but afterward, I pretended to be mute and immobile per Silas' instruction and repeated threats. Lucien did not know. I was sure of it. And Silas, he just had a way of knowing everything. I did not know how until just now, when you told me about your adventures serving Adonai and defying Xhormas."

She took a sip from her water while everyone processed the unfathomable story. The shocked expression on Liara's face told Leon that she had not even known of Silas' evil. "But mother, that was three years ago! That was going on this entire time?" Liara asked.

"Yes. Silas took it upon himself to 'care' for me. All the while he gave me daily reminders of what was at stake if I defied him. In time, it became almost a game for him. To think me helpless, and tempt me to defy him. He had intercepted every letter between us. He started to read me some of the letters when we were alone, but I was sure that some of what he said were lies. Then, at night when Lucien would talk to me, unaware of what was going on under his own roof, I would have to fight to hold my tongue and not confess everything!"

She clenched her teeth and continued in a cold fury, "Imagine being trapped every day, for years, forced to simply sit and do nothing. Say nothing. Be nothing. Otherwise, your loved ones would be tortured to death in front of you before you yourself are killed. But I beat him in the end. I did what was needed to protect my children, and I would not hesitate to do it again."

Leon couldn't imagine the pain and suffering that she had dealt with on a daily basis. "How did you get through it?"

"I defied Silas in other ways. Claimed small victories. I already knew about his ability to manipulate emotions, so I remained as emotionless as possible. No matter what he said to me, or threatened me with, I bore it all." Lady Erika's eyes narrowed as she spoke of her defiance. "I–I had a lot of time to sit and think on things. A mother's love can do wonderous things. It allowed me to realize that our emotions are a reaction to the things around us. That our emotions, and the reactions we have to situations, are always a choice. We can choose to be angry, or choose to not let our situations get to us. It was a realization that I wished I could share with Lucien. But what is done, is done, and now we forge ahead."

With that last statement, Lady Erika pulled the letters out of a pocket in her dress. The stack of envelopes and parchment were wrapped in twine, and almost all were uniform in size. It contained all the messages that Leon had sent to his family over the past five years. She placed them next to her at the table and patted it – almost as though it was a loved pet.

"Now we can catch up. With what little time we have left."

Once it appeared that she had concluded her story, everyone began to speak all at once. Leon felt sickened by what Silas had done, but that didn't stop him from asking the first question. "What happened at Liara's engagement party? I could have sworn I saw you in the window."

Lady Erika smiled warmly at him, "You did, dear child. I got to see you all grown up for a brief moment." Her smile faded, "Silas and Lucien were in a rage. Nobody expected you to be there, but then Silas boasted to me that you would be dealt with."

Leon recalled the Mazzikin who had been ordered to influence him to take his own life that night, but his mother's words also caused him to remember something Silas uttered near the end of their battle. "That's because Silas had wanted me dead before. During our fight, he said that he sent the dragon after the *Dawnfire*!" Leon turned to Princess Schalae who stood, listening in shock. "He was the one responsible for our crash and Prince Gelan's death!"

Princess Schalae's reaction to this revelation was understandable. She had been engaged to the crown prince, Leon's captain on the *Dawnfire*, and was lied to and misled about Gelan's death for months. She hadn't known the truth until the day Leon told her what actually occurred. While their marriage had been arranged, their love for each other was real. Leon had discovered that during his harrowing trek with Gelan to Agaprya, after the *Dawnfire* had crashed. Prince Gelan had confessed to Leon that he was eagerly anticipating his nuptials to the elven princess. More so than his coronation, in fact. It was one of the many things they had discussed to keep themselves occupied on their tragic journey.

Princess Schalae fought back tears as she hurriedly excused herself from the gathering. The braided tail she kept her evergreen colored hair tied in whipped around as she spun and hurried down the stairs. Leon couldn't fault her for her reaction. He really hadn't had any time to process this discovery either. All the guilt that he had borne over surviving, and having been the one to end Gelan's life to ensure he didn't come back as undead, felt like a complete waste of time. Leon thought he should feel some relief now that the real culprit had been found and eliminated.

Why am I still so unsettled? He asked himself. Justice seemed to have been served, save for the fact that Silas looked as though he had welcomed death at the last moment. Leon felt as though he was missing something. Something important. But he couldn't quite figure it out. Leon wanted to voice his concern to the group, but didn't want to further alarm his mother. She had been through enough.

Miala turned to Liara and spoke up next, "What about the deceased Baron? You were supposed to be married to him, right? Was he part of the plot?"

A look of revulsion crossed Liara's face. "I couldn't believe father arranged for me to wed that man."

Lady Erika interjected herself into the conversation, "He was a pawn, just like the rest of us. Lucien needed Halomir's lumber to build ships himself – so that he could then use them to threaten King Garinth."

Threaten the king?

Everyone exploded at that bit of news. Lady Erika's voice rose slightly in defense, "Well, I assumed you knew about that already!"

"Why would we?" Gionna replied.

"Because you are already on your way to stop Laric from becoming king! That is why we are going to Last Bastion, right?"

Everyone began talking at once all over again, and after much confusion Miala asked Lady Erika, "What has Lucien and Silas' plan been exactly?"

Lady Erika made an attempt to piece it all together for them. "Lucien's lust for more power began a little over twenty years ago, before he met Silas. Together, they created a plot to overthrow the king by usurping his power, and then demanding the throne. Prince Gelan dying was merely one step in the process to them. Building the dreadnoughts was, again, another piece. The real confrontation happened when Lucien cornered King Garinth, and demanded that Laric wed the princess and be crowned king. Failure to comply would mean the destruction of the fleet, assault on the kingdom by the dreadnoughts, and that the undead horde would wipe out the last of the living."

Everyone processed the depravity of Lord Lucien Rhise. How could a man be willing to throw away so many lives for mere power? Gionna broke the silence, "Silas could control the undead!"

Lady Erika nodded. "Lucien was promised by Silas that when he and Laric controlled the kingdom, the undead horde would be easily defeated by the dreadnoughts and the fleet of airships. Then the Rhises would be in power, and this kingdom could start again under their leadership."

"I have no doubt that Silas would never have kept that promise. He served Xhormas. The god of corrupted undeath. He wanted all the living to be consumed." Leon continued down that line of thought aloud, "Lord Lucien and my brother Laric were being used."

"Are being used." Lady Erika corrected. "I can confirm your suspicions. If this Xhormas entity is truly what Silas served, then there is no doubt that at some point Silas would have double crossed them and continued to turn the whole world into undead."

"He had already started betraying Lucien by not taking you and Liara to join them and head to Last Bastion." Leon added.

“Why though? Why didn’t he?” Duamé asked.

Gionna tapped her glasses as she thought aloud, “Because the horde was already attacking. Silas’ plan was already in motion. He must have kept you ladies at the manor because he knew we were coming.”

Duamé threw his hands up in the air. “Again. How in tha bloodstone did he know we were comin’?”

Leon already had an idea of how Silas had known. “The Mazzikin must have told Silas. Or Xhormas. There was a clay idol of Xhormas in his room that I destroyed before we left.”

Duamé pinched the bridge of his nose with his fingers. “Ugh. This is makin’ me head hurt. Can we take a break?”

They all agreed to finish lunch, and reconvene their meeting at dinnertime. This allowed Leon to take the time he needed to get out of his armor and clean off in one of the secured washbasins. The sweat and grime of the past couple days washed away, but Leon’s cares remained. So much had happened in such a short amount of time. So much had been lost: the capital, his home, Calvin, Gezado, even some of the *Esperella’s* crew.

After redressing in simpler clothes, Leon sought out Miala. Walking through the lower decks, and back through the galley, he passed by Duamé who was in the midst of an animated conversation with Gérda. She was vigorously scrubbing the lunch pans, and occasionally handed a smaller dish over to one of the mancer children. The little girl, Brigid, worked with the gnomish lad, Tyne, to clean the smaller dishes. Sam, the orcish teenager, completed the task by drying them with a rough towel.

All three children glanced silently amongst themselves while Gérda and Duamé openly talked about them. From what Leon could glean as he walked by, the disagreement revolved around their safety. Gérda occasionally gestured at Duamé with the scrub brush she held, flicking drops of soapy water on the floor every time she waved it at him.

“Don’cha tell me what I can or cannot do with these kids! They need ta learn a trade, an’ cookin’ is about as useful as ya can get!” She ranted. Her blond braids shook with fervor as she scrubbed a large stock pot.

Duamé didn’t seem to want to listen. “I’m jus’ sayin’, they’re powerful kids, but they also are likely ta have families who miss ‘em! If’n they’re still alive, we should give 'em back. We can't just adopt 'em inta tha crew here. This is a warship!"

"Just where do ya think it's safe ta drop off three little ones in tha middle o' tha end o' tha world?" She countered.

"Maybe tha village o' Springfield will have space fer 'em! No offense ta tha kiddos, but they don't need ta be on board a ship that's takin' on tha horde!" Duamé exclaimed.

Leon tried to just walk past their bickering, but was roped in by Gerta's raised voice behind him. "Oi, Judge person!"

Sighing, Leon turned and saw her pointing the scrub brush at him, "It's Leon."

"Wotever! Wot are yer plans fer me an' tha wee ones? We ain't part o' yer crew, but 'short, dark, an' handsome' has a point."

Leon tried not to smile at the spluttering Duamé while he pondered her question. Both of them had a point. Leon's conscience couldn't reconcile bringing the kids along to every fight they engaged in, regardless of how powerful they were. Gérda had taken responsibility for them almost immediately, and the three children had acquiesced to her care. The words from the letter Calvin left Leon rang through him though. These children were somehow important to the future, and Leon did not want to leave them in potential danger, out of his reach.

The children looked at Leon nervously as he walked over to them. Brigid edged closer to Gérda, and hovered just behind her stocky frame. Their potential fate was in his hands, and he didn't want to make the wrong choice. Leon crouched down in an effort to seem less imposing as he asked, "Do any of you have any family waiting for you somewhere?"

Three heads shook silently, and the teenage orc, Sam, spoke up, "We are all we've got, sir."

Deciding that it wasn't vital to make this decision immediately, Leon got up and announced, "We should be passing Springfield on the way to Last Bastion. Right now, the safest place in the Kingdom is here on the *Esperella*, next would probably be Last Bastion. We will see how Springfield fares once we start to pass it, but I would be loath to leave you there undefended. Last Bastion, being the fortress that it is, would probably be the next safest bet."

The answer appeared to satisfy everyone for the time being, and Leon placed a placating hand on Duamé's shoulder as he left and the dwarves resumed their conversation with Duamé asking, "So… Short, dark, an' handsome, eh?"

Leon continued moving out of earshot as he resumed his search for Miala. He quickly realized there was a much better way to find her. He climbed the stairway to the upper deck with a smile on his face. Nodding to a few crew members as he passed, he stepped onto the top deck and felt the welcome warmth of the afternoon sun as it shone down on him. A few things immediately caught his eye. Since he had last been up here, someone had roped off the damaged area where a crossbow turret had been ripped from the ship's surface. There were also a few less people, with the most notable absence belonging to Gezado. A few crew members were still stationed at the turrets, and Ophelia stood at the helm. However, Leon found who he was looking for nearby. Kelleren stood on his rear legs, with his front paws resting up on the ship's railing.

Kelleren's tan fur wafted in the wind as his tongue lolled happily while they flew. Leon approached the companion, and while Kelleren briefly glanced at Leon, he promptly resumed his joy-filled activity. "Hey Kelleren, do you know where Miala is?"

A small whine escaped from the dog as he left his position and descended the stairwell. Leon followed after him, and passed Gionna and Magnus as they talked quietly in an alcove on the gun-deck. Kelleren led him to one of the two bedrooms located next to the crew hammocks. The door was slightly ajar, and feminine laughter could be heard behind it. Kelleren scratched at it and an amused voice called out, "Come in boys, it's ok."

Opening the door, Kelleren went over to Miala who sat in a chair that was bolted to the floor. She scratched behind his ear, causing his leg to start thumping against the floor in delight. Leon was surprised to see his sister and the Princess also in the room. The two of them occupied another chair and one of the two simple cots against the wall. They all sat with amused looks on their faces. It prompted Leon to ask, "What?"

Miala waved a dismissive hand, "Nothing. Did you need something?"

"I was hoping to talk to you."

"Oh, what about?" Miala asked innocently as she arched her brow at him. The amused looks of the women persisted, and Leon could feel heat rising in his neck.

What did I want to talk to her about again? Leon's mind went blank from the scrutiny of the room. Flustered, he looked at Liara and Schalae, and gestured awkwardly as he muttered, "Um, I was wondering if–"

Princess Schalae stood quickly, and Liara followed suit as Schalae announced, "I will, oh, WE will just leave you to talk. See you at the meeting tonight."

Liara walked towards the exit, and leaned over to whisper in Leon's ear, "I like her."

Leon couldn't help but grin sheepishly as Liara closed the door and he heard their suppressed laughs from outside. Turning back to Miala, she too held a grin hidden behind her hand. Leon complained, "Hey, quit it. This isn't easy for me."

"I'm sorry. I'm–" Miala made an ample effort to hide her mirth, "I'm sorry. What did you want to talk to me about?"

"Well, I was just wanting to thank you for your help with the manor, and see if you were okay after everything that's happened. We haven't really had the chance to talk much lately." Leon sat in one of the wooden chairs opposite hers. "Are you okay?"

Miala looked amused at first, then resigned, as she stated, "I'm… tired Leon. We just seem to jump from crisis to crisis with no break in between."

"When we are done, I figure we can find some time to take a nice vacation somewhere."

"What? You mean like a honeymoon?" Miala asked as her smirk returned.

Leon felt the heat rise in his neck again from Miala's jest. In the eyes of some dwarves, and almost every entyrnet troll, they were married – but no knot had been officially tied yet.

"I feel I would have to officially ask for your hand to do that."

Miala's eyes narrowed as she said, "Why haven't you?"

Flustered by the unexpected path their conversation had taken, Leon tried to think of something to say. Until Miala saved him by laughing again. "Don't worry about it Leon. I was just giving you a hard time. I was questioned by your sister about our relationship earlier."

Relief washed through Leon. "She said she likes you."

"I know. Kelleren overheard." Miala stated as she rubbed her companion's forehead, "I asked her if I had to be a noble for us to be wed or something, since you are one."

"Well, I… uh, hope you told her that since my father disowned me, that I am a commoner just as you are. Rank doesn't play a factor in our… relationship."

"You interrupted our conversation before we could get that far, but it's nice to hear your answer." Miala stood, approached Leon, and grasped his hand. She was still warm, and her green eyes were piercing, "I… I have no family anymore. No father that you would need to seek permission from. I am my own person."

Leon knew of her tragic past, of the home that was burnt to the ground when she was but a child. She had put that past behind her, and Leon gave her a sympathetic smile.

Miala continued, "You told me back at Masterwork Halls that you wanted us to be together."

"I–I still do." Leon said as he also stood, resolute in his feelings toward her.

"I think that would be… nice."

Leon's heart fluttered when she raised up on her tiptoes, and met his lips in a brief tender kiss. Just as quickly as it started, Miala broke it off and turned to leave the room. As she walked out the door, she called back to him over her shoulder, "You'd better do something about that then… Preferably sooner rather than later."

Kelleren tilted his head at Leon before he whined quietly, and trailed out the door after her.

Women are confusing. Leon thought through the thudding of his heart.

Chapter 11: The Plans

Later that evening, after having taken time to digest all of the information that had already been shared, everyone once again converged in the designated meeting area. General Xiphos was in attendance this time, shadowed by her guard, Lorog, who listened in from his post at a nearby wall. The general bore a tired, frazzled look as she walked them through her own experiences leading up to the battle of Agaprya. "We were told that if we couldn't beat their forces outright, then we were to hold the undead at bay until the general populace could evacuate. After that the military forces could flee using the airship armada. Once those instructions had been given, King Garinth, Princess Giselle, and lords Laric and Lucien Rhise all left for Last Bastion."

"When was this, exactly? When did they leave?" Kérik asked.

"A little over two days ago."

Kérik's puffy white hair waved as he nodded to himself while working through some math on his fingers. "A good headwind, an' they could make it ta Last Bastion in three an' a half days… Four tops."

"They traveled there on the *Golem*." Magnus added.

Leon couldn't help but notice that he had again seated himself next to Gionna. Their short gnomish frames leaned into each other, and it seemed fairly apparent to him that they might be rekindling their old flame.

Good for them. He thought.

Kérik winced at Magnus' revelation. "Maybe two an' a half days then. That's a fast ship if there ever was one."

Leon was trying to think everything through. "This means they are almost there, while our own journey to Last Bastion will take just under three days. So, by the time we arrive, Laric will have already married Princess Giselle and been crowned king."

“I wouldn’t be too sure about that.” General Xiphos interjected. “The horde’s presence has changed the timeline for the wedding and coronation. When we were forced to evacuate Agaprya, plans had to be altered. Both ceremonies would necessitate the presence of nobles, commoners, and guards. The general populace and the military are still en route to Last Bastion from the evacuation efforts. I doubt that they would hold either event without the presence of as many witnesses as possible.”

The consensus within the room was that Xiphos was correct; it would be unlikely for them to proceed with either the coronation or the wedding without the presence of Xaelon’s population, however dwindled that might be. “Knowing my brother, he would want to make it as big a spectacle as possible.” Leon mused aloud.

The general held up a hand, “What are your intentions here? Stop the wedding? Overthrow the crowning of a new king? Regardless of what happened between King Garinth and Lucien Rhise behind closed doors, are we seriously discussing treason and sedition?”

A dark pall fell over the room, as everyone grew silent at her words. The questions Alexandra Xiphos asked chipped away at Leon’s resolve. Yes, his brother and father’s actions were reprehensible. After everything that had occurred, Leon felt as though he was fulfilling the role that had been laid out for him by his father. He was truly becoming what the heralds had originally accused him of: a bandit who had committed crimes against the crown.

“Preventing Laric and Lucien Rhise from using the crown to strengthen their power is a battle that I will not force any of you to join me in. My former father’s dark dealings have far reaching consequences, and I feel… I know, that he must be stopped.” Leon turned to look directly at the general, “If you choose to help me, then I thank you for it. If you only wish to destroy Xhormas and his undead hordes, then I thank you for that too. I would not ask you to betray your king and country lightly, General. If King Garinth was coerced into handing over the throne, as per Lady Erika’s account, then I feel my duty is to stop my brother and father. No matter what.”

A dour look crossed General Xiphos’ face, and it appeared to Leon as if she struggled with what her duties to the crown would deem necessary.

Kérik Silverspine tapped one of the steel pauldrons on her armor, "We've been servin' Agaprya fer a long time, Alex. Until tha coronation, our duty is ta protect King Garinth. From enemies both outside, an' within. I know ta tha public Lucien Rhise is some great leader. Takin' in refugees from tha Lost Lands, an' givin' em jobs. He's got influence throughout tha heralds, an' they make 'im inta some kinda hero. Trust me Alex, he's not."

"I know. I KNOW!" She burst. "I would see his private dealings at council meetings. I just never said anything. Never went to his majesty about it. I didn't think it would get this bad. Yet, now we must protect the king from him." General Xiphos nodded to Leon, "What is your plan?"

Leon grinned, "I figure swooping in and saving the day might work."

A few chuckled at his response, until Gionna rapped her cane against the table to get everyone's attention, "Our task becomes all the more perilous if Laric has been crowned before we get there. Assuming that happens, then he will have all available military resources to stop us… Plus the king's personal bodyguard."

"Emirah." Miala muttered loud enough for everyone to hear. Several of those who were gathered knew of the galvamancer's reputation. Over the years electrified smoking husks of would-be assassins and kingslayers had been a testament to her powers.

General Xiphos reasoned aloud, "Some of us know her reputation more than others. We can present our best possible case to her, and hope for the best that she doesn't fry us all. Between myself and Admiral Silverspine, we should hopefully be able to talk our way through whatever obstacles come our way from the Agapryan military."

"And if my Laric hasn't ascended to the throne yet?" Lady Erika asked. She had been quiet throughout this meeting, and still looked exhausted from sharing her emotional story earlier in the day. Her appearance could easily be due to something more though. They were talking about overthrowing her husband. Her child. Such discussion could wear a person down.

"Then it will be all the easier to stop him and Lord Rhise." The general assessed as she stood up, her armor creaking. "Our goal should be to do this quickly, and with minimal resistance. I can reconcile preventing the Rhise family from obtaining the crown with myself, but I will not fight against my own soldiers. Especially not with the undead horde heading towards Last Bastion. This… this could mark the last days of the living in our world. It may be the final stand of the Dead Wars. I would not doom us all due to infighting."

With that, the older woman turned and walked away from their meeting, Lorog following close behind her. Their planned actions weighed heavily on Leon, and mixed with the already potent emotions that fought within him. General Xiphos' points were all valid, yet he still felt that this was the correct course of action. He knew that this part of Silas and Lucien's plan had to be foiled.

For the next few hours their group continued to talk about strategy, Last Bastion's impressive defenses, and the undead horde that was coming to consume them all following their retreat from Agaprya. As the discussion swirled around him, Leon couldn't help but notice the parallels between Agaprya and the Elvenwood. The lush forest, once home to numerous elves, was now nothing more than a smoldering ruin. Agaprya had been overrun by the undead in much the same way, and Leon wondered if it would ever recover should they prove victorious.

Night had fallen, and after everyone dispersed from the meeting Leon felt that a shift at the wheel might help clear his head. He was still coming to grips with so much of what had happened, and he found Ophelia more than eager to relinquish control of *Esperella* so she could rest. She sighed in relief as she lifted her leather cap to scratch her scalp. Her short black hair was briefly exposed with the motion, but disappeared just as quickly when she jammed her cap back on. "Thank you, Captain." She said, before she made her way below decks.

Leon was calmed by the familiarity of standing at the ship's helm and the smooth grain of the wheel's wood as it skimmed across his palms when he made slight turns to maintain their northeasterly course towards Last Bastion. Stars shone overhead, and their light joined with the glow of the airship's hull. They mapped his way as he began to think over recent events.

It didn't take long for Liara and his mother to also appear above deck. Both women wore borrowed coats to fend off the chilly night air. When Leon left Rhise manor and began this journey it had been the beginning of springtime. Now, a few months later, as the more temperate summer nights took hold, the evening chill had become less on an issue. Still, Leon had to remind himself that his family members were not used to such conditions.

"Leon, can we talk?" Liara asked as she came to his side. Their mother, Lady Erika, sat on a nearby crate that housed crossbow cartridges for the turrets. In the glow of the airship hull, he could see that both his mother and sister had worried expressions on their faces.

"What is it?" Leon asked, the relaxation he hoped for while piloting *Esperella* replaced with concern.

Liara constantly stole glances at their silent mother as she spoke, "Well, Mother and I have talked, and frankly, we are a little worried."

"About what?"

"Well, this whole 'Adonai' business that you're involved in. It sounds a little crazy doesn't it?"

Of all the people who had doubted his beliefs, Liara's hurt the worst. She was his sister. His childhood confidant. "You do realize that it is equally crazy to believe that a man who lived in our house for twenty years was bent on wiping everyone in the world out, right?"

"Our point exactly. How could a just and loving God allow all of this to happen?" Lady Erika added.

Leon remembered his lessons from Rohiel – both the ones he received with his friends, and the ones he learned while dreaming. Even these hard questions that were being presented to him had answers. So, he spent the next several minutes sharing more about Adonai and His desire to see everyone be saved from the corrupted undeath that Xhormas brought.

"Ultimately, it's not that Adonai is allowing this to happen. The machinations of those who wish us harm, combined with our own rebellious choices, made the world the way it is right now. I choose to live by, and believe in, a better way. You could too. The world would be quite different if we all lived the way Adonai intended. Not only because it would eliminate the Dead Wars, but because we would just… be better people."

They listened to Leon, and watched Revelator glow brighter as he spoke more about Adonai. It continued to brighten when he shared that the way to begin following Adonai was to acknowledge that all had fallen short of His standards, and to personally seek His forgiveness with true repentance. Leon could see that his sister was gaining understanding, her emotions had always been easy for him to read. Perhaps it was due to the years spent hiding behind her false paralyzation, but unlike his sister, Lady Rhise's face was an emotionless mask that Leon couldn't decipher.

"So… What are these tenets that you live by now?" Liara asked with interest.

Rohiel had made Leon memorize them, which allowed attributes that guided how he should live to flow freely from his lips. "Love. Joy. Peace. Patience. Kindness. Goodness. Faithfulness. Gentleness. Self-Control." Then, after a brief thoughtful pause, Leon added, "You could live by them too, you know. If you both followed Adonai… We could follow Him… As a family."

"But what about Laric? Father? Does Adonai love them too? Would you accept them if they chose to follow this God of yours?" Liara asked with downcast eyes.

This was a question that Leon had struggled with before. For a long time the only feelings that he harbored towards his brother and father were ones of contempt, which he had paired with a resolve to never be like them. He had vowed to never strive for power and control in the manner they did. His anger towards them, and specifically the hatred he felt towards Lord Rhise, had been a hindrance to his walk with Adonai. Leon had to change his way of thinking. The hatred was hard to let go of, and harder still to not allow back in.

"Of course Adonai would accept them. Adonai would accept any who truly turn to Him. It is our choice to believe in Him or not, and follow Him or not." Leon sighed as he thought about his next words. "I-I would like to think that Laric and Father would choose to believe in Adonai one day, but if they have chosen to ally themselves with Silas and Xhormas… I-I just don't know if they will."

Their mother chimed in, "Lucien never talked about… I do not know if his level of involvement with Silas went deep enough for him to know about Xhormas."

Well, there's that at least. Leon briefly thought about what it would be like if a situation arose where he could talk to his brother and father about Adonai.

"Regardless, they aren't here right now, and we are. So how about it? Want to not rise as undead? Would you want to follow Adonai for yourselves?" Leon implored his sister and mother.

"It is a tempting offer, to be sure." Liara admitted, still casting glances at Lady Erika, who appeared to wipe a tear from her eye.

"I… I cannot." Their mother said simply.

"Wh-Why?" Leon fought the urge to leave the ship's wheel and hug his mother as she cried.

She kept trying to demurely wipe her tears away as she explained, "My mistakes are too great. I could not protect my family. My children. It is all my fault. If I had only–"

Leon understood guilt over past decisions, and tried to head off her trail of thinking, "I've been down that road mother. Blaming yourself for everything that has happened. It's not healthy, or even accurate for that matter. You're not the only person who made decisions regarding anyone's past or future. The burden isn't yours to bear. It's Adonai's. He can take it from you. He can take it all."

Their mother wouldn't hear a word of it. She dismissed Leon's plea with a wave of her hand and went below decks for the night. Liara stayed with Leon a little longer, enjoying the night air and the clear cloudless sky. They silently watched the world, until Leon suddenly blurted, "I got your package. The bundle that you sent to me on the night I was kicked out… From the engagement party, remember?"

Between the glow of the airship, and Revelator's light, he could see the beaming smile that his simple statement brought to his sister's face, "Really? I-I wasn't sure that Telon could get it to you. I hope it was useful."

Leon remembered the letter, blanket, soap, and coins that had somehow made it past Silas' notice. The bundle was dropped to him from Countess Serena's carriage as it traveled down the road. Liara's letter had explained how she asked the boy Leon met that day, Telon, a young staff member, to deliver the bundle. Thoughts of Telon caused concern to rise within Leon as they had just left the manor – and the undead host that had been dispatched there. "The boy, Telon. If memory serves, both he and his mother worked in the manor. Did we just–"

Liara laid a reassuring hand on Leon's arm as he kept the ship's course. "They left the area a couple weeks ago – along with the populace of Everbright. When Bulwark Fortress fell, a lot of towns and villages started evacuating to either Agaprya or Last Bastion." She shivered, despite the warm fur lined coat that covered her. "This world is getting scarier every day, brother. How can you stand it?"

Leon's response was near automatic, "I told you. With Adonai."

Silence stretched between them before Liara asked, "What… what would I need to do to follow Him?"

Leon led her through her first prayer to Adonai in the quiet night, and rejoiced when Revelator's light pulsed slightly in response to Liara's newfound faith.

Well after Liara descended below decks, Kérik and Duamé came up the nearby stairs, conversing between themselves. Leon figured their approach was prompted by the approaching shift change at the helm. Looking at the two of them together was a story of contrasts. Duamé's dark dreadlocks shook next to Kérik's white puff of hair. Though late at night, they were having a heated argument, which would be problematic for those trying to sleep below decks. Kérik then pointed a finger at Leon, which presented another issue altogether.

"–bein' completely daft, an' what's worse, is ya know it!" Duamé finished saying.

"Like I said, let's ask tha Judge! He's a Judge, so he'll know!" Kérik retorted.

They walked up to Leon, who grimaced at their volume, and hissed, "People are trying to sleep you two!"

"Lemme take tha wheel." Kérik suggested, as he all but shoved Leon out of the way, "That way, ya can give Mr. Onyxwill yer full attention when ya tell him his head's made o' pumice. I wanna be able ta say ya weren't distracted."

Duamé was visibly irritated with Kérik and on the verge of another retort, before Leon interrupted him. "What's going on? Duamé, c'mon. It's me."

Kérik Silverspine spoke over his shoulder, "He's collapsin' his own mineshaft is wot he's doin'!"

"Oi!" Duamé exclaimed. "He was talkin' ta ME!" Duamé continued in a growl, as he sat on the same crate that Leon's mother had occupied. He huffed and crossed his arms, muttering to himself as he looked into the night sky behind them. "I–I got a question fer ya."

A tense silence descended before Leon finally commented, "Typically questions are supposed to be asked so that the person can give you an answer, Duamé."

"I'm gettin' ta it!" Duamé snapped before leaning over on the crate to address Kérik. "Ya know, he's only a kid. He ain't gonna know."

Leon tried not to take offense, "I'm almost twenty one years, I'll have you know."

Leon could hear Kérik grit his teeth as he said, "Just ask him, Onyxwill."

Duamé scoffed, "Tch. Yer still just a kid, but yer tha Judge. So, here we go." With a scoff, Duamé rolled his eyes and continued, "What does Adonai say 'bout remarryin'?"

Taken off guard by the odd question, Leon racked his brain and his memories – only to realize that Rohiel hadn't said a thing to him about marriage, much less remarrying anyone, "Why do you ask? Is… is it about the rescued dwarven cook that you were talking to? Gérta?"

"Ha! Told ya." Kérik crooned.

Duamé shushed them both again hastily, and looked around to see if there was anyone else near them before he spoke. The closest crew members were the few late night scouts, and a mancer on a turret, near midship, so he continued, "Keep yer voices down ya– Aw, flint an' feldspar! Look, we just met. She's a pretty lass, but she ain't Rozella." Duamé sighed after he spoke his deceased wife's name. Leon had felt horrible for his friend's loss when he first learned that she died giving birth to their daughter Esperella. It was no less heartbreaking hearing Duamé speak of her now, though he quickly moved on with his explanation. "Gérda caught me eye is all. An' complimented me looks, an'-an' it's been a while since anyone did that. I just don't want ta be betrayin' me Rozella and Esperella's memory by… by goin' after something that ain't right. That's all."

Leon tried to understand what Duamé's thought process stemmed from, only to blurt, "Your head's made of pumice, Duamé."

Kérik's cackle at the helm of the ship was louder than the verbal assault the dwarven smith launched at Leon. It took Leon a few moments to calm Duamé back down, "Look, you're right Duamé. I'm probably not the best person to ask, but it seems like a pretty simple question. Do you think that Rozella and Esperella would want you to be happy?"

Kérik called back again, "Almost verbatim wot I told ya, wasn't it?"

"Ugh! Quit it already!" Duamé bantered, before turning back to Leon with a quick subject change. "Enough about me. Ya saved yer ma an' sister. Now we're gonna go roll a stone over yer brother an' da's plans… How are ya feeling boyo?"

"Fine, I guess." Leon replied, amused by the talkativeness of his friend. "I keep circling back to when Silas died."

Duamé scoffed, "Good riddance."

"It's not just that, something was off. Not too sound ominous, but it was… too easy." Leon remarked.

"Ya call that easy? Didn't ya tell me he was steppin' on yer head?" Kérik asked.

"Well…" Leon trailed off before his friend cut him off.

"Yer just bein' cautious. Nothin' wrong with that mind ya, but take tha time ta celebrate yer victories. Like me takin' yer da's trophies. Any o' them magical?"

Leon resisted the urge to laugh, "I don't know, Duamé. I'm not the best person to ask."

"I'll find out, boyo. I'll find out."

"Ya better get some sleep while ya got tha time, Leon. Tomorrow ain't far off." Kérik interjected.

"Yes, sir." Leon took the hint, and accompanied Duamé down the stairwell to rest. As they tromped down the stairs, past the gun-deck, and quietly through the other sleeping forms of elves and dwarves, Leon noticed a few more empty hammocks than the previous night. Once again he lamented that day's loss of warriors and friends.

Settling into a hammock, Leon bid Duamé a tired goodnight before falling into a dreamless sleep.

Chapter 12: The Issue

The next morning, Leon awoke slightly concerned that he hadn't dreamt of anything. *Was that some sort of message from Rohiel and Lochemetel in and of itself?* He questioned. He couldn't shake the sense of foreboding he felt. It was that sense of unease which made him buckle his scale-mail armor on, and strap his shield and Revelator to his back almost immediately upon waking. Something was off, and the feeling persisted as he greeted people in passing on his way to the galley.

Grabbing a couple buttered rolls and two mugs of java, Leon carefully made his way to the top deck, where he found Kérik still at the helm. He first passed one mug, and then one roll, to the older dwarf. Kérik drank the entirety of the java before his face contorted in a grimace. "Ugh, still tryin' ta get used ta it. Better than tha alternative I suppose."

"How was the rest of the night shift?"

"Hpmh. Uneventful. Which is always a good thing. Should pass over tha city o' Springfield later today at this rate. How was yer rest?"

"Uneventful. Which may not actually be a good thing." Leon remarked, as he sipped his java and surveyed the ship.

The warm air and clear skies allowed them to comfortably look over the picturesque landscape that passed below. Leon had always thought the dense forests were a sight to behold, but as the sun continued its climb through the eastern sky its glare forced him to shift his gaze elsewhere. Looking around, Leon watched as the ship's crew members began to file onto the top deck. Some took the time to enjoy their breakfast in the fresh morning air like him, while others appeared to be all business and headed directly to their crossbow or mancer turret stations.

It was strange. He could almost feel a tension in the air, though everything around him was indicative of a laid-back atmosphere. Everyone went about their morning as if it were just another day. Currently, their only objective was to arrive at Last Bastion, and that only really required effort from the scouts and whoever was piloting the *Esperella*. Most of the other crew members appeared to be treating the morning as one of rest – a welcome reprieve from the tension and stressful battles that had plagued the past few days.

Is this really somewhat of a day off for us? Leon thought.

Leon walked along the deck towards the bow of the ship, where he saw a small figure looking through a gap in the railing. The wind whipped through the little gnome boy, Tyne's, hair as he stood there. No taller than a human toddler, the boy at least had the good sense to fasten himself to one of the ship's metal eyelets with a leather strap. Otherwise, Leon would have feared a small gust of wind might carry him right over the side. The young gnome's pronounced angular features made it hard for Leon to determine if he was thin for a gnome, sickly, or both. Either way, he was glad to see Tyne show care for his own safety.

As Leon drew closer to the gnome, he reflected that the boy might actually be in his early teens. Gnomes were known to live a lot longer than humans, which made him wonder if Tyne didn't speak much because he had not learned many words yet. Perhaps it was because he only had the mental development equivalent to a four or five-year-old human child. Leon joined the boy, and they looked silently off into the distance. The scenery was beautiful. Soon the forest would give way to lush green fields, then those would transform into the farmlands that surrounded the city Springfield. Leon lost himself in the beautiful morning, and almost didn't notice when the small gnome spoke to him.

"You can feel it, can't you?"

The tiny boy stared at him with large innocent eyes, though something was hidden behind his gaze; a sense of fear that was conveyed within his unexpected statement.

"What is 'it'?" Leon asked, before realization struck him and he continued, "There is… a discomfort that I feel. A foreboding I sense. Is that what you are talking about?"

"He is coming soon." The boy replied.

Leon tried to get the cryptic young gnome to clarify his statement. "Who is coming?"

"Multiple airships sighted! High, port side!" An elven scout shouted, pointing up and to the left. Many sets of eyes, including Leon's, shifted to where the airships of varying sizes had been spotted. They were headed towards them, coming from the west. Leon grabbed a nearby spyglass and focused it on the group of ships. The group consisted of three attack ships, numerous mail carriers, and the undeniable shape of one of Lucien's dreadnoughts. The three attack ships were almost as large as Leon's old ship, *Dawnfire,* and the mail carriers wove an intricate unseen web as they zipped about them. Lucien's enormous dreadnought brought up the rear of the envoy. All of the airships flew high, and angled their path to intercept the *Esperella*.

"Are they friend or foe?" General Xiphos yelled.

"They're higher than we are! All I can see are their hulls!" Kérik replied.

"All hands, prepare for battle! NOW!" Leon screamed as he surveyed the dreadnought's damaged hull. Between the dirt and earthen marks scraped along its bottom, and the westerly direction that it flew from, Leon had arrived at a safe but chilling conclusion.

"That's the dreadnought that crashed at Mancer Academy in Agaprya!"

A flurry of activity erupted as Leon unclipped Tyne from his position at the bow and carried him back towards the ship's aft. Warriors rushed towards the turrets preparing to either use them or guard them. The clack of the crossbow turrets being armed, and the spark that leapt between mancer hands and branches of elvenwood filled Leon's senses as he ran along the deck.

"All fighters ta yer stations! Cannon crews, round shot in both sides! Everyone on board who can't fight, find a place ta hunker down! An' stay there!" Kérik shouted into the speaking pipes next to him.

"That means you, Tyne. Go find Gérda and get to safety." Leon quickly instructed the boy, as he deposited him at a rear stairwell and pointed downward. The yellow-haired gnome gingerly climbed down the stairs and Leon rushed to the ship's wheel. The elderly dwarf was at the tail end of his shift piloting the *Esperella*, and even with the surge of adrenaline that battle brought thrumming through his veins, Leon knew Kérik shouldn't be at the helm much longer.

"I'll relieve you, sir." Leon said, as he put a hand on the wheel.

Kérik nodded, but instead of leaving the top deck to rest, added himself to the growing throng of warriors coming up to fight. He brandished the curved double-headed axe that normally rested slung across his back, and used his own spyglass to survey the incoming fleet. Leon saw his friends scramble up the aft stairwell that he had just sent Tyne down. Miala, Duamé, Schalae, and Gionna all joined Kérik and positioned themselves near Leon – circling the ship's wheel to defend him as he flew.

"Where's Kelleren?" Leon asked Miala.

"Below, guarding the children and your family!" She replied.

Not sure of how much longer they had, he shouted, "Everyone secure yourselves where you can! Strap in!"

The clink of small metal S-shaped hooks latching onto eyelets echoed throughout the airship while Leon checked his own. When he finished, he looked at the fleet of airships that drew ever closer and watched as they shifted their flight path, angling themselves to become slightly more parallel. They were easier to see without a spyglass now, and Leon noticed that no dragons or gryphons had accompanied them. He felt a momentary sense of relief until it was promptly shattered by the sound of a distant boom that came from the enemy fleet's direction. A few seconds later, Leon heard the careening whistle that accompanied cannon fire as a ball flew past the *Esperella's* port side.

"Bow chasers!" Kérik shouted. "Get us higher up!"

Leon immediately pulled back and up on the wheel. The control levigem in its center worked with its larger counterparts, and the ship climbed in altitude in an effort to escape the cannon fire. One cannonball struck a glancing blow to the *Esperella's* aeonyte hull, and the resulting crash of metal against metal sounded like a reverberating gong. Leon looked at both Kérik and Gionna and asked, "What's the damage to our hull?"

Kérik hopped up to the speaker pipes to shout the question, but a dwarven voice blared through it before he had a chance, "There's a dent in tha hull, but looks like no other damage!"

“Well, that’s good at least.” Leon commented.

“Oi! Not fer me! I gotta repair that rustin’ dent!” Duamé protested.

“I designed airships to stand against the undead, dearie! Not other airships!” Gionna raged beside him.

“Well, if all they can do is dent our hull–”

Gionna poked Leon’s side with her cane. “If those cannonballs damage the levigems embedded in the hull, or destroy us here at the helm, then we’re all done for!”

Before Leon had time to process her grim assessment, a shout came from a nearby elven scout. “Mail carriers incoming!”

Leon kept the *Esperella* in a steady upward climb, angling away from the attacking ships, but the enemy fleet simply rose to match their elevation. Casting a glance over his shoulder, Leon saw that a slew of mail carriers bobbed and careened toward them at a much faster pace than the dreadnought and other supporting ships. In less than a minute’s time, those carriers would catch up to the *Esperella* and continue their harassment of the ship.

Princess Schalae stood near Leon at the helm, and looked through a spyglass to enhance her already excellent elven sight. Her next words sent a chill throughout all who could hear, “There are multiple undead fighters on those mail carriers.” She handed the spyglass to Kérik before she took hold of her bow and concentrated. Over the rushing wind, Leon heard the clear snap of wood as she broke it in half, and saw the vine-like string shrivel back into the wood. Both curved halves crunched further as the wood compacted and hardened under the guidance of her hortimancy, forming two curved, sharp-edged swords. “I think they mean to board us!” She announced.

“Boarders!” Kérik shouted across the deck. Elves and dwarves who weren’t manning turrets quickly swapped whatever handheld projectile throwers they had for curved swords or axes.

“Turrets, get ready! Cannon crews, stand by!” Leon shouted. There was no reason for the cannons to fire at the smaller, rowboat sized mail carriers. Those manning the gun-deck had bigger ships to bring down. Leon leveled off the ship, and angled their flight away from the pursuing fleet towards the northeast. "Aft turrets, fire!"

He heard the thrum of two mancer and two crossbow turrets as they fired at the incoming mail carriers. "How many are there?" He called out.

"Nine rustin' mail carriers!" Kérik replied, "Down an' port! Now!"

Leon jerked the wheel to the left and pitched it forward, relishing the immediate responsiveness of the *Esperella*. A few seconds later, a mail carrier dove down from the exact spot their ship would have been had it stayed its course. Leon caught a quick glimpse of the fast moving boat that was packed with armored undead. Their red glowing eyes disappeared from his view when they abruptly maneuvered below the ship. Just as that carrier descended from his line of sight, another mail carrier careened into the *Esperella's* starboard side. Leon heard the splintering of wood as the second carrier crunched against them.

"They're tryin ta ram us too!" Kérik shouted as Leon turned the wheel again.

"And push us back into range of the bigger ships!" Gionna exclaimed amidst the chaos. Leon could hear the distant booms of cannon fire increasing in pace, and tried to dodge everything that was being sent their way.

Another couple of mail carriers flew overhead and dropped undead from their ships onto the *Esperella*. Leon spotted plate mail encased shamblers wielding long swords, and a few thin wretches as well. A few of the undead missed their mark entirely, and their forms collided with the hull or dropped through the empty air near the ship. The ones that landed successfully immediately wreaked havoc on the deck. Defenders clashed against the undead; blades crossed and bodies shoved, while Leon tried to keep the ship steady for the sake of everyone's footing.

Then a mail carrier actually crashed into the ship's top deck. Hit by a mancer turret's blast, it whirled through the air until it collided with the *Esperella*. All of the undead on board the small ship were crushed by the impact, as was an elf who manned a mancer turret. Their unsecured, lifeless bodies all slid towards the ship's defenders, creating unexpected stumbling blocks. Leon growled in frustration at the losses they were already incurring, and knew they needed a better plan of action. Between the swarming mail carriers, and the barrage of cannon fire from the larger ships, the *Esperella* would soon be downed if they didn't do something. Leon analyzed the threats that surrounded them while he rammed a mail carrier that had passed in front of the bow.

"We can't lead these ships to Springfield, Last Bastion, or any populated area. We need to deal with them now!" He yelled to his friends.

"We're outgunned! If they hit our levigems, or a shot hits us here at the controls–" Kérik warned before shouting, "Head's up, a wee mail carrier is comin' our way below an' starboard!"

Gionna's eyes grew wide as she yelled, "Wait! Yes! Turn us around!"

"You have a plan?" Leon asked.

"Yes! They boarded our ship to disable us, so we need to disable them first! Turn us around, dearie! Assault them! The aeonyte can take it based on the dent left from the one ball that connected with it."

"WHAT? Ya done lost yer mind ya–" Kérik roared as a mail carrier flew directly over them. An armored shambler dropped directly in front of the older dwarf, interrupting whatever he was about to say. Kérik swung his enormous axe and cleaved into its legs, while Duamé knocked its head off with such gusto that it went sailing off behind the ship. As the dwarves made quick work of the threat, Leon saw that the last of the other undead on board had been dispatched. A blast from one of the turrets brought down another mail carrier, and three more of the undead vessels flew in formation preparing to cross over the *Esperella's* bow.

"Are you sure the hull will hold?" Leon asked the genius gnome.

"It's iron cannonballs against aeonyte! The hull will be fine, just protect the levigems!"

Understanding the urgent need to evade the small vessels that still swarmed them, Leon yanked on and pivoted the wheel, causing the *Esperella*'s aft to swing wide. Pushing the ship's wheel forward again, Leon angled the ship directly towards their attackers.

There are no good options for running, and we can't hide. Leon thought. *So that means we must attack.*

"She's right! We have to fight!"

"We're outnumbered!" Duamé objected.

"Wouldn't be the first time!" Leon retorted.

A few questioning stares turned his way from both his friends and the crew, as they waited for him to address them all.

"Everyone listen up! We need to down the mail carriers that are still chasing us, but we're also going to attack that group of larger airships! Don't worry about the numbers! We have a better crew, a better ship, and can withstand anything they throw at us! We WILL bring those ships down. For Adonai!"

"For Adonai!" Came the scattered but resounding shout back.

"Haha, we're a worship warship!" Duamé quipped.

As if understanding their intentions, the three attack ships moved to evade the *Esperella* as she barreled towards them. Though the attacking airships were smaller, their speed appeared to be evenly matched. Leon thought that was likely due to them having only two levigems protruding from their lighter wooden hulls, versus the four levigems that came from the much larger hull of the *Esperella*. The large dreadnought stationed behind the attack ships continued to hover in place, though it slowly began to turn its bulk. Its large side, with gun ports open, showcased twenty cannons that threatened to bombard them at any moment.

Miala broke away from the group and positioned herself at the nearby starboard railing. She re-clasped her leather strap and shouted to Leon, "Get us closer to those ships and I can try to bring them down!"

"Duly noted! Everybody, hang on!" Leon yelled back as he brought the wheel up and to the right. The ship responded in kind – just as distant blasts could be heard from the dreadnought. Cannonballs whizzed past the *Esperella*. The three other attack ships closed the gap that had been created by their evasion maneuvers, and their singular bow chasers fired in tandem with the dreadnoughts. More gong-like sounds rang through the air as cannonballs from the onslaught connected with *Esperella's* hull. Leon prayed the aeonyte would hold against the pounding force before he shouted, "Ready, port cannons!"

A few moments passed before a tinny dwarven voice shouted from a speaker pipe, "We're ready, Captain… Judge… sir!"

Leon turned the wheel ever so slightly and lined their cannons up to broadside the three attack ships climbing towards them. Their attackers rapidly approached, and as soon as they were within range Leon leaned into the speaker pipes.

"Port cannons… FIRE!"

The blasts from the cannons below caused a familiar ring within Leon's ears, as ten solid metal cannonballs launched from the *Esperella.* They arced towards their targets, and Leon saw more than a few make direct strikes. The damage was both visible and audible as their cannonballs penetrated and splintered the wood of the enemy ships. Several of the crew cheered as the turrets fought off the remaining mail carriers, while others, Leon included, watched the results of their salvo. Grinning viciously, Leon continued flying forward and turned to starboard – bringing the other side of the *Esperella* into firing range.

"Port cannons, reload! Starboard cannons ready!"

Tense moments followed as the turrets around them continued to fire at the fast moving mail carriers while the cannon crew readied their weapons. Leon checked on the attack craft that approached and saw that they bore many undead on their decks. Most of the undead appeared to be former naval military, and their black and blue uniform leathers were marred by the death wounds they had received. With the closeness of the attack ships, Leon could clearly see the vacant stares of their red glowing eyes as they waited to assault and board the *Esperella*. As they were only a few ship lengths away, Leon was able to see them crowd against their railings with weapons drawn.

Wait a second, naval issued weapons are…

"Crossbows! Get down! Everybody get down!"

No sooner had Leon called out the warning, than crossbow bolts plunged into the aft area. The crew, along with Leon's friends, hunched behind the ship's railing and turrets. Still, a few of the crew were hit and their cries of pain filled the air. A bolt thudded into the ship's wheel, and another deflected off of the shield strapped to Leon's back. As the volley of bolts continued, Leon yelled towards the speaker pipes from his crouched position.

"Starboard cannons! Fire at their ships. Try to hit their levigems, but if you have any shot, take it!"

Leon looked back and tried to line the starboard side of the *Esperella* up as best he could. Peeking over the railing, Leon saw the attack ships were also turning with the intention to broadside them. With four cannons to a side, at this close of a range, Leon knew survival was only a matter of who fired first.

"Turrets! Fire!"

Pulses of brown and green tinged light shot from the mancer turrets on the starboard side. Leon's vantage point allowed him to see the destruction they wreaked on the undead who stood at the attack ship's railing. Balls of mancer light hammered into their vessels, causing wood to chip and splinter from every point of impact around their levigems and hulls. Then Leon heard the *Esperella's* cannons fire. Cannonball after cannonball was launched, and all hit their marks. A few holes were made in hulls, but an altogether distinct sight and sound followed the impact of some of the heavy iron balls.

The cannon crew of the *Esperella* had focused a majority of their salvo on two of the attack ships. The eight foot long levigems that adorned the nearest sides of those ships took multiple direct hits from the cannonballs and mancer turrets. Cracks grew within the gems, and the sound of shattering crystal followed the barrage as the gems fractured and broke apart. Robbed of their full flight capability, the weight of the wooden vessels proved too much for the singular intact levigems on their far sides to handle. After listing for a few seconds, gravity took hold and they fell from the sky to the ground below.

Cheers erupted from Leon and the *Esperella's* crew just before the final attack ship fired. Leon felt his stomach clench as the ball launched from its hull hit one of the *Esperella's* levigems. The gem took the impact with a crystalline crunch, and Leon felt a jolt pass through the wheel as the ship tried to list. He turned the wheel in the opposite direction, which seemed to temporarily compensate for the unbalanced pull. Another iron cannonball whizzed towards his head, and he ducked reflexively. He looked back just in time to see it fortuitously smash into the last remaining mail carrier that had lingered the far side of the *Esperella*. The mail carrier crumpled as it split into fragments, and there was no longer anything to hold the undead on board aloft. They fell through the air, and Leon returned his focus to the final attack ship. That was when he saw that the dreadnought was once again moving forward to intercept them.

Miala yelled in a battle rage as she stood and leveled her braided wand at the last attack ship. White-hot fire burst from its tip and shot like a beam towards the enemy vessel, joining the multitude of turret blasts that also flew through the air. Her lance of fire didn't merely burn the enemy ship when it connected, it punched straight through all of the wood it touched. The white-hot line crept up their hull, leaving only black char in its wake. It continued its destructive path until Miala shifted her focus, and aimed towards the ship's aft. Leon looked and saw a bisected undead at the helm. Its upper half was splayed over the ship's wheel, pushing it forward as it dropped out of the sky.

The undead that stood at the ship's railing continued their effort of firing crossbow bolts at the *Esperella*. They gave no regard to the fact that they careened towards the ground. Leon saw one bolt knock the wand from Miala's hand, promptly extinguishing the lance of fire as it tumbled from her grasp. She scrambled to grab it before it could bounce off the *Esperella's* railing, and would be lost to her. She leaned over the railing as far as she could to try and reach it, but all that did was leave her exposed. Leon immediately saw the danger, and yelled, "Miala, get down!"

His warning was too late. From Leon's higher vantage point, he saw when their undead attackers fired more crossbow bolts at her and he yelled to Kérik, "Grab the wheel! It's listing, they hit a levigem!"

Miala still dangled over the railing when her cry of pain reached Leon's ears. It took every ounce of restraint for him to await Kérik's shouted response, "I've got the wheel! Someone check that gem!" Then he took off, scrambling towards her with Duamé on his heels. Together, they pulled her back over the railing and laid her on the deck.

Leon's eyes swept over her as he tried to assess her injuries. A cut ran across her cheek and some of her lustrous red hair had been clipped, presumably by a bolt that must have grazed her head. As he pressed his hand against the wound, he noticed another bolt. This one had lodged near her heart, and only its short shaft and fletching poked out from her. The brown robe that surrounded it was already stained with far too much red, and Leon quickly pressed his other hand against it in an effort to stem the flow of blood. A hiss and cry came from Miala and her panicked eyes locked onto Leon's. Pain and concern marred her features. Leon had seen wounds like these during his service. They were invariably fatal.

"It… it hurts." Miala moaned.

Leon could dimly hear Duamé shouting, "Schalae! Schalae, we need ya!"

The elven princess rushed over, accompanied by a streak of tan fur. Kelleren's frenzied barking joined the panic that had settled in Leon's chest. The canine companion whined in obvious concern, when Miala cried out in pain once again. An elven hand closed over Leon's, and at Princess Schalae's gentle urging he moved it away from Miala's wound. Schalae's eyes roved over the pyromancer, and her expression was grave as she observed the blood that saturated the front of Miala's robe. Hurriedly, Schalae said, "We need to get the bolt out before it does more damage or in case it's poisoned! Hold her down!"

Duamé's short but muscular stature pinned Miala's legs, while Leon leaned over and placed his blood stained hand on her shoulder. The chain-mail protection she had made him with Duamé rustled as he rested his other hand on her cheek. "Everything is going to be fine. Just look at me. Miala, keep looking at me!"

Her frightened eyes teared up as she whispered, "Leon… I- I love you."

"I love you, too." Leon's voice was laced with both conviction and fear as he felt a shift in the *Esperella*. They were moving again, and he heard Princess Schalae's voice tremble as she counted, "One, two…" and then all Leon could hear was Miala's scream of pain as the bolt was withdrawn.

Schalae hissed urgently as she pressed down on the wound, "It looks like the bolt wasn't barbed or poisoned, but it went between her ribs. Leon, use the spear! See if it can heal her!"

Leon frantically unsheathed Revelator from his back and held it against Miala. The blue tinged aeonyte metal wasn't shining due to the daytime hours, and it didn't look as if it was having any effect. Miala shakily lifted a hand to Leon's cheek and started to speak, but then her eyes drooped and fluttered. The muscles that held her hand up gave out, and her arm flopped limply to the deck. Leon panicked. "No no no, stay awake Miala. MIALA!"

Miala's form was still as Schalae moved to her other side, facing Leon. The elven princess leaned over and pulled one of her eyelids back, letting out a short groan at what she saw. Schalae sounded frantic as she yelled, "We're losing her. We're losing her!"

Cannon blasts sounded in the background before they heard Kérik shout, "It's tha dreadnought! Everyone brace yerselves!"

The *Esperella's* hull rang like a gong as the ship shook from the severity of the cannonball's impacts. The unexpected movement must have forced Schalae to steady herself, because she reflexively grasped Revelator's shaft as Leon held it over Miala's still form. A low hum sounded as they held it together, and for a brief moment the spearhead emitted a bright light. It winked out again when Schalae quickly took her hand away.

"No! Do that again! Schalae! Duamé! Grab hold!" Leon shouted, hoping and praying for a miracle to occur.

The elf and dwarf both grabbed hold of the old spear, and the hum returned – this time at a different pitch. Brilliant white light came from the spearhead and made it hard to see Miala's face. The only thing that was clearly visible was a silhouette of the א that adorned the blade's center. When Leon turned his head away from the bright light, he saw Gionna hovering close by. At some point, she must have hobbled over to see about Miala's status. She came forward, and her tiny gnome hand caught the end of the spear's shaft.

As soon as she grasped it, Revelator's already bright light grew almost blinding, and the loud hum turned into a musical chord that built upon the edges of Leon's hearing. At an urging that he couldn't explain, Leon brought Revelator to rest on Miala's still form. He grasped her limp wrist, and held her limp hand against the spear as well.

The divine chord changed in pitch again, and Leon heard Adonai's voice fill the air surrounding him. It was a calmer, gentler voice than Adonai had used when had spoken to him at Masterwork Halls. Words of love, empathy, and kindness flowed around them. The words were accompanied by Miala gasping in a lungful of air as her eyes shot open. She immediately raised her free hand to shield them from Revelator's brilliance. Though a battle raged around them, and a dreadnought bore down on the *Esperella*, Leon heard Adonai speak with clarity.

"Daughter, your faith has made you well."

Chapter 13: The Dreadnought

A thunderclap sounded as the light from Revelator suddenly cut off, and the aeonyte spearhead returned to its normal blue-tinged hue. When its light extinguished the heavenly sounding chord stopped, leaving Leon and his friends speechless over what had transpired.

Miala's wounds, and all of the blood that stained her robe, had disappeared. Moreso, her robe had been transformed. What had once been a nondescript light brown was now white. Every link of the fine chain-mail that adorned her shoulders had broken apart, and the small links were being carried away by the gentle wind that passed over her. As Leon looked at her face, he saw that a thin white scar marked her cheek where one of the crossbow bolts had grazed her.

Gionna quickly tapped at the bridge of her intricate glasses as she analyzed Miala's recovery. "Wounds are gone, bloodstains gone, even your robe is mended! This… is impossible!"

Impossible. Leon thought.

Or miraculous.

Or both.

"What… What happened?" Miala breathed.

Leon and Schalae helped her to her feet, and Kelleren hopped up on his hind legs, barking with an unmistakable joy. Duamé managed to choke out, "Did… Did anyone else hear… Adonai?"

"He… He talked to me." Miala said, "Healed me."

"You were dying. You were about to die, and He…" Princess Schalae began as she looked at Leon, and pointed at Revelator. "What… What is that thing?" The nearby sound of cannon fire interrupted their conversation. Everyone dropped low to the deck, and some of the launched cannonballs thudded into the aft of the *Esperella* while others whistled past overhead. "This is not over!" Schalae yelled.

“We’ll table the discussion!” Leon replied as he looked behind their ship. The dreadnought was turning back from its broadside, once again in pursuit of the *Esperella*. Kérik still stood at the helm, but was speaking to Ophelia, who had placed her hand on the wheel. It appeared that she was taking it over from the tired-looking dwarf. The hours Kérik had already spent piloting the ship throughout the night had taken their toll on him, and Leon was thankful the dwarf had possessed the presence of mind to hire her. Ophelia currently had much more energy than Admiral Silverspine, and after a bellow of, “All cannons reload!” Kérik willingly relinquished control of the vessel.

Leon and his friends clambered back to the *Esprella’s* helm, and found that General Xiphos and Lorog had stepped in for them to defend the pilot. Ophelia handled the ship’s wheel expertly, and Kérik gave direction at her side whenever it was needed. The dreadnought that was in pursuit was close enough to successfully fire cannonballs at them, but far enough that the multitude of undead onboard couldn’t fire crossbow bolts. Still, the huge ship continued to launch salvo after salvo from its bow chasers as it trailed them.

“What’s the damage to the levigem?” Leon asked Kérik over the din.

Kérik looked back at the dreadnought as he replied, “It cracked, but didn’t shatter! As it is, I don’t know if we should risk tryin’ ta broadside tha dreadnought though!”

An enemy cannonball picked that exact moment to crunch through, and destroy, a valuable mancer turret at the aft. The dwarven geomancer who had been manning it died instantly, and the cannonball, along with all the debris it caused, tumbled over the railing to the ground far below. “This isn’t working!” Leon exclaimed to his friends after Duamé let loose a frustrated cry at the loss of his brethren.

“What do ya propose? As soon as we turn ta broadside it, we’ll give ‘em a big fat target at this close a range!” Kérik replied.

“For once, I agree with the puffball! We would be blown out of the sky.” Gionna added.

Leon was becoming frustrated by their lack of options. "Well, we can't just let them follow us to Last Bastion! They are matching our speed, and will eventually hit another levigem, or the ship's wheel."

"If we had another ship… like my mail carrier… we could distract them by diverting their attention! Just saying…" Ophelia complained.

"I apologized about destroyin' yer mail carrier already, but we had ta think fast–" Kérik began before the young pilot waved off his explanation.

"It's okay, sir. Just lamenting my vessel, that's all."

Leon's mind worked furiously as he stared at the dreadnought in their wake. Running and hiding were still not options. They also couldn't afford to lose the *Esperella*, much less her crew. Every life lost endangered their mission more.

As his thoughts continued to spin, Leon looked around. First he noticed the exhaustion Miala was clearly fighting off. While her injuries had been miraculously healed, it did not appear to have gifted her renewed energy. He shifted his focus to the crew, and observed that their dwindling turrets and hand crossbows would not be able to successfully take the dreadnought down. The risk of turning the ship to fire had already been discussed, and Leon agreed that it was too dangerous at this close of a range. While Leon tried to sort through what options were left to them, another salvo was launched from the dreadnought's bow chasers, and hijacked his thoughts once again. Ophelia swerved in a serpentine motion attempting to avoid the incoming cannonballs. Her maneuvers, combined with the dreadnought's poor aim, prevented the *Esperella* from incurring any further damage. Leon knew that though the cannon balls had missed their ship this time, they couldn't avoid their shots for long.

Ophelia's skill at the wheel brought Leon's thoughts back to their flight, and the northeasterly direction they were heading. He still didn't want to lead the dreadnought any closer to Springfield, in case the people there hadn't already fled to Last Bastion. They couldn't turn too much to port or starboard without being broadsided, and neither grounding nor climbing higher into the thinner unbreathable air were options.

That leaves one direction left to go.

An idea formed in Leon's mind based on his previous experiences, and out of a desperation to not lose anyone else. He cast a calculated look back at the dreadnought – it would be farther than he had ever jumped before.

If I could get there, I could distract the undead so they couldn't broadside us...

Leon raised his voice to his friends around him, "Alright, new plan. When you get the chance, after the next salvo is launched from their bow chasers, turn and broadside them!"

"That is quite literally exactly what we DON'T want to do! They have twenty cannons to blast our levigems with!" Gionna gesticulated wildly with her cane at the monstrosity chasing them. "What do we have?"

"It's like Ophelia said. We need a distraction. I'll pop over there, and you fire at their ship once I've gotten their attention."

Everyone's reactions to his declaration lived up to his expectations. Leon suffered through the various questions about his sanity and proclamations that he would die. Then he bit back with, "Anyone else have a better idea?"

When nobody answered, Leon walked from the aft to the middle of the ship. He unstrapped the shield from his back, and affixed its straps to his wrist and forearm. He turned to see that Miala had followed him. Her weary eyes searched his face as she grasped his arm and asked, "Are you sure?"

Even with the small scar that now ran along her cheek, Leon couldn't help but think that she was the most beautiful woman in the world. The air whipped her fiery red hair around her face, and he felt the urge to reach out and touch it one more time. He stepped close to her and she reflexively leaned into him. Leon captured her mouth in a brief kiss before he whispered, "I'm sure. It's the only way."

Gionna turned from looking at the dreadnought with her spyglass, "They have crossbows just like the other ships. Find cover where you can! I'll try to monitor your progress with these!" She tapped at her multifocals and her spyglass.

"This is madness!" General Xiphos yelled from the aft. "What do you mean you'll just 'pop over there'? We can't just turn around and board them!"

That's right. Some of them haven't seen this trick before. Leon would have chuckled to himself if he hadn't been about to launch himself right into the midst of their enemy.

"Everyone, make a hole!" Leon yelled, causing both elves and dwarves to clear a path from his location all the way to the aft railing. He grasped the spear in his right hand and shouted instructions to Ophelia at the ship's wheel. "When I tell you, bring the ship higher in elevation!"

"Uh, sure thing? Not exactly sure what you're gonna do there, but…"

"Jus' trust tha bloodstone buffoon! Yer gonna do great, meat shield! Turn 'em all ta salt!" Duamé encouraged.

Leon couldn't help but smile at Duamé's use of his nickname, even as he set his eyes on the flashes coming from the dreadnought's bow chaser cannons. Six cannonballs arced towards the *Esperella*, but after Ophelia jerked the wheel only two of them remained a threat. They both bounced off the aft of the hull right as Leon screamed, "Now Ophelia!"

The ship lurched as it climbed. Leon didn't want the dreadnought to have an opportunity to match their elevation and waste whatever advantage their higher ground would give him. Taking a few quick breaths, Leon ran. His legs moved swiftly, and his arms pumped furiously while holding both spear and shield. The aft came up quickly. He passed the shocked faces of the General, Lorog, and Ophelia, and never broke his stride as he moved to jump up to the railing. Leon grasped Revelator in both hands, and when the levigem in his gloved palm made contact with the elvenwood of the spear he felt instantly lighter.

He knew the leap between ships would be great, and that his faith would have to be greater still. However, after having witnessed Adonai's power save Miala from the clutches of death, Leon knew his faith had never been stronger. He felt the fullness of his faith shine brightly – just like Revelator's light. As Leon launched himself from the *Esperella's* rail, he trusted in Adonai, and that his faith in Him would carry him all the way to the pursuing dreadnought. Startled shouts from those who hadn't witnessed his ability before, sounded behind him. The wind quickly captured the sounds and pulled them away as he left the *Esperella* behind. Leon refrained from looking at the several hundred foot expanse between himself and the ground as he flew through the air; unwilling to allow anything to sow a seed of doubt in him. Instead, he fixed his eyes on the dreadnought, confident of where he would land.

The prominent brow of the ship was made up of the six recently-fired bow chaser cannons, and manned by an assortment of undead shamblers and wretches assigned to them. They were all busily reloading the cannons for another salvo, and for a split second Leon believed his jump had gone unnoticed. Then he saw a group of four wretches, to the right side of the bow, aim their crossbows at him. Leon angled his aeonyte shield to be more in front of his frame as he reached the peak of his jump. Based on his current trajectory, he gauged that he would land in between the four wretches and the bow chaser's cannon crew.

A wide stairwell descended into the dreadnought behind where the wretches were located. Leon decided that once the initial forces that had spotted him were dealt with, the ship's interior would be a good area to limit the angles from which he could be shot at. Bolts fired from hand crossbows began to tink against his scale-mail armor and shield, their angles of impact ineffectual. As Leon aimed for a clear spot to land, more undead began to make their way across the top deck towards him. He landed in the midst of them, knowing he had little time to spare as they swarmed towards him.

"Adonai, guide me." Leon whispered as he engaged his enemy in battle.

The naval leathers that the wretches wore hung loosely on their thin frames. These once-soldiers were now essentially skeletons, with little muscle and tightly stretched skin. Their needle-like fingers held hand crossbows that they struggled to reload. Leon moved towards the easy targets and swept Revelator in a diagonal slice upward. Its hard metal tip easily pierced and ripped through the leather armor they wore, and a flash of light foretold two of the wretches being permanently dispatched. Salt sprayed from undead flesh, only to be blown away by the wind that swept across their deck.

Leon recognized that a stationary target made an easy target, so he charged at the remaining two wretches who had abandoned their hand crossbows for close-combat short blades. Their foot long swords were unsheathed to meet Leon's charge, but the reach of their blades was nothing compared to that of a spear. Leon jabbed low and used one wretch's deflection to guide his spear in a slice that penetrated the adjacent one. Revelator's blade buried itself within the second wretch's leg. Beneath the wound, the wretch's leg turned to a useless pile of salt, causing it to fall on the deck. Not losing any forward momentum, Leon bowled into the last wretch left standing. With a swift movement, he brought his shield upward, violently knocking its head back. The much lighter wretch practically flew over the ship's railing from the forceful impact, and Leon turned back to finish the immobile wretch as he surveyed his surroundings.

A mass of shamblers and wretches rushed towards him from across the dreadnought. All were armed with swords, shields, and hand crossbows. Desiccated undead flesh moved in mindless fury, each creature fully determined to end his life. Seeing the nearby bow chasers, Leon made the decision to run in their direction instead of to the stairs below. He needed to prevent any more salvos from launching at the *Esperella*. Crates and barrels of supplies were stacked near each of the cannons. With three undead manning each cannon, and six cannons in total, Leon understood that he would have to be both smart and systematic in his attack. He was thoroughly outnumbered by the cannon station's undead, and the enormous lengths of the cannons themselves served as obstacles he would have to maneuver around.

Leon's mind whirred, and he struck where he could. He downed two undead before he was forced to jump over one who dove low at him. The lightness from the combined spear and levigem had dissipated, and Leon's feet landed hard as he delivered a downward strike against an one shambler's upraised linstock. The long torch-like stick snapped in half from Revelator's force. He then turned the shambler to salt with Revelator's blade, and the burning end of the linstock clattered to the ground before rolling under a cannon.

Leon fended off two more shamblers sporting their own burning club-like linstocks, before a crossbow bolt whizzed by in front of him. He backpedaled in an attempt to disengage as another bolt clanged off his shoulder pauldron. The mass of undead were closing in, and Leon instinctively knew that if he didn't find cover within the ship's belly, he would be overwhelmed. The last swing he made with Revelator knocked another burning linstock down, causing it to roll against one of the crates near the cannons.

Leon's mind raced as he turned and fled down the stairwell that led into the dreadnought. The next level down held more undead, and was laid out similarly to the bow chasers area on the top deck of the vessel. Mindless shamblers were under the direction of various wretches, and charged with maintaining the cannons. The smell of decay mingled with the smoke of spent gunpowder that hung in the air, and Leon fought the urge to plug his nose.

The nearest undead shambler was an overly large ogre who had a wide frame covered in layers of fat and muscle. A dangerous foe even when alive, its outfit did not depict it as a former member of the military. The undead ogre was covered by a large canvas that had been roughly stitched together. Joining the dark stains and holes in its outfit were dried and caked on mud splatters. Leon could tell with very little observation that this ogre had probably come from working one of his father's mines.

Whether the ogre formerly unearthed levigems from Lucien's floating landmasses, or worked deep in the mountains extracting iron ore, Leon couldn't tell. It was clear, though, that this ogre wasn't the only miner onboard the ship. Leon saw that there were other humans, orcs, even a gnome and a few goblins, on the gun-deck of the dreadnought in the similar drab mining garb. How were there so many miners spread among the military personnel? Clearly, something was off, but Leon couldn't focus on it at the moment.

All crew members were undead, of course, and with the undead forces from the top deck about to descend, Leon knew he had to move fast. He held Revelator in both hands again, and felt lighter when the levigem's influence took effect. While the dreadnought's interior was in actuality wider than the *Eperella's*, it still felt quite tight as almost half the space on one side was taken up by the overly large orge.

Leon leapt up, and almost cracked his head on the ceiling when he practically flew into the air. He impaled the back of the ogre, and salt spread from the wound near the massive ogre's spine. His forward momentum propelled him through the air and into the ogre, causing its bulk to crash into the ground. While it proved fortunate that the ogre's mass provided a temporary blockade against any pursuing undead until its salty transformation finished, the crash of its body caused any undead who hadn't noticed Leon yet turn and fix their glowing red eyes on him.

As more enemies scrambled to subdue him, Leon pulled on every skill and strategy he had learned from his dream-training with Lochemetel. Her strikes during their sessions had been quick, relentless, and designed to make Leon learn how to defend against successive attacks. By the time that he finally bested the angelic warrior, their matches lasted minutes instead of seconds. Whether it was one shambler with a club-like linstock, or three wretches with short swords, all fell before Leon; undead limbs, bodies, and salt piles littered the ground around him.

When Leon saw the wretches with crossbows who had followed him down the stairs, he parried a club swing from a shambler and kicked its body into them. Most of the group was knocked into a tangled mass that writhed on the floor. Leon speared one wretch who had moved out of the way and remained upright. It managed to fire its crossbow at him while its shoulder turned to salt, but the bolt pinged harmlessly off his aeonyte shield. After finishing that wretch off, Leon turned and dispatched the ones who were still struggling to regain their feet. More undead poured down the stairs in pursuit of him, while another horde scrambled up from the level below to also engage in the combat.

Seeing that the only reasonable path was through the gun-deck, Leon leapt over a nearby cannon. A few undead immediately greeted him, but they were not nearly as many in number as the horde that barrelled in from the upper and lower stairwells. Leon slashed through one shambler as he landed and used his shield to shove another back. Feeling exposed in his current position, Leon dove forward, aiming toward the ship's center. A few more bolts were fired as he moved, all aimed directly at the spot where he had just stood. Slicing on the upswing of his roll, Leon caught a gnomish undead's head causing the rest of its body to collapse.

The telltale booms of distant cannonfire announced that the *Esperella* had turned to fire upon the dreadnought as Leon had instructed. He could hear wood splinter behind him, and jagged holes punched through the dreadnought. Suddenly a deafening explosion sounded from above decks, followed by a shudder that rippled through the boards at Leon's feet. He promptly realized that either a shot from the *Esperella,* or one of the flaming linstocks, must have ignited a black powder supply near the bow chasers! Leon turned to look back and saw that many of the undead who had been chasing him were knocked down, and flames licked at the upper stairwell's opening. Any possible escape route won by *Esperella's* attack had been cut off from him by the flames. This knowledge only reinforced Leon's earlier decision to get through the gun-deck and exit near the dreadnought's aft.

"Time to go!" Leon announced to no one but himself, before he ran towards the smaller group of undead that converged ahead of him. Several undead cannon crews had abandoned their positions to attack him. Mindlessly, they tried to either climb over the cannons that blocked their way, or move around them towards the central aisle of the ship. After engaging in a few stabs and one block with Revelator, Leon's footing was forced to change. The angle of the decking tilted downward towards the bow that had just exploded. The ship was nosediving, and Leon was still inside.

Loose cannonballs and uncoordinated undead rolled past Leon as the ship's angle of descent increased dangerously. The stairwell that led to the aft of the ship was still too far away, so Leon grasped Revelator in both hands to activate his jumping ability. He launched himself diagonally upward – towards the vessel's hull and away from the undead that tumbled past him. Planting a foot on the hull's side where he landed, Leon jumped again and made it to a stout, rounded pillar. It was one of the central pillars that were spread throughout the ship, which ran through all the decks. Hugging it tightly, he watched as more of his adversaries fell past him from the ever inclining pitch of the ship.

The explosion must have damaged the front levigems. Leon's thoughts raced as the undead made futile attempts to swipe at him as they sailed past. The screech of heavy cannons beginning to break from their frames sounded throughout the gun deck as the pull of gravity overwhelmed their bracings. The metal guns soon broke free, and slid across the level with savage force.

They crashed against any undead, wooden crates, or structural supports that stood in their path indiscriminately; the effects of their brutal slide appeared to be devastating to both the undead and the ship. Still braced against the pillar, Leon saw broken bodies and cannons all careening into the far end of the ship – which resembled a fiery furnace more and more with each passing second.

How was he once again on a ship that was crashing with flames covering its bow? There was no nefarious dragon to blame this time, just the orders and actions that had come from himself. The irony of his situation didn't escape Leon, but once again, an escape desperately needed to happen. Fixing his eyes on a stairwell that was a ways ahead of him, Leon planted his feet and jumped. His supernatural ability only carried him part way towards his goal, and he directed his landing to a small section of the starboard hull. His error was instantaneously made clear to him when he saw a cannon careening towards him. Leon leapt again, before it could carry him to a fiery doom.

Soaring upward, Leon jumped from one final foothold and was able to grab hold of one of the stairwell's steps with his left hand. Using every ounce of straining muscle he possessed, Leon cried out from the exertion of hoisting his lower half up the stairwell. Revelator remained secure in his right hand and sheer desperation fueled his thoughts. Arm and stomach muscles exhausted from the strain, Leon made it to the exit and found footing outside the stairwell. He was near the aft of the ship, and grabbed hold of the dreadnoughts railing so he could quickly assess his surroundings.

The dreadnought was literally falling out of the sky. The ground was fast approaching and, looking about, Leon could see no sign of the *Esperella*. What he could see was an undead fiercely pulling back on the ship's wheel at the nearby helm – the wretch was fighting against the ship's dive. Movement near the helm suddenly caught Leon's eye. Two dark robed figures dangled in the air from their securing lines. One held its palms outstretched at Leon, and the glowing red eyes that shone from its raised cowl left no doubt as to its identity.

"Rust!" Leon exclaimed, as he let go of the railing and slid back into the stairwell. He stopped just inside the opening, tucked out of view from the top deck, as two small blasts of magic slammed into the railing where he had been. The wooden railing splintered under the impact of what appeared to be magical cannonballs. They floated in the air unnaturally for a few moments before they snapped out of view as they flew back to where they had come from. Leon didn't dare poke his head out from the stairwell for the two liches to aim at again. He knew he had to do something though, because in a few minutes they would be a pile of fiery rubble on the earth.

The wooden decking near him crunched from the impact of things hammering against it and while Leon couldn't see what caused it, he suspected the liches didn't care about the ship's integrity in their effort to kill him. His suspicion was confirmed when the wooden wall that made up part of the stairwell cracked and splintered from the force of successive blows. Leon ducked and braced himself behind his shield just before a cannonball exploded from the wall and slammed into it. The impact knocked him to the base of the stairwell, and just as he feared, he was about to slide all the way into eventual oblivion. Leon instinctively hooked Revelator through the base of the stair railing and held on for dear life.

The cannonball snapped out of sight, returning once again to its sender. Leon could hear more destruction of timber, and saw chunks of planking and wall falling towards him. Within seconds an opening was made between himself and the two dangling liches. He watched as they controlled the floating cannonballs by flinging them in a direction with incredible force, before then summoning them back to themselves.

Leon clung to Relevator at the base of the stairwell, as he continued to stare at the two liches through the newfound opening. They held their cannonballs in their extended hands, and Leon could do nothing to protect himself as they adjusted their aim towards his prone form that dangled in the air. Suddenly, Leon saw a flash of movement behind them. As magic coalesced around the cannonballs, the head of a hammer smashed into the side of one lich's robed head, while a sword blade severed the other's as it turned.

The familiar faces of Duamé and Lorog appeared as they destroyed the liches before once again darting out of view. Leon couldn't comprehend how they were present, when he saw them reappear at the top of the stairs.

Lorog lowered himself down the sloped stairs yelling, "Grab my hand!" Not needing to be told twice, Leon swung himself up and reached out with his shield arm. The orc's rough muscled arm connected with his, and Lorog pulled as Leon climbed. Duamé stood at the top of the stairs, and grabbed them both to help pull them the rest of the way up.

"What are you both doing here?" Leon yelled over the wind.

"Savin' yer saltshakin' hide!" Duamé retorted.

"The older gnome lady said you needed help!" Lorog clarified.

"Where's the *Esperella*?" Leon asked.

"There!" Lorog pointed towards the ship. The distinctive aeonyte hull was circling around from the dreadnought's aft. Though it was leveled off, the Esperella was descending, and Leon saw they planned to run alongside the dreadnought where the railing had broken apart. The aim of the ship was clear: retrieve the three of them before the dreadnought slammed into the ground.

"We need to jump now!" Leon yelled as the farmland around Springfield rapidly approached. At their current speed they would crash within seconds.

Lorog, Duamé, and Leon ran up to the dreadnought's broken railing and leapt. Their yells were drowned out by the air that whistled around them, and the thudding of Leon's heart. For a moment it looked like the *Esperella* wouldn't be able to catch them, but the bow of the top deck scooped underneath Leon's feet just in time, and they landed safely with a few rolls and tumbles.

The terrible sounds of a gigantic crash and splintering wood filled the air as the *Esperella* angled upward, and peeled away from the dreadnought. Leon looked behind him and a massive explosion filled his vision when the flames finally ignited the powder magazines. Surely if they had jumped but a moment later, they would have been engulfed in that inferno.

"Well, tha dreadnought's… naught." Duamé droned from the floor of the top deck. He still hadn't stood up from his tumbled landing. The rest of their friends converged around them, anad Leon kept reassuring everyone that he was alright. Between the amazed observations at what they had just accomplished, Leon heard laughter begin next to him.

Laying on the deck near the dwarf, Lorog was laughing uproariously. His muscled arm slapped down on Duamé's shoulder as he rumbled, "Naught."

"Ah! Ooh! Think I twinged me shoulder."

Leon saw his sister make her way towards him through the crowd. Liara didn't look happy, but still grabbed him for a quick hug. "Liara, thank Adonai you're safe. I–"

She disengaged from him, and Leon felt a hot sting on his face as she slapped him. Hard. The anger in her voice was clear, "I'm glad you're safe, but don't ever do that again." Then she hugged him again and walked off through the snickering crowd.

"Are you… alright?" Princess Schalae asked.

"I'm… wondering why everyone I care about slaps me."

"Oh, I haven't hit you yet, dearie." Gionna said between laughs.

"Ta be fair, I didn't slap ya, but I did punch ya in tha gut once." Duamé clarified, "But I can fix that as soon as me shoulder is better, if ya like."

"No thanks, Duamé."

"Ya sure? I could just use me other arm."

"It's fine, Duamé!"

Chapter 14: The Inspired

Once the amazement of his survival wore off, Leon took command of the ship and situation. As captain, it was Leon's duty to lead his crew in a eulogy for those who had been lost over the previous days. Every crew member participated in the moments of respectful silence and remembrance, and Leon ruminated on their fallen comrades. So much death had occurred during their recent battles, and he could only assume that the conflict at Last Bastion would result in even more.

After the ceremony, Leon and the others took time to examine the village of Springfield as they passed over. It was the largest village in Xaelon Kingdom, and therefore shocking to see it completely deserted. Homes lacked any sort of cooking or warming fires, standing in stark contrast to the blazing dreadnought that lay further and further behind them. Barren roads and streets contrasted the fields overflowing with grains, fruits, and vegetables that circled the village. What Leon could clearly see, and what they followed in their low altitude flight, were the multitude of tracks and carriage ruts that exited from the northern gate of the village.

Springfield's residents had clearly evacuated towards Last Bastion, though the exact time of their departure remained uncertain. Leon assumed it must have been within the past few days, and General Xiphos confirmed his suspicions when she reminded him of the emergency council meeting she had attended with his father. That had been when the king ordered the evacuations, commanding everyone to head for the mountain fortress. Leon's naval service hadn't taken him there personally, but 'impenetrable', 'safe', and 'unassailable' were consistently used to describe it by his fellow soldiers who had been.

Relieved that the populace of Springfield were as safe as possible, Leon gave the order for the *Esperella* to resume course toward Last Bastion with all haste. Racing against both the undead horde and Laric's coronation, the faster they arrived at the fortress, the better. With their renewed sense of urgency fueling their rapid speed, Kérik assessed that they could reach the fortress by midday of the following day. After a brief discussion, it was agreed that they would also need to maintain a lookout for more airships throughout their final night of flight. Whether friend or foe, they needed to be prepared for whatever might come.

The rest of the day passed as Duamé and Miala completed makeshift repairs to the top deck before then moving down to the hull to try and tackle its dents. After whacking the dents with the largest hammer he could find, Duamé reported that it proved virtually ineffective at repairing them.

"The cannonballs were iron too, but they were flyin' at high speed. Whackin' with this gal just ain't cuttin' it!" He explained, as he lifted the maul from Masterwork Halls that had replaced the one he lost in the Archives.

Gionna cocked her head slightly before she suggested, "Don't you have any spare aeonyte sheets in that blasted forge downstairs? Why not reinforce the maul with one of them? You might have better luck with repairs."

Duamé stared at her with his mouth hanging open for a few seconds before he tapped Miala's shoulder, said, "Come on!", and raced into the belly of the ship. A short time later Leon heard the telltale ringing of a hammer striking against an anvil. Dwarven efficiency, paired with mancer heat, brought a unique combination to their unusual forge. Leon only hoped that the two of them wouldn't accidentally set fire to the ship in their zeal to work.

Kérik and Princess Schalae approached Leon as he sat near the ship's wheel to rest his tired legs. The two leaders sat next to him as he propped himself against a crate full of crossbow bolts. He pulled his thoughts away from Miala to look at the elven princess and dwarven admiral. Their expressions were serious, and Leon's relief shifted into something that more closely matched their concern. "What's wrong?"

The princess sighed deeply before she spoke. "Your spear, Revelator. May I see it?"

Without a word, Leon withdrew the spear that had been sheathed into the strap on his back after he sat to rest. The princess grasped the spear, and for a brief second while they both touched it, the strange hum once again permeated the air. Leon released his grip, and the sound abruptly cut off. The princess held the spear in both hands, closed her eyes, and furrowed her evergreen colored brows in concentration. Leon half expected Revelator's blue tinged metal to flash, or perhaps burst into a brilliant light. Instead, it remained unchanged as Schalae sat there.

"Any idea what she's doing?" Leon asked Kérik.

"Not a clue, lad. Though, I wanted ta talk ta ya about the crew's morale."

Leon's attention shifted from the elven princess to focus on the admiral, who stressed every word that he next spoke.

"We're comin' up ta tha endgame lad. Whatever that may be. These people, yer crew, have been with ya through a lot recently. We don't know what's comin' at us at Last Bastion. So we need ta take care o' morale tonight."

Leon thought he followed what Kérik meant. "You want to throw a celebration? Now?"

Kérik's nod jiggled the puff of white hair around his head. "It wouldn't hurt lad. A celebration fer those that have gone. Fer those o' us still here. Any way ya want ta spin it."

Leon could see the admiral's point. They had all been through multiple battles, and some of the warriors had traveled with Leon and his friends for weeks. The Northern Elvenwood, Masterwork Halls, Agaprya, Rhise Manor, even the undead airship battle they had just survived. There hadn't been many opportunities for them to stop and celebrate hard won victories. So long as no more engagements against aerial undead or enemy airships occurred this evening, Leon couldn't see a reason why everyone shouldn't relax for a bit.

Gazing at the various crew members within his line of sight, Leon had to admit that they looked tired. Stressed. Who could blame them? Danger followed their every move, everyday, like an obedient puppy. They needed a break, and a bit of relaxation sounded wonderful. This promise of a nice time came from Kérik Silverspine though, and that posed a possible concern. Kérik's idea of a celebration, back in Leon's naval days, had always led to the severe inebriation of everyone who participated. Only after

Leon's imprisonment at Masterwork Halls a week or so ago, had Kérik thrown his flask into an underground lake; it had been a physical act to commit himself to stop drinking.

"It's a good idea, Kérik. But I need to ask, you don't have any…"

"Nope. It's a dry ship, an' like I told ya before, I'm done with that nonsense. Me head's clearer than it's been in years, an' I feel twenty years younger. No need ta worry there, lad." Kérik glanced at the princess with a quizzical expression as he stood up, "I'll spread word among tha crew. Ya can deal with her highness."

A few minutes after Kérik left, Princess Schalae broke herself from whatever trance she had been in, and opened her eyes. She gazed at the spear in her hands with an unreadable expression, and slowly held it out to Leon.

"What happened? Are you ok?" Leon asked, as he took hold of the spear.

In all the time Leon had spent in the princess' company on their journey, he had never seen her look so unsettled. Her shoulders trembled slightly, and she breathed a response that he couldn't quite hear. Her royal composure seemed completely shattered, and she asked just a touch louder, "Do you… know how old the elvenwood from this spear is?"

For all its miraculous powers, Leon still didn't know very much about Revelator's history. Beyond having been told that Calvin had originally deposited it in Rhise Manor, the spear's origins were a complete mystery to him. He was eager for any information or insight the princess could share.

"Go on. What did you find out, Your Highness?"

"It is… incredible. It's older than my Broken Bough, and my bow has been handed down for centuries. This comes from before the Dead Wars… before anyone remembers. I… I think this spear could be…" Her voice trailed off as she shook her head in apparent disbelief. "I think it could be from the tree of life."

"The tree of life?" Leon repeated in confusion. He had never heard of any such thing before.

"It's an old tale, about origins. The origins of us all. Judge Leon, I know multitudes of different trees. This is something older. Something different. The wood is not even native to Xaelon. It's similar to acacia wood, but lighter, and it has not turned grey with age. Whatever the wood is, it comes from the Lost Lands beyond our borders."

Each of their neighboring kingdoms had been forced to slowly shrink their borders until they were eventually completely overrun by the undead hordes, and disappeared altogether. Their cultures and peoples were gone; the undead had left nothing resembling life in their wake. Someone would have had to have intentionally brought it to Xaelon for the spear to make such a trek across distant lands. For that matter, Revelator was an exact fit for the Judge's room table within the Agapryan Archives. Magnus had even mentioned that the Judge's section of the Archives outdated everything else in Agaprya. All of these details certainly lent credence to the idea that Revelator was not just old, but ancient.

Leon ran a hand along the spear; its stout wood had never bent or broken during his travels. In fact, the wood appeared unchanged since he first picked it up months ago. The fact that the spear could be centuries old was unfathomable to him.

How could a weapon of war survive for so long?

Of course, the answer came to Leon immediately: Adonai was all-powerful and could make any artifact, such as Revelator, last for however long He wanted to. If the artifact had been created to help Leon fulfill his role as Judge, or possibly even help other Judges throughout history, Adonai would ensure it survived the test of time. Leon recalled the pictures carved on the entryway wall to Masterwork Halls. Whichever Judge helped free the enslaved dwarves from the giants who had terrorized them, had been in possession of a weapon that was indistinguishable in the worn picture. If that had indeed been Revelator, then the spear had a much more storied past than Leon first thought.

Princess Schalae looked as if she were patiently waiting for Leon's response as he processed the information that had been given him. "If Revelator comes from beyond Xaelon, then I have no idea where from. The last time I crossed into the Lost Lands, I was onboard the *Dawnfire* with your betrothed. We were scouting for any survivors, and for undead hordes to destroy."

Princess Schalae's elven features twitched at the mention of her dead prince. Her head hung a bit lower, and Leon felt the need to boost her spirits.

Kérik did say to take care of morale.

"He was a role model to me. Gelan was the best person that I had ever met. Kind, selfless, everything that I aspire to be."

"Do not disparage yourself, Judge. You exhibit those traits as well. I can see him in you." Schalae sighed as she looked away briefly, "I miss him."

Leon couldn't help but empathize with her, "Me too."

Miala returned from below decks, and found her way over to the two of them. She silently sat next to Leon, slipped her hand into his, and their fingers interlaced as she tried to lean her head against his pauldron. It only lasted a few seconds before she gave up with a playful push on his shoulder. "Your armor's uncomfortable."

"That's because the padding is on the inside." Leon snarked.

"Kérik told me about tonight's festivities… You should bathe."

Leon was confused by the sudden turn in the conversation. "Is it really that bad?"

"We've been through a few battles, Leon. It's bad. We're all taking turns, and you should definitely take yours."

Leon did some mental calculations of their water supply. "I'm surprised that we have enough water for everyone to bathe."

Miala's smile grew broader as she explained, "Well, it helps when you have a powerful aquamancer on board like Brigid. She's quiet, but an amazingly gifted mancer. After Gérda and I talked to her, she coalesced ice. Then I melted it. If you hurry, it might still be warm."

Leon couldn't resist planting a quick kiss on Miala's cheek before saying, "You're brilliant. If you would both excuse me."

He left the ladies to continue their conversation, and made his way down towards the gun-deck where crew members were packing up supplies from the recent battle. The dwarven cannon crew brought a swift efficiency to the task, cleaning the cannons with wet and dry rags in a flurry of activity. More than a few of them gave Leon pats on the back and congratulatory thumbs up, exclaiming their thanks for his efforts in the fight. Leon tried to humbly accept their gratitude before he continued his trek down to the washrooms that were located in the belly of the ship. As he descended the next set of stairs, Leon saw his mother speaking with Gionna. They stood apart, in an uncrowded corner of the ship, and spoke in hushed whispers. Their conversation drew to an abrupt halt as soon as Gionna caught sight of him. He gave them an awkward wave, and once they waved back, continued down the stairwell – knowing full well that their business was their own.

Leon finally made it to the level he sought, and proceeded to take his time in one of the *Esperella's* washrooms. He made sure to not only clean himself, but his armor as well. He ran a hand over the stiff stubble of a dark beard that had returned to his face, making him look far too much like the bandit from the wanted posters spread throughout Agaprya. Even during his tenure in the airship navy, Leon had preferred a close cropped look; he felt long beards were best left to the likes of Duamé and Kérik. Now, out of sheer necessity, Leon took the extra time to shave. It was imperative that he not reveal his true identity until the time was right – until he could confront his father, and denounce him.

Thoughts about the navy brought Leon's mind back to Prince Gelan. The enigmatic man had been a massive influence on Leon's life both during and after the time they had known each other. From the first moment they met Leon had felt a connection to him, and strove to live up to his expectations.

Two years ago…

"It's been a while, Leon." Dawes grinned and offered an outstretched hand, though his smile didn't quite reach his eyes. "Glad you're joining the crew."

Leon couldn't help but smile in return as he shook the extended hand and hoisted his pack up on his shoulder. Back when they trained together he and Dawes had been quite competitive, working hard to vy for the training admiral's favor. Kérik Silverspine ended up ranking Leon at the top of their graduating class, though Dawes had come in at a very close second. Once they graduated, their careers had taken them down widely different paths. Leon's first three years following training had brought him to several different ships and battles against undead. He even helped with a few evacuations of the Lost Lands survivors and villages who had tried to hold out against the undead forces.

Dawes' career had been less tumultuous. He was able to land a midshipman position on the flagship of the fleet after a battle with a pyromancer lich scrapped his first ship. Despite their prior rivalry, it felt good to see the man again. Dawes' short stature forced him to crane his neck back slightly to meet Leon's eyes, and even though he smiled and offered his hand, Leon couldn't help but notice that the midshipman seemed slightly standoffish.

Leon was resigned to be good natured, whether Dawes wanted him to be part of the crew or not. Breaking the handshake, Leon gestured behind Dawes, towards his latest ship assignment. The *Dawnfire* was spectacular, and he couldn't wait to feel the wind against him when he took to the sky as one of the ship's newly promoted officers. "It's beautiful."

Dawes' face lit up, a genuine smile taking over, as he too looked over the ship. "Top of the line. The best ship. The best crew. The best captain."

"Don't you mean Prince Gelan?"

Dawes held up an admonishing finger as they ascended the gangplank to the top deck of the ship. There Leon saw a few more of the crew: humans, elves, a couple dwarves, even an orc and a goblin. Many different races, all wearing the same black and blue of the Xaelon airship navy, and all trying to steal glances at him in an effort to size up their new officer.

"That's rule number one on the *Dawnfire*. The captain prefers to be just that, captain. Everyone's treated with the respect they've earned here. Best not forget it." Dawes hooked his hand under a strap and pulled Leon's pack from his shoulder. "I'll go ahead and stow this in your hammock. The captain has asked to speak with you in his chambers. Down the aft stairwell, and furthest door in the back."

"Thanks for the advice, Dawes. I look forward to working with you again." Leon nodded to the man, but within the span of a breath Dawes had already turned and carried Leon's pack towards the bow stairs. Hoping their rivalry wouldn't deepen further, Leon nodded to a few passing crew members as he headed towards the captain's cabin.

The Dawnfire was larger than the other vessels he had served on, and he marveled at the wide corridors and stairwells he stepped through. Knowing that there would be time to tour the vessel later, Leon felt it prudent to not keep Prince Gelan waiting. He briskly approached the closed cabin door and knocked.

"Enter." A strong-timbred voice called from within.

Leon pushed the door open and found the cabin to be decorated more simply than he would have imagined. There were no royal cushions or frilly accouterments to be found, just a mattress in one corner, and a map depicting the border of Xaelon and the Lost Lands pinned against a wall. Two people sat on the edge of a sturdy table that was bolted in the middle of the room, and they both looked at Leon as he entered and shut the door behind himself.

The Prince was easily distinguishable. While both men wore a leather naval uniform, the prince's bore a purple ribbon that encircled his shoulders and lapel. Prince Gelan was approximately ten years Leon's senior, the bottom of his angular face was covered in a close cropped dark beard, and straight, shoulder length, dark hair effortlessly framed his features. Before Leon could take anything else in about his new captain, he exuberantly leapt up from his seat on the table and stood beside the other officer.

"Second officer Leon reporting for duty, sir." Leon stood straighter as the two older men inspected him.

"Thank you, Officer Leon." Prince Gelan gestured to the man next to him, "May I present the first mate of the Dawnfire, Ebaret Jiasse. Ebaret, Leon."

They all shook hands and exchanged pleasantries while Leon sized up the ship's first mate. He was a slim, middle aged man, who appeared to have received too many sunburns. His reddish skin and somewhat blotchy complexion paired with the dark hues of his naval uniform to create an interesting image. An exotic accent flowed from the first mate's lips as he asked, "No family name?"

Before Leon could deliver a prepared speech he had given to the numerous other ship captains and commanders, Prince Gelan interjected, "Leon's a special man who's risen up through the ranks thanks to hard work, with no family behind him. Ebaret, please launch the ship on a course for the Lost Lands. I'd like to speak to our new arrival alone… Give him a brief rundown."

Ebaret snapped to attention and affirmed his orders before taking his leave. Leon suddenly found himself alone with royalty for the first time in his life. As soon as the door closed, Leon quickly uttered, "Thank you, Captain."

"Not a problem, Officer. The Admiral made me aware of your situation. I assume that you have parchments for me?"

"Yes sir." Leon reached into a breast pocket and produced a short folded stack of parchments. As he handed his naval history to the prince, along with a letter from Admiral Silverspine, it once again struck him how odd it was that his year of training and three years of service could be boiled down to a few meager leaves which could be handed to his superiors.

The Prince took the offered papers and paced around the room as he reviewed them while Leon stood in silent attention. A few minutes later, following some muffled shouts from outside, Leon steadied himself as the Dawnfire lifted into the air. Prince Gelan didn't even break his stride as he moved about the cabin.

"Well, this all seems in order." The Prince declared, as he handed Leon back all of his papers except for the letter from Admiral Silverspine. "You won't be needing this one again."

That the Prince would withhold Admiral Silverspine's letter of introduction confused Leon. "Sir?"

"This is the last ship you'll be sent to serve on Leon. I can promise you that. I expect much from my crew, but where much is expected, much is rewarded. Officers are to not lord their positions over the rest of the crew. Each person on this ship is integral to its function and our mutual survival. Of course, from your deployment history, it doesn't look like I necessarily need to explain that to you. You've seen plenty of action in your career, and while on this ship, you'll continue to. We are men and women of action, and we will always do our part in the Dead Wars."

Leon couldn't help himself, "A question, if I may, Your Highness?"

The Prince's expression was unreadable as he replied, "'Sir' or 'Captain' will do just fine, Leon. What's your question?"

The prince's informal nature was a bit unexpected, but his declaration that the flagship was one of action was even more so. "Well, Sir… you're the prince. Aren't you supposed to be taking over the Kingdom from King Garinth soon? Why risk your life in the wars, Sir?"

For a moment the prince didn't respond, as if he was thinking of an answer. When he did, he gestured for Leon to sit in a bolted seat at the table. Taking the seat, Leon was surprised by the wooden chair's comfort. The prince sat across from him and leaned forward as he spoke.

"Leon, a simple concept that the majority of the world has failed to grasp is this: we are in a war. Like it or not, want to be or not, every single person is a part of it. I learned long ago, with the passing of my mother, that no one escapes death." He sighed before he continued, "It was a lesson that was hard to learn, but it gave me a resolve to make Xaelon a better place. A safer place for all of the living that this world has left in it.

"I know that I must ascend to the throne soon. Schalae and I will lead this kingdom to a brighter future, and if I must personally seek out and destroy every threat to its security for that to happen, then so be it. It is a responsibility that I bear as a prince. I must safeguard this land, and that charge is one I ask every man and woman who serves with me to share in. Tomorrow is not promised to any of us. Thus, we do what we can today. Do you understand, Leon?"

Leon had heard many speeches from the mouths of previous captains, training officers, and even Admiral Silverspine. His father had even been known to deliver long diatribes describing his disappointment over Leon's behavior and failings. The prince's words were something different than anything he had heard before. They were inspiring, a rally call to do better. To be better. This was someone Leon could follow.

"Absolutely, Captain."

Present day…

Leon entered the dining hall that, while sparsely decorated, was filled with crew members who brought joy and life to the area. A few stopped their conversations to nod at him or lightly pound his shoulders in camaraderie. He took the time after washing to quickly polish his armor. Having to present himself as both Captain and Judge to the crew, any celebration would quickly sour if he arrived coated in the grime of battle.

The festivities had already commenced before Leon's arrival, evidenced by groups of elves and dwarves talking and laughing in varying volumes. Platters of food were spread on some of the nearby tables, while Duamé sat with a few others at one further away to inspect the decorative weapons and armor he liberated from the walls of Rhise Manor. Keeping Kérik's advice in mind, Leon took the time to visit with each congregated group and speak words of encouragement and thanks for their ongoing efforts. It had been a lot to ask that anyone go to war with him, especially one with such a slim chance of success after the centuries of destruction that had been wrought. A few minutes of his time spent talking to each member of the volunteer crew was the very least he could do.

A few dwarves seated at one of the nearby tables started to drum out a beat with their hands and feet. It was a simple enough rhythm, and soon enough it spread throughout the hall prompting a few of the other dwarves to stand and dance together. Never ones to be upstaged, elven crew members began to join the circling dwarves, and a raucous jig began to form. Laughter and smiles abounded as Leon weaved his way through the outer edges of the crowd. As he moved, he spotted his mother and sister watching the festivities with rapt interest. They still wore the dresses they had on when rescued from the manor, but they appeared to have been cleaned of the soot, and the damaged hems repaired as best they could be.

Plopping on a bench next to Liara, Leon leaned close and asked with a smirk, "Would you hit me again if I asked for a dance?"

Liara's stony-faced exterior cracked as she cast a sideways glance at Leon. "You put yourself in extreme danger… You leapt some great unfathomable distance due to some sort of miracle-power, based on what your friend Miala told me, fought countless undead in a falling airship, THEN would have died had it not been for the intervention of your friends."

Leon couldn't resist the quip that came from his mouth. "Sounds like just another day to me."

The scowl that formed on Liara's face mirrored the one displayed on Lady Erika's. Before any further protest could be made, Leon continued, "We're in a war, dear sister. In a war there are soldiers, and everyone, myself included, must do their part. I would be a pretty poor Judge if I asked others to risk their lives before I was willing to risk my own."

"You can't expect me to be happy about that!" Liara protested.

Leon thought back to the words of wisdom that had once been spoken to him, "Tomorrow is not promised, Liara. Therefore, we must do what we can today. That includes destroying undead, trying to save everyone who still lives, and," Leon held out his hand, "sometimes dancing, to celebrate the hard won victories."

Receiving nothing but a flat stare, Leon tried one final tactic to coax his sister off the bench. "Come on Liara, I never did get to dance with you at your engagement party. Now's our chance."

Liara's resistance crumbled; her hand slowly left the table as she raised it to meet Leon's. She rose to her feet with his help, and he immediately started to twirl her in tight circles to the dwarven drum beat. As they spun, Leon caught sight of other familiar faces dancing nearby. Duamé and Gérda's hands were clasped together as they swung across the floor, while Magnus and Gionna had climbed onto the top of a table and moved gingerly to the rhythm. Others, like General Xiphos and Lorog, watched from the sides of the crowd – interested in the dance, but not engaging in more than tapping their feet to the beat.

The dance Leon shared with his sister continued until joy finally broke through her somber shroud. They circled and swayed through several different percussion beats that came from the dwarven table. Leon could almost feel a tangible strengthening of their sibling bond once again. Each dance step, each drum beat, seemed to breathe life back into their relationship. Before long, they found themselves laughing and dancing with abandon. When one rhythm reached its end, all of the dancers around them changed partners. With a warm smile and a polite nod, a new partner stepped in to take Liara's place.

Leon bowed respectfully to his mother as the dwarves began to pound out a new beat. Lady Erika swayed in place with him as they talked. "It is nice to see you and Liara together again. You were always the best of friends as well as siblings. Reading through some of the letters that Silas stole made it clear that the bridge you two built never truly broke, it just needed some minor repairs."

"At some point, when things calm down, I'd like to see those letters." Leon replied.

"With everything that may occur when we reach Last Bastion tomorrow, 'calm' might prove impossible for a while." Lady Erika warned. Concern clearly laced her features, and though she still danced, her mind was obviously elsewhere. Her mental distraction caused a few missteps, and after stepping on Leon's boots for the third time, she apologized. "I guess I have just gotten used to not moving at all. It has been a while since I have had the opportunity to dance."

"Are you alright, mother?"

Worry lines creased her brow as she gave a small shake of her head but remained silent. Wanting to see the wounds within his family healed, Leon tried to break through the wall she had erected to hide her discomfort behind. He racked his brain to come up with a topic that could take her mind off of whatever was bothering her.

"I saw you talking to Gionna earlier, she's nice isn't she?"

Her eyes widened slightly before once again becoming guarded. "She is a very lovely… very observant… person."

Leon laughed at the understatement. "That she is. She picked up on who I was almost as soon as I met her. What did she say to you?"

"I… would keep that to myself for now." Lady Erika replied, destroying their thread of conversation.

The awkwardness that encompassed their dance grew as the silence stretched between them. Their relationship felt strained, as if all of the confessions and disclosures that had been made hadn't fully cleared the way forward for them. Leon couldn't help but feel as though his mother was still holding something back. Maybe she was just too used to keeping to herself. Regardless, a rift still existed between the two of them, and it was becoming clear that it wouldn't be easily mended. The song ended, and Leon's mother stepped back before nodding her head at him. With a few quiet words she excused herself, departing before Leon even had a chance to respond.

Before the concern for his mother could fester, Leon turned to find that Miala had stepped up behind him. Without the need for words, they clasped hands and began to dance to the newest dwarven beat. Song after song they continued. As the evening grew late Miala rested her head against Leon's chest. His heart began to thump faster though the pace of their feet had slowed. Leon wished the dance would never end so he could hold her close in his arms forever. Reality crept back in after their second slow dance drew to a close and Miala squeezed him in a tight embrace before stepping back from him .

"I love you." Leon blurted, not wanting her to go.

Miala hid a yawn behind her hand as she responded, "I figured."

Leon feigned shock as Miala gave him a tired smiled. "I love you, too. It is, however, Kelleren's and my bedtime. We have a long day ahead of us tomorrow."

"I… understand."

"Sweet dreams, Leon."

"Goodnight, Miala."

The remainder of the night's celebration continued to be filled with merriment, Kérik's idea for raising morale proved a resounding success. Following another hour of revelry, more and more of the crew began to filter out of the party in search of their beds. When only half of the original attendees remained, Leon formally announced the conclusion of the festivities, and suggested everyone get whatever rest they could. Shortly after his announcement Leon dragged himself to his own hammock, confident that Rohiel and Lochemetel would invade his dreams with one of their cryptic messages.

Chapter 15: The Bastion

The next morning brought an end to the merriment. In its place confusion had taken root.

Why didn't I dream? Leon questioned for the umteenth time as he sipped his morning java. He had grown quite used to the bitter concoction, and saw that many of the crew also carried their own mugs of it. His thoughts continued to spin around the absence of his spiritual advisors; he couldn't understand why they were being less involved than before. Here they were, about to reach Last Bastion and confront his father, but Rohiel and Lochemetel were nowhere to be seen. It wasn't as though he could shirk his duties as the ship's captain, sleep whenever he wanted, and try to force them to meet with him.

I wonder if I did something wrong.

Leon walked to the helm and relieved Ophelia, keeping the *Esperella* on its northeasterly course. The morning sun bathed the top deck in a soft glow as more of the crew filed upstairs. Mancers and warriors moved about, and began to position themselves at their assigned stations. Miala and Gionna came to stand near Leon, while Kérik, General Xiphos, and Lorog formed their own small group close by. Duamé was noticeably absent, having headed to the ship's forge in the early morning hours to begin working.

A few uneventful hours passed before the elven scouts spotted any noteworthy activity. As the *Esperella* approached the lands surrounding Last Bastion, they finally caught sight of the caravan that had fled from the village of Springfield. Leon arced the ship in a wide turn to grant a better vantage point for seeing the refugees. Numerous wagons, carriages, and small flocks of cattle all moved closely together along the wide dirt roads.

Their progression stirred a trail of dust as they progressed, which was caught on the breeze and formed a faint cloud behind them. Traveling through that cloud, at a low altitude, was another airship. Leon and the scouts all spotted the ship at the same moment, noting that it was moving towards the *Esperella* on an intercept. The ship didn't appear to have been harassing the caravan, but instead, escorting it. Their assumption was confirmed when the elven scouts reported that the ship's top deck was populated by people who moved about without the jerky motions common to the undead. While they looked at the ship a shout of alarm arose from one of the scouts who was frantically pointing over the bow. "Another ship in front of us! Approaching from higher elevation and descending!"

"Flint an' feldspar, here we go…" Kérik muttered loudly.

Leon and a few of the others focused their attention on the new ship. It approached from the direction they were heading. As its descent continued, the ship that had been escorting the refugees began to draw along the *Esperella's* starboard side.

"Steady lads and lasses! Let's stick ta tha plan. Everybody's friendly 'til they're unfriendly." Kérik called out.

Both vessels were smaller than the *Esperella*, and Leon noticed that, with the exception of the captains, their sparse naval crews all stood along the rails. Once their ship had drawn near enough to be heard, a middle-aged woman with a fair complexion and twang to her voice hollered across the open air.

"Ahoy there! You were at the battle of Agaprya. Who are ya'll anyway?"

Kérik sauntered toward the railing. "Captain Kendra, I'd hope ya hadn't forgotten me that quickly."

The short distance between the ships allowed Leon to see the almost comical expression of shock as it registered on the woman's face. "Silverspine! This is your ship, Sir?"

"I'm tha First Mate fer it. Tha captain here is tha Judge o' Xaelon." Kérik replied with a finger pointed at Leon.

Leon waved to the other ship, and the bewildered people on board it. The break in their conversation allowed the second Xaelon airship to pass the *Esperella,* turn sharply, and draw along the first ship's far side. A series of hollered introductions, and restatements of peaceful intentions, followed. Finally reassured, the second ship peeled off to take charge of the caravan's escort. Meanwhile, the attack ship captained by the woman named Kendra, continued to fly right alongside the *Esperella.*

After assurances about Kendra's integrity from Kérik, Leon agreed to allow her to board and catch them up on current events. Upon closer inspection, following her boarding, the woman appeared to be in her mid-forties. Bleached hair and burnt skin told of her many years spent in the sun. Her eyes constantly roved over the ship, only pausing periodically to stare at Leon. Had Kérik not vouched for her, the scrutiny of her gaze would have caused every muscle in his body to coil in anticipation of an attack. After all, there was no way for him to know who was under his father's influence, or might have been assigned to assassinate him – like the mail carrier pilot at Masterwork Halls.

"Begging your pardons, but a lot of the survivors assumed y'all had been overwhelmed and destroyed after the retreat from Agaprya. Our ships regrouped, and what's left of our fleet is either already at the Bastion, or escorting any stragglers there before the big fight comes."

"And the undead horde?" Leon asked.

"Mail carrier scouts report they spent time ravaging Agaprya. Unless things have changed, they're about two days from the Bastion. Then we either grind them to dust, or…"

"What's the situation with the coronation? Is the king still in power?" General Xiphos interrupted.

To Leon's relief, Captain Kendra nodded her head. "Rumor was, they were holding out hope for the new royal's mother and sister to arrive. When they also never showed, folks figured they were dead. The coronation is scheduled for tonight – before the undead horde can get there. The heralds say a new king will give us new hope. With all the undead, chimeras, dragons, giants, and now airships under their command aligned against us, I don't see how a new king helps. But, I guess you do what you must to survive, right?"

The captain's words presented an opportunity Leon couldn't let pass. "We have the good fortune of not just having both the Admiral and General on board, but we also found and picked up the king-in-waiting's family." This statement earned him a few quizzical and wide-eyed looks from his friends before he continued, "We were heading straight to Last Bastion in an effort to deliver them, before then helping with the defenses."

The airship captain's eyes lit up in delight at the news. "That's wonderful! Too many families have been torn apart of late. Nice to see that at least one can be put back together. We're about an hour from the Bastion, so keep going in this direction and you should get them there in time for the ceremony."

"Fair enough." Leon replied. "Thank you for the information, Captain. We'll let you get back to your escort duties, and will see you at Last Bastion soon."

"No, thank you for your help, Judge. You, your crew, and this ship will all be very much needed in the days ahead. Anyway, y'all take care now!"

They bade their farewells, and deposited Captain Kendra back on her ship. She promptly peeled away to join the other airship in escorting the caravan over the final leg of its journey. Leon continued to steer along their plotted course while he explained his reasoning for the information he disclosed.

"I figured that if other ships know Lucien Rhise's wife and daughter are on board, they won't dare attack us."

"One would think they wouldn't attack us anyway, with Admiral Silverspine and myself present." General Xiphos stated.

"With my father pulling the strings you can never be too safe. Besides, if you'll recall, he tried to have me killed." His companions' taut faces reflected the tension that permeated the air. An unease, similar to what he felt prior to the undead airship assault, once again settled in the pit of Leon's stomach. One way or another, the end of their arduous journey was fast approaching. As he looked over his friends, he realized they could all use some reassurance. "Look, everything will be okay. We've got Adonai on our side. We'll get there, stop the coronation, expose my father's plot, stop the undead army, and save the day. The plan is going great so far. We just need to see it through."

Even as he spoke the words, Leon's insides churned. For all their planning, it would only take one split second for everything to go wrong. There was no real way to know how thoroughly Lucien's influence had already permeated Last Bastion's ranks in preparation for him and Laric to take full control of the kingdom. While the possibility of him attacking the *Esperella* before they could land existed, the visibility of such an act made it an unlikely option. That said, the two dreadnoughts in existence were almost certainly operated by Lucien's people. If his mother's instincts were correct, then should Laric not be crowned, anyone in his father's employ would show little hesitancy towards attacking other people.

"Wot's goin' on now?" Duamé asked, as he climbed the rear stairs to join them. His large maul, now covered by a thin plating of light blue aeonyte, was firmly clutched in his hands.

"We're discussing the best way to pass through the airship fleet that is guarding Last Bastion." Then, distracted by the huge hammer in Duamé's grip, Leon asked, "Just finished it?"

"Yeah, boyo! Yer deadbeat dad didn't have any other nice weapons er armor on his walls, so I took Miss Gærheart's idea an' put a layer o' aeonyte over me hammer. Whatcha think?" The dwarf all but shoved its massive head in Leon's face.

"Looks amazing, just like all of your work."

"Who knows? It might just spit salt better than yer shaker there!" Duamé joked, prompting chuckles from the group around them.

Leon took the jest in stride, and forced himself to refocus on the problem of getting through Last Bastion's airship fleet unscathed. "What are everyone's thoughts on doing some heralding?"

He began to explain the idea that had formed in his head, and was glad that everyone seemed to love it. Duamé even erupted in laughter at its audacity. "Now yer using that big ol' Rhise head o' yers!"

General Xiphos nodded her head, tapped Lorog's shoulder, and walked off into the ship's hold with him. When they returned, Liara and Lady Rhise followed in their wake. They had ascended the stairwell near the bow, and though a few glances were cast in Leon's direction, they did not approach. Leon couldn't help but wonder why they were keeping their distance.

Maybe they don't like the plan.

Maybe Mother is just not in a talkative mood.

From the aft's raised platform, Leon watched the flat grasslands below change into low rolling hills as they drew nearer to the mountainous region. Isolated farms were still sporadically dotted across the hillside, and Leon knew they would be the first structures lost to the fast approaching undead onslaught.

The scouts stationed at the front of the ship began to shout reports of having sighted their destination, but Leon had already recognized the unmistakable dots of airships that filled the air around it. Vessels hovered in tight formations; they patrolled at differing elevations and distances from the mountain range, unified in their mission to protect the city.

Leon had never been to Last Bastion before, but as he approached the stronghold, he could see why it was so defensible. The sight was awe inspiring. It looked as though the top half of the mountain had been cut completely off, and in its place was a plateau where stone structures had been built. A large ziggurat stood at one end. Each of its levels sat slightly askew, which caused it to spiral as it rose in elevation. The other side of the flattened space held only a small cluster of buildings. Walls and short towers, that jutted from the mountainside itself, could also be seen as they drew nearer. Their odd placements gave Leon the impression of spines on a massive beast.

"They're coming ta take a look at us!" Kérik warned when multiple airships began flying towards them.

Everything will be fine. Leon told himself. *We battled alongside them at Agaprya. They know we are allies... Everything. Will. Be. Fine.*

"Is everyone ready?" Leon shouted.

The incoming aircrafts all zipped over the city that sat nestled at the fortress' base. Smaller than Agaprya, it was shaped like a crescent, and abutted a deep gorge that ran along the fortress base. A large stone bridge appeared to be the only way to cross the chasm and access the mountain's interior. Leon appraised the pillars of rock that supported the bridge, concluding that in an emergency they could be destroyed and successfully cut off all ground access to the stronghold. Overall, Last Bastion looked unassailable.

Which means Xhormas has a plan to crack it.

Redirecting his train of thought, Leon knew their more immediate issue was the airships that were headed directly toward them. Attack craft, transports, even mail carrier ships were all converging on the *Esperella.* A few airships remained stationary in their distant formations, and the noticeable pair of now-familiar dreadnoughts continued to hover close to the ziggurat. As mail carriers were the fastest vessels, they intercepted the *Esperella* first. They began to slow down when they spotted the *Esperella's* crew waving their arms and trying to get their attention.

That's when Leon's crew took their cue to begin shouting.

"Important passengers for the royals!"

"General Xiphos is alive! We're bringing her to the King!"

"Oi! Tha Judge o' Xaelon is here!"

Multiple crew members bellowed out the importance of the passengers on board to the circling mail carriers. They started to disperse, passing over some of the larger and slower ships, and must have repeated what they heard. With relief, Leon saw some of the ships break off to fall back into their previous flying patterns. Others, however, including a few attack ships, continued heading straight towards the *Esperella.* They would intercept them in mere minutes, which prompted Leon to shout out, "Everyone, be ready for anything!"

As they held their course, the *Esperella* began to pass above the crescent-shaped city. Its outer rampart walls were wide and held varying defensive siege equipment. Behind the walls, simplistic stone buildings of varying heights were clustered tightly together in a twisting maze of alleyways. The tight passageways would decrease the effectiveness of the undead's numerical advantage. The view was reminiscent of the maze that the Northern Elvenwood had shifted into while under attack. This maze-like layout was made of stone buildings though, which would be far less malleable than the trees that had defended the Elven Grove.

Leon tried not to tense as larger ships crowded near to get a closer look at the *Esperella.* While their cannons didn't appear to be pointed at them, one misunderstanding could cause a firefight that would end any chance of success. Leon had almost gotten their ship to the plateau, where they would have an opportunity to land. There were a couple of visible clearings, but the only one large enough to land the *Esperella* rested between the ziggurat and clump of other stone structures.

Kérik edged towards Leon and spoke in a low voice. "Easy on the wheel. Remember tha plan, lad. I'll take over once ya disembark. I know wot ta do. Ya do wot ya need to."

"Thanks again for everything, Sir."

Kérik shook his head. "Don't mention it, lad. Just end this nonsense once an' fer all."

Leon's unease persisted as he approached an opening between the two dreadnoughts and saw the crew on both ships' decks. Many of them stood at the railing, unmoving, and simply stared at the *Esperella*. They passed through the shadow of one of the ships, and whether it was due to slightly colder air, or the nervousness inside of him, the experience sent a chill down Leon's spine. The dreadnoughts remained stationary where they hovered, which thankfully allowed the *Esperella* to thread through them faster.

Leon let out his held breath in an explosive whoosh once they finally passed through the dreadnoughts unchallenged. Pleasantly surprised by the lack of confrontation, Leon slowed the ship and landed in an open courtyard. A couple of shouts sounded from the scouts at the bow of the ship, alerting Leon that a group of Xaelon soldiers were heading towards the *Esperella*. They had to appease these soldiers quickly, and move on. The longer they delayed the greater the chances were of something not going to plan. They had tried to cover solutions for every possible scenario during their in-flight meetings, but nothing was foolproof.

At least we didn't have to fight our way here. Leon reassured himself.

Kérik took control of the wheel, while Leon straightened the spear and shield slung across his back and hustled to the extending gangplank. Duamé, Miala, Kelleren, Gionna, and Princess Schalae stepped next to him. No words were exchanged between them, but Leon felt their love and support all the same.

Before long, the group of soldiers arrived at their ship. Tabards of blue and black flapped lightly in the breeze, and while their weapons were not unsheathed, Leon recognized their questioning, if not unfriendly, stares. Human, orcish, elven, dwarven, and even gnomish guards held their hand at the ready on pommels or lowered crossbows, while their commanding officer stepped forward. The middle-aged officer, who had short curly hair and an oddly-sculpted short beard, raised his loud voice to address them. “Ho there! Unknown ship, state your intentions!”

As the captain of the ship, Leon would normally be responsible for responding. However, their group had already agreed upon who would handle the obstacle of being challenged by Xaelson’s military. General Xiphos stepped to the *Esperella’s* railing, her dented plate mail polished to a shine, as she yelled back, “Garrison Commander Ciaye, thank you for the reception!”

Leon enjoyed seeing a few of the soldiers' eyes widen with the recognition of their leader before then whispering her identity to those who were unaware. Stances straightened, and the soldier at the base of the stairs visibly winced before coming to attention. “General Xiphos, ma’am. We’re glad to see you alive. Reports suggested otherwise.”

“Thank you, Commander, I assure you I am quite well.” She replied, as she descended the gangplank. Lorog shadowed her, with Leon and his friends close behind.. Huddled at the very back of the entire group were ladies Liara and Erika Rhise. While Leon noticed his sister’s demure demeanor as she walked, he was truly struck by how extremely nervous and uncharacteristically fidgety his mother was.

General Xiphos continued to speak when she reached the ground. “What is the report of our forces?”

The soldiers shifted as the garrison commander answered, “Ma’am, the city and fortress are secure. The populace of the kingdom has been processed and housed within the city. You-you should know ma’am that…um…”

“Spit it out, Commander.” Xiphos interrupted.

“Well Ma’am, it’s ‘General Ciaye’ now.”

A tense silence followed his pronouncement as General Xiphos raised a brow. “I’ve been replaced? Already?”

“We needed to have a command structure in place. Especially since you disappeared after Agaprya. You were presumed dead, as were many of the defenders. I-I can brief you on our forces and defenses once we present you to His Majesty–"

"Garinth or Laric?" Leon blurted a little too loudly. This was received with questioning glances – especially from General Xiphos, whose all too wide eyes conveyed a silent admonition.

"May I present the well rumored 'Judge' that you may have heard about." General Xiphos exclaimed testily. "His question is a valid one. Is King Garinth Galcyon still on the throne?"

"Until tonight, yes. The wedding between Lord Laric and Princess Giselle will happen in a couple of hours. From there, they'll move to the coronation. But I would just like to–"

"Wonderful. I would like to present myself to His Majesty immediately, with the Judge and my other guests." General Xiphos gestured towards Leon and his friends. Duamé tried to give his best friendly smile, but Leon thought it just came off as creepy.

The other general must have thought so too, and said, "Look, it is perfectly acceptable for you to report to His Majesty, but these… people…"

Leon interjected again, to head off any objection. "General Ciaye, with respect, we also have the fortune of bringing some of Lord Rhise's family, whom we rescued." Liara curtsied to the general, though Lady Erika appeared distracted.

"But–"

Princess Schalae stepped forward next, to clear up any possible further confusion. "I am Princess Schalae of the Northern Elves, formerly betrothed to the late Prince Gelan. I can vouch for the Judge and our fellow companions' peacefulness and good intentions."

After a respectful short bow to her, General Ciaye cast a cursory glance over Leon and his friends, which stopped almost immediately. "You look familiar. Have we met before?" He asked Leon.

While they had never met when he served in the airship navy, Leon could guess the unspoken question that the general was actually asking. *Am I the bandit named Leon, from the wanted posters?*

“He’s the Judge of Xaelon, with an important message for the King.” General Xiphos interjected smoothly, “He’s been protecting Lord Rhise’s family.”

“Nice to meet you.” Leon nodded to General Ciaye, who raised a questioning brow.

“We’ll be the judge on you being a Judge or not. The heralds all say that you’re a myth.”

“If I am a myth, then it begs the question of whether or not you’re hallucinating.”

The general grunted, and then continued to eyeball the group. “You seem to be a mancer based on your dress, young lady. Who are you?”

An official posing such a question would normally be cause for concern, as Miala had been branded a deserter in Agaprya. Mancer Academy had since fallen though, and much of the capital city’s military had died in the battle there. So, without missing a beat, she stuck her thumb out at Leon and replied, “Miala. I’m his bodyguard.”

“She guards the body.” Leon stated, trying not to smile.

When General Ciaye’s eyes met Duamé’s, the dwarf offered, “Duamé Onyxwill. I’m jus’ tha comedic relief.”

Miala snorted, masking a smile behind her hand. It was one of her habits that Leon found adorable. Kelleren barked and padded around the new general. He sniffed around a bit before he finally sat on his hind legs and barked once more. Miala interpreted, “He says he’s Kelleren, and he wants to know where to find more of the bacon that you had this morning.”

General Ciaye’s mouth opened and closed a few times, though no sound escaped his lips. An amused expression crossed his face, followed by a moment of slight stammering, before finally, a look of resignation settled over his features. He gestured to his contingent of Xaelon guards, and they fell in line on either side of the new arrivals. Once the general was satisfied with their formation, they began escorting the group towards the ziggurat structure in the distance. Leon was thankful that everything had gone well so far, and took a moment to lift a silent prayer of thanks to Adonai. They trudged towards the structure along an old, but solidly built, path. Leon felt the wind shift behind him, and turned to see the *Esperella* ascend into the air. Kérik piloted the vessel up and away, to initiate his part of their plan.

Leon's eyes constantly scanned their surroundings for hidden dangers. Most of the soldiers appeared relaxed, but a couple still held one hand on their pommels as they continued towards the ziggurat. If the soldiers moved to attack before they made it to the king, his group would be in dire circumstances. Leon was so preoccupied by his thoughts that he didn't even notice they had crossed the distance until the opening at the base of the ziggurat was right in front of him. The entrance had no doors, and was framed by giant stone slabs that looked similar to the other megalithic sites they had seen. The huge blocks fit tightly together, and stretched all the way to the structure's uppermost layer. It was very reminiscent of the Agapryan Archives, and the towers at Masterwork Halls.

Miala must have also been observing the architecture. "It's the same type of construction…"

"We think that long ago it was some sort of temple for giants." Ciaye commented. "So much history has been lost since the beginning of the Dead Wars. There may be answers for you here, in the new Archives, but at the moment there are more pressing matters than the history of Last Bastion's fortress."

"It's solid construction, though." Duamé said.

There was something in his voice when he said that. Leon thought before he said, "Oh, really?"

"Yeah, good stonework like this…" The dwarf continued.

Here it comes...

"Ya jus can't take it fer granite." Duamé quipped, then smirked as several groans sounded.

Just inside the ziggurat was a large room that acted as a guardhouse. Tables lined the walls and were laden with stacks of armaments and shields for the soldiers stationed there. Tapestries of Xaelon's landscapes were regularly interspersed along its walls. Passageways, that led further into the massive structure, branched from either side of the room. Soldiers constantly filed in through them, though Leon stopped attempting to count their numbers once he reached fifty. Many sets of eyes rested on him and his friends when General Ciaye turned to address them.

"Your weapons, please."

Their various protests were drowned out by Ciaye, who raised a hand and spoke over them, "I appreciate your concerns. While I know General Xiphos, and of Princess Schalae, the rest of you are untried, and going to be in the presence of royalty. I can assure you all that while I am in charge of this rock, and for everyone's safety, you will abide by my rules or your journey will come to an end."

Leon knew they only had seconds before their hesitancy would cause suspicion to grow in all of the soldiers' minds. They had already objected once, if they protested further it would be cause for concern at the very least. Their weapons were their protection. If Lucien had already bought these people then General Ciaye was right: their journey would end here. They would be defenseless if attacked. However, if they insisted on keeping their weapons, they would likely provoke a fight anyways. They were surrounded, and the possibility of turning potentially friendly people into definitively unfriendly ones was a big risk to take.

"Of course." Leon stated. "Guys, it's fine. We'll hand them over."

Duamé grunted, rolled his eyes, lifted his newly plated maul, and deposited it in a soldier's waiting hands. The soldier was unprepared for the sudden weight of the weapon, and had to bear the chortles and laughs of those around him when the large hammer brought him to the floor. Duamé continued to withdraw the other hammers he wore around his belt, and they clanked when they fell to the floor around him. After loosing the fourth one, he held up a tiny hammer that had been in his belt, "This is fer jewels. It ain't a weapon. Unless ya think I could smash a few fingers an' toes wi–"

"Just keep it." General Ciaye breathed in exasperation, as he pinched the bridge of his nose. Duamé gave a satisfied grunt and put the jeweler's hammer back in his belt, enjoying his small victory. Meanwhile, everyone except for General Xiphos and Lorog had relinquished their weapons.

Even Gionna had to trade her metallic cane for a less threatening wooden stick. "What else would you take from an old lady? You want my glasses too?" She railed at a soldier. She quieted when the person holding her cane accidentally activated it. A female orcish guard yelped when a small crossbow suddenly unfolded in her hands. Everyone who was unfamiliar with the contraption stared at it in amazement. Instead of embarrassment at the revelation of her weapon, Gionna just became more ornery, "What? A lady has to protect herself!"

Leon tried not to think too hard about confronting Lucien and Laric without Revelator at his disposal. He slowly withdrew it from his back strap, and the spearhead flickered to life. Its glow caused cries of alarm from the surrounding soldiers. Leon lamented his lack of forethought about the likelihood that the spearhead would glow inside the ziggurat – which was clearly built by Nephilim giants. After much placating from Leon and his friends, the soldiers calmed down. Trying to figure out a way to mitigate the loss of the spear, while still keeping Revelator nearby, Leon held it out to General Xiphos.

Her hand paused over the spear as she looked into Leon's eyes. The general looked as though she needed some sort of confirmation. He gave her a short nod and told her the spear was safe to touch. Thinking the spontaneous hum that occurred when two believers simultaneously held the spear might raise more questions, Leon simply tipped Revelator towards her and let go. The spear didn't react to her touch when she caught it, instead the glow flicked off. Whether that indicated a lack of faith on her part, or not, Leon couldn't tell.

After everyone had relinquished their weapons, and Miala had been instructed to keep her hands at her sides, Leon once again turned his attention toward General Ciaye. "Well?"

"Alright." The General sighed. "Let's go see the king."

Chapter 16: The Father

Their group was escorted down a short hall, further into the structure. As they continued on, a few attendants and courtiers were seen hurrying through the passageways, each focused on their individual tasks. A soldier hustled up to General Ciaye, his ring mail jangling underneath his tabard, and they had a whispered conversation that was beyond Leon's hearing. Knowing that Kelleren could probably pick up what they were saying, Leon slowed a bit so he could find Miala behind him. He slipped his hand into hers, and she gave it a squeeze. Leaning into him, she whispered, "They suspect you. You look similar to the man in the wanted posters throughout Agaprya. They're being cautious."

"Thanks." Leon whispered back. He leaned down and scratched Kelleren's head as they walked, which caused the dog to close his eyes and lean into the gesture.

They soon entered another room. This one was rectangular in shape, and filled with symmetrical rows of long wooden benches that lined either side of a long central walkway. Large vases filled with bouquets of mountain flowers adorned the walls, and several people were draping white fabric along the camber's outer edges. Everything about the space looked extravagant, even more so when an exceptionally dressed courtier or noble would flit in and out of it. None of their faces were familiar to Leon, but then again, he hadn't been invited to many court functions while growing up. That honor had been reserved for Laric and Liara.

Leon looked back at his sister and saw that both she and Princess Schalae were eyeing the decorations. His mother, however, had escalated from nervous fidgeting to full blown hand wringing. Concerned, Leon discreetly approached her, "Mother, are you–"

"I don't know if I can do this." She interrupted, before collapsing onto a nearby bench and beginning to slowly rock her body back and forth. Liara and Gionna immediately sat on either side of her. The elderly gnome patted his mother's arm, the gesture highlighting the friendship they had formed during the flight. When their convoy of escorts drew to a stop Leon turned to General Xiphos and asked, "Can you give us a minute?"

She still held Revelator in one hand and nodded solemnly. "We'll move a little further ahead. Don't take too long."

"We'll try not to." He then turned to Duamé, "Take care of everyone else, we'll catch up."

"Right." The dwarf replied, before he left with Princess Schalae and the rest of their entourage. Miala remained behind with him, and Kelleren laid his head on Lady Erika's legs. By now, Leon was intimately familiar with the dog's innate instinct to cheer others up. He whimpered quietly a couple of times until Leon's mother relented, and scratched behind his ears. Kelleren's tail thumped against the ground in delight, but it didn't seem to raise Lady Erika's spirits at all.

"Mother, what's going on?" Liara asked.

"It's… been years. I can't face him. Not like this. I thought I could, but I can't!"

Leon's thoughts turned to the many times where his mother had borne the brunt of his father's anger. There had been days where Leon could handle no more bruises. Those were the days when she had occasionally stepped in. It had been over five years since he had left the manor, and three years since Silas had shoved her down the stairwell. Lady Erika still carried those years of physical, and then psychological, abuse with every step she took. Leon had thought she was strong enough to overcome it, but a dwarven saying he heard at Masterwork Halls said it best: even a diamond will shatter if hit correctly.

"Mother, we can face him together. All of us. Your past doesn't have to define you. You don't have to shoulder this pain alone anymore." Leon reassured her.

"You… you just don't understand, Leon." Lady Erika shook her head with tears in her eyes. "None of you do!"

"Then explain it to us, Mother! Please!" Liara pleaded.

"I… can't!" Lady Erika wailed.

Gionna stood up on the seat and addressed them, “Alright dearies, everyone go on and catch up to the others. I’ll talk to her.”

Liara tore her gaze away from their distressed mother to look at the elderly gnome. “With respect, Miss Gærheart, this is a family matter.”

“Gionna is family to me, Liara.” Leon asserted.

The old gnome affectionately patted Leon’s hand before looking at Liara. “Don’t worry, dearie. I can help your mother because I know what she is dealing with. None of you do, so just hurry along.” Gionna then fixed her multifocal gaze on Leon before she emphasized, “Trust me.”

The sound of low muffled moaning filled the air, coming from his distressed mother’s covered face. Leon couldn’t imagine what she was feeling. Gionna’s persistent silent prompting motivated him to stand and offer a hand to his equally concerned sister. Liara still hesitated to leave their mother, but Leon added, “Trust her, Liara. Trust in Adonai.” Glancing at Miala, he continued, “He’s really good at healing people.”

That seemed to convince her. Liara slowly stood and laid a hand on their mother’s shoulder. “It will be okay, Mother. Everything will be okay.”

They slowly walked away from the two older women, and Miala told Kelleren to give them privacy. Leon faintly heard his mother’s, “I’m so embarrassed!”

“I know, dearie. I know.” Came Gionna’s reply, before their voices faded beyond hearing.

They quickly saw that their group stood in a hallway up ahead, and had not traveled very far from the ornate room. Miala snuck her hand back into Leon’s, and turned to reassure him and his sister, “She will be okay. I know she will.”

“How can you be so sure?” Liara asked. “I’ve never seen her like this.”

“Gionna is the perceptive one of our group. If anyone knows what to say, it’s her.” Miala explained.

“She’s also the most brutally honest.” Leon countered.

Liara huffed and all but threw up her hands in exasperation. “Who knows? Maybe that’s what she needs at this point.”

They rejoined the others, though Leon’s mind lingered on his mother’s distress. Soldiers had moved to the sides of the hallway, allowing them access to their friends. Princess Schalae promptly filled them in, “The King, Princess Giselle, and most of the court are just inside – including Lords Lucien and Laric Rhise. Apparently, we are about to be announced… individually.”

Leon was baffled, “Who’s idea was that?”

“Mine actually, meat shield.” Duamé whispered. “Leave em’ in suspense. Make em’ sweat a little.”

Leon looked over his friend’s head, and saw the herald in lavish frippery standing just past the line of soldiers and Generals Ciaye and Xiphos. Frilled sleeves and puffed pantaloons made the herald look absolutely ridiculous. His oversized hat did him no favors either. Leon and Miala stared at each other, rendered speechless by the absurd costume. He was speaking animatedly with the generals, until Xiphos audibly growled, “Just do it, Kazave!”

So this was the fabled Headherald. Presumably in Lucien’s pocket, this man was responsible for perpetuating the false narrative of Leon’s banditry. This was the person who, with the use of a few convincing words and heralds in his employ, had dismissed Leon’s news of Adonai. Kazave flinched from Xiphos’ threatening tone. The man picked at an invisible piece of lint on his costume, sighed in disdain, then turned to the room beyond and announced in a loud, nasal voice, “Generals Ciaye and Xiphos of the Xaelon forces.”

The murmur of voices that came from the room suddenly rose in volume. Ciaye turned to three nearby soldiers, motioned towards Leon and his friends, and ordered, “Keep guarding them.” He then accompanied General Xiphos, who was followed closely by Lorog, into the room. Leon couldn’t quite make out what the voices were saying from his position in the hallway. Amidst all of the chatter, he picked out the timbre of Xiphos’ voice as she responded to someone. Leon leaned in to ask Miala if Kelleren had heard anything specific, but was interrupted when Princess Schalae stepped forward.

Headherald Kazave’s eyes grew wide when he saw the elven princess in her armor. The rough edges of the black bark plates did nothing to mar her regal stature. With her back held straight she followed the generals into the room, barely allowing the Headherald time to announce, “Princess Schalae of the Northern Elvenwood.”

The murmurs grew even louder, and Leon surmised that not just King Garinth, but virtually the entire noble court must be inside. Knowing that their fates were tied to their reception by those in the next room, Leon turned to face his friends and sister. He looked into each pair of eyes as subtle nods and short words of encouragement were shared. With his mother still absent, Leon hugged Liara and asked in a low voice, “Are you alright?”

She whispered back, “This needs to happen, Leon. I’m behind you all the way.”

“We are all with you.” Miala added.

“So, who are these people?” Leon overheard Headherald Kazave ask one of the soldiers. Leon turned to address him, but Duamé proved faster.

“Right ya frilly fluorite, this here’s what ya should say...”

After a bit of debate, Liara persuaded everyone that she should wait to enter until Lady Erika was present. Leon stepped past her, and studied the room through its entryway. It was far more spacious than he had imagined, and clearly the ziggurat’s main chamber. Lit by a combination of torch sconces and sunlight that passed through holes in its incredibly high ceiling, Leon was surprised at how warm and inviting it appeared. As the sunlight streamed down, it bounced off of a central crystalline chandelier which, unlike the one at Rhise manor, wasn’t enchanted to glow.

The entire floor looked like it was made of a single enormous slab of rock. The only variations he could see were where small grates had been installed under the ceiling’s openings, likely to drain the water when it rained. A few passages branched off from each of the massive room’s sides. Leon guessed they led to more guardrooms, living quarters, kitchens, and other useful chambers. Currently, servants and other workers flowed back and forth through many of them in preparation for the upcoming wedding. They carried food trays and earthenware cups in all states of fullness. It was quite evident that their group's unexpected introduction had interrupted a pre-wedding celebration honoring Laric and Giselle.

How poetic. Leon thought as he recalled his sister's party.

Duamé harangued the headherald until his nasal voice finally shouted, "Duamé Onyxwill of Masterwork Halls, son of Ignys Onyxwill of the Nonagint!"

Duamé entered, waving to no one in particular, while Headherald Kazave continued, "Pyromancer Miala."

Miala held her head high and a confident smile was spread across her face as she gazed around the room. The conversations near the entrance died down, and almost every pair of eyes in the room stared at where they stood. Kazave's prolonged silence caused Leon to look at him. The puffed up herald was visibly sweating in his outlandish clothes. Duamé's proposed theatrics wouldn't prove effective if the Headherald didn't finish, so Leon quietly commanded, "Say it."

"I-I cannot! You cannot–"

"Say it. Now." Miala's calm but firm voice ordered. Kelleren growled at the herald with his tan hackles raised, and Kazave yelped.

Duamé slid close to the herald, and under the cover of their soldier escorts, firmly clapped him on the back, "Why don'cha walk with us? I'm sure that yer heralds would want ta get yer firsthand account o' wot happens here. Just tell 'em all what we said. Exactly like we told ya."

Kazave's body shook as they began to slowly walk forward. He raised his voice once again, "C-Captain of the *Esperella*, the first airship from Masterwork Halls! Protector of the Northern Elves!"

With each pronouncement, their group progressed further towards the center of the room. Small groups of well dressed nobles hurried out of their way, leaving them with a clear path forward. Capturing the attention of every attendee possible, Kazave's voice and their footsteps became the only audible sounds as they drew near to the throne.

King Garinth Galcyon sat on what must have once been the throne of a giant. The original seat had been broken and refashioned to accommodate much smaller occupants. Its excess stone had then been used to craft two additional, smaller, seats positioned on either side of it. A simple golden crown sat atop the king's mostly grey hair, which framed a face that was marked with deep set worry lines. Dressed in a fine, royal-purple robe, he didn't look like the frail, trapped king Leon had imagined him to be.

"Scourge of the undead!" Kazave continued.

Princess Giselle sat next to the king, on one of the smaller thrones, looking lovely in a gemstone studded white gown. Her delicate features, reputed to have come from her late mother, were topped by blonde hair that had been pinned up in cascading ringlets. She had been speaking with Laric, but their conversation paused when they turned to look at the approaching group. Leon locked eyes with his older brother and couldn't deny the enjoyment he felt when Laric's flirtatious smile fell from his face like a crashing airship. In its place was a look that resembled sheer, wide-eyed panic.

"Slayer of giants!"

Leon spotted the fabled protector of the royal line standing near the thrones. Galvamancer Emirah Exiosa looked upon them with only a vague interest. She was the one General Xiphos had warned them of during their planning sessions aboard the *Esperella.* They couldn't know who's side she was on. Lucien's pockets ran deep, and his sphere of influence was vast. If she had been bought, and their confrontation turned sour, then she could prove to be an incredibly deadly adversary. Her blue and black robes were lined with several copper strips. Leon didn't know whether it was due to her power, or his nerves, but the hairs on the back of his neck raised a little. This mancer exuded power, even without the stories of lightning that coursed from her.

"Destroyer of dragons!"

As their group reached the center of the room, Princess Schalae grinned at them from where she stood with both generals nearby. Ciaye stared openmouthed, and Leon couldn't help but wink at the general. Xiphos was all business as she stepped in line with them. The sound of her clanking plate mail joined the shuffling that came from people at the outskirts of the room. All attempts at conversation around them had ended. Instead, people jostled for the best position to get a good look at the new arrivals.

Leon watched his former father, who stood close to the thrones with an impassive expression on his face. The only tell that indicated Lord Lucien Rhise was full of rage at the moment was the way his fine goblet shook in his clenched fist. Gone were the days of Leon's youth when he feared those fists. Months had passed since he had finally forgiven Lucien Rhise for his abusive actions.

"Th-The Judge of Xaelon!" Kazave continued, bodily quivering from what Leon assumed was an unfamiliarity with telling the truth.

Leon and his friends all stopped when Xiphos did. The general knelt on one creaking knee and bowed her head towards the king. Headherald Kazave gave his final instructed pronouncement, then darted out of Duamé's reach.

"Leon… the bandit!"

A cannon could have exploded, and nobody would have heard it over the tumult that stemmed from Kazave's words. Leon calmly stood through the cries of alarm and the multitudes of swords being unsheathed by guards. The galvamancer stepped in front of King Garinth and Princess Giselle with her fists raised. Leon raised his empty hands in a gesture of surrender from where he stood, and glared at Lucien. Lord Rhise's veins began to bulge across his forehead. His jaw muscles flexed as he clenched his teeth, and his face began to redden as he walked towards the panic-stricken Laric, clearly enraged.

As King Garinth sat on his throne, looking deep in thought, Leon was painfully aware of the many armed soldiers closing in. Knowing that the herald's pronouncement needed clarification, Leon shouted, "I am here to defend the King! I have always tried to defend Xaelon from all threats! Please," Leon directed his words to the monarch, "let me explain."

Lucien Rhise's words dripped poison as he pointed at Leon and shouted over the din, "Restrain him! Do not let his lies sully the ears of this court!"

"I mean no harm to anyone here! Please, listen to me!" Leon shouted.

As soldiers reached to detain Leon and his friends, General Xiphos raised her voice, "Soldiers hold!" Turning to King Garinth, she stated, "Your Majesty, you should listen to what he has to say. He saved my life in Agaprya, as well as the lives of many of our forces. Hear him out."

"Nonsense! Take that murderer away!" Lucien bellowed.

"Everyone, be silent!" King Garinth roared, glaring daggers at Lucien. "What do you mean, murderer?"

As the murmurs of the crowd continued around them, Leon's soul felt crushed as Lucien seethed, "Why would you listen to the man who killed Prince Gelan?"

The effect of his words on the King was visible. His shoulders slumped as if a weight had settled over them, and a mask of depression and malaise washed over his face. "What?"

"Crimes against the crown, Your Majesty. The bandit Leon is guil–"

"Bandit? You're the one who branded me a criminal!" Leon shouted.

Incredulity and confusion burst over the crowd as everyone started to talk again. King Garinth, in his sad state, grew visibly agitated and once again asserted himself, "I said SILENCE!"

The air around Leon grew dry and carried an odd smell as galvamancer Exiosa opened one of her fists wide. Lines of lightning coursed between her fingers in an unspoken threat, as the short white hairs on her head raised on their ends. Soldiers with drawn swords backed away from her, but Leon felt as if he shouldn't move with the galvamancer's gaze on him. Dwarven made or not, Leon was clad in metallic armor, and it would not mix well with her powers. Glaring at everyone present, she closed her fingers into a fist again and the lightning cut off with a pronounced zap.

"Thank you, Emirah." King Garinth said through gritted teeth. His heavy gaze turned back to Leon. "You walked in here with many titles, bandit Leon. Many claims. At the moment, I am interested in only one. Did you kill my son?" The King asked in a low voice.

"Your Majesty, may I–" Princess Schalae tried to speak.

King Garinth waved her off and raised his voice at Leon. "Did you kill Prince Gelan, yes or no?"

This wasn't going the way Leon had thought it would in the least; Lucien's false narrative was quickly taking control. The king was obviously still distraught over his son's death, and Leon knew that sharing the truth would hurt the mourning king even more. The truth however, was what

Adonai required of him. He could only hope that he would be able to phrase his answer exactly right.

"Out of mercy, and at his command, yes. Prince Gelan was slowly dying as a result of the wounds he received when the *Dawnfire* crashed. He was about to turn undead, and asked me to prevent it. Afterwards, I made sure his body was brought back to Agaprya. Your Majesty, I am so sorry. More sorry that you could ever possibly know."

The King's eyes were furious as he stared balefully at Leon. Leon knew there was much more that needed to be said and tried to continue, but King Garinth spoke first, "Kazave!" His voice cracked like a whip, causing the older man to yelp and jump where he stood.

"Y-yes, Your Majesty?"

Garinth's voice grew even colder as he asked, "Why am I hearing a conflicting report on the death of my son? You told me he died in the crash. That there were no survivors."

The Headherald wrung his hands as he stuttered, "W-well, um, Your Majesty, I-I am sure that the bandit would say anything he could t-to escape justice."

Leon knew that this was the moment that would either prove his innocence or condemn him. "Your son told me the advice you gave him, Your Majesty. You told him to lead with love, because love conquers all."

Shock splayed across King Garinth's face at the words that came from Leon's mouth. The advice that King Garinth had once given his son had been passed to Leon. Gelan would have to have known him well to entrust him with that mantra, nothing else would make sense. Leon could almost see the king's thoughts reach the same conclusion. "He told you… that was… you… you truly did serve with my son?"

"I was the first mate on the *Dawnfire* when it crashed, and had served in the airship navy for five years, Your Majesty." Leon made sure to watch Laric and Lucien as he spoke his next words, "Admiral Silverspine would vouch for me, but he is currently rallying those loyal to the crown. As we speak he is surrounding the two dreadnought vessels loyal to the Rhises, forcing them to surrender and stand down. They were poised to fire on the populace should Laric not gain the throne. I can assure you I am not conspiring against the crown, Your Majesty. I am trying to save it."

As soon as he revealed what Kérik had been doing on the *Esperella*, Laric tried to bolt for the exit. Shouts of alarm and cries of, "Stop him!" rang throughout the room. Guards immediately jumped into action, cornering and capturing Laric mid-flight.

Lucien drew a well-crafted gladius from a sheath on his leg, and pointed it at the king with a snarl. "We had a deal, Garinth! We–!" He shrieked as a thin lance of lightning leapt from the galvamancer's hand and connected to the tip of his straight-edged sword. Lord Lucien's muscles contracted, and limbs convulsed. He collapsed on the floor, groaning incoherently, before Emirah cut off her attack. Generals Xiphos and Ciaye, along with several other soldiers converged around him, and Princess Giselle ran into her father's protective arms.

Have... have we done it? Is it over? Hope bubbled within Leon as he watched his former father and brother be restrained. The other nobles of the court gave the soldiers surrounding the disgraced lords a wide berth.

The king brought himself to his full height and growled, "You threatened my people, my kingdom, and all of our futures with your lust for power. You told me you would rain destruction on us all if I didn't bend to your will. This boy's testimony renders your threats hollow, and you will both be held to account for attempting to usurp my kingdom!"

Laric screamed in rage, "Leon! I will kill you!"

"Stop it!" A new voice shouted from near the entrance.

Practically everyone in the throne room turned, and Leon saw his mother and sister with Gionna Gærheart at their side. They walked briskly across the space, and didn't stop until Lady Erika reached the thoroughly confused looking father and son.

"H-h-how are… you-you are both alive?" Laric asked them.

Lucien looked even more confused. "You… walk? Talk?"

King Garinth spoke up as she approached, "Lady Erika… I had heard that you were paralyzed. Struck mute by a seizure."

There was no way for Lucien and Laric to fake their reactions to Lady Erika's surprising revelation. They hadn't known of her true condition.

Whatever trepidations had been bothering her were evidenced only by her red-ringed eyes and tired face. Lucien looked confused from the moment he saw her, all the way up to the moment she strode up and slapped him across the face.

The crowd gasped as Lucien staggered from the force of the blow, and was immediately gripped tighter by the soldiers who held him. Uncaring of their audience, Lady Erika pulled the wedding ring off of her finger and deposited it into one of Lord Rhise's coat pockets. "I never stopped being able to walk or talk. I was a prisoner within my own home. Your business partner threatened the lives of my children and myself if I said anything about it. For years. But he is gone. Your plans are over, and I am not afraid anymore."

Leon was shocked by his former father's next words. Blinking and shaking his head as if trying to clear his confusion, Lucien breathed, "Silas… is dead? That is… impossible."

"Yes. He is dead. Liara and I were rescued. Not by my soon-to-be-ex-husband, who got me into the horrible situation in the first place, but by my son and his friends." She pointed to Leon as she continued to berate the dejected and defeated Lucien.

The murmurs and whispers once again rose in volume, as people couldn't believe their ears.

"Wait, the Judge is also a Rhise?"

"She was okay this whole time?"

"Who is this Silas fellow?"

King Garinth turned slowly to Leon, his eyes wide, as if seeing him for who he was for the first time. "You… You are Leon… Rhise?"

"Yes, Your Majesty. I am so terribly sorry our first meeting is under these circumstances."

The king didn't seem to be listening. He was surveying the entire Rhise family, his eyes roving over them several times until he raised his voice. "Everyone who is not a part of this… farce, will leave this room. Immediately."

The next several minutes consisted of the Xaelon nobility expressing muted outrage at being excluded from the dramatic entertainment. Even so, they obediently filed out of the room alongside the courtiers, servants, and guards who were not assigned to Kazave, Laric, and Lucien. Leon and his friends remained in the room with both generals, galvamancer Exiosa, the rest of the Rhise family, both princesses, and the king. King Garinth pointed at Headherald Kazave, “I have no use for heralds who cannot give me the truth. Get him out of my sight.”

Kazave started to blubber and cry as he was bodily hauled out of the room. Laric whined, “Mother… help me, please!”

Lady Erika shook her head as she responded, “I love you, dear child. You have chosen this path with your father, and I will have no part of it.”

“You started all this!” Lucien bit back, rage dripping from his voice. Several people, including Leon, immediately began expressing their confusion over his statement. The only ones to remain silent were Gionna, King Garinth, and Lady Erika. As soon as there was silence, Leon asked his mother, “What is he talking about?”

She sighed, shook her head, and closed her eyes. “I am sorry, Leon. For years I blamed myself, I held myself responsible for all of this. But my marriage had turmoil long before…” Lady Erika trailed off. She squared her jaw and turned towards Lucien with a resolute expression on her face. “I have been quiet for too long, and you have no power over me anymore."

After her declaration, she then spoke to King Garinth. “I turned to you in confidence when my husband's greed and lust for power began to change him. You turned to me for comfort after my friend, your wife, Queen Dionne died. What we did was wrong, but–”

“You brought shame upon our house! You BETRAYED ME!” Lucien screamed.

Stunned silence filled the room and Leon felt his world begin to crash around him. He barely registered when Miala slipped her hand into his, and whispered, “Be strong. It will be okay.”

He couldn’t pay attention to her, because his focus was riveted on his mother.

She... was unfaithful... to my father... with the king?

Lady Erika stood as tall as her small frame would allow, slowly looking at everyone present. Her eyes rested on each of her family members, lingering on Liara and Leon. When she once again looked at the king, his sorrow-filled eyes met hers, and he gave an almost imperceptible nod of his head. With a newfound calm, she turned back to her husband.

"I acknowledge my mistakes, and Adonai has already forgiven me for them. I am no longer ashamed and no longer afraid. There stands the undeserved gift of my indiscretion all those years ago."

As she spoke, her arm raised.

Lady Erika was pointing directly at Leon.

Part Three: The Truth

"The people living in darkness have seen a great light; on those living in the land of the shadow of death a light has dawned." - Matthew 4:12 NIV

Chapter 17: The Royals

Leon's knees almost gave out as numbness flooded through him. The revelation of his true parentage was not only unexpected, but it also brought mixed feelings of awe and sorrow. So lost in his own thoughts, only had a dim awareness of everyone else's reactions filtered through.

"Mother! You did what?"

"Leon's a prince?"

"He's a ROYAL meat shield?"

All Leon could think was: *no wonder!*

It was no wonder Lucien had given him such a hard time throughout his childhood. All of the shouting, fighting, and abuse stemmed from the fact that Leon wasn't really his child. Every time Lucien looked at him had been a reminder of his wife's betrayal. Pairing that newfound knowledge with Silas' presence and powers of influence over emotions, Leon was able to view his upbringing from an entirely new perspective. Upon deeper reflection, he even recalled multiple occasions when Silas had lingered in the background during volatile arguments. Though silent, the man had almost certainly been twisting Lucien's mind. Throughout the majority of his life, Leon's entire family had been mere pawns in Silas' sick game.

Was the anger Lucien held against my mother and I enhanced beyond what he had originally felt?

Leon felt the hands of his family and friends as they gently supported him. Conversely, at the King's command, he watched as the hands of guards bodily hauled away the now subdued Lucien and Laric. "Count yourselves lucky that you are only headed to the dungeons!" King Garinth yelled after them.

Bodies were crowded around Leon, but it felt completely different than when he was surrounded by others in the midst of a battle. These people had drawn close in an effort to comfort him while the foundation of his life crumbled to dust. An emptiness began to swell within him as he realized that the feelings of friendship and care he had felt for his captain and prince were actually feelings felt towards his sibling. Quick on that realization's heels was a darkness that tried to permeate his mind as it then dawned on him exactly who he had been forced to kill under the oak tree all those months ago. Reliving the moment made Leon feel sick. Looking over at his mother, all of the anger he had banished by forgiving his former father came roaring back to life. "This? This is why I was treated the way I was? Because I was an illegitimate son?"

She bore his anger with a humble dignity, simply walking over and wrapping him in a gentle hug. "I am so sorry, Leon. Sorry that the truth was hidden from you. From all of you. You were not alone in your torment or treatment. My unfaithfulness was constantly used as a weapon against me. It was like a wound continually being ripped back open. Not a week went by where our house was not mired in the past. There were times when Lucien did try, when he made an effort to forget and forgive. But then Silas would twist him and his mind once again."

"This is all so… overwhelming." King Garinth watched Leon's face as he and Princess Giselle descended from their thrones. Being examined so closely by the king, his true father, unnerved him. He found Princess Giselle's stare even more unsettling though. Her notable timidity was displayed through every effort she made to avoid his attempts at eye contact. She hadn't spoken much throughout the entire exchange, and it took a moment for her to realize that she was being addressed.

"Yes?"

"My dear, would you be horribly offended if I called off your engagement? It does not seem altogether right, or indeed necessary, anymore." The King jested.

"Oh. Yes, of course!"

"Of course. Of course!" King Garinth repeated, patting the back of her hand as he turned to Leon. "It seems the whole kingdom has heard of your exploits. Giants, dragons, I… I would love to hear all about it, truly, but the horde arrives tomorrow. I do not know if we have the time we would need to talk at the moment. Time to catch up on all the things that need to be said, need to be heard."

"Well, there's no longer a wedding to perform, so how about a strategy session with the Judge instead? He has shown great capability for tactics. He may be able to bring new insight." General Xiphos suggested.

The king nodded his head in agreement with her suggestion, and asked the generals to facilitate converting the throne room into a war room. As orders were barked at the various guards and officials, Xiphos took a moment between tasks to hand Revelator back to Leon with a wink. The bustle within the room became more militaristic in nature, and in the midst of it, King Garinth pulled General Ciaye aside for a few quiet words. Leon could tell, based on their body language, that he and his friends were once again the topic of discussion. Soon thereafter, the General approached them with an apologetic expression, proving his earlier assumption accurate.

"Um, Your Highness, by any chance do your friends have any sort of military background?"

It took Leon a moment to register that he was the person the general was speaking to. "First of all, I am simply Leon, or Judge. I would not be comfortable using a title I haven't earned. But yes, my friends have fought by my side through many battles against the undead. Why do you ask?"

"Yeah boyo, jus' spit it out." Duamé commented.

"We have plenty of military minds in here… What we really need are people who can get ahead of the rumors that are probably already spreading about what just occurred."

"You want us to go tell people about Leon… being a lost prince?" Miala asked, as a smile slowly pulled up on the corners of her mouth.

Duamé began to chuckle, then cackle, before he finally calmed enough to explain his mirth. "Oi. Wot ya need is a new Headherald! Ya sacked tha last guy fer lyin' through his lodestone tha whole time. Ya need someone ta tell people tha right story!"

"You're… volunteering?" General Ciaye asked, with a look of hopeful confusion plastered on his face.

"I was tha person who started tellin' people about tha Judge in tha first place, doncha know."

After staring at the smiling dwarf for a few moments, the General turned to King Garinth, "Your Majesty, this dwarven fellow–"

The king halted the conversation he had been engaged in with his daughter and Leon's mother to look over at them. "Yes?"

Duamé leaned in and interjected, "Duamé Onyxwill."

"–is offering to be the new headherald. To help spread the word."

"Already been doin' tha job fer ya."

King Garinth was clearly bemused as he waved a dismissive hand, "As you wish. After all, we may all die tomorrow, so what harm could there be?"

"Great! Now about me pay…" Duamé rubbed his hands together.

Miala rolled her eyes at their friend's antics. "Kelleren says he wants a good walk anyway."

When Duamé, Miala, Kelleren, and Princess Schalae left to spread word of the throne room confrontation, Leon found himself keenly aware of the void their absence left. His friends helped him during times of trouble, and he had not come to grips with his newfound lineage yet. All of his friends had not left though, Gionna had remained behind. She hobbled towards Leon, looking as if she were preparing to speak. He headed her off, trying to keep the accusatory tone from his voice. "You knew, didn't you?"

The gnome let out a heavy sigh, "I suspected, dearie. However, it wasn't until I observed your mother's odd behaviors that I asked her about it. The unreasonable antagonism toward you by Lucien Rhise, the similar coloring both he and your mother shared… You look very much like King Garinth, your father, did when he was younger."

A prick of betrayal stabbed Leon before he asked, "Why didn't you tell me?"

"It wasn't my secret to tell. Your mother confirmed my estimation, and I urged her to tell you as soon as possible. While her admission certainly clarified a few things, she had her own issues to work through before she could share the truth with you."

While still mostly numb from the shock, an irritation began to take root within Leon. Gionna knew, his mother knew, and he was fairly certain that his angelic tutors had known as well. *Is this why they haven't visited in the past couple days?* Leon questioned. The dreams that usually accompanied his travels had been sorely lacking of late. While his advisors had honestly been nothing but helpful, Leon still couldn't help but feel hurt by their prolonged silence.

His brooding continued until Kérik sauntered into the room. The dwarven admiral managed to enter just as the conversion from throne room to war room was completed. He beelined straight for Leon, and barely suppressed a grin beneath his enormous beard as he gave a short bow.

"Quit enjoying this, Sir."

"O' course, Yer Highness."

"Master Silverspine!" King Garinth crooned, as he approached the older dwarf. "Can you ever forgive me for the poor decision of letting you go? I must admit that my opinion of you was greatly tarnished by the words of a traitor to the kingdom."

"No harm done, Yer Majesty. In fact, if it weren't fer yer dismissal o' me service, we wouldn't even be here." Kérik replied, bowing low to the king. "You'll be happy ta know that tha city is safe fer now. Tha two dreadnoughts, an' crews fer 'em, surrendered an' were grounded after we surrounded em. Course, tha problem is now we don't got enough trustworthy people ta fly em… Seein' as how we're shorthanded already. Fer now though, it seems tha insurrection against ya is over. I caught up with Princess Schalae, an' she filled us in on wot happened here. Apparently ya had a decent swing o' tha pick yerselves."

While he spoke, a medium sized wooden table, topped with a miniaturized map of Last Bastion and its surrounding area, had been brought in. The mountain ranges to the north of the city were depicted as tiny jagged mounds that ran along the northern coastline of the kingdom. The corner of the map showed the plateau that housed the upper portion of the city and the ziggurat. As Leon studied it, he noticed that the cliffs and gorge descending from the plateau seemed so small compared to the real thing. While the map didn't go into detail of each individual building, the to-scale model also showed an accurate layout of the city nestled at the plateau's base.

As the generals and admiral crowded around it, Leon looked over to where his mother and sister were quietly conversing. Liara still looked shocked by the revelation of their mother's infidelity. She stood with her arms wrapped around herself, and her shoulders quivering. Their low whispers continued, and Leon's attention was pulled back to General Ciaye whose voice was raised as he tried to give an account of their situation.

"Before you all arrived, we covered this with Lord Rhise. The undead horde outnumbers us approximately five to one after we whittled their numbers down during the battle of Agaprya. Unfortunately, our forces were also impacted, as a vast portion of our airship navy was destroyed. What we are left with is no more than ten attack ships, fifteen transports, and a score of mail carriers. We had the two dreadnoughts, but now without crews they are useless, unless we shift manpower to them. Maybe from the transports?"

"We were also thinking to even our odds by conscripting from the general populace. People of all ages: women, children, anyone who can hold a sword." King Garinth sighed at the distasteful idea. "I do not want it done, but this will be the battle in which we either survive, or face total annihilation. The future for all of the living will be decided tomorrow. What are your thoughts, Leon?"

It was obvious to Leon what the king was trying to do. Including him in their battle plans, and asking for his opinions, were poorly veiled attempts to both ingratiate himself to Leon, and test his mettle. Leon could feel the king's probing gaze as he awaited a response. Beside him, his half sister, Giselle, looked on with an unreadable expression. Her planned ascension to Queen was over, and Leon wondered if she held onto any animosity over that development.

Setting aside his royal ponderings, Leon focused on the problem at hand. "I can't condone children fighting on the frontlines, or being in any avoidable danger at all for that matter. If they can help with preparations, fine, but that is the extent of what they should do. Beyond that, any additional help from able-bodied men or women would be appreciated."

A pall fell over the room as his words were absorbed, "Could we have the populace help with fortifications?" Ciaye asked, "How much could actually be accomplished in only one day?"

General Xiphos replied immediately, "Barricades. Caltrops. Trip wires. Sharpened stakes."

“I’ve seen villagers in the town of Everbright fight the undead off with pitchforks and torches. If the villagers and refugees can organize, give them weapons and point them where they need to go to defend Last Bastion.” His recollection prompted him to ask a question, “Everbright supposedly evacuated here. Did they make it?”

Ciaye nodded. “They’re here. One of the first villages to make it here, despite the distance.”

Leon breathed a sigh of relief. *Thank Adonai they’re safe!*

“With citizenry complimenting our armed forces, we will still be outnumbered, but to a lesser degree.” Ciaye’s grim frustration was expressed with a sigh before he continued, “We also know an aerial force of dragons, gryphons, and an unknown number of captured airships are coming against us. One of our older reports suggested that the undead had captured the third dreadnought.”

Leon cleared his throat, “They did. Along with three attack ships and about a dozen mail carriers. Those won’t be a problem. The *Esperella* took care of them.”

Their looks of unbelief were Leon’s only reply before Gionna cleared her throat and clarified, “Well, technically you crashed the undead dreadnought.”

“After he leapt onto the ship and single-handedly engaged the undead crew onboard.” General Xiphos added. The wide-eyed stares continued, and Leon felt all he could do was give a modest shrug.

“I couldn’t have gotten out of there alive without Duamé and Lorog’s help.”

Lorog, who had remained silent at Xiphos’ side, stood a little straighter and grinned a little broader following Leon’s rebuttal. “But that brings up a good point.” Leon continued. “If we can down their airships, and kill their remaining gryphons and dragons, that would eliminate any aerial forces they have. Xaelon has survived for decades on Miss Gærheart’s inventions due to their superiority against ground forces. If we can destroy Xhormas’ air forces, then our airship navy can focus on grinding the undead on the ground to dust.”

Kérik winced before he contributed, "That'll be tough ta do without tha two dreadnoughts on our side bein' operational. Or even with havin' ta shift personnel from tha other ships ta them. At this point, we will need every body we can get."

General Xiphos looked at him and asked, "Where are the turncoat dreadnought crews now?"

Kérik turned to General Ciaye, "Bein' detained by yer folks."

"Those traitors will fill the dungeons, right next to Lucien and Laric Rhise." King Garinth said darkly.

"How are we on munitions? Arrows and bolts? Cannonballs? Black powder?" Gionna asked.

"All well stocked. Both for airships and Last Bastion itself. Strongarm Smithy took over the operations here and have been churning out weaponry at an unbelievable pace." Ciaye reported.

Leon and his friends chuckled, and the questioning looks from others prompted him to clarify, "Duamé will be happy to hear that. He's part owner, along with the husband and wife."

General Ciaye blinked a few times before he dismissed the statement, "Be that as it may, we've got all sorts of undead heading towards this rock, and every person that dies here will add to their numbers. As we are outnumbered already, this will be a difficult fight."

"Unless the rumors about you are to be believed."

Everyone turned towards Princess Giselle, but she just stared at Leon following her unexpected comment. Her quiet voice forced him to lean in to hear better, and she looked painfully aware of all the attention that was focused on her, but she continued anyways, "There are rumors that the Judge of Xaelon possesses a secret that prevents the living from turning undead."

"What? More rumors? From where?" King Garinth demanded.

"People talk. Nobles. Soldiers. Even townsfolk." Giselle explained.

"It's not that much of a secret, really." Leon replied. "It requires placing your faith in the one true God, Adonai. Believing in Him, and following His teachings, is what stops you from turning undead."

King Garinth's reaction to the news seemed more promising than those of the others who had not heard Leon talk about Adonai before. "That… would be incredible. How come some of us have never heard of this until now?"

Judging there was no better time than the present, Leon told all who were assembled about the unseen war being waged around them. He shared how beyond the undead and the living who warred against each other, there existed a war between Adonai and the beings Rohiel had called the 'b'nei ha'elohim' – the fallen entities who rebelled against Him. Leon filled them in on how Xhormas had risen as the leader of the fallen, and as the god of corrupted undeath, he waged a war to cover the world with undead and ensure that Adonai was completely forgotten.

From there, Leon launched into what he and his friends found within the Archive at Agaprya. From the weird to the wondrous, their adventures were a testament to Adonai's faithfulness. As much as the odds were stacked against them, Leon knew that they could, and would, overcome the undead horde. With the conviction of his beliefs forming a solid foundation beneath him, he shared the truth of Adonai with those that were present. As he spoke he found that thanks to Gionna and General Xiphos' occasional input, it was a bit easier to share his faith than it had once been.

King Garinth listened with patience and grace, but at the earliest opportunity gave a dismissive wave. "This is all very fascinating, illuminating, and a bit far-fetched. If what you say is true, how would we even get knowledge of this… Adonai… to the general populace? If the defenders did not turn when killed, we would stand more of a fighting chance."

"It is true Yer Majesty. We've seen it fer ourselves." Kérik assured.

"As far-fetched as it seems, Your Majesty, the facts remain – no matter how uncomfortable they are." Gionna replied.

Wanting to capitalize on their discussion about Adonai, Leon asked,

"Is there any way to assemble the populace? Bring the hope of Adonai to them right now?"

General Ciaye looked extremely skeptical. "They are busy preparing for tomorrow. Then, after this strategy meeting concludes, they will help with building defenses."

If left to choose between physical defenses and spiritual awakening, Leon felt their choice was clear. "I can assure you, the best defense that we have is hope and faith in Adonai. He would protect you from Xhormas' tainted influence forcing you to rise as undead. This is something that everyone needs to know. If it were up to me, I would forgo an hour or two of preparation to prevent every citizen I possibly could from turning undead."

The king's gaze roved over to his generals, who both nodded their approval of Leon's proposal. "Then let us address the populace. On the day before a battle, a public address just makes sense anyway. Especially seeing as nobody is getting married or coronated today, the people deserve an explanation."

The next hour was a blur of activity. Guards and heralds rushed to spread word throughout Last Bastion of the upcoming royal address. Leon took an opportunity amidst all of the chaos to snatch food from a few nearby platters. An officious looking courtier stepped close and offered him a royal robe to wear.

Leon had no words. He certainly didn't feel like a royal; Prince Gelan was the prince. Casting a look between his mother and the king, who watched him from afar, Leon knew he couldn't, and wouldn't, try to fill Gelan's boots. With a dismissive wave, Leon shook his head at the courtier. The confused individual hesitated before finally exiting down a hallway with the robe in hand.

Gionna tugged on Leon's sleeve and told him she would go inform Magnus of everything that had happened. Kérik escorted her out, promising to take her to the new Archives by way of the *Esperella*. Lorog whispered a few quiet words to General Xiphos, and was then dismissed to find his family in the city. Everyone who remained was instructed to round up as many citizens and military personnel as possible, then bring them to the wide bridge that led into the mountain. One of the mountain fortress' crenelated protrusions was located directly above the main gate, and Leon had been assured he could address the people from there.

The king and princess followed Leon practically everywhere, which meant their galvamancer bodyguard also always hovered nearby. Leon privately suspected that his majesty's overprotectiveness could be attributed to their newfound kinship. Their close proximity allowed them to discuss his values, his history in the military, and the time he had spent with Gelan. It was not nearly enough to make up for twenty years of lost time, but it was a start. When Leon's stories came around to Miala, King Garinth was quick to perceive his feelings. "You love that woman, the pyromancer."

"Yes, Your Majesty. Emphatically."

With a sigh, the King continued, "Matters of the heart are complicated for royalty. Take what happened between your mother and I. Grief caused us to do something that… well… should not have happened. Because of your and Giselle's stations, a future alliance within the court may very well hinge on your… availability."

An unsettling irritation towards King Garinth ignited within Leon as the monarch broached the topic of relationships. Hours before, he had been ready to wed Princess Giselle to Laric. Now he dared question Leon and Miala's relationship? Before he could stop himself, Leon whirled on his newfound father and said in a low voice, "There are no other kingdoms to ally with. Even Princess Schalae's Northern Elvenwood is gone. Tomorrow, there could very well be no kingdom at all, even if we survive. So, you will forgive me, Your Majesty, if I choose to love and be with the woman I chose for myself before I met you or knew of my lineage. Besides…" Leon continued, "according to the Entyrnet trolls, Miala and I are already married. We might as well keep up appearances."

The blood seemed to drain from King Garinth's face even as Princess Giselle's cheeks flushed. His lips moved to form words, and an expression of outrage was written across his features from being addressed in such a manner. Galvamancer Exiosa stood nearby, a small smile betraying her while she shook her head. Finally, King Garinth managed to choke out, "Entyrnet trolls?"

"They relocated to Masterwork Halls, along with the elves. Great fighters. Odd culture. Avoided a misunderstanding by–" Leon explained.

"Causing misunderstandings?" King Garinth arched a brow.

“Professing my feelings.” Leon finished.

A soldier approached, whispered in the galvamancer’s ear, and waited. Emirah relayed the information to King Garinth in wooden tones, “Your Majesty, the traitorous Rhises, along with the dreadnought crews who followed them, have filled the dungeons to capacity. Ladies Erika and Liara have requested a visit to speak with them.”

“A monitored visit, of course.” The king replied. The soldier bowed and left quickly – just as their royal entourage was escorted towards the parapet.

They traveled through spiraling passageways and oversized rooms, all made of the enormous monolithic blocks. Multiple corridors branched from each room they encountered, making this mountain fortress less like the cavernous Masterwork Halls, and more like a giant maze. Every so often sunlight pierced through the ceiling, and Leon realized the mountain must be peppered with impossibly precise holes that allowed the shafts of light through. Confused as to how the holes could be so effective, Leon decided to ask General Ciaye about them. The man stroked his odd beard as he continued walking.

“We certainly didn’t bore any holes into Last Bastion. From our limited research, the holes have little mirrors that run along the walls that line them. Those surfaces catch the sunlight at just the right angles to reflect it all the way down here. It’s another fascinating aspect to the fortress, because we don’t have a clue how it was done.”

Leon lost all sense of direction as they continued through the mountain’s many twists and turns. Eventually their group arrived at a fairly large room, lit with only the barest amount of sunlight from both the ceiling and a nearby corridor. It was the fortress armory. One side of the large space was covered in racks that were nearly bare of their swords, pikes, and other deadly instruments of war. The other side housed depleted racks of defensive gear; only a sparse scattering of helms, shields, and chainmail armor remained. The absent equipment was undoubtedly in the hands of the fortress’ defenders. The faint ring of a hammer striking an anvil echoed from an adjoining passageway – likely from the blacksmith repairing or maintaining the weapons and armor housed here. Their escorts turned away from the sound, and instead brought them to a wide corridor that opened to the outside.

Leon stepped out onto the defensive parapet that was located directly above Last Bastion's massive stone gates with the rest of the royal entourage. Shielding his downcast eyes as they adjusted to the sunlight, his gaze landed onto the cannons and their munitions clustered at the front of the space. They were angled to point at the large stone bridge that stretched across the gorge, and would be heavily used if the undead's ground forces broke through the city. While other defensive structures poked out from the mountain in various places, this one had a key vantage point.

The warm sunlight shone across the breathtaking view of the stone bridge and the cityscape beyond. Buildings of varying sizes and shapes filled the crescent shaped city, and a large stone wall bordered the gorge that separated the mountain and the city. Water from the Sigrit river flowed far below, its current swift and frothing as it crashed against boulders and debris in its path. High above the river, the crowning jewel of the entire scene, stood the wide stone bridge that looked as if it could support the multitudes. Even now, groups of people, families, and individuals all approached the mountain fortress. Young and old, soldier and civilian, all headed towards Last Bastion's massive gates.

As time progressed, more and more citizens showed up. Transports, mail carriers, and attack ships all began to converge nearby. Soldiers lined their railings, trying to get a good look at the royalty who were about to address them; at the new 'prince' that had appeared and disrupted the crowning of Laric Rhise. Leon was high enough above the bridge and the fortress doors that he couldn't distinguish any faces, but at the urging of King Garinth, who had stepped next to him, they waved to the crowd at large.

After almost an hour, the stone bridge was packed full with a mixture of all races. Those that couldn't fit on the bridge crowded around the walls on the other side of the gorge, or were on the airships that hovered above. Leon picked the *Golem* out from among the various ships, and waved at the crew who had carried him and his friends to the Northern Elvenwood. The living had gathered together by the thousands, unified in their need for survival, waiting to hear the words that desperately needed to be said. There was a choice they could make, one that would give each individual not just hope, but also faith and a power to believe in; a power that could defy Xhotmas and prevent undeath.

A massive, hollow, curling horn was brought out on a wheeled dolly. Its base opening was as wide as a person, and it curved and twisted before ending in a sheared-off tip. Leon's private doubts about how the populace would be able to hear anything they said were quickly dispelled. King Garinth stepped near the opening of the horn, raised his arms to gain the crowd's attention, and spoke.

"My people! Children of Xaelon! Hear me and rejoice! The rumors that you have heard are true. The Judge of Xaelon is here and a new prince has been found!"

Amid shouts from the populace, Leon grit his teeth at the spectacle that was being made of him. He was not some prancing steed to be gazed at, prodded, or preened. His frustration must have been evident because Princess Giselle drew near and whispered to him away from the massive horn their father was speaking through.

"It gets easier."

"What does?"

"Being used as a pawn. Not having a say. You get used to it."

Leon couldn't help but stare into his half sister's sad eyes. It was clear she was speaking from experience, and the more Leon thought about it, the more he found her opinion had merit.

Younger than Prince Gelan, Giselle was almost certainly consigned to a life of service through an arranged marriage. Even after Gelan's death, she hadn't been trusted to lead the kingdom in his place. Rather, she had been forcibly used as a bargaining piece in Laric taking the throne. Now, with Lucien's plan thwarted, and Leon in the picture, he could see through the forced public smile that she displayed.

"You… you think he would deny you your right to rule? That I would be chosen?" Leon asked, unable to comprehend the audacity of such a thing.

"Our father was right about one thing: his time to rule is over. Either the kingdom is destroyed tomorrow and all life ends, or we somehow survive with new leadership in place to nurture a new beginning. What better leadership than the opportune prince? One who served alongside the originally intended king?"

As she adjusted her golden hair in the slight breeze, Leon pondered over the princess' predicament. Here was a woman only a couple years older than himself, who was every bit as trapped in her assigned role as he was in his. Due to the circumstances of her birth, she was overlooked and overruled. Ironically, Liara had fallen into that category as well. Laric had been the focus of Lucien's instruction, while Liara was only used to further Lucien's agenda with hardly a voice or say in the matter.

"I'm… sorry." Leon stated.

"For what? You did not do anything to me." The Princess replied.

"I suppose I empathize with you and your situation. No wonder you get along with Liara."

Giselle's smile turned real. "She is a confidant of mine with regards to our similar situations, yes. I would welcome you to our small support group, but should we all survive, your position would be more… elevated than ours."

The king glanced back at him before turning towards the horn. "–and so I present to you, the Judge of Xaelon!"

Amid the resounding shouts and applause the king's pronouncement drew from the crowd, Leon barely heard Princess Giselle whisper, "Good luck." Then she was clapping as well.

Leon numbly stepped toward the behemoth horn, as King Garinth stepped slightly to the side. He looked as joyous as his people, and clapped as Leon approached.

Addressing the town of Everbright, the Northern Elvenwood, and Masterwork Halls paled in comparison the sea of faces that he looked upon now. What must be tens of thousands of people watched Leon, waiting for him to say what they needed to hear. This was the first address from their future would-be king, and all of their faith and hope was placed on him.

With a slow, calming breath Leon lifted a silent prayer, and began to redirect their faith and hope to the one who truly deserved it.

Chapter 18: The Imprisoned

A deafening roar rose from the crowd as cries, cheers, and chants of 'Ad-on-ai' filled the air. Leon had spoken from his heart, conveying the message that he had told time and again. Words came to him unbidden as he shared the experiences he'd had as a Judge. Of seeking forgiveness from Adonai for his failures. Of the tenets that he lived by. Of how the Dead Wars had begun, and how the undead could be stopped. Mostly, though, he shared how people could be spared from turning undead by placing their faith in Adonai. Leon felt as though he spoke for hours, trying to impart the good news to the best of his ability. He also tried to not be disheartened when he saw some of the onlookers begin to file away from the back and edges of the crowd.

Leon mentally reassured himself that they were likely leaving to prepare the city's defenses. It was already early afternoon, and much still remained to be done in anticipation of the looming attack. Their pressing timeline only motivated him further to tell anyone who had ears to hear about Adonai and his power. The awesome power that had caused the undead horde to retreat from Masterwork Halls. The power of life, and of peace over undeath.

After Leon's impassioned speech, King Garinth cast furtive glances at him before speaking through the horn himself. "Now let us go and prepare for tomorrow! For Xaelon!"

A mixture of 'For Xaelon' and 'For Adonai' were the shouted responses to his final words. For a moment Leon thought the king looked baffled, before a guarded expression once again closed over his face. "Not a bad speech. Not the direction I would have gone, but if there is something that people can believe in to help get them through this, then why not let it be this Adonai?"

“Why not?” Leon scoffed in disbelief. “I’ve told you about Adonai twice now Your Majes– Oh forget it! You’ll find out later.”

Blank, confused stares from guards and royals alike met Leon as he explained, “Sundown. You’ll see at sundown.”

“Why sundown?” King Garinth asked, but Leon’s only reply was a knowing smile.

They walked back into the fortress and were met in the armory by Ladies Erika and Liara. Their red-rimmed eyes told of the recent tears that had been shed by them both. A handkerchief passed between them, each taking a turn dabbing their eyes while Leon approached.

Leon embraced both his mother and his sister, remembering that prior to his speech they had been allowed to visit Laric and Lucien in the dungeon. “What’s wrong?”

“It is nothing to concern yourself with.” His mother replied. “The part of your address we caught was quite lovely.”

King Garinth stepped forward, “Lady Erika, what happened with Lucien? What did he say to you?”

Fighting back another tear, she shook her head, “He said hardly a word. It… is Laric. I am afraid that he has… gone mad. He kept giggling and babbling nonsense while Lucien just sat there in silence. I… I do not know what to do!”

Laric had come so close to gaining the throne before then falling so far from grace in a matter of mere minutes. That would certainly have been an understandable shock to his senses. To have gone insane though? Leon truly didn’t believe his brother’s mind would be that fragile. Despite his constant attempts to surrender the anger he felt to Adonai, he could still feel the undercurrent of ill-will he carried toward Lucien and Laric. That anger had reared its ugly head during their confrontation in the throne room, and even though they had been carried off to prison, Leon still didn’t feel as though justice had been served. The matter between his brother and former-father remained unresolved, and it nagged at him.

His lifelong struggle with animosity towards them had prevented him from performing his duties as a Judge in the past. Leon knew he should not do anything that would stoke the fires of anger and resentment within himself on the eve of battle. Unfortunately, his brother's mental state was clearly distressing both his sister and mother. Leon knew that he would do whatever he could to at least grant them some semblance of peace.

"Maybe it's best if I talk to them?" He suggested.

"You foiled their plans, and now you want to talk to them?" General Xiphos asked in confusion.

Various others in the room expressed their hesitancy over the idea. The more Leon thought about it though, the more convicted he was to go see them. Moments ago he had explained to the remainder of the living world who Adonai was, following the decades Xhormas had spent ensuring He faded into the anonymity of their non-remembrance.

Who am I to deny Laric and Lucien the same opportunity to know Him? Leon thought.

"They deserve to hear the same message I just shared with everyone else. Plus, as much as I hate to admit it, I am still in need of some answers – which I believe only they can provide."

King Garinth frowned slightly as he mulled the idea over in his head while pinching the bridge of his nose. "If I were to agree to this, then you would need to take some guards with you. The traitorous dreadnought crews are also being housed in the dungeons. It would be dangerous and foolish for you to go alone."

General Xiphos cleared her throat and addressed the group, "I would go with him, Your Majesty."

King Garinth nodded to his general. "So be it. When you are finished I will need you to join General Ciaye in continuing to set defenses."

"As you wish, Your Majesty."

King Garinth's gaze lingered on Leon, his thoughts unreadable until it finally shifted towards Lady Erika. Leon thought he would speak to her, but in the end, the king turned on his heel and exited with his retinue – walking down the hallway they had entered through earlier. Princess Giselle, who had been talking with Liara, promptly followed her father with the royal galvamancer, Exiosa, in tow. The royal retinue had no apparent qualms about leaving Leon with General Xiphos, his mother, and his sister. Liara immediately cast an impish smile at their mother.

"What?" Lady Erika asked.

"You know what, Mother! What was that look about?"

Lady Erika shook her head vigorously at her daughter. "It was nothing, child. You are imagining things."

"Um… Even I noticed that one, Mother." Leon joined in the ribbing.

Their mother's eyes, still red from her recent tears, grew wide as she pointed an accusatory finger at both of them. "You are to both stop this nonsense at once! Our family has been through too much in the past day, and I do not have time for your fantastical notions or delusions." Quick on the heels of those chastising words, however, her regal demeanor slipped back into place. She gently smoothed her singed dress, and gave a disgusted sigh at the state of her appearance. "Ugh, never would I have thought that I would be forced to wear something like this in front of royalty, or at the end of the world for that matter. It is… I just…," she gestured to herself, "A burnt dress!"

Liara's expression brightened as she motioned to her own attire, "Well, that is something I suffer from as well. It is also something that, with a bit of determination, can be easily rectified."

Leon gaped at them in disbelief. "You're going shopping? Now?"

"What could we possibly contribute to the war effort?" Liara asked. "Besides, it is not as if we know how to build fortifications."

"You… do have a point."

"Judge Leon, we should be going." Xiphos chided.

"You're right." Leon agreed before he turned back to his family, "I'll see you both later."

"Be careful, Leon." His mother cautioned.

Leon snorted. "I will be. After all, I'll be on the good side of the bars."

General Xiphos directed two passing soldiers to aid Leon's family in finding a seamstress, and then ordered another two to escort Leon and herself. She then strode off, with purposeful strides, her plate mail jangling with each step she took towards their destination. Leon followed her through the giant-sized passageway's many twists and turns, and could tell that their path led further and further into the bowels of the mountain. The soldiers that Xiphos had ordered to accompany them kept glancing at Leon warily.

Upon his initial arrival at the fortress, those who escorted him had been a bit nervous because his identity and his intentions were unknown. Now, Leon assumed the nervousness stemmed from the discovery of his true parentage.

Dust and mold assaulted Leon's nose as their journey deep into Last Bastion finally came to an end. Before him was a long chamber with a vaulted ceiling, capable of accommodating giant-sized beings. The area Leon and his guards entered was quite wide and showcased several soldiers lounging around wooden tables. They were all either engaged in cards, dice, or reading books. Another guard entered the opposite side of the room from where Leon stood, and a long row of normal-sized prison cells stretched behind him. Pitted and rusted metallic bars that formed a lattice pattern ran down either side of the entire corridor's length. While their voices were mostly kept low, the prisoner's hands, arms, and feet occasionally poked from the holes in the bars as small acts of defiance.

"General Xiphos!" A guard at one of the tables exclaimed, causing the others to leap up and stand at attention.

"Relax, soldiers. The Judge is just here to talk to our special prisoners." General Xiphos replied.

"Yes ma'am." A few of the guards automatically replied, their postures only halfway relaxing. Only one guard sat back down, while the rest busied themselves with useful tasks like dusting crumbs off of tables, or oiling their armor and weapons.

"This way, your Highness." The guard who had just walked in from the prison cells said. It took Leon a moment to register that he was the one being addressed, and then he wordlessly acknowledged the guard before following him. Xiphos, and the two soldiers who accompanied her, remained close behind him as they walked between the cells.

The cells themselves were bigger than the small, cramped ones at Masterwork Halls. Each one could hold three to four people, though there were two cots per cell. The spaces were filled with individuals, some in naval uniforms and others in the rough clothing of miners. These were the traitorous dreadnought crews. They had been bought and paid for by Lucien, and were loyal only to their employer. There were some humans, but also many orcs and goblins, and mixed in were even a few elves and ogres; all of whom looked positively miserable in their current state. As Leon passed by more than a few of them met his gaze, and their eyes followed him and his escort down the hallway.

Predictably, Leon found his half-brother and Lucien in their very own cell at the far end of the hall. The man whom Leon had once thought to be his father currently sat unmoving on his cot with head in his hands. His coat with the levigem pin on its lapel had smudges of grime in places, and his off-white shirt was wrinkled and untucked. His belt and ascot were gone, and the buttons around his neck were undone. Leon had never seen Lucien so disheveled and distressed before.

But he was calm in comparison to Leon's half-brother.

Laric paced the small cell's open space, and the crazed, wide-eyed stare Leon received from him was downright unnerving. Laric's clothes were torn, ripped, and ragged in places. He must have put up a fight while being detained because an ugly bruise was developing near his temple. Laric didn't stand and stare at him for long before rushing at, and colliding into, the bars with a clang. He reached an arm out frantically trying to grab at Leon, then groaned when he realized his effort was futile.

"Traitor! Usurper! It should have been mine! It has always been mine!" Laric seethed as he rattled the metallic bars in their frame.

"We had to knock him out on the way here. I'm sorely tempted to do it again." The guard who led them to the cell said, before he turned back to the once again yelling Laric. "Hey! Pipe down!"

"Maybe this wasn't such a good idea." Xiphos muttered to Leon.

"I still need answers." Leon told her, before he turned back to the cell's occupants and addressed them in as neutral a tone as he could muster.

"We need to talk. I have some questions for you both."

Laric's eyes grew crazed once again and he pointed at the guard, "He just told me to 'pipe down' but we have so much to discuss!" He then shook his head repeatedly and muttered, "No no no. Not yet. Not the time."

Laric continued to shake his head until he suddenly cocked it at an odd angle. He then turned in a slow circle, stepped backward from the bars, and collapsed to the ground. Leon watched his half-brother curl into a ball and rock himself slowly back and forth, while he quietly muttered to himself. A small piece of him felt pity for his older sibling. Their rivalry had grown into a bitter feud over the years, but Leon had never thought that it would end like this

"See what you have wrought, boy?"

Lucien's tone dripped with the scorn and bitterness that had poisoned him for so many years. He sat up straighter on his cot, and glared at Leon with obvious contempt. "I hope that you are happy with yourself. It looks like you have gotten everything that you wanted."

Leon knew better than to give in to the goading tone, or to the resentment that threatened to worm its way back inside. He had grown since his time at the manor, and would not play Lucien's games. "This isn't exactly what I wanted."

Lucien flinched at Leon's use of the contractions that had been forbidden for so long in their home, after all the Rhise family were not to use the common language. Leon suspected the real reason for his former-father's dislike of abbreviated speaking was that it reminded him of the dwarven dialect. The dwarves were who Silas hated, and who Lucien had so thoroughly betrayed. Laric had apparently also picked up on the hatred of abbreviated words, growling, "Is not. Is not. Is not!" before falling silent again.

Leon figured that if he wanted to get any answers at all, he would have to be less antagonistic. He gestured to General Xiphos, and motioned with a nod of his head for her to give them some more privacy. She assessed the situation, and with a few words had the guards around them move back down the hall, away from Leon. While they were not far, the low chatter between the other prisoners provided some semblance of white noise.

Mindful of his phrasing, he once again spoke to the man he had thought to be his father, "Please help me to understand. Did you know this whole time? About my… heritage."

For a while, Leon thought Lucien wouldn't answer. The man simply sniffed, shook his head, and stared at the wall. Then Lucien replied without bothering to look at him, "I do not owe you an explanation."

"But I want to hear it. Tell me why. Why did this have to happen?" Leon pleaded.

Lucien Rhise heaved a heavy sigh. It was a sigh that Leon hoped indicated the beginning of the unburdening of the man's soul. Sure enough, it seemed that Lucien could talk to him if he didn't look at him.

"Erika was a noblewoman at court, and I had my heart set on her from the first moment I saw her. I was not the only one though. I made my case to my father, explaining that the mercantile empire her family built could be melded with our mining company, benefitting us all greatly. The arrangement was made, and we were wed. We were happy. She was happy. I… I was sure of it."

"When my father passed, the Rhise mines and business fell to me to manage. I knew how to maintain it, but I did not expect how much time would be required to do it all. Managing the financing of the materials in the mines. Sifting through the constant influx of refugees turned workers. Managing and maintaining consistent output from the mines. Still, I am not one to whine or shirk my duties. Erika managed the household, while I took care of our enterprises. When Laric and Liara were born, I thought we had everything I had ever wanted. I thought we were still happy together. Then Dionne died."

Lucien sighed again before he continued, "Erika was one of her ladies-in-waiting while growing up at court, and they were good friends. Naturally we attended the funeral, where Garinth…"

He leapt off the cot and rattled the bars of the cell in frustration. A sneer spread across Lucien's face as he spit, "I knew when we were young Garinth fancied Erika! I knew, and I won her heart first. He had no right to her. None! Yet, in the depths of all our woes and drinks over the loss of the queen… After only one day of grieving… He…"

Leon was shocked that he had never heard any of this before, and would have voiced as much, but they were both interrupted by Laric shouting, "No! I do not want it. I do not want it!"

A guard hollered down the hallway for Laric to quiet down. Leon wasn't sure if Lucien's scoff was in response to the guard, to his son's apparent madness, or to Leon himself. It could very well have been due to all of those things, but Leon quickly urged Lucien onward in his tale.

"I was made a fool. I did not know until months later – until your mother was expecting you. She told me she made a mistake. That she was sorry. She begged for forgiveness and to not be shamed for her infidelity. It took everything in me to not throw her out the door. So, out of the love that I still had for her, I let her stay. But I needed distance. I needed time. Especially after you came."

Lucien went from pointing at Leon to gesturing grandly. "You can see now how I was the victim in this tragedy. How I am not the one who was wrong, but the one who was wronged. So yes. I knew the whole time. I even made an effort to include you in our family. To show you what a proper upbringing and good sense could produce. I tried to make you a Rhise. Instead, you brought it all to ruin."

The tug of pity towards the man Leon had thought he knew was gone. Several times Leon had wanted to point out the flaws in Lucien's logic. His victim mentality refused to admit to the root of his issue. His business had been his first love for so many years. It had been his first 'wife', while his family only got what was left over. That was the problem his mother had explained to him when they were reunited.

Yet what would be the point in arguing with Lucien? What good would come of it?

Leon had more questions, so he pressed forward. "How did Silas fit into all of this for you? You do know he was the one who threw mother down the stairs, right?"

Laric erupted in a shrill giggle on the floor as Lucien shook his head. "Is it true? Is Silas really dead?"

"Mother cut off his head."

"Silas told me he could help my family gain more than I had ever thought possible. He said he could give us the power to change the kingdom for the better, to rebuild the world in a better image. He was an idealist."

"And so he gave you the Diviner ring? Helped the Rhise family find iron deposits?" Leon asked.

Lucien scoffed. "We found multiple sites. Ironically, not far from the levigem mines. After the ring served its purpose Silas took it back. He told me an associate of his would hang onto it."

So that's how Rhoxmas played into this. Leon thought. With his power and influence over the undead, Silas must have had some awareness or connection to the alukah. Utilizing that connection would have kept the ring out of sight, and left no one the wiser about its location.

"And you didn't ask Silas about his associate? You just blindly trusted him?"

"Blind!" Laric sang discordantly, as he interjected. "Blind. Blind. Blind. Darkness all around! Closing in!"

Leon stared at Laric with mixed emotions. While he desired justice for his half-brother's involvement in the conspiracy, a seed of pity implanted itself within Leon. No one deserved to have their mind shattered, not even Laric.

Lucien interrupted Leon's thoughts by slamming his fist against the iron bars of the cell. Clearly frustrated, he answered Leon's question. "Silas proved useful enough over the years. He had some strange habits and ideas to be sure, but his suggestions had all panned out. Had I known of his duplicitous intent to not follow through with what we discussed…" The fallen lord trailed off, shaking his head in dissatisfaction.

"You have absolutely no idea." Leon agreed. He then told Lucien what he knew of the man and of whom he served. Leon spoke of the carved idol of Xhormas in Silas' room, of the tenets Silas had followed, and of the resultant decades-long manipulation of their family. Lucien Rhise took it all in without so much as a grimace. Laric, however, had developed some sort of facial tic throughout the course of their conversation.

"The fact is, you basically invited evil incarnate into our home, and then stood by while he played with our lives for years. To top that all off, he was an empamancer. He could control and influence emotions just as easily as you could pluck strings on a lute. Had you looked hard enough, you probably would have been able to see it over the years. So, save me your sanctimonious diatribe, because the god he serves wants nothing more than destruction and death. And you helped him accomplish that!"

Leon reigned his emotions in once more, beating down the anger that simmered just beneath the surface. After a few calming breaths, he continued, "Luckily for you and Laric, I have a solution to the problem that Silas caused, and I–"

"You mean your so-called 'God of love', Adonai?" Lucien drawled.

Leon didn't think Lucien's response could have surprised him more if the man had started to hurl entyrnet troll insults at him. "Wait, you already know about Him?"

Lucien's voice was as cold and hard as ice, "As soon as I found out that you were the Judge, I had my sources gather everything they could find out about you. What you said. Where you went. It was easy to sort fact from fiction. I have heard all about your 'God', and am not interested in your fanciful tales."

An eagerness to try and pierce through Lucien's misconceptions of who Adonai was filled Leon. Who knew what wild information Lucien had gleaned by not coming to the source. While Leon remembered every beating and every abuse he had suffered at the hands of the man before him, he had already privately forgiven those actions.

If he could just seek forgiveness for himself...

"You must know the gift that is available to you, to Laric. Even now, here, in this very cell. He can meet you here. All you have to do is believe in Him. Follow his ways. Ask Him for forgiveness. Then you could–"

"Forgiveness?" Lucien scoffed before chuckling derisively. "Have you not listened to a word I have said? What do I need forgiveness for? I am the one who was slighted! I was betrayed by those whom I trusted. All I am guilty of is exacting the vengeance that was owed to ME!"

The jangle of armor accompanied the sound of footsteps as guards approached with Xiphos. "Is everything alright here, Your Highness?" She quietly questioned.

"She is talking to me. Right, Father? I am supposed to be royalty today!" Laric sang as he rose from his seated position on the floor.

Leon wasn't really sure what he had expected when he initially proposed coming to speak with Lucien. He had received most of the answers he sought, but somehow he still felt defeated by Lucien Rhise's rejection. *I've been rejected by this man my whole life. Why should it bother me now?*

Leon asked himself. Perhaps it was because Leon wasn't actually the one being rejected this time.

"Everything is fine, General. We were just about to leave." He assured her, before turning and beginning to walk away from the men in the cell.

"I do regret one thing, Leon!" Lucien hollered after him, halting his steps. "I regret not ending your life sooner!"

Leon didn't even bother looking back at his father or brother. Instead, he chose to ignore the hatred that spewed from the bitter man's mouth. He comforted himself with the knowledge that he had tried, despite Lucien's abject refusal. Leon shook the proverbial dust from his boots as he left the man who raised him behind. Laric's shrill laughter pierced the air, mocking Leon's failure to open Lucien's eyes to the truth.

"Just ignore him." General Xiphos muttered, as they continued past the cells. The raucous laughter continued, causing Leon to almost miss a high pitched voice calling out two cells down from Laric and Lucien. Hearing it the second time, Leon turned and saw a small goblin waving and shouting, "Hey you!" to get his attention.

The young looking goblin wasn't dressed in naval academy gear, but was instead covered in a ramshackle assortment of rags and clothes, which Leon assumed marked him as one of Lucien's many miners. Long tufts of unkempt black hair sprouted from his head, ears, and eyebrows, which did little to detract from the confusion on his face. The goblin's bulbous nose twitched as he asked, "Oi, you… you the Judge?"

Bemused, Leon couldn't help but stop and nod at the imprisoned goblin. The small, green goblin nodded enthusiastically with Leon and asked in his high pitched voice, "You… you can get us out, right? We… we ain't with that Rhise fella over there no more. Honest!"

Surveying the other prisoners, Leon assessed the men and women who had made up the dreadnought crews. They looked miserable – which was understandable in their given circumstance. Sullen faces and heads hung in defeat were what resulted from their choices to follow the Rhise family. Leon knew that a majority of the miners were probably refugees from the Lost Lands, just trying to support themselves. A few people in naval uniforms, who were housed in a nearby cell, simply stared off into space as the gravity of their decisions crushed their souls.

Leon smiled faintly at the young goblin. “I can’t get any of you out of the prison. I’m sorry.”

The goblin, along with many others, were visibly and audibly disappointed. Leon turned to continue making his way out of prison when the goblin asked, “What about that ‘Adonai’ feller you were talkin’ about over there? Could He get us out?”

An irresistible urge rooted Leon’s feet in place. He knew he couldn’t take another step forward without addressing the goblin’s innocent question. Turning back to the prisoner, the goblin pointed to his head and explained, “I got big ears, see? I heard ya talkin’ about someone called ‘Adonai’ over there. Can he get us outta here?”

An idea began to form in Leon’s head; one that just might help them even their odds in the battle against the horde. But first, he had to tell the prisoners all about Adonai.

Chapter 19: The Dinner

"You want to do WHAT?" King Garinth roared.

Leon and General Xiphos once again stood before the king and princess in the throne room. Galvamancer Exiosa was also present, but remained unobtrusively nearby. A few of the older lords and ladies flitted around the edges of the room, though many of the younger nobles were absent as they had either been conscripted to help build defenses, or had joined in weapons training. Soldiers rushed back and forth as they hurried to their own practice drills, or to check on the defenses. All of the activity meant that plenty of people were present to watch as even more drama unfolded at Leon's feet.

"I thought it might be a good idea to release the dreadnought crews from prison so they could help with our defenses." Leon repeated.

"They were going to help Lucien Rhise overthrow our kingdom! They were going to do it by firing on our own ships and people!" The King growled.

Leon tried to reason with his newfound father, "They were only following orders, which is what all good soldiers do. Tomorrow, they can either hope to live while fighting alongside us, or die trapped in their cells should we lose. Our chance of surviving is much better with the two dreadnoughts supporting our cause! Besides, it is not likely that they would fire on anything but the horde once the fighting begins."

King Garinth clenched his teeth as he seethed, "I have made my decision. I will not have traitors roaming freely, let alone with some of the most powerful vessels we possess at their disposal."

General Xiphos subtly tried to motion for Leon to stop arguing with the king. Leon, however, had never been one to refrain from speaking his mind, so he plowed on, "Better that than both dreadnoughts sitting uselessly on the ground while the rest of us are slaughtered!"

“That is enough!” The King cut Leon’s protestations off with an angered wave of his hand. “The traitorous crews will remain right where they are. We will make do, and the dreadnoughts will be held in reserve as additional cannon defenses for the mountain. I will hear no more of this.” His voice lost its edge as he continued, “I thank you for everything you have done thus far, Leon, and for everything that you will do still. You have turned into a fine leader despite the… uncommon… message you bring. This, however, is still my kingdom, and as such, I will judge the traitors within it. Do you understand me?”

Leon still felt that the king was making the wrong choice, but finally heeded General Xiphos’ unspoken advice and nodded his head. “Perfectly.”

“Wonderful. Now, can anyone tell me the status of our defenses? The day is pressing on and not much time remains. Where is Ciaye?”

“I’ll go and get him, Your Majesty.” General Xiphos volunteered. As she turned to leave the room she cast a hard-eyed stare at Leon, which clearly said *don’t cause any more trouble.* Then, with a swift turn, her metallic steps rang across the stone floor as she made her exit. With no one addressing him directly, and nothing of import occuring, Leon felt the awkwardness of not knowing what to do creep in. The obvious attempt all of the nobles made to not capture his attention only added to his unease. All except for one; she not only caught his gaze, but held it and gave him a small smile and wave.

Leon strode towards the elderly Countess Serena, and her smile broadened at his approach. Dressed in a slim black gown, her silver-grey hair was sculpted into a style that resembled a short bush atop her head. The courtiers who had been hovering around her suddenly recalled other duties which needed their attention, and gave her short bows with whispered excuses before hastily making their exits. By the time Leon reached her, their section of the room had emptied of every other occupant.

“You make them nervous, Your Highness. They do not quite know what to make of you. You are both an oddity, and the talk of the town, as they say.” She inclined her head slightly while Leon respectfully bowed his. The countess had always been cordial to Leon and his siblings during his childhood. Her good nature continued to show forth as she said, “It is good to see you Leon. Thank you for coming to our aid.”

“It is good to see you too, Countess.” Leon’s thoughts traveled to a recent time when she had greatly, though unknowingly, helped him, and he continued, “I must thank you for your excellent choices of employees.” When she reacted to his greeting with a quizzical expression, Leon clarified, “The night of Liara’s engagement to Baron Halomir. Your carriage driver delivered something to me on the road as you left. When, or perhaps if, you see him again, please do thank him for me.”

Countess Serena’s pale eyes brightened. “Oh, you must mean Reginald. Yes, he is quite a good man. He is helping secure the defenses with his new wife and son. They should be in the city below somewhere.”

Leon found himself confused, as his mental calculations did not add up. “A new wife and son! That’s wonderful… but don’t those things normally take longer than a few months?”

“Normally, yes. But Reginald took in and married a widow who had a young son. I believe you may also know them from that day. They left the employ of Rhise manor and found their way into my service. It did not take long for the widow and Reginald to fall in love. Soon thereafter they were wed, and that was that.”

Leon racked his brain in an effort to remember the boy’s name. “Telon!”

“Yes. Smart young man, and eager to learn too. A good combination to be sure.” Her warm, tired eyes were downcast as she continued, “I only wish we could ensure that he will live to see the days that follow tomorrow.”

Her fear was made plain through her trembling voice and arms. Looking about the court, Leon could see the fear that marked many. The undercurrent of it permeated the air, and though the fear washed over and around Leon, it did not enter him. He had learned how useless it was to give in to fear over the past few months; it paralyzed good people into a state of inaction. With the horde due to arrive the following day, fear had found an easy point of access into most minds, and would strive to tear apart any positive morale that had been built from sharing the truth of Adonai.

“I wouldn’t worry, Countess. Everything will be okay. You’ll see at sundown.”

“Sundown?” She questioned, as confusion marked her wrinkled face.

“Yes, in an hour or two from now. Just have faith in Adonai.”

“Your speech was inspiring, Judge, but I am too old to believe in fanciful tales and mystical last minute rescues.”

Leon tried to smile through her dismissal of his beliefs, knowing the light from both the *Esperella* and his armaments would convince at least a few of the skeptics. Hopefully the Countess would be one of them.

Before Leon could respond further, Xiphos and Ciaye entered the throne room. He excused himself from the countess, made his way back towards the royals, and stood near Princess Giselle while Ciaye reported on the day’s progress.

“I was pleasantly surprised, Your Majesty. The populace really stepped up and helped our soldiers create barricades throughout the city. They also managed to form several traps and chokepoints. The city now has multiple defensive hardpoints to wear the undead down, before our men then fall back to their next mark. We have the ability to implement those tactics all the way to the fortress if necessary. We’ve been preparing for this invasion for some time, but the progress that has been made in a single day… I couldn’t ask for anything more.”

King Garinth was among many in the room who released a sigh of relief at the news, but General Xiphos held up a hesitant hand, signaling Ciaye to speak again. “This plan is completely contingent on our ability to maintain air superiority throughout the battle. If the horde overwhelms our airships, then our ground forces will easily be cut off from any chance of escape.”

Leon’s newfound father closed his eyes and clenched his jaw, “If you are about to ask me what I think you are about to ask…”

“We need those dreadnoughts airborne tomorrow, Your Majesty.” General Xiphos stated.

“They are all traitors! Every last one of them!” King Garinth roared.

“And yet, they may be the key to our survival.” Leon opined. “No one is saying you have to make the decision to release them right now. But if we want to be ready, then you need to make it soon.”

“Father, they can no longer betray us, or our kingdom, if we all die tomorrow.” Princess Giselle added.

"Enough!" King Garinth stressed. "I will state, for the final time, that I will hear no more of this. Thank you for the report Ciaye. If we are as prepared as we possibly can be, I ask that you grant any citizens, or soldiers who have families, the evening to rest. We will all need to be at our strongest tomorrow."

Nobles, courtiers, and soldiers alike showed signs of relief and thankfulness to King Garinth, as more than a few filed out of the throne room. Leon couldn't blame them for their rapid departure. Many of them knew this could very well be their last evening alive. As questionable as King Garinth's decision regarding the imprisoned dreadnought crews was, Leon knew this display of mercy was right. When he met his father's eyes, he saw that the tired king's gaze was filled with the weight of all that was to come. At that moment, Leon also knew his decision to dismiss people, and allow them to spend time with their families, was not a decision made for them, but for him. It was his simple attempt to show Leon what good leadership looked like. Perhaps the king's action was good, but to Leon it was just another decision made for the wrong reason.

Maybe his half-sister, the princess, was right. Maybe the king's time to rule had come to an end. Thus far, Leon's personal experience with King Garinth's leadership ability had left much to be desired. Leon had no aspirations to replace his father as king, but it seemed as if the king was determined to make him fill that role. Instead of the deserving Prince Gelan, or the maddened Laric, Leon found himself singled out for the position. He felt unprepared, undeserving, and truly without any desire to fill the honored position of king.

A courtier who had remained behind approached the king, prompting Galvamancer Exiosa to raise a few fingers in response. The courtier froze with his empty, placating hands held aloft. The mancer finally nodded, granting him permission to continue. A few whispered words were spoken, and of all the things Leon could have heard, the words he caught spoke of a small feast to be held. The audacity of hosting such a thing on the evening before a battle baffled him.

Yet, sure enough, the courtier disappeared down a hallway and returned with several other well dressed workers in tow, each helping to carry wooden tables and benches into the throne room. Wood scraped against stone as the well crafted tables were arranged in a circular formation, before the throne. Fine quality earthenware settings were carefully arranged once the table placement was finished. Leon watched the preparations unfold, mesmerized by the bustle of the workers. They flit about the conversing courtiers, who either ignored, or were oblivious to, their presence. Occasionally, a cup or goblet was claimed from the table, and that noble would hold it out for a worker to fill with whatever request they had whispered.

Looking back on his time in the service, and the months since then, Leon couldn't think of an occasion where such opulence and class differentiation had been so openly displayed. The last recollection he had of such behavior was from when he still lived at Rhise Manor. He wasn't sure at what point his conviction struck him, but he stopped a nearby worker who stared wide-eyed at him as he asked, "Any way that I can help?"

A few low chuckles from nearby nobles accompanied the worker's confounded look. He shook his head vigorously before stating, "No, Your Highness, we-we are almost done. Thank you for the offer, but it is–"

"Not your place." King Garinth finished from behind Leon, as he clasped Leon's shoulder. The worker gave a short bow and quickly exited. King Garinth leaned in and whispered low in Leon's ear, "You are royalty now, son. You have a lot to learn should we live beyond tomorrow."

Unease stirred within Leon as he replied, "I have a lot to teach, too."

When the tables were finished being set, the workers moved along the edges of the room replacing torches that had burnt out or low. Their light was a welcome addition, as the holes in the ceiling that had provided sunlight were bereft of their glow. Sundown was approaching, and Leon knew that those who hadn't seen the aeonyte glow would be in for a treat. Once all of the torches were replaced, a majority of the workers exited down one of the halls. Meanwhile, some new arrivals began to file in through the main entrance.

The small forms of Magnus and Gionna entered arm in arm, and Leon noticed Gionna's metallic cane had been returned. Magnus wore his archivist robe, with his sash signifying his leadership, and Gionna's many-pocketed leathers appeared to have been recently cleaned. They beelined toward Leon and King Garinth and bowed. The King asked Magnus, "I hope you found your personnel and the new archives well, Master Magnus."

"I did, Your Majesty. Xieth led them in my absence, and she did a good job of it too." Magnus replied.

Leon couldn't contain the burning question he had from watching their behavior towards each other the past few days. "Are my eyes deceiving me, or are you two back together again?"

"Your eyes are fine, dearie. I mean, Your Highness." Gionna corrected herself. "Over the past few days we have had time to hash out our differences. We realized that our hearts have kept bringing us back to each other over the years. Despite our shortcomings, I think we are willing to give it another go."

Magnus smoothed the front of his robe. "She saved my life recently, Your Majesty. Such a thing gives a man perspective."

"It certainly does. I hope your relationship flourishes for the rest of your years." King Garinth smiled warmly as he nodded to them. The two gnomes gave a respectful bow in return, and found their nearby place settings as another of Leon's friends entered.

Princess Schalae strode into the chamber with purpose; her dark bark armor was still on, and she was dressed for battle. Her braided green hair provided the only color to her outfit, and its shade matched the clothing of those who walked in behind her. Leon's mother and sister were both resplendent in their dark green gowns, both of which were reminiscent of the dress Liara had worn during her engagement party. Their gowns shimmered in the torchlight as they turned to look back at where they had entered. Kelleren weaved between them all and let out a bark that caused a slight echo in the open chamber. The sudden sound made several of the nobles look at Miala's companion. While they all focused on the happy, golden haired dog, Leon's gaze traveled a little further behind him, where it locked on Miala.

Leon's heart began to pound a little harder in his chest as he took in the fact that Miala Mytheriyan had traded her mancer robe for something much more feminine. A red satin dress showcased her bare arms and shoulders.

Her crimson hair had been lightly curled at its ends and styled to perfectly frame her face. Her eyes looked about the room, as if searching for something. Or someone.

She was the first, within the group of ladies who had entered, to spot Leon and start walking toward him. The closer Miala came, the more Leon was convinced that she was the most beautiful woman in the room, or perhaps the world. Her green eyes held a mischievous light as she approached him, but he had a hard time keeping his gaze focused on them due to the way her dress swished as she walked. Mesmerized, Leon could do nothing but stare as she sidled up to him and asked with a newfound confidence in her voice, "So… What do you think?"

Leon was speechless. "I–You…You're…Wow…"

His reaction seemed to be exactly what she was looking for. Miala smiled as she held his hand. "Cute." She responded.

Leon turned to introduce her to King Garinth, but it looked as if he had also been entranced by a lady who was also walking towards them. Lady Erika was trailed by Leon's sister, Liara, and Princess Schalae. Knowing smiles adorned their lovely faces, and they curtseyed to King Garinth who had remained next to Leon. The King proved more eloquent than Leon, and Leon's mother took all of his small pleasantries in stride.

Their back and forth gave Liara an opportunity to critique Leon. "You did not change into something more formal?"

"I didn't realize I needed to." Leon admitted.

"Neither did I. Although, it does not matter as I do not have anything else to wear." Schalae added.

Liara discreetly rolled her eyes and addressed Miala, "Did he like the dress we picked out?"

"I think we broke him." Miala laughed as she hid a smile behind her hand.

"I'm right here, you know." Leon advised.

"Why, yes. Yes, you are." Liara needled.

Miala's attention was suddenly pulled away. With a quick, "Excuse me for a moment," she headed over to talk to Galvamancer Exiosa. They spoke in halted, hushed whispers while a boisterous shout came from the room's entrance.

Duamé had also changed outfits, and was dressed in a deep blue silk shirt and pants. The sleeves of his shirt were rolled up, revealing his dark skin and well defined arm muscles. He sauntered over to their group and exclaimed, "If only me ma an' pa could see me now. Ya will never believe wot happened out there. Remember tha smithy couple? Girard an' Josephine?"

"The royal smiths you taught the dwarven forging techniques to?" Leon asked.

The dwarf nodded and chortled, "Yep! They made it here safely an' set up shop already. Been takin' over every smithy in wot's left o' tha kingdom. They bought out me share o' tha business today. Told me I can collect me earnings after tha battle tomorrow."

Awestruck by the dwarf's good fortune, Leon offered his heartfelt congratulations. In the time they had known each other, Duamé had gone from a dwarf who had lost everything he cared about, to building a new life and career for himself from the ashes. He couldn't be more happy for his friend who was currently engaged in greeting King Garinth.

"So you are the fellow we have to thank for Strongarm Smithy's production!" The King exclaimed joyously. "I must confess that without your guidance, I daresay we would not have had enough ammunition nor supplies to make our stand here tomorrow. Your position and fortune are both well earned, Mister Onyxwill. Xaelon cannot thank you enough." Garinth shook the beaming dwarf's hand, and Leon watched as the bridges that were once thought burned with Masterwork Halls were rebuilt right before his eyes.

The aroma of roasted meat and potatoes wafted through the air, prompting those who were in attendance to sit for the meal. Most of Leon's friends sat near him on one side of the table, though Miala occupied the seat directly next to him. Across the table sat Duamé and Leon's family. They all stared at him as he maneuvered Revelator and his shield off of his back harness, and propped them at his seat. "We do have an armory where you can store those, you know." General Ciaye stated, as he arched a brow at him from a few seats down.

"I would prefer to not part with these particular items. But thank you for the offer." Leon replied.

The workers brought trays of food around the table, and Miala waited for them to depart before she leaned in to whisper, "Exiosa claims she didn't know about the Dark Room, and Kelleren thinks she is secretly glad that the Academy has fallen."

Leon's joy at Miala's closeness to him turned sour as she gave him the barest of nods. Galvamancer Exiosa sat nearby, close to Princess Giselle and the king. She dug into her food with a set of wooden utensils, as opposed to everyone else's metal knives and forks. She constantly surveyed the room for threats as she vigorously sawed at her steak.

While he ate, Leon tried to think of ways to see if the silent but powerful mancer would open up a little. Raising his voice slightly, Leon asked, "Miss Exiosa, I know that tradition dictates you guard the royal family, but will you be joining the fighting tomorrow? You would be a great asset to our defense."

The short haired woman took the time to thoughtfully chew on a bite of her food before her gravelly, feminine voice responded, "I go where I am ordered."

Emirah looked to the king with a hopeful expression as he cleared his throat. "We will see what tomorrow holds." King Garinth stated. It was clearly an issue that the king didn't want to deal with at the moment, instead resuming his conversation with Leon's mother and Princess Giselle. The galvamancer tilted her head at Leon with a lopsided smile, as if to say that she had expected that answer. Leon didn't feel as if he learned anything from their short exchange, so trying again, he asked, "What made you decide to serve the king?"

"Necessity." She replied tersely. As Leon continued to look at her, the galvamancer must have realized that her answer wasn't satisfactory. She explained, "My talents were not wanted once I graduated from the Academy. I was told my power was too volatile. Uncontrollable. In my wanderings after leaving the Academy, I happened to be in the right place, at the right time, and saved his majesty from an assassin. My overzealousness in electrocuting the would be king-killer turned out to be a great deterrent for any future assassination attempts. So, I was hired on the spot."

King Garinth's eyes bulged at the mention of electrocution, and he jumped from his conversation to Leon and Emirah's. "And of course we are continually glad and thankful for your protections, Miss Exiosa. The next king will surely need them when the dust settles after the battle."

His words were quite telling, and Leon's eyes met Princess Giselle's as she imperceptibly shook her head. Quite innocuously, King Garinth had effectively announced his intentions to have Leon succeed him. Not even a full day after their relationship had been revealed, his fate had suddenly been decided. The prospect of leading the entire kingdom weighed heavily on Leon, causing him to send a panicked glance at his friends to see if they had picked up on what he heard.

Duamé stared at Leon for a moment, then shifted his food to one side of his mouth and said, "Oi, ya mean Leon? King? Only if ya want tha whole economy o' tha kingdom ta collapse."

The clink of silverware against plates ceased, and all general conversation fell silent as everyone, including King Garinth, turned their attention to the dwarf. "Whatever do you mean by that, Master Onyxwill?" King Garinth asked.

Duamé pointed at Leon with his fork, "Beggin' yer pardon, Yer Majesty. It's just that 'Meat Shield' over here doesn't really have a head fer negotiatin' when it comes ta money. We've been tryin' ta teach him, but Leon jus' wants ta pay askin' price fer everything."

"I blame his sheltered upbringing, and his subsequent stint in the airship navy, where he really didn't have to pay for anything. I firmly predict he would crash the Agapryan economy irreparably." Gionna piped from nearby.

The king's eyes widened in alarm as he looked between Leon and Duamé. "Truly?"

"What is so bad about giving people the payment they want? They set the price there for a reason." Leon explained, genuinely confused.

Princess Giselle tittered in a fit of giggles nearby, and if the king's eyes had been wide before, they were now bulging. "Is… is he serious? Surely this is some jest."

Leon would have been offended if he hadn't understood that Duamé was creating a reason for him to not be crowned. He would have even pushed the matter further had a soldier not burst into the room, heading straight for Generals Xiphos and Ciaye who were seated next to each other. Leon watched the hushed exchange until Ciaye exclaimed, "It's doing what now?"

"It's a perfectly natural effect of the aeonyte. Quite beautiful, actually." Xiphos commented.

"What is going on?" King Garinth asked.

"Thank you, soldier. Resume your post please." Ciaye advised the messenger. "It seems, Your Majesty, that the Judge's ship is causing a bit of a stir within the fortress and the city. It began… glowing a few minutes ago."

"It what?" The King asked as he stood. The scrape of multiple benches against the floor followed, as most of the court stood with the king out of respect. "What is going on now?"

"Sundown is when aeonyte starts to shine when under the right circumstances, Your Majesty." Leon clarified as he also rose from his seat. He grabbed his shield and Revelator, causing the aeonyte elements within both of them to give off a pale glow. Startled exclamations accompanied the radiance of his armaments, and Leon held the items up for those around him to see. "I've found that the glow of aeonyte reacts to the faith that one has in Adonai. As I said before, the metal turns the undead, giant, and draconic flesh it comes in contact with to salt. But the most visually impressive attribute of aeonyte is its light."

Leon watched the king as he stared at the glow coming from Leon's armaments. Numerous nearby nods from Leon's cohorts affirmed his words, and the wonder of the glowing weapons was conveyed when Princess Giselle breathed, "They are lovely. But, what is that symbol in the spearhead and on your armor? What does it signify?"

Magnus, who had remained mostly silent, piped in with exuberance. "Ah, um, it is the symbol of the Judge's mark, Your Highness! I can assure you that this young gentleman, Leon, is the real thing!" He launched into an abridged version of his meeting Leon at the Archives, and connecting the symbol with the Judge's section of the Archives. The place Rohiel had called the Sanctuary.

Leon capped off the gnome's explanation with an offer, pointing to the spearhead and the symbol etched into it. "Revelator itself has a few other attributes and powers I've seen, but the *Esperella* is quite beautiful when glowing at night. You are all welcome to see it."

Heartily agreeing to the idea, King Garinth, held out an arm for Giselle as he stood. The two royals left the dinner table, and the remainder of Leon's family followed with Emirah in tow. Those who wanted to see the shining airship with the king either immediately joined in a group behind him, or scarfed down as much food as they could, and caught up. Leon and his friends led the way outside of Last Bastion's ziggurat. Close to the structure's entrance, in an open courtyard, were parked the two dreadnought vessels. Next to them, towards the edge of the plateau, sat the *Esperella* – shining for all the world to see. From their current proximity, Leon could see a crowd of soldiers huddled around the ship. They chatted among themselves while Leon and the royal group walked closer. The א symbol near the aft of the ship also shone brightly, and Leon enjoyed seeing his true father's reaction to the metal's glow.

"What do you think?" Leon asked those around him.

"It is breathtaking." King Garinth agreed somberly.

"What is that clanging sound?" Princess Giselle asked.

The faint klink of metal against metal could be heard in the air, prompting Duamé to sputter, "Rust!" before clambering up the ship's gangplank. A few moments later, both he and Kérik were walking back down, and Duamé carried his two handed maul over his shoulder. The hammerhead was glowing, though very faintly when compared to Revelator.

"I was only finishin' wot repairs I could, boyo." Kérik muttered to Duamé, as they walked back.

“Ain’t no trouble. As long as she knocks tha dents out.” Duamé replied, “Normally I’d tell ya ta never touch another dwarf’s tools, but I was busy.”

“Admiral Silverspine. We missed you at dinner.” Princess Giselle smiled warmly.

“Beggin’ yer pardon lass, but I had some last minute work ta do on tha ship.” Kérik lamented before he turned to Leon. “The turrets an’ cannons are stocked, set, and ready fer tomorrow.”

“Turrets?” King Garinth asked.

Gionna’s eyes lit up almost as brightly as the aeonyte. “A recent invention, Your Majesty.”

“Care to take a tour aboard the ship, Your Majesty?” Leon offered.

The glow that came from the *Esperella*, Revelator, his shield, and Duamé’s hammer allowed Leon to clearly see the interest on the king’s face, which was mirrored in the faces of the few others who had not yet been on board.

“I thought you would never ask.”

Chapter 20: The Transformation

After a thorough tour of the *Esperella*, everyone present was dismissed to rest before the upcoming battle. Though the other nobles and royals left, Leon insisted that he remain with the ship. His mother and sister accepted the offered guest rooms located in Last Bastion, but Leon knew he wouldn't be comfortable in unfamiliar surroundings the night before a battle. Miala and Duamé also stayed on the ship, while some of the others, such as Magnus and Gionna, departed for lodgings located in the fortress or the city. Leon couldn't hold their departures against them, some people were just not built for resting well on a warship.

As Leon lay in his hammock, he took one last look around the sleeping area and counted too many unoccupied hammocks. Too many warriors and friends had been lost in their recent skirmishes, and Leon hoped those who remained would be enough. He closed his eyes, resigned in the knowledge that their current numbers would have to suffice.

Leon was surprised to once again find himself in the grey dreamscape as soon as he drifted off to sleep. The absence of his angelic advisors had weighed heavily on him over the last few days, and he felt as if his whole life had been upended since they had last spoken. Leon found himself somehow dressed in his armor, and the scale-mail faintly reflected the light that shone from above. Although the massive sphere of light radiated warmth and light overhead, a small rolling mist had settled around his feet. Neither Rohiel and Lochemetel were visible, but Leon knew they could hear him.

Why else would I be here?

"Why didn't either of you tell me about my real father?" Leon yelled into the seemingly empty expanse. "Come on out Rohiel! Lochemetel! Where are you guys?"

A crash of metal hit the floor behind Leon, causing him to spin around and see Lochemetel as she collapsed to one knee in her aeonyte armor. The glow from her hidden facial features was more muted than normal, and her golden eyes pierced right through him. The look was an unspoken plea for help – probably for the heavily armored individual who hung on her arm and collapsed with her.

Rohiel.

His aeonyte plate armor was rent with jagged holes in various places, and his bulky form was unmoving. Leon ran to them. He quickly helped Lochemetel lower Rohiel to the floor, before his unsupported weight could make her drop him and collapse. Rohiel was heavier than he looked, and the thin layer of mist parted around where he laid on the grey floor. The light that emanated from his face was also dim, but still managed to hide his facial features. A small echoing groan escaped from Rohiel's hidden lips, providing the only indication that the angel still lived.

"What happened?" Leon demanded, his previously asked question still unanswered, but no longer at the forefront of his mind.

"Judge, summon Revelator! Quickly!"

The desperation in Lochemetel's voice caused him to falter for a moment before he gathered himself enough to hold out his hand in the dreamscape. Focusing his will, Revelator suddenly appeared in his hand, and he brought the spear above Rohiel. Leon expected Revelator to shine and hum as it had when it healed Miala. The aeonyte blade, however, did not change from its telltale light blue color until Lochemetel grasped the shaft of the spear with him. A blinding flash accompanied the hummed chord, which seemed to vibrate the very air around them. The glowing sphere above exploded in a wave of light that washed over each of them, and a rainbow of color infused both the spearhead and the rents in Rohiel's armor. As the light poured over the angel and his wounds, Leon heard Rohiel whisper:

"Heal me, O LORD, and I shall be healed; Save me, and I shall be saved, For You are my praise."

The multicolored light lingered like a residue over Rohiel's armor, and the glow that emanated from both his and Lochemetel's faces grew brighter. Their voices repeated the prayer of healing together, in harmony with the chord that resonated from Revelator. Leon thought it was perhaps the most beautiful sound he had ever heard. As soon as Leon memorized their words he joined in the chorus of praise, and the lingering rainbow residue that covered Rohiel hardened. The hue and the sound from Revelator then faded, leaving the unblemished form of Rohiel laying on the ground.

It took the combined efforts of both Lochemetel and Leon to help hoist Rohiel onto his feet. The angel's grip was firm, even though he had lay grievously wounded only moments before. It appeared to Leon as if Rohiel had never been injured at all. Lochemetel placed her gauntleted hand on her counterpart's shoulder in a comforting gesture. Stepping back, Leon saw the unspoken camaraderie between beings who had lived and fought with each other for thousands of years. He didn't want to intrude on their moment, but broke their silence out of concern for his friend.

"Are you okay, Rohiel? What happened?"

"The prince."

Whatever Leon had thought Roheil might say, he hadn't expected something so cryptic. "Prince?"

"The descendant of Xhormas delayed us. The dark prince." Lochemetel explained further.

Leon became even more confused, until the answer finally dawned on him. "Wait, Silas? He's… He's dead though!"

Rohiel's voice was patient, teaching him like always. ***"Silas Anakim is a Nephilim. His spirit endured after his physical death. He rallied many Mazzikin, and waged battle against us and Adonai's forces for days. Have you not felt it?"***

Memories of his recent unease, and the vision he had seen of the Malakim and Mazzikin engaged in fierce battle over Agaprya, all came rushing back. In a war that had lasted many times longer than the Dead Wars, it stood to reason that the fierce fighting would continue in the unseen realm all around them. Could that unseen war somehow be linked to the discomfort Leon had been feeling?

"Where is Silas' spirit now? Did you kill him?"

"The dark prince escaped in the fray before we could deliver the final blow. We know not to where." Lochemetel said.

"He just… disappeared in the middle of a battle?" Leon couldn't believe it.

"Rohiel threw himself into the fray to protect the rest of us from the dark prince's fury. After Silas Anakim injured him the Mazzikin rushed us."

"Why would you do that Rohiel?" Leon lamented his concern for his teacher. "What made you take such a risk? Why would you take on Silas and his Mazzikin alone?"

Rohiel grunted before responding, ***"There is no greater love than this, Judge: that one should lay down his life for his friends."***

Lochemetel explained, ***"His spirit ran off while we were dispersing the Mazzikin cloud and rallying to Rohiel. Whether his departure was due to cowardice or conniving, I am certain we have not seen the last of the dark prince."***

Leon couldn't shake Lochmetel's ominous words. He agreed with the warrior's assumption that the struggle against Silas wasn't over. The man had worked towards his revenge for as long as Leon had been alive. Possibly before that, too. Leon had no idea how long Silas had been contained in his coffin-like prison, or what he had done to end up there. All he knew is that even after Silas' physical death, his spirit was still causing mayhem. Leon currently had no idea how to stop him, but there were many other things to contend with at the moment. After all, in the morning they would be going to war.

"Judge Leon," Rohiel interrupted Leon's thoughts, ***"you have a question. Ask."***

Leon had come into the dream with just one question, but had put it aside for obvious reasons. Not wanting to beat around the boulder any longer, the question that had burned and festered within him poured from his lips before he could stop it.

"Why? Why didn't either of you tell me who I really was? Did you know that Lucien Rhise wasn't my father?"

A long pause permeated the dreamscape when the two angels didn't say anything in response. Leon felt their stares, and the compassion that radiated from them through their light. He was beginning to think that the angels simply wouldn't answer him, until Rohiel heaved a heavy sigh.

"There is a difference between knowledge and wisdom, Leon."

"Are you telling me you didn't know?" Leon asked, indignation rising within him as his eyes grew wet and his vision began to blur. "Are you saying you never knew the cause of what I endured throughout my entire life? That nobody but Adonai knew? That through this entire journey you couldn't have told me that I had… killed my own brother?"

Even in a dream, Leon could feel the depth of his heartbreak. The weight of his actions had been lifted from him once before. Now it came crashing back down on him, threatening to crush him. Leon collapsed to his knees as he started to cry, unable to quench his wracking sobs. He no longer questioned if it was acceptable for him to cry in front of his angelic teachers. Roheil already knew all of the hurt and sorrow that had filled his life. It had been replayed for him on the first day they met.

The shuffle of feet and the clink of armor was Leon's only indication that Rohiel had knelt with him. A gauntleted hand clasped his shoulder and another sigh was released, this time close enough to send a slight gust of breath against his tear stained face.

"We knew of your heritage, Leon. Your parentage. And I tell you truly, that you are every bit as much a son of Adonai as you are the son of the king. Your life has been a struggle, yes. Because all have struggled and fallen short. But, as a fire can refine and make metal stronger, so the struggles of your life can strengthen you for what will be needed ahead. It is easy to be consumed by the evil of this world when you have not been tempered to stand against it. An arrogant noble youth could not have driven back the darkness as you have. But a refined young man, purified through his trials, is someone whom Adonai can use. Your life has been full of pain, yes. That pain prepared you for what you have faced. What you will yet face."

The words all made sense to Leon, and he could see Roheil's reasoning, yet they did not completely remove the sting of his past. Lochemetel then added her own wisdom to Roheil's.

"One cannot become a warrior without training. One cannot face darkness without light on their side. Adonai has given you a purpose, and a promise. His promise is of a day to come when there will be no more strife. When His everlasting Kingdom will be full of those who share your tenets. Love. Joy. Peace. Patience. Kindness. Goodness. Faithfulness. Gentleness. Self-Control."

Through his sorrow, Leon felt the weight of his life's struggles begin to once again melt away. He repeated the tenets of his faith over and over in his mind, seeking to replace his memories of pain and suffering as a youth with them. Over and over, Leon sowed words of life into himself. As he focused on Adonai's truth, another wave of light pulsed and washed over him. In the midst of his prayer for guidance and wisdom, Rohiel murmured, ***"Rise, Judge."***

Rohiel hoisted Leon to his feet with one hand as he said, ***"Thank you for helping to heal me. I know Adonai would want me to give you a gift in turn."***

"A… gift?" Leon repeated.

A strange fluttering sensation built in Leon's chest as Rohiel placed his other hand against the Judge's mark that adorned the center plate of his scale-mail armor. The symbol itself did not change, but the metal around it began to corrode and age right before Leon's eyes. The steel changed color, pitted, and flecked; the effect spread until a green and then brown sheen of rusted armor covered his entire body. Leon didn't dare move, lest the armor Duamé made him would groan and fall apart.

"Wh-why did you–"

"Let the old pass away, and the new come!"

Rohiel slapped his palm against the chestpiece again, and the rusted armor flashed. A wave of multicolored light spread from the Judge's mark, flowing all around him as it shifted and resolved into a new scale-mail armor. It was built identically to the prior suit, save one difference: each scale and plate was now light blue. The suit of armor was both lighter and stronger now that it was made of aeonyte.

When the transformation was finished, Leon marveled at the results. More than the external change though, was the shift he felt internally. His sorrows that stemmed from his prior life were gone, in their place sat a steely determination. He now had a drive to not wallow in the regrets of his past, but to instead focus on living his new life.

"Thank you, Rohiel. It's… beautiful. But…"

"But what?"

"What will my armor be when I wake up?"

A hearty rich laugh came from Rohiel, and Lochemetel spoke once more. ***"Who is to say that you are not already, finally, awake?"***

✦✦✦✦✦

When Leon awoke, he immediately fell out of his hammock and checked on his armor. He couldn't help but be surprised when he saw the change that had occurred in the dreamscape also appeared in real life. Through his awe, Leon began to don his armor for the momentous day. The aeonyte scales certainly felt similar to their previous counterparts, though they were much lighter. The creases and minor damage that the previous armor had suffered were gone, and as Leon's head came through the opening in his chest armor, he was greeted by Duamé, Miala, and Kelleren's slack-jawed stares.

"Flint an' feldspar, wot did ya DO?" Duamé cried.

"I didn't do anything. It was Rohiel."

Leon explained his dream while he finished putting on the rest of his scale-mail. Duamé fretted and fussed over each scale in detail, and Miala attempted to hide her amusement over his reaction behind her hand. Kelleren wagged his tail and barked at Miala, but she waved him off dismissively. "I'll help you into your doggie armor later, Kelleren."

"Well?" Leon asked the dwarf.

"I cannot figure out how he did it! Transmutin' metal? Turnin' it inta rust first? Some sort o' geomancy I suppose."

"You know, we could just chalk it up to a miracle and leave it at that." Miala commented while she blatantly looked Leon up and down. "A good looking miracle at that."

Leon felt a flush creep up his protected neck as he replied, "Well, um… you look nice in your new… robe."

"Alright, lovebirds," Duamé commented, "Let's get through today first, then ya can ogle each other all ya want."

"Oh, whatever! How're things going with Gérda?" Miala shot back.

Duamé rolled his eyes, "We're gettin' through today, then we'll ogle at each other later too."

They all laughed while Leon finished strapping himself into the scale-mail. The silence that followed was slightly awkward, as the unspoken side of their conversation was a weighty one. After the upcoming battle only some, or perhaps none, of them might be alive. Kelleren whined softly, giving voice to their silent concerns. Leon impulsively grasped both Duamé's and Miala's shoulders as they huddled in a tight circle. Even Kelleren nuzzled his way into their small ring.

"It will be okay. We can do this. We can beat them." Leon stated.

"Yeah we can." Miala joined in.

"Woof."

"Is this yer idea o' a pep talk?"

A small chuckle came from each of them as their huddle turned into a hug. As they disengaged, a couple dwarves and an elven mancer passed by, giving them respectful nods and greetings. Their eyes all lingered on Leon's armor as they passed, and Duamé chortled, "Pretty soon, everyone's gonna want one."

"He has a point." Miala chided.

"No, HE has a point." Duamé thumbed at Leon while he lifted his aeonyte plated maul. "I have more of a bashin' implement."

The joke prompted more chuckles, and Leon's friends hugged him one more time before they turned and followed the other crew members up the stairs. On the next landing, Leon watched as the gun-deck crew scrambled about the cannons on either side. Muscular dwarves heaved cannonballs about, and checked the munitions crates. Continuing on his way through the *Esperella*, Leon stood in a line that weaved through the galley and up to the top deck. Crew members patiently waited to receive a light breakfast and a mug of water or java before the day's events unfolded.

Leon graciously accepted the small roll of bread and dark liquid that was handed to him. The roll was plenty, as he never felt the need for large meals before a battle, and the java helped prevent his tired eyes from shutting. Leon watched Gérda and the three mancer children diligently working in the kitchen, to keep up with the crew that passed by. Leon met their inquisitive eyes as he shuffled past, and asked Gérda, "What… What are you all doing here? The city–"

"It's not half as safe out there as this flyin' metal tub. Plus, tha kiddos insisted." She gestured wildly to the quiet children. Her blond braids flew as she turned to point at the orcish teen, Sam. "Although ya are most definitely NOT fighting in tha battle!"

"I agreed, didn't I?" Sam moaned, as he rolled his eyes and vigorously went back to washing cups. Brigid's icy stare at Leon would have given him the creeps, had it not been for the even creepier vacant stare Tyne directed his way, which caught him completely off guard. Leon knelt down to the gnome child's level, and asked, "Are you okay?"

The gnome's eyes seemed to pierce right through him, as the child repeated words spoken to Leon only a few days earlier. "He is coming."

Brigid cast a weirded out look at the boy, as she broke her silence. "Who?"

"Xh-Xhormas. He is coming." Tyne replied.

Leon finally drew a conclusion based on the behavior he observed from the gnome. "You… You're a chronomancer, aren't you, Tyne? You can see the future?"

"We needed to be on the ship." Tyne stated, answering the question without even acknowledging it. The young gnome nodded his head to no one in particular, then turned to walk into the ship's larder beyond the galley. Leon and Gérda watched the young gnome go, as the dwarven maiden commented, "He was most insistent on us bein' here. Guess he has his reasons, but don't go gettin' us inta more trouble than we need ta be. Ya hear me, Judge?"

"Yes ma'am." Leon rose from his crouched position and munched on his bread roll, dismissing himself from the galley and heading up to the main deck. The morning sun broke through the few mountains that remained in the east, and illuminated the predominantly overcast sky. Clouds churned overhead, and Leon wondered if they would end up having to fight in the rain.

Airships of all sizes and shapes crowded the skies around them, but mostly they were a mixture of the smaller transport ships and mail carriers. Leon counted only four attack ships hovering in the air, and the two dreadnoughts still rested on the plateau. The glint of the rising sun off of numerous vessels' levigems caused Leon to squint and redirect his eyes to where he was walking.

Elves were stringing their bows and adjusting the quivers strapped to their backs, hips, or legs. Princess Schalae looked to be helping Miala outfit Kelleren in the wooden bark armor he had received back in the Northern Elvenwood. A contingent of dwarves passed behind them, making their way towards the *Esperella's* bow with their axes and hand crossbows. Their short husky frames jingled from their chainmail and hooks to latch themselves onto the ship. Lightly armored mancers headed to their turrets, looking out from the ship at the sights all around them.

Leon felt the slight shift under his feet as the *Esperella* slowly rose from its resting place on the plateau. The movement caused him to glance back and move towards the aft of the ship, where Duamé stood talking with Olivia at one of the crossbow turrets. It was her turn at the helm, but instead of her manning the wheel, Kérik was there. Leon had thought the dwarven admiral would survey the battle from Last Bastion, not that he would remain on the warship – much less that he would pilot it during the battle. As Leon weaved through the warriors who were preparing themselves on deck, he drew close enough to Kérik to ask, "What are you doing here, Sir?"

"I prefer ta be in tha thick o' tha battle, an' I piloted this girl through Agaprya, so I might as well do it here too. So here I- what happened ta yer armor?" Kérik asked as one of his bushy eyebrows rose into the tufted mane of his white hair.

"It's… a long story, Sir." Leon replied as Kérik gently turned the vessel, giving them a good look at a large dust cloud in the distance. "Has the enemy been sighted?"

"Should be here within tha hour. Scouts came back an' reported. Nine attack ships, a couple transports, an' a dozen mail carriers controlled by tha horde. They got a lot o' gryphons an' dragons as well, but that pretty much covers their aerial forces. Should be interestin'." Kérik replied, as Olivia pulled a spyglass from her leather harness and handed it to Leon.

Peering through, he saw that the dust cloud was dotted with several small shadows that were still too far away to make out. Thanks to their high vantage point, Leon could see the multitudes of undead horde approaching on the ground. It was like a dark stain upon the earth itself, rapidly approaching to end all remaining life at Last Bastion.

Handing the spyglass back to Olivia, Leon saw a mail carrier rise above the railing near the aft of the ship. The pilot of the small craft maneuvered it to be adjacent to the *Esperella*, and he saw that Generals Xiphos and Ciaye were both aboard. They hailed their greetings towards everyone on deck before General Ciaye spoke up.

"I'm glad we caught you all before the battle started. There have been a few developments." Ciaye scratched at his beard and turned to address Leon. "Your family is taking shelter with King Garinth, at his request. They send their good wishes, and between the guard stationed at the Bastion, and Galvamancer Exiosa, they will be well protected."

Leon couldn't think of a better place for his family to be, and gave a silent thanks and prayer to Adonai for their continued safety. "Thank you for telling me." Leon nodded.

Ciaye held up a hand, "You should also be aware that after the report detailing the enemy's numbers, King Garinth has made an official decree offering a full pardon to any of the dreadnought crew that wish to fight against the undead for our survival."

Leon's heart leaped up into his throat as his spirits lifted. "Truly?"

Xiphos joined in the conversation. "The truth of the matter is, we are already outnumbered, and we need the dreadnoughts as airships rather than additional defensive points for the Bastion. The offer is being made presently, and whomever answers will be suitably equipped and rushed to the ships. Both Laric and Lucien Rhise are excluded from the pardon, of course."

Leon stepped to the railing to look down upon the two parked dreadnoughts outside the fortress. Soldiers carrying supplies were hastily being brought onto the ships. With their firepower, the *Esperella* and other airships stood a much better chance of bringing down the undead's aerial forces. Shifting his focus to the mountain itself, he saw that its many protruding fortifications were all equipped with soldiers preparing cannons or ballistae.

General Ciaye's attention turned to Kérik as he asked, "Admiral, will you be overseeing the battle with us?"

Kérik shook his head. "No lad, me place is here in tha thick o' it."

The generals' objective now complete, they bade them farewell, and their mail carrier zoomed away. Leon's thoughts turned to others who were missing. "Where is Gionna? Magnus?"

Miala walked up to stand alongside him at the railing, and pointed. "She told me yesterday that she was going to help Magnus organize and lead the archivists who came from Agaprya as they establish their new facility. They are helping with the city's defenses, and I believe Lorog was assigned to guard them."

Leon knew the crescent shaped city that hugged the gorge at the base of the mountain had several defensive chokepoints and structures woven throughout it. His eyes followed where her finger pointed, and he saw a conical tower near one of the many chokepoints. It appeared to have its own short wall around three sides of it, and the cliff's edge along the fourth. The structure had terraces on many of its levels, and from Leon's vantage point he could faintly make out several robed individuals flitting about its exterior. Hopefully Gionna, Magnus, and Lorog would be safe there.

The voice of his father, King Garinth, filled the air as he spoke through the behemoth's horn. "Fight for your lives, your families, and your kingdom! For on this day, we end the Dead Wars! On this day, we crush the horde!"

As before every battle, Leon felt his adrenaline surge as his heart began to rapidly pump the blood through his veins. The king spoke rousing words of inspiration and glory, while more and more people exited the ziggurat and headed towards the two parked dreadnoughts. Leon saw many of the prisoners, as well as a few soldiers who escorted them, file into the massive ships. As the *Esperella* hovered near the plateau's edge, a slight breeze caressed Leon's face and swept his short dark hair back. Leon ran his hand through it, and scratched at the stubble that had formed along his jaw as he surveyed the freed prisoners. He was glad to see that the goblin he had spoken to in the cells hurried towards one of the dreadnoughts.

"–A new future is upon us! A hope and a future that will be assured once we get through this last remaining struggle." King Garinth continued.

A deep, sonorous horn sounded three times from nearby; it was the universal sign for an undead horde attacking. Leon looked towards the bow of his ship, and saw the massive horde had become much closer. Their aerial forces pulled ahead of the ground forces that followed below. The two bulky dreadnoughts rose alongside the *Esperella*, and Xaelon's airship navy spread out to meet the oncoming attack. Leon exhaled slowly in an attempt to calm his nerves before the battle commenced. This conflict would determine all of their fates. As Leon unsheathed Revelator and his shield, his father uttered the final words of his speech.

"So let us rise, children of Xaelon! Rise to overcome this challenge! Rise and fight!"

Chapter 21: The Battle

Now that they were closer, Leon could see much larger figures leading the horde's advancing ground forces. Numerous Nephilim giants, their stature at least three times the height of a man, made up the advance force of the undead army. Their bronze armor glinted in the sunlight and caused Leon to shift his gaze up to the aerial undead. Above and ahead of the giants, multiple dragons winged their way through the air, accelerating towards the city. While none were as large as the horde's former draconic leader, Nachash Seraph, the flying lizards were large enough to pose a threat to any airship.

Leon once again borrowed Ophelia's spyglass to take a closer look and confirm his suspicions. The dragons flew close to the ground, while the captured airships and gryphons remained above them to provide cover. Though they would be upon the city within minutes, what concerned Leon the most was not the dragons themselves, but what they carried in their huge claws. Their enemy was using the same tactic that had worked for them in Masterwork Halls. The dragons would drop their undead cargo directly within the middle of the city, bypassing many of their defensive fortifications.

Indecision momentarily wracked Leon. If they allowed the dragons to fly over the city, they would come within firing range of some of the fortresses' impressive defenses. While this could bring a quick end to some of their adversaries, it would cost the lives of numerous soldiers and citizens who were still housed within Last Bastion's city. If they instead chose to fly out and meet the undead's aerial charge, then any ships they lost would weaken Last Bastion's aerial superiority.

Adonai, what do I do?

Reaching a decision, Leon turned towards the older dwarf at the helm, "Kérik! We need to stop the dragons from flying over the city! They're carrying undead warriors in their claws. We can't wait for them to come to us. We need to attack!"

"Right! Everybody, hang on!" The older dwarf replied, as he pushed forward on the ship's wheel. The *Esperella* lurched forward and rocketed away from the other airship defenders. The wind picked up with their newfound speed, and whipped through Leon's hair as he steadied himself against the railing. Glancing back, Leon saw that a few of the transports and attack ships had begun to follow the *Esperella* into the fray. Other ships then began to follow those, until finally the entire airship fleet moved en masse to engage the enemy beyond the city. Undead voices eerily chanting their god's name grew steadily louder as they approached.

"Xhormas. Xhormas. Xhormas."

"Portside cannons ready!" Leon shouted when the nearest dragon was only a few seconds away. He could clearly see an undead soldier squirming in each of the dragon's claws. The flying beast had set its sights on the *Esperella,* and winged its way towards them. Kérik shouted that he was turning, and the ship quickly drifted to position its cannons directly at the dragon.

"Canister shot! Fire!" Kérik yelled into the helm's speaking pipes.

They had alternated the cannons' ammunition types, causing every other cannon down the ship's left side to thunder at the dragon as it twisted in the air. Five of the ten cannons loosed their ammunition, and a majority of the canister shots hit their mark. The dragon's ridged spine and wings were suddenly riddled with multiple holes, and the flames held within its maw died out. Leon didn't have time to celebrate their victory though, because the sounds of their crossbow and mancer turrets began to thrum on the starboard side. Turning, Leon had just enough time to see another dragon, with its own mouth full of fire, dive towards the *Esperella.*

White tinged spheres of green and brown mancer power slammed into the dragon as it flew over the *Esperella.* Its claws opened, releasing two heavily armored shamblers onto the deck. One landed in the midst of dwarven warriors, causing them to fall in a tangled up heap. They immediately devolved into a mass of limbs, blades, and blunt objects as they attempted to strike out against the vulnerable shambler. The other undead had managed to land on its feet. Armored plates covered its entire body, except for the two eye slits in its tight fitting helm. Tall and imposing in its plate mail, the undead was a menacing sight, even without the huge two handed sword it carried. Leon and Duamé both ran towards it as it hefted its huge sword, aiming for one of the mancers at a nearby turret.

Leon yelled and dove. He tackled the armored figure to the deck just as the ship turned and angled upward. Duamé then swung his aeonyte maul sideways, connecting it with the undead's huge sword. As the armored shambler tried to scramble onto its feet, Leon brought Revelator's shaft down against its neck. Using his upper body weight, Leon pinned the undead to the deck. As he continued to press Revelator down on the shambler's desiccated neck, a blast of heat bloomed behind him, making him turn to see what had happened.

Dragonfire engulfed the ship's aft, causing Leon's heart to sink. His friends… Miala… They had all been where the orange and red flames now tried to devour the ship. The aeonyte hull would remain unharmed, but his friends appeared to have all been incinerated. Leon pushed against the undead soldier's neck with a renewed vengeful force, until he heard bones break and his adversary stilled. The fierce anguish he felt only lasted for a moment though.

The dragonfire churned and coalesced, spinning tighter and tighter into a white hot ball that continued to grow in size as more and more flames fed into it. As nearby turrets hammered the dragon's hide, one singular ball of light didn't move. The ball was molten, made of dragonfire, and held securely between Miala's hands. Those within the area that had been covered by the flames remained unharmed. Miala had used her ability as a pyromancer to take control of them and make them her own. The dragon winged away from their ship, having been dealt several grievous wounds, and dipped below the *Esperella* as it fell to the ground.

A familiar hum brought Leon's attention back to the armored undead pinned to the deck. Ash flaked away from the dead exposed flesh at its neck, causing Revelator's wood shaft to push completely through it and rapp against the deck. As the helmeted head of the undead fighter rolled away, Leon gathered himself up to join Duamé. His friend hammered away at the second undead soldier who had regained its feet alongside the other upright dwarves. The ring of their hammers continued to sound against its dented steel armor, even as Leon deflected a swing from its sword. Leon immediately followed the deflection by bringing Revelator down at an angle and piercing the aeonyte head into the undead's collar, driving it to its knees.

Before Leon had a chance to deliver a finishing blow, Duamé swung his maul sideways, connecting its aeonyte plated end with the shambler's upper body. Due to the *Esperella's* upward and angled trajectory, the blow caused the undead warrior to slide towards the ship's railing near one of the turrets. Its large sword clattered to the deck, and Duamé followed the initial strike by taking a step forward, grunting, and landing a powerful overhead blow. The aeonyte coated maul easily caved the undead's helmet in, and Leon watched the red lights in its eye slits wink out.

"Deck secure!" Leon shouted.

"What am I supposed to do with this?" Miala shouted, as she raised the large ball of dragonfire still held in her hands.

"Look alive! Here comes the rest o' em!" Kérik reported.

The skies were an absolute tangle of dragons, airships, and gryphons. As the turrets on the *Esperella's* top deck increased their firing speed, cannons from nearby airships, both friend and foe, also fired repeatedly in an irregular staccato beat. The cacophony of noise was enough to overwhelm even the most seasoned warrior. A nearby attack ship lined directly up with the *Esperella*, and Leon barely had time to register its existence before Kérik shouted, "Starboard cannons fire!"

The resulting cannon fire between the two ships portrayed a stark contrast in outcomes. The shots that connected with the *Esperella's* hull rang against the aeonyte, causing little to no impact. However, flying shards of wood flew from the attacking ship's hull as the *Esperella's* cannon fire tore through it, leaving numerous holes of destruction. Kérik veered the *Esperella* away from the crippled ship and Miala launched the large fireball she held at the enemy vessel. Leon watched the projectile fly straight into one of the holes that now riddled its hull, and disappear. The fireball must have struck a black powder magazine stored within the belly of the ship, because a concussive explosion soon filled the airspace, leaving only burning pieces of rubble to fall to the earth.

Several beasts and airships wove in an intricate and fatal dance throughout the airspace around them. As their ship turned once again, the *Esperella's* turrets succeeded in keeping the gryphons and other airships at a decent distance. Their defensive strategies didn't, however, deter the undead horde from attacking the other vessels engaged in the massive dogfight. Two nearby transport vessels crashed into each other, and bodies of both the living and the undead fell from them to the ground below. A red-eyed undead dragon breathed fire onto an unfortunate attack ship's aft, causing the ship to careen down and crash amongst the oncoming horde that covered the ground beneath it.

Other airships, as well as a few dragons, broke away from the fighting and flew towards Last Bastion's city. Leon's heart lurched as too few of the defending vessels maneuvered to head the enemy off. He stabbed Revelator through the air, pointing towards the enemy that approached the city, and yelled, "Kérik! The city! We need to stop them!"

"Aye Captain! Comin' about, everyone hang on!" He shouted as he leaned and spun the wheel. The *Esperella* made a hard turn, and only those who could brace against something, or were secured via their straps, were able to remain standing. Duamé wasn't so lucky, and with a startled exclamation he tumbled head over heels across the deck, until a few elves and dwarves were able to stop him. Even Leon almost lost his grip on the railing as the ship jerked forward and careened toward the enemy's air forces.

Too many enemies were breaking through their aerial lines. As powerful as the *Esperella* was, it was just one ship. While the other defending ships were still entangled with the undead's main airborne attack fleet, the *Esperella* angled towards the nearest invading ship. Leon knew they would never be able to stop all of their enemies from flying over Last Bastion's city's outer walls; the dragons would begin to drop their undead cargo, and the undead-controlled airships would either bombard the city or crash themselves into any defenses they could find.

Leon spotted a small, singular mail carrier flying from the plateau near the ziggurat directly into the enemy forces that headed towards it, and knew that the tiny ship would be consumed. He couldn't fathom what would cause the ship's crew to so boldly head to certain doom. The carrier came upon a dragon who had released its undead into the city below, and the beast used its empty claws to reach for the smaller vessel. They were too far away to help, and Leon resigned himself to only being able to watch as the mail carrier wastefully sacrificed itself.

A light flashed within the grey clouds overhead, perfectly timed with a bolt of lightning that leaped from the doomed mail carrier. The bolt was aimed directly at the dragon, and the blast forked through its head, wing, and one of its claws. The little mail carrier swerved to avoid the dragon's limp smoking bulk as its lifeless form careened out of the sky. Moments later, lightning sprouted from the tiny ship again, this time raking across a transport vessel. This bolt scored across the wood of its hull before finally coming in contact with the levigem on its side. The blast shattered the gem and caused the ship to twist and angle sharply downward. Unrecoverable, it crashed into the city below.

Thunder rolled through the clouds above. Emirah Exiosa had been set loose.

Amid blasts of lightning, the *Esperella* once again entered the fray and caught up to an enemy attack ship. It was unloading cannon fire into the city, causing some of the stone structures to crack or crumble under the weight of its assault. Leon and Kérik simultaneously shouted for the port cannons to fire, and the thunderous cannons shot their payloads toward the attack ship. Turret fire also raked across the enemy vessel, and the cannons from Last Bastion's mountain began to fire at the undead force which had strayed too close.

The barrage was enough to cripple the enemy vessel, but it seemed the undead pilot understood its eventual outcome. The ship started to turn towards the *Esperella*, and though Leon and other crewmembers shouted for Kérik to avoid the ship, it managed to match their every move in an effort to intercept them. Amid the shouts to brace for impact, Leon grasped Revelator in both hands and touched the levigem he carried to the spear's shaft.

"Be right back!" Leon yelled over his shoulder.

"Wait, what?" Princess Schalae called in confusion.

Taking advantage of the weightlessness that the combined gem and the spear provided, Leon accounted for where the attack ship was heading, and jumped. The distance wasn't that great, and with his new aeonyte armor weighing less than it had before, his flight was not hindered. Leon soared through the air, his faith in Adonai's abilities guiding him to his destination at the aft of the attack ship. Multiple undead fighters dotted the vessel's damaged decking, and as he began to descend from the apex of his leap, he was reassured that his trust in Adonai had not been misplaced. His landing point would be right by the ship's wheel, where only a few undead stood.

A wretch, dressed in naval armor, was skewered by Revelator when Leon landed on its fragile body. Its red eyes winked out, and its body slid a short distance, turning to salt with Leon still on top of it. As their slide stopped, Leon brought up his shield to deflect a sword blow from a nearby decomposing shambler. Absorbing the impact, Leon retaliated by thrusting his shield upward, and throwing the shambler off balance. A swift kick sent the undead over the ship's railing and into the city below. Leon quickly turned and jumped a short distance to the helm of the attack ship, where another wretch was steering it to ram the *Esperella*.

Slamming into the wretch with his outstretched shield, Leon knocked the thin undead off balance. It maintained its grip on the wheel even as its desiccated face, now missing a few teeth, began turning to salt. Due to the momentum of Leon's charge, the wheel was pulled sharply down and to the left, causing a sudden shift in the airship's direction. The vessel's bow dipped sharply downward, just barely missing the *Esperella*, and turret fire pulsed and hammered the undead that remained on the deck. The smoking attack ship continued its uncontrolled dive, and it passed over the outer wall toward the massive horde of ground forces.

Feeling the sensible and immediate compunction to get off the doomed ship, Leon braced himself against its angled wheel. Grasping Revelator again, Leon leapt towards another vessel high in the air. This one, another undead transport, was descending towards the interior of the city, just inside one of the main gates. Behind and below him, Leon heard the crash of the attack ship as its wooden frame crunched against whatever unfortunate undead lay underneath its bulk.

Ahead, Leon's trajectory had brought him to the bow of the transport ship, but it had altered its elevation to be slightly higher than when he initially jumped. Shifting Revelator to his left hand, where the levigem was in its glove and the shield was on his arm, Leon reached out and grasped the transport's railing with his right. Still lighter than normal due to the effects of the levigem, Leon hoisted himself upward with a grunt and rolled onto the deck at the front of the ship. Shamblers and wretches filled the deck, standing almost shoulder to shoulder, and all of their red glowing eyes were locked onto him.

"Aw, rust." Leon muttered, taking a page from Duamé when he saw how outnumbered he was.

The undead lunged towards him and Leon reacted. He stabbed low to trip up limbs, and retaliated after strikes against his shield. The butt end of his spear proved useful for follow-up strikes whenever Revelator's blade parried. Leon even pinned undead against the rail of the ship in order to cripple or toss the enemy over the edge. No matter what maneuver he utilized, salt continued to spray from every cut, stab, and bash that he made.

A few times the undead scored lucky hits against him. When Leon knocked the sword out of one shambler's hand, another of its cohorts, who was engaging him at that moment, swept its own blade down. Leon couldn't raise his shield at the needed angle fast enough, and the blade cut against the scaled aeonyte at his shoulder. Another gnome-sized undead cut against Leon's shin armor before he then kicked the offending undead up and away like a ball in a child's game. The damage from either blow was minimal, and Leon barely felt the force of their impacts. Had he still been in Duamé's alloyed steel armor, the damage he incurred would have been much worse.

A series of crossbow bolts pinged against Leon's upraised shield before Leon realized that enough of the undead on deck had been dispatched to allow firing room. Leon raised his shield to protect his face as he stabbed toward an overly large ogre shambler whose every footfall vibrated the deck as it advanced. Revelator's spearhead connected just above the ogre shambler's beefy shin, further salting the deck, and throwing it off balance.

A large cleaver of a blade was brought down on Leon's shield, and the unnatural strength of the undead ogre was enough to send Leon to his knees and a shock through his arm.

As the undead ogre raised the cleaver to strike again, a ball of mancer light slammed against it. Knocked completely off balance, it crashed against the decking with a thud. Like the ogre in the dreadnought days before, Leon dove behind its bulk to shelter himself from the bolts and balls of mancer light that flew all throughout the air. Tracking the balls origin, Leon saw that the *Esperella* had followed him. The turrets on his ship launched blast after blast at the undead who were firing at him with their crossbows. As he salted the ogre who struggled to rise again, Leon saw his opportunity to jump back over to the *Esperella*.

While he flew through the air towards his ship, Leon saw that Duamé and Schalae had mounted a defensive attack against a multitude of undead gnomes and goblins that had boarded. The small critters had invaded the bow of the ship, and were slicing and hacking their way towards the back. A few of the turrets near the front of the *Esperella* were unoccupied, and just before he landed Leon saw some of the crew's unmoving bodies near them. They had been assaulted and trampled over by the smaller undead invaders.

A heat rose up Leon's neck as his rage built. He had known that many could, and would, die today, but he had a responsibility to protect those that served on his ship. What started as a gambit to prevent the *Esperella* from being rammed and suffering casualties, had still resulted in crew members being lost anyway. As Leon gained his footing, the righteous anger within him continued to build, and he ran towards the defending line of dwarves and elves. He would save whomever he could, and bring any undead that stood in his way to salt.

Meanwhile...

The din of the battle outside was faint in the foul depths of the cramped cell where Lucien now resided. Hatred and resentment for both King Garinth and his illegitimate spawn roiled just beneath Lucien's silent exterior. In truth, he had hardly slept a wink the night before. Everything that he had worked so hard for was ruined; a disaster that had culminated in the doom of not just the Rhise line, but the living world as he knew it. If it hadn't been for that self-righteous brat Leon, his Laric would be king now. With his careful oversight, Lucien was sure they could have guided the kingdom into beating back the horde. Or at least they would have dug into Last Bastion and survived.

Lucien sat on his dingy cot, disgusted by his present circumstances. Laric had fallen unusually silent since the horns outside had sounded to announce the undead horde's arrival. The ramblings, odd yips, and squeals had lessened. Only an occasional muffled 'no' or 'please' escaped Laric's lips now. Lucien reflexively smoothed his hair backward after noticing his son's disheveled appearance. Laric had not slept in his cot overnight either, choosing instead to stay curled up in a ball, in the corner of the cell. Almost silent for at least the past hour, Lucien thought his son had become content to just stare off into thin air.

It's not as if they had anything else to do, or anyone else to talk to. Even the airship and mining crews that Lucien employed had switched allegiances. A couple of guards had returned earlier with General Xiphos, and the flat, unfriendly stare she had given him preceded her ridiculous offer to everyone else housed in the dungeon. She offered royal amnesty for their crimes against the crown, and a restoration to their prior positions, should they choose to defend the kingdom once more. All Lucien made out from his vantage point within the furthest cell was the squeal of cell doors opening, and the shuffle of many pairs of feet, indicating that many must have accepted the offer. These were people that had lined their pockets with Lucien's pay. Those whom he had employed!

Traitors. All of them.

A low chuckle came from Laric, breaking his silence. It built louder and louder until the eerie cackle grated Lucien's nerves. A lone guard hollered from down the prison hallway, "Hey! Pipe down!"

"Be silent, child." Lucien hissed at Laric.

Laric blinked a few times before he slowly stretched his legs. Chuckling, he used the cell wall to pull himself upright, and once standing he immediately locked eyes with Lucien. "Hello, my good friend."

The outright lack of decorum and respect caused Lucien to bolt up from his cot. "I do not care if your mind is gone or not. You will address me with the respect that I am due, son."

Laric shoved a finger in his ear and wriggled it, seeming to have no care of Lucien's response. "Laric is a bit busy at the moment, and I need to discuss a few things with you, my good friend."

A shiver crept up Lucien's spine as he recalled only one person had ever used that form of address with him. A reportedly dead person. Yet, Laric wouldn't have the gall to address his family in such a manner.

Lucien's mind reeled with confusion as he whispered, "Silas? How–"

"It matters not how, Lucien, just that I can." Laric smiled as he looked about. "We seem to be in quite the predicament here."

"W-what have you done with Laric?" Lucien asked, as concern for his son crashing through his thoughts.

"He is restrained. It turns out that Laric had been conspiring against you for quite some time. He planned to betray you as soon as he was crowned. He was even conspiring to kill you once you fell asleep. I stopped him for you. You are quite welcome, my good friend. Now the plan can come to fruition."

The calm, collected manner in which Silas was speaking did nothing but further infuriate Lucien.

"The plan? What plan? You mean the plan you abandoned when you failed to bring my wife and daughter to Agaprya with you before we left? Or, how about the plan where the undead would be defeated once Laric was crowned king? That plan? IT SEEMS TO BE GOING GREAT SO FAR!"

Lucien roared at his colleague who was somehow speaking through Laric. Temper lost again, the guard at the end of the hall rapped against the iron bars on one of the cells and yelled, "Hey! Be quiet down there!"

An insufferable smirk was all that Silas displayed on Laric's face, as he asked in a low voice, "Do you still remember the note I sent you before you left Agaprya?"

Lucien set his rage aside momentarily as he recalled the simple, yet confusing, message that Silas had sent before he left for Last Bastion. "What are you going on about now? 'To gain power, be ready to sacrifice the son to Xhormas.' That message? In case you have missed it, the king's son, Leon, is out there while we are trapped in here!"

Laric's smile grew even wider. "That was not the son my message referred to, my good friend."

Realization of what Silas was asking him to do hit Lucien, and just as he was about to protest, Silas struck. Within a single heartbeat, hands closed around Lucien's neck and Silas' bored voice said, "Oh dear, your son seems to be gaining control again."

Lucien tried to pry Laric's hands off of him, but his son's grip was too tight. Though Silas was the one who spoke, Lucien still had a tough time reconciling his business partner's mind being in control of Laric's body. Confusion churned within Lucien's own mind as he started to fight back against his tormentor.

Is Laric really trying to kill me?

Or is it Silas trying to trick me?

Lucien shoved Laric back against the cell's stone wall, and the force caused Laric's arms to release him. Stepping back and cradling his aching neck, Lucien heard Laric's voice from the shadowy corner of the cell where he had huddled the night before.

"You can still beat them. Still get your revenge, and gain ultimate power to boot. My master is waiting for your sacrifice, and he will not be denied. It is up to you, my good friend, to fulfill this one last task. Kill Laric in the name of Xhormas, before he kills you. No one will dare betray you again."

Before Lucien could question Silas further, Laric's body lunged forward with outstretched arms. Amid confusion and heartbreak, Lucien realized that he would indeed have to fight for his life against his only son.

Chapter 22: The Enemy

The fatigue of battle would have weighed heavily on Leon had it not been for the thought that they were finally wearing down the enemy's aerial forces. After helping Duamé and Schalae dispatch the undead gnomes and goblins who had boarded the *Esperella*, they began coordinating their strikes with Emirah's mail carrier to defeat each of the enemy attackers who breached the city's airspace.

The small ship that carried Emirah Exiosa was too quick for any of the enemy to corral her. On occasion lightning would flash from the rolling clouds overhead and strike the galvamancer, recharging her powers. Thunder crashed after each burst of light, and she immediately focused her deadly ability on whichever undead foe pursued her. When she passed close to the *Esperella* Leon could see the electricity that coursed up and down her outfit. Her hair stood on end as she impaled the second-to-last dragon that remained over the city with a beam that shot from her outstretched hand. The beast tumbled to the streets below, one of its wings completely obliterated from her powerful blast.

The defending line of airships had moved into the airspace above the city, and Leon saw that both sides had suffered considerable losses. There were just a few gryphons left within his field of vision, and while only half of the airships that had fought at the beginning of the battle remained, the two dreadnoughts were among them, and they continued to pummel the enemy forces. Help also came from the defensive points that had been built into the face of the mountain. Any enemy ship that flew within their range suffered from the volleys of cannonfire that assaulted them from multiple directions.

Accomplishing one of their main objectives seemed to be within reach. If Xhormas' aerial forces could be destroyed, then any of the remaining airships assigned to Last Bastion could focus on the enemy's ground forces.

That was a tried and true tactic in grinding the enemy's foot soldiers to dust. The fortress' horn hadn't sounded again, which meant the enemy had not yet breached the city's outer wall. While pockets of undead, who had been dropped from dragons or enemy airships, were in the city, the main bulk of their horde continued to pound away at the thick, high wall that had prevented their entry.

At Leon's direction, Kérik angled the *Esperella* to skirt the edge of the city so they could check on the status of the wall's defenders. Boulders were being launched from catapults, and arrow bolts pierced through the sky, as the soldiers repeatedly fired on their enemy from the ramparts. Nephilim giants scooped up the grounded boulders and sent them crashing back into the wall with forceful throws. An explosion near one of the wall's ramparts ahead caught Leon's attention. Trying to discern what had occurred, his eyes widened when a giant globule of earth rose up and cracked against the already burning structure.

In the midst of the undead horde's battering attacks, the undead mancer's were also launching their powers against the wall and its defenders. They were apparently being used for the siege itself, instead of summoning more dragons as they had in past battles. Leon prayed that the wall would hold against the combined attacks of the Nephilim giants and liches, but couldn't figure out a way they could give their kinsmen any aid.

"Enemy ship dive bombing the wall!" A scout yelled, as he pointed up towards a burning transport airship. Chunks of the ship's hull were missing, and the levigem on its port side had been knocked askew. The ship spiraled downward on a path that would cause it to hit an already damaged rampart. The tower built within the walls was already all but destroyed. Such a gap in their defenses could provide the undead hoard their much needed opening to flood the city.

Kérik jerked the ship's wheel towards that section of the wall, but the speed of the falling, burning wreckage was too great. Leon's mind flashed back to the *Dawnfire* crash, when he and Prince Gelan had fallen from the sky in a similar manner. The *Esperella* flew close to where the impact would occur, and he shouted a warning for everyone to find cover just before the burning ship collided with the wall. As the transport ship connected with the rampart, it set off an explosion that sent out a massive wave of heat. Stones and wood sprinters flew in every direction, peppering against the *Esperella.* A brief moment of panic struck Leon, and he raised his arms and shield to protect Miala and Duamé from the shrapnel. He had seen the damage wooden shards could inflict; the one that had pierced Gelan's arm had ultimately claimed his life.

Everyone on the top deck crouched low and covered any flesh their armor left exposed as best as they could. Leon felt small rubble rain down on his aeonyte armor, and his concern shifted to relief when he saw that no one had been injured from the blast. Recovering from his momentary panic, he scrambled to the railing to survey the damage that had been wrought by the destroyed airship.

A deep scar had formed in the wall, and the horde of undead were already rushing to pour into the newfound opening. Multitudes of red eyed shamblers, wretches, and chimeras all wormed their way through while Nephilim giants ran to either side of the gaping hole. The giants pulled at the stones along the damaged edges, enlarging the opening as they broke and tore each oversized handful apart. A low blast from the ziggurat's behemoth horn sounded twice – a signal that the enemy had breached the outer wall.

At Leon's command, the *Esperella* flew in tight circles, raining destruction from their turrets down on the enemies who filled the wall's opening. Return fire came from the liches within the horde, while the giants also hurled large stones at the ship. The exchange was vicious, but gaining air superiority would mean nothing if the city were breached and its populace slain. Miala staggered to one of the now-unoccupied mancer turrets at the front of the ship. Orbs of her white fire joined the brown and green ones that hammered at the invaders. Their turrets only had a few seconds to fire before the *Esperella* would turn and the ones on the other side would fire from slightly farther away.

Alternating their salvos, and interspersing them with cannonfire helped to grant them a tactical advantage. A couple of gryphons tried to dive at the deck, but Leon, Schalae, and Duamé easily dispatched the chimeras. Duamé's maul crushed the head of one of the beasts, abruptly cutting off its squawk, and sending a burst of salt from its limp lion-like body. Schalae danced with her blades in a more surgical fashion. As Leon pinned a wing from the last gryphon, Schalae precisely slashed at her opponent before slicing through it with a deadly maneuver. She looked up, and her gaze caught on something over Leon's shoulder. Pointing with her razor sharp Broken Bough she exclaimed, "Leon, look!"

Leon turned and his eyes locked on a shock of yellow hair that was next to red braids. Tyne and Brigid were at the top of the bow's stairwell, peeking through the railing unnoticed by anyone else. They were close to Miala's turret, where she was about to start firing at the wall's opening, when Leon began to run with a shout over the din of battle, "Miala, the kids!"

Miala did a double-take, and tried to reach for them just as Leon noticed the teen orc, Sam, using his frame and unnatural strength to block Gérda and Kelleren from the stairwell. The dwarf and the dog were both trying to get past him as Gérda screeched, "Kids! Ya need ta go back below! It's dangerous out here!"

"We're just doing what Tyne said we needed to do!" Sam growled.

Kelleren barked furiously, and Duamé sauntered over, having just noticed the situation. "Oi, wot's goin' on?"

"Wait!" Brigid imperiously commanded everyone, her hands outstretched towards their group. Tyne had his tiny gnome hands cupped to her bent ear, whispering something. She nodded at whatever the gnome said, but didn't relay anything further. Her minimalistic use of words didn't prove especially helpful to anyone at the moment, as she simply extended her arm over the railing of the ship and pointed at the gash in the wall.

"Get them out of here!" Schalae cried out.

"No, wait! Look!" Miala exclaimed.

Wisps of white tendrils were rapidly coalescing in the middle of the fissure. The undead still scrambled through, either oblivious to the mancer power, or ignoring what converged above them. A giant, covered in bronze plates and armed with a tree trunk that had been carved to sharp points at both ends, began to climb through the hole. Its glowing red eyes took note of the rapidly changing air in front of its face, and twisted its neck to look up at the *Esperella.*

Leon wouldn't have believed it if he hadn't seen what happened next for himself. Just as the giant reared back to throw the sharpened tree trunk at the ship, the wisps of white thickened into a solid mass of ice, and dropped onto the giant's foot. It only had an instant to howl in pain and grab for the frozen boulder before it began to rapidly grow. Spikes and shards randomly sprouted from it in all directions, forming deadly crystalline patterns. Within moments, an entire glacier had grown. It ran the full length of the hole in the wall, fully encasing the pierced and unmoving Nephilim giant, and blocking any more undead from gaining entry into the city.

Brigid's small form sagged from the massive exertion of her mancer powers, and Sam raced over to catch her before could fall and hurt herself. Leon and the others could only stare and marvel at the massive feat the young girl had just accomplished. The hole in the wall had been plugged, and the flow of undead that had poured through it was momentarily stopped. Though Brigid had once again passed out, Tyne rather casually announced, "We can go back below now. Our task is done."

As the children calmly passed the wide-eyed Gérda and filed below, Leon realized his earlier suspicion about the mysterious gnome mancer had been confirmed. Based on Tyne's words, and the children's actions, he appeared to be Calvin's chronomancy successor. Tyne was the last to descend the steps, but before he did, he turned to address Leon. "He's coming. Don't be afraid."

Bewildered by the statement, Leon silently watched as the gnome turned and resumed his trek down the stairs. He looked at his friends who merely shrugged at him, as they also didn't comprehend the meaning of Tyne's words. The unease that had plagued Leon over the past couple of days, however, returned in full force. Unsettled by the child's pronouncement, he turned to survey the battle that still raged all around the *Esperella,* puzzling over what the gnome could have meant.

Leon watched as the undead who had gotten through the hole spread throughout the city below. They snaked through alleys and corridors, but whatever defensive maneuvers needed to occur were out of Leon's hands, and entrusted to Generals Xiphos and Ciaye. The barricades and strategic placement of troops within the city's tight quarters would have to hold the enemy back for the moment, as the *Esperella* had to fly back into the aerial battle over Last Bastion. There were less than fourteen ships still churning in the air, and other than the two dreadnoughts, Leon could not yet discern which were friend or foe. The dreadnoughts looked to have taken some damage, but their cannons still fired towards the splintering and shattering ships that remained. Multiple airships had fallen onto the city, and plumes of smoke rose from the wreckage all around.

The skies were overcast as far as they could see. The already existent clouds had begun to darken further though, and at first, Leon thought it was due to Galvamancer Exiosa's continued draw of lightning from them. Then they began to churn violently, turning nearly black as they shifted and folded into each other. The late morning sunlight that had been trying to break through the overcast sky was muted further, and only a dim light filtered through all around. Had Leon not known what time of day it was, he would have been inclined to think that night was fast approaching.

Unexpectedly, the *Esperella's* hull, and all of the other aeonyte around, began to glow. Duamé's hammerhead, Leon's armor and shield, even Revelator's spearhead lit up at the same moment – which was not typical during the daytime hours. Leon would have taken a moment to admire the beauty of the sight, had the unease residing in his heart allowed it. Somehow that feeling had burst, and a cold chill flooded through his entire body, despite the warm air they were flying through.

Something was wrong.

The dark clouds dipped slightly over Last Bastion's spiraled ziggurat, and Leon blinked as thousands of winged creatures flew in circles above it. Uncountable numbers of mazzikin melded in and out of the cloud, causing Leon to clutch at Duamé's chain mailed shoulder and point at it with Revelator.

"Do you see that?"

"What is that?" Miala exclaimed.

"Wot' tha hematite is goin' on NOW?" Duamé demanded.

"Come on!" Leon responded to them.

Duamé joined him, though Miala stayed at the nearby mancer turret. They headed down the length of the ship, making their way towards the helm at the aft. The rest of the crew stood, mesmerized by the atmospheric display. Many were slack jawed at the sight, and Leon couldn't fault them for it. He had to fight to tear his own eyes from the foreboding imagery, in order to watch where he was going. On his way to the aft he turned back to look, and the swarm of mazzikin were gone. While that surreal vision had ended, the slow swirling clouds remained with their bottom end clearly hovering over the top of the ziggurat.

"Kérik!" Leon yelled when he had almost reached the aft.

"Don't say 'get us closer'. Don'cha dare say 'get us closer', boyo!" Duamé warned loudly.

"Get us closer?" Kérik hollered back.

"Aw, rust!" Muttered Duamé.

Leon nodded to Admiral Silverspine. "Cut through the dogfight! We need to get over there now!"

Another horn blast sounded from the ziggurat, only to be abruptly cut off.

Dread wriggled its way into Leon as he latched himself onto the railing. A sudden burst of speed forced him to grab for Duamé. The dwarf had almost fallen over, but Leon's hands had been able to latch on to the head of his maul, and he swung his grunting friend toward the rail next to him. Duamé's hand fumbled to latch onto an eyelet and pull himself up as they stared towards their destination.

The *Esperella* dove low under the skirmishing airships, racing just above the cityscape. The dark skies seemed to amplify the fires that raged from burning vessels, and the forks of lightning that Emirah continued to conjure. An attack ship dipped into their path just ahead, and broadsided the *Esperella* as they flew towards it. Their cannons must have been loaded with canister shot, because the spray that hit the bow of the ship peppered against it like a gong. A shot or two must have also been aimed above the decking though, because multiple crew members were hit by the iron spray.

Leon watched as two more turrets, one crossbow and one mancer, were obliterated by the rounds, and their crew slaughtered by the debris. A few of the warriors on the deck also succumbed to the broadside attack, their strong forms crumpling under the cannon fire. Princess Schalae cried out in pain and spun, she still held onto one of her swords but had reflexively raised that hand across her chest to her now-injured shoulder. Leon could do nothing but watch as her bark armor splintered and fell away from her damaged upper arm.

Kérik pulled upward, in an attempt to maneuver over the attack ship, but it had already advanced forward and was angling to fire again. Undead were scattered across its top deck, and they brandished various weapons and crossbows as they formed a firing line. Before they could do more than posture, Miala fired successive blasts of white fire that ripped holes through their ship. Her retaliation came from her lone turret near the bow, but the few remaining turrets on the starboard side were quick to join her efforts until Kérik shouted, "Starboard cannons return fire as you bear!"

Concussive blasts ripped the enemy ship apart, and the *Esperella* zoomed past its falling debris. They swerved past other vessels, and flew near the squat tower that housed the new Archives. It appeared undamaged, but due to the unnaturally dark skies Leon couldn't see if any battles were being waged at its base. As they passed over the gorge, Princess Schalae was helped toward the aft by a few of the remaining elves. She still cradled her arm, and before Leon could ask, she announced, "I'll be fine. My shoulder is dislocated, but I'll be fine."

Her eyes told him a different story though. While she may have only suffered from a mild injury, many others now laid unmoving across the deck. Almost half their turrets were gone, and the *Esperella's* crew had taken quite a beating. Schalae was not 'fine' with their losses, and neither was Leon. In war there was death, but each loss of life on the *Esperella* weighed on Leon. These people had known the risks and dangers this battle would pose, but had still entrusted him with their lives. With each felled crewmember the feeling of having failed them grew – even though he knew there was nothing he could do differently.

When the *Esperella* arced up and around the spiraled ziggurat, Leon noticed dark tentacles of shadow wriggling from the structure's small holes. They grew outward and upward, continually spreading. An entry tunnel had been built into one of the mountain's protrusions, and a contingent of soldiers had been stationed with a few cannons there. One of the dark tendrils burst from the passage, and each soldier it passed through simply disappeared. Concern for his family, both newfound and old, wracked Leon.

The *Esperella* continued its turn, and was about to fly over the plateau where the entrance to the ziggurat was, when a mass of people fled the structure. They headed toward a small trio of mail carriers that were parked where the dreadnoughts had rested at the beginning of the battle. Agreeing with Kérik to take the risk and land, the *Esperella* made a swift descent towards the mail carriers as thunder rolled overhead.

"Ready the gangplank!" Ophelia yelled, scrambling to grab the long boards at the railing with a few other crew members.

As the *Esperella* landed, Leon and Duamé quickly unlatched and hustled down the gangplank that was being pushed out. Miala waved her arms, wildly gestured at Leon from the front of the ship. He hazarded a guess that she was asking if he wanted her to come with him, and addressed everyone present, "Everyone stay here, we are picking up some passengers. Watch the skies!"

Nods of assent, as well as a few, "Aye, Captains", were his reply before he all but ran down the steep gangplank.

Upon reaching the hard packed earth and stone of the carved mountain, Leon waved to a group of people who were hesitantly approaching. "This way! Over here!"

"Oi, ya louts! Get yer rustin' behinds on board!" Duamé shouted.

The group of people ran over, and to his great relief Leon saw that his mother, sister, King Garinth, and Princess Giselle were among them. A few nobles, some workers from the fortress, Countess Serina, and only a handful of soldiers, were also present. Hundreds of people were missing.

Every person present was either breathing heavily, or out of breath entirely, as King Garinth ordered, "Women first!"

"What happened? Where are Xiphos and Ciaye? All the other people stationed here?" Leon asked wide-eyed, dreading the answer he knew was coming.

Silent sobs came from his mother and sister as they passed by, while others appeared to just be mentally absent. Whether due to shock, or perhaps trauma, the people numbly hurried up the gangplank while King Garinth and his few soldiers remained behind. Leon's father cast an odd glance at his glowing outfit before waving a hand towards the ziggurat. "They are gone. All gone. It, whatever that is, has been spreading throughout the Bastion fortress. The shadows just swallow people up and they disappear!"

Leon barely had time to register the loss of so many lives, some of whom he had spoken to mere hours ago. With the generals gone, and Last Bastion's fortress compromised, their defense was left to the city itself. They no longer had the ability to fall back into the fortress, and their chances of survival were dramatically reduced.

King Garinth continued, "It came up from below, and–"

"Your Majesty, look!" A soldier cried out with a pointed finger.

Everyone looked at the writhing mass of shadows filling the ziggurat. More dark tentacles had sprouted from the holes within the spiral structure. The lazy, swirling, funnel of dark clouds continued to reach farther down, and some of the oily black tendrils stretched upwards to meet it. The soldier, however, was not pointing to the sky, but outward.

Leon could faintly see a lone figure slowly walking towards them from the ziggurat's entrance. Even from a distance its bright red demonic eyes shone clearly, but the figure itself was cloaked in shadows. A cold fear ran down Leon's spine, and he didn't dare turn away from the approaching figure as he ordered those nearby to board the ship immediately.

"Everyone, get on the *Esperella* and take off! Now!"

The soldiers began to escort King Garinth up the gangplank, but he shrugged them off and placed his hand on Leon's shoulder. "Son, you are coming too."

Leon wanted nothing more than to go with his family and friends; to clasp hands with his newfound father, and run into the relative safety of the glowing ship. In his heart though, he knew that he was the only one who could face the approaching entity. If Tyne's warning held merit, then the fallen b'nei ha'elohim, Xhormas, had arrived. No one else would be able to face the god of undeath but him. As Leon tried to pull away from his father, King Garinth's grip tightened on his armor. "What do you think you are doing?" He demanded.

"I have to face it, Your Majesty."

"I forbid it!"

Leon sighed resolutely, "I have to try."

"I WILL NOT LOSE ANOTHER SON!" The King roared.

Red rimmed eyes full of pain and loss met Leon's, and his heart broke. On some level, he understood the king's plight. However, if Prince Gelan were here, Leon knew full well what he would do.

"My duty is to defend you and the kingdom, Sir. It is the same duty I had while serving with Prince Gelan. My brother. Your son. I would have died to protect him, just as I would die to protect this kingdom. But my goal isn't to die, it's to stop that… thing." Leon pointed at the approaching man.

"I'll… look after him, Yer Majesty." Duamé volunteered as he hoisted his maul.

A bestial scream of rage came from the shadowy figure, and it flicked a hand to its side. As it drew closer, Leon could see a wickedly curved glaive in its hand. The long polearm's axe head dripped shadowy flames that emanated from the weapon.

"Ya know, on second thought, ya got this meat shield. Ya don't need me fer this one."

Leon could hear the fear in Duamé's trembling voice, and knew the dwarf's short range of attack would hinder him. Before the king could stop him, Leon forced himself to step forward and challenge the shadowy figure. Calling over his shoulder, he said, "Take care of them, Duamé."

"Milord, we have to go!" The soldier who had pointed out the approaching figure implored.

Leon listened as his father was escorted up the ship's gangplank behind him. His mother and sister shouted his name, pleading for him to board the ship. All he could do was raise Revelator high above his head, acknowledging that he heard them, and hope that he would see them again. Their cries turned to screaming his name as the *Esperella* took off and headed towards the battle.

Leon could also dimly hear Miala's voice, as she shouted her own protests. Powerful as her pyromancy was, Leon couldn't risk her safety against this mass-murdering foe. He couldn't risk anyone's safety. He was the Judge, and it was his duty to protect them. Not taking his eyes off of the figure that continued to walk towards him, Leon's thoughts turned to Miala's smile, their shared kisses, and how they supported each other.

Next came thoughts of his family and friends, and each step he took towards his adversary was fueled by the fierce desire to protect them. Determination filled him, reinvigorating his aching muscles. Revelator's spearhead shone brighter, as the glow from Leon's shield and armor amplified. Soon his battle fatigue melted away, just as it had at Masterwork Halls, leaving Leon feeling refreshed and ready to face this entity.

The shadowy figure, that now stood just a short distance ahead, was slightly taller than Leon. Though it seemed to simply be a manlike figure, the shadow that cloaked its form appeared to absorb light. Tiny ropes of darkness, just like those that came from the ziggurat, stuck out from the person in odd places. These small tendrils reached out almost as if to grab the air, and pull it in. Bright red glowing eyes shone from the shadowy figure more intensely than any Leon previously encountered.

Leon could feel the evil that radiated like a wave off of the entity before him. He had felt this way once before – in a dream that seemed as if it had occurred ages ago. A dream where he had been trapped, unable to move, and conversing with–

"Xhormas." Leon spoke, guessing at the entity's identity in front of him.

"Not quite yet, Judge." It replied.

Surprised, the sound of the entity's monotonous voice grated on his ears. Haunting and chilling, it actually sounded as though two voices spoke at the same time. Voices that Leon had heard before. "Wait, Silas?"

"And one more guest." Came Silas' response as the shadows peeled back to reveal a pale face. A face with damp, dark hair plastered to parts of it. A face with inky black tear tracks coming from its red glowing eyes. A face that was locked in an expression of complete and utter brokenness. Still wearing the outfit from his prison cell, Lucien had no armor. Only the simple formal jacket with his levigem pin on the lapel, covered him. His face once again became obscured by the shadow that flowed over it.

Whatever fate Leon might have imagined for his father, hadn't been this. When Phonz Jasperfoot had been possessed by a Nephilim spirit it had remained hidden and manipulated him behind the scenes. The way Silas controlled Lucien was entirely different. This was overt, visible, blatant, almost flaunting the dominion that Silas had over him. To be inhabited and controlled by Silas, was far worse than any prison cell Leon could have left Lucien in. The man had cut all familial ties with him when they last talked, and had openly confessed to desiring Leon's death. Even so, no matter the animosity between them, Leon didn't believe his abusive father figure deserved this.

But there was another in his cell. Leon reminded himself.

"What have you done with Laric?" Leon asked.

Silas, or Lucien perhaps, slashed the glaive through the air in front of him. The whoosh of displaced air and the speed at which he moved was entirely too unsettling for Leon.

"He was the first ritual sacrifice. Now Xhormas approaches, and he will not be stopped. All will hail the dark god as he assumes his rightful control over creation. All will bow at his feet, and glorify Xhormas in perpetual undeath and torment!"

Silas lifted Lucien's limbs and shadow dripped off of his raised arms. ***"Adonai has lost, and the world of the living is doomed!"***

Rage built within Leon. Laric was dead, Lucien was possessed, and Xhormas was coming. Silas had indeed outwitted them all. He felt used, and now Xhormas was supposedly going to enter their world. Glancing up at the ziggurat's peak again, he saw that the clouds still swirled and the funnel still descended. If Leon had to guess, the storm, the ziggurat, and Laric's sacrifice were all somehow linked. He couldn't think of a way to stop the storm itself though. All Leon knew he could do was face the enemy that stood before him.

Silas was also responsible for the injuries Rohiel had sustained. In his Nephilim spirit state, this man contended with beings more powerful than Leon could imagine.

How in the world can I stop a being such as this? Leon thought.

I... I can't. It's no use. I–

Wait.

With a cold realization, Leon remembered that while alive, Silas had been an empamancer. Controlling thoughts and emotions had been part of his capabilities, and to top it off he had ordered the Mazzikin to try to tempt him into harming himself on his very first night away from the manor. The night Leon had been called to become a Judge.

Who is to say he isn't trying to do that now?

The more he thought about it, the more Leon realized the truth of the situation. Silas was trying to win their fight before it had even begun, through intimidation and head games. Aware of what was actually going on, Leon realized he could almost feel the waves of fear Silas sent towards him. Though the former empamancer continued to try and manipulate his emotions, Leon forced himself to ignore it. After all, he knew power that opposed fear.

Love. Joy. Peace. Patience. Kindness. Goodness. Faithfulness. Gentleness. Self-Control. As he reminded himself of the attributes Silas couldn't corrupt, his armor and weapon began to glow brighter and brighter. Silas hissed in frustration as Leon leveled a hard stare at him. Raising Revelator to point at Silas, Leon announced, "That didn't work the first time, and it won't work now."

Baleful, hate filled glowing eyes met Leon's, and a few of Silas' dark tendrils slid towards the glaive he carried. They braided together and hardened to a glossy black sheen over the wood. Silas lowered the weapon's head closer to the ground with its blade facing up. Silas and Lucien's combined voice growled in a taunting discordant harmony. ***"Xhormas will enjoy your sacrifice."***

Leon shifted his spear and shield into a readied position, gently tapping Revelator's shaft against the levigem in his opposite hand. A familiar weightlessness settled in his gut, joining the grim determination he felt. For a few moments, neither opponent moved. Thunder rolled overhead, and the distant sounds of battle and cannon fire punctuated the silent stillness between them. Then Leon burst forward, his spear extended against his foe once again, determined to finish this fight once and for all.

Chapter 23: The Judgement

Silas had been no pushover the last time that he and Leon fought. Moreso, while in the spiritual realm, Silas had been strong enough to injure Rohiel. The Nephilim was certainly a skilled opponent. Knowing this, Leon fully expected his stab with Revelator to be dodged. However, the speed at which Silas moved out of the way was completely unexpected. Only by lowering his head while rolling did Leon avoid a killing stroke from Silas' shadowy weapon. Turning and raising his shield, Leon was just barely able to block his opponent's instantaneous follow up strike.

When the shadow glaive crashed against his aeonyte shield, salt sprayed everywhere. Some of the shadowy tendrils recoiled from the flash of light that burst from the shield's face, and Leon took that opportunity to jab Revelator in an upward sweep. Silas sidestepped it though, and he had to quickly bring it back down. Continuing his offensive attack Leon stabbed Revelator low, attempting to trip, or at least pin Silas in place, but the shadow glaive's end parried Leon's strike. Silas cackled as he retaliated in a flurry of blows and strikes that Leon was barely able to dodge and protect himself against.

They continued to trade blows and dodge strikes, neither seeming to gain an edge over their opponent. Every time the shadows clashed against aeonyte though, salt sprayed and Silas grunted in frustration. The Nephilim spirit's quick strikes against Leon were all aimed at his joints or exposed skin. One cut directed at Leon's neck grazed his flesh, and a chill seeped into his bones as death and failure came too close. Desperation to end the fight festered within Leon as he swept Revelator towards Silas. The man crouched under the attack, and taunted, ***"Everyone you love will suffer and die. I will make sure of it."***

He is still trying to get into my head. Leon thought. The desperation building inside of him was momentarily tempered by his self-control as he blocked a strike. Rather than respond to Silas' goading, Leon diagonally sliced Revelator down. When Silas moved away from the strike, Leon leapt towards him, closing the distance between them. Tackling the former seneschal with his outstretched shield, Leon stabbed into the earth to stop his momentum towards the ziggurat. The deadly tendrils that sprouted from the structure flailed through the air, and one slammed down just outside of Leon's reach, far too close for comfort. The impact jarred the ground, and Leon launched himself toward where Silas had rolled out of the way.

Their fight had grown ever closer to the ziggurat, and Leon registered that it was likely an intentional maneuver from Silas. It took almost all of Leon's concentration to just keep up with the man, also dodging the shadowy tentacles would be nigh impossible. Silas must have noticed Leon's hesitancy and began to press his attack. Leon matched Silas blow for blow, striving to take every step he possibly could away from the ziggurat. When an opening finally presented itself, Leon tapped the spear against his levigem and leapt a short distance away. Quickly turning to face Silas again, Leon was surprised to see that his opponent hadn't run after him. Instead, Lucien's body remained rooted in place, and the dual voices spoke.

"Ah. That is how you do it. Interesting."

The shadows peeled back slightly to reveal the levigem pin Lucien always wore on his lapel. Silas plucked it from his jacket, and with a sadistic grin across Lucien's possessed face, he clenched the pin in his fist and leapt towards Leon with an outstretched glaive blade. Leon dove sideways, narrowly escaping the surprising attack. He instinctively felt danger behind him, and thrust Revelator backward as he stood. The defensive maneuver saved Leon's life. Silas had once again leapt in pursuit of him, and was forced to parry Revelator as he landed.

An intricate dance of cat and mouse followed. Numerous blows were exchanged as the two supernaturally leapt towards and away from each other over and over again. The ring of metal clashing against metal resounded constantly, as neither of them gave their opponent an opening. Whenever Silas leapt away from Leon a shrill laugh would come from his and Lucien's overlapping voices. At other moments he continued trying to goad Leon.

"Your God hates this world and all its iniquity. He has abandoned it to an inevitable fate."

"The city will fall, just like all the others."

"You have failed your people. Their iniquity is too great."

"Xhormas cannot be beaten. You have already lost."

Leon knew the intention of each taunt was to influence his thoughts. His recurring rebuttal was silence as he reminded himself of the tenets Judges were called to live by. Leon would remain faithful to Adonai. God hated sin, but loved people. Adonai had protected him thus far, and He would continue to do so. No matter how hard Silas tried to worm his way into Leon's head, he shook the assault off. He blocked, parried, and dodged Silas' strikes time after time, and the Nephilim spirit's rage boiled hotter with every second that passed.

Glaive held in both hands, Silas repeatedly hacked downward – his motions too fast for Leon to do anything other than block with his shield or Revelator's shaft. Each impact shuddered through Leon's limbs, and one particularly jarring blow brought him to his knees. The next strike knocked Revelator from his grip, and the spear's glow winked out as it clattered to a stop a short distance away. Just as he had during their first fight, Silas disarmed him. Before Leon could dive to retrieve Revelator, Silas struck. With a leap towards Leon, Silas stabbed the glaive's blade at his chest.

Leon failed to raise his shield in time, but somehow managed to bring his hands up and clasp the glaive's shaft just behind its blade. The momentum of the jab threatened to bring him fully to the ground, but he miraculously managed to remain on one knee. Leon tore his eyes from Silas' face to look down at the weapon. Silas applied more pressure, causing the tip of the glaive to dig into his scale mail. Leon desperately tried to shift the glaive's edge away, but his poor angle and footing didn't give him the needed leverage. He could only watch as his arms quaked from the effort it took to hold the weapon in place, while Silas and Lucien's blended voices taunted him.

"Just give in. Give in to death, Leon. It is okay to stop struggling. It is okay to fail."

Leon looked up at Silas' red glowing eyes, widened in their eager anticipation of his demise. The effort to prevent himself from being impaled was quickly sapping his strength, and though he knew he couldn't give up, he also knew he wouldn't last much longer in his current position. He would defy Silas, and Xhormas, and any other fallen entity who had the audacity to stand against Adonai, to his last breath. Leon's aeonyte shield and armor pulsed brighter when his thoughts turned to Adonai. Silas' eyes narrowed, and he tried harder to push the blade into Leon. It must have slipped between a gap in two of his armor's scales, because the pressure against his chest morphed into a hot, piercing pain. The combination of pain and anger caused him to scream out as he desperately tried to wrench the glaive aside.

Wood crunched. The glaive's shaft splintered and broke apart where Leon grasped it. The snapping of the wood freed his tired arms from their strain, and the broken head of Silas' weapon remained in one of Leon's hands. Silas' shocked face rapidly fell towards him as the force pushing against him and the now broken glaive suddenly disappeared. The glaive's broken shaft glanced off of Leon's armor, and Lucien's shadowy body partially collided with Leon's shield, as they both tumbled to the ground..

Salt erupted.

Leon thudded against the ground with such force that the wind was knocked out of him. He lay helplessly on his back, staring directly into Silas' shocked red eyes. His adversary didn't move. With a grunt of effort Leon rolled the still body off of him knowing, against all appearances, their struggle wasn't over yet. Shifting away from his foe, Leon saw that the glaive's blade had penetrated through Lucien's mid-abdomen, and exited near his spine. The shadows that enveloped Lucien's still form quivered as his mouth soundlessly opened and closed. Not wanting to waste a second, Leon scrambled towards Revelator's nearby resting place. A brilliant light burst from its tip when he grabbed hold of it and turned back to Silas. The body remained unmoving, and Leon leapt towards it to finish their fight.

Dual voices screamed out a desperate, "Noooo!" as an inky black cloud tore from Lucien's body. Silas' spirit left its most recent dwelling and hovered in front of Leon, its red luminous eyes wide and panicked. Leon ran after the cloud that he knew to be Silas, but it flitted out of his reach towards the ziggurat. A shrill, ethereal laugh trailed behind the retreating spirit as it entered into the safety of the ziggurat's gigantic, flailing, dark tentacles.

"You are too late, Judge! It is TIME!"

Silas' laughter grew louder and deeper as his dark cloud zipped toward the structure's peak. He disappeared within the swirling cyclone that had descended upon the top of the fortress during their battle. Disheartened, Leon realized that their skirmish had merely been intended to delay him. Silas, once again, had played him like a lute. The air around Leon grew heavier as the grey sky darkened further. Color and light faded into a pinpoint of pure black darkness at the peak of the ziggurat. Then the pinpoint began to grow larger and larger as the surrounding cloud swirled and fed into it. Its growth continued until it was a black gaping hole above the ziggurat. Over the din of the still raging airship battle, the undead voices cried out their enthusiastic chants even louder.

"Xhormas! Xhormas! Xhormas!"

An otherworldly shadow burst out of the black opening and merged with the dark tendrils that reached up from the ziggurat. The thunderous crack of stone being ripped apart sounded as the ziggurat collapsed on itself, forming the foundation for a gigantic living shadow that reached into the sky. A familiar pair of large, red-glowing eyes opened in the entity's center. They roved over the cityscape, and a terrible fear tried to worm its way into Leon's heart as he once again heard Xhormas' voice.

"This creation is now mine. Adonai himself could not stop me, and neither can anyone here. Surrender and worship me."

Every word Xhormas spoke was like an assault on Leon's ears. His voice was maddening, and it caused a part of Leon to want to curl up and sob uncontrollably. How could he stand against a god? Why should he even try to fight when there was no longer any point to it? They had lost. All Leon could think about was how he had let everyone down.

I'm sorry, Miala and Duamé.

I'm sorry, Lochemetel. Rohiel.

I'm sorry, Adonai.

Movement in the sky caught Leon's eye, and when he looked up, he saw that only three airships remained from the nearby aerial battle. One of the dreadnoughts had managed to stay aloft, even though it smoked from several places along its hull. Leon also recognized the sleek profile of the *Golem,* which flew in close proximity to the shining *Esperella.* All three of the ships were converging to launch an attack on Xhormas. A deep sense of helplessness filled Leon as he stood and watched the ships fire cannonball after cannonball into the shadowy god's form. Nothing seemed to work, until an arc of lightning suddenly leapt through the air and skittered across Xhormas' shadowed surface.

A loud echoing grunt came from the b'nei ha'elohim after Emirah Exiosa's conjured lightning struck. A spark of hope lit within Leon as he watched the galvamancer and the dreadnought fly close to the pillar of darkness. Emirah's repeated blasts spoke of the living's defiant stance towards Xhormas. Leon's faith was briefly bolstered by Emirah and the other airships' attacks.

That same blooming hope was quickly quenched though, when shadowy tendrils began to hoist the ruined ziggurat's huge megalithic blocks. They floated throughout the dark cloud, giving the appearance of dense pockmarks across Xhormas's surface, before being forcefully launched in multiple directions. Boulders that had once formed the focal point of Last Bastion now crashed into the defiant airships, the city below, and even into the exterior walls.

The sound of the heavy stones crunching against the airships might as well have ripped a hole through Leon's heart itself. The dreadnought was pulverized into smoking fragments, causing it, along with Emirah's mail carrier, to fall into the gorge that separated the city from Xhormas. Screaming at the loss, Leon was then forced to tear his eyes away from the galvamancer's plummeting ship when boulders began to assault the *Esperella*. The metal airship shook under the onslaught. Dents and other damage spread across its surface as the ship was battered off its current course. The levigem that had been damaged in their previous battle was struck again, causing the airship to dip violently.

Helplessness once again enveloped Leon, as he could only watch while the *Esperella* barreled toward where he stood on the plateau. Xhormas flung more boulders towards the city and its walls, all while emitting a maniacal, chilling laugh that grated against Leon's ears. Their defenses were crumbling. Walls were being breached, the undead were about to pour in, and a heavy sense of defeat consumed Leon. His last hopes were obliterated when the *Esperella* crash-landed on the plateau. With a shriek of metal against earth, the ground rumbled as the ruined ship slid in his direction. Leon leapt over the bow and its massive aeonyte fist masthead that pointed towards him, only to land on a deck strewn with people who clung to each other for dear life.

He quickly spotted his friends and family huddled together near the ship's aft. Duamé was clasping hands with Kérik, while Miala, Schalae, and Liara were sprawled on the deck, bruised but alive. He landed and surveyed the area. A few of the other mancers and soldiers had survived, but there weren't many people left on the top deck. Anxiety over the danger his friends and crewmembers were in filled him as he struggled to maintain his footing while the airship slid to a stop. Groaning and gashed bodies surrounded Leon, and the aeonyte that surrounded them visibly dimmed as he ran the short distance to his friends.

Concern for their well-being consumed him. Everyone in the living world was about to die, but all Leon could think about was protecting those he cared about as much as he possibly could. Even if it would only provide them a few moments longer to live, he felt a stirring, a duty, to do whatever he could to defend them.

What was it Rohiel said? Leon asked himself.

No greater love…

Leon moved towards Miala, tears welling in his eyes, and saw that she had begun to stir and rub her neck. Knowing that time was short before Xhormas would continue his assault, Leon locked eyes with her and placed Revelator on the deck so he could gently hold her face. Shock and panic clouded her eyes, and Leon put every ounce of feeling he possessed into his next words.

"I love you more than words could hope to express." Then he tenderly kissed her.

A newfound resolve filled his heart, and Leon tore himself from her. He grasped Revelator in his hand once more, his heart aching as he tried to memorize every curve of her face and every strand of crimson hair. Then he turned away as she stammered, "L-L-Leon? Wait."

He couldn't. Every second mattered. He took one final look at his loved ones before he forced himself to put one foot in front of the other. As he walked away, he shouted over his shoulder, "Get to safety however you can."

Looking up at the huge pillar of shadow that he knew to be Xhormas, Leon leaped away from the *Esperella,* towards the dark god. Xhormas had continued to launch boulder after monstrous boulder at the city and its walls, pulverizing everything that he could. When Leon hit the ground and ran towards the ruined ziggurat, he saw shadowy tendrils hoisting the gigantic stones closest to him. At any moment they would be hurled towards the *Esperella.*

Leon waved the dim spear, yelling taunts as he ran closer.

"Hey! Huge, dark, and ugly! Xhormas!"

The dark god seemed to pointedly ignore Leon's bait as more boulders were propelled into the city. Distant screams of terror and despair joined the cacophony of noise that came from the undead horde who had breached the walls and flooded the streets. Their defenses were in ruins and Xhormas was winning. Still, Leon felt the need to stand against him and defy the b'nei ha'elohim as much as he could.

"Even if you kill us all, you'll never be able to overthrow Adonai!" Leon hollered, as he ran inside the range of Xhormas' tentacles of darkness.

The dark god's glowing red eyes shifted to stare at Leon balefully. Their slight narrowing was all the warning Leon received, before a boulder crashed down on the spot where he had just stood.

Pour it on, Leon. He hates the name of God.

"Your entire war against Adonai is pointless, Xhormas. You made your choice to rebel against Him, and you chose wrong!"

Dodging, leaping, and continuing to evade Xhormas' repeated attacks, Leon poured every ounce of his righteous indignation into the words he yelled. He knew he had to keep Xhormas' focus on him and not the others.

"What kind of god can't even hit a simple Judge?"

"You'll consume the world and then what? You still won't be able to beat Adonai!"

"The true God will wipe the floor with you, Xhormas!"

Leon felt the earth around him shake as one huge tendril, which was entirely too close, blocked his path. Xhormas growled as he crashed another tendril down behind Leon. ***"Insect! I will torture your soul for a thousand years."***

Leon looked up, and saw that a third shadowy tentacle was flying down towards where he stood while the two other tentacles also slid towards him. Leon's body tensed, and he pictured his friends' faces as he braced for the end. Pressing his eyes shut, Leon hoped that his small distraction had given his loved ones enough time to recover and flee. Sonorous, sinister laughter echoed all around him as the darkness closed in.

Suddenly, the laughter was replaced by a familiar hum that grew louder and louder.

A light pierced through Leon's closed eyelids, and he cracked them open to peek through them. Scintillating light burst out of the aeonyte that covered him. Brighter than ever before, it reacted violently with the tentacles that attempted to bind him. Mere inches from his face, the tentacles shook fiercely from the light's contact. Salt and ash swirled, falling like rain all around him, and Leon began to relax his muscles in amazement that he was not dead.

A still small voice in Leon's right ear pierced through both Revelator's hum, and the now faint, though still somehow thunderous, scream of rage that came from the dark god who sought to crush him.

"I AM love, and there is no greater love than that one should lay down his life for his friend."

The unquestionable voice of Adonai blew like a rushing wind both around and through Leon. Hope blossomed within him like a fire that had been stoked back to life. The resignation of defeat melted away as the light that came from his armor and weapons held Xhormas at bay.

Before the words asking for help and strength could even form on his lips, Leon heard Adonai's voice again.

"I AM always with you, even to the end of this age."

Tears flowed freely from Leon's eyes as the awesome power of the God he served washed over him. Even when it seemed that he was about to lose everything, Adonai's promises and mercies never failed.

Willing himself to stand firm, and basking in the glow of the radiant aeonyte, Leon once again lifted his weapon. The א in Revelator's spearhead was a molten rainbow of light as he stabbed it upward. Xhormas screeched as a column of light pierced through, and cut off, the tendril hovering over Leon. The dark god must have recoiled his appendages, causing the darkness that surrounded him to fade, and revealing the plateau and ruined ziggurat upon which Xhormas had enthroned himself. Xhormas' red glowing eyes stared at Leon, widened in shock, as his cut shadowy tentacle dissolved away into salt and ash.

Xhormas' eyes narrowed again, warning Leon a split second before another tentacle threw a boulder at his location. Leon dove through the air and leapt up as the projectile cut through the air in its effort to obliterate him. He angled himself towards another one of the tentacles, which was delving into the ziggurat's ruins, presumably to pull out more boulders. No longer afraid of the massive god's shadowy appendages, Leon leapt and punched straight through the darkness – causing his spearhead and aeonyte to both flash.

Landing, Leon was first aware of the salt and ash that blew away behind him, then he immediately knew that he needed to move again. A rumble of rock repeatedly crashing into the nearby ground accompanied the vaulting leaps and bounds that Leon attacked with. With each boulder dodged, Leon retaliated. Slicing piece after piece of Xhormas' writhing figure off.

Over time, Xhormas grew visibly frantic and desperate. Multiple megalithic stones came crashing down at him, but Leon ducked, leaped over, and even propelled himself off of some of them. Grim, implacable determination fueled every leap he took toward danger. Leon knew that Adonai was with him, and with that knowledge there was nothing Xhormas could do that would make him waver. With each strike against the shadows, parts of Xhormas were dissolved and carried away on the wind. When Leon's jumps brought his ship into view, he could see that the *Esperella's* dented and ruined hull had begun to glow brighter, purging the darkness around it.

In fact, Leon was almost certain that Xhormas was shrinking. The leaps he made using his spear and levigem were becoming lower to the ground, and he found himself able to attack the direct mass of Xhormas more frequently. The hum that sounded from Revelator grew in intensity, and upon landing from his most recent assault Leon bellowed.

"XHORMAS!"

Leon ran and leaped straight toward the god of undeath with Revelator outstretched. As with the many times before, Leon didn't feel the blade meet any resistance. It just passed straight into the shadowy substance that formed Xhormas, and the dark god cried out in protest. Shadow coalesced, constricting down like a bubble around Leon and the light that radiated from him. Like two giant hands that were trying to hold Leon at bay, the darkness attempted to restrain him. The darkness, however, could not overcome the light. Leon continued to step forward, dissolving Xhormas with each footfall, tearing the dark god apart, until its red eyes were all the way down to Leon's level.

Higher pitched, but no less menacing, Xhormas' voice cried out, *"This... this changes nothing! You will all be nothing but tools. That is all you are. Tools and playthings! He does not care–"*

"Except He does care. Adonai cares, and you do not. That is why you need JUDGEMENT!"

With another step forward, Xhormas' scream was cut off, and Revelator's hum faded. Light exploded outwards from Leon's shield and armor, from the nearby airship, and from Revelator. A wave of light, once only found in Leon's dream, exploded all around him, expanding and leaving particles floating in the air. The dark clouds above parted and were dissipated by the light. Sunlight shone down from the sky, basking Leon in a warmth that he was all too familiar with.

Beyond the stone bridge, the wave of light rolled through the city. Leon could see flashes erupt along the ground in the distance, and puffs of salt filled the air above the streets. The undead horde was being annihilated by the light wave that washed through the town. The warmth that filled Leon's heart confirmed what his eyes were witnessing.

They had won.

The war was over.

Distant cheers accompanied his rush back to the airship, but a wet cough from nearby snagged his attention. Running towards the sound, Leon saw it had come from the body of Lucien Rhise. He scrambled over to the broken man, saw that his chest barely rose and fell with shallow breaths, and his face, though deathly pale, had eyes that were still moving. Those eyes locked on Leon, and another cough escaped Lucien's lips as Leon knelt over the man. Leon wondered how Lucien had survived this long with the blade of his glaive still stuck in his abdomen.

"L…Le–" Lucien began, but Leon saw the blood staining his teeth.

"Don't try to talk." Leon soothed. The man who lay before him had caused so much hurt in his life. So much pain. Just the day before he had wished for Leon's death.

Why am I tearing up over him?

Lucien blinked a few times, and wheezed once more. He persisted in his effort to speak, and slowly the words came, "I-I'm… s-s…"

A lump formed in Leon's throat, and tears rolled down his cheeks unchecked.

"Sor-ry." Lucien whispered, as moisture filled his own eyes.

Leon sobbed tears that represented the many years of hurt he had suffered. How long had he waited to hear those words? His whole life. For some reason, they were uttered here. Now. The victory he had felt in his heart was tinged with a hint of bitterness. Lucien had caused so much pain, and had helped orchestrate this entire battle. Willingly or unwillingly, Lucien had been a tool that inflicted pain upon pain on countless people, not just Leon.

Even so, Leon knew his charge. He knew what had to be done, regardless of how hard it was.

"I… I forgive you." Leon shut his eyes to blink them clear of the tears that kept flowing. Sniffing, Leon tried again, "I forgive you. Just as I am forgiven. You are forgiven too if you just accept it. Lucien, accept Adonai, and everything will be okay for you! Just–"

When Leon's eyes opened he knew that Lucien Rhise was gone. His body no longer held his soul. Leon didn't know if his former father would rise as an undead within minutes. He didn't even know if that would still happen to anyone anymore. Xhormas was a defeated foe, and the dark god's lingering influence at this point was unknown. The day before Lucien had rejected Adonai, but maybe Leon's voice had gotten through to him in his last few moments. Maybe with his last thought he had welcomed Adonai into his heart.

All Leon knew for sure was that for whatever reason, even as the cheers of the living rose through the town and by the *Esperella*, he couldn't stop crying over the unchanged body of Lucien Rhise.

Chapter 24: The Reunion

When Leon finally felt ready to stand and depart from his father's lifeless form, he noticed a small group had gathered in the distance. Liara and his mother stood holding hands, their silent tears a sign of their shared grief. Hugs of sympathy, along with tears of joy, could be seen all around. Leon joined his mother and sister, and they solemnly stood together – their loss weighing on them amidst the sea of joy. After a few minutes, Leon turned away to let his mother and sister grieve with each other. He headed towards Duamé, Miala and Kelleren, who were all respectfully waiting for him. Leon cast them a tired smile, and with arms wide open they clasped each other's shoulders, forming a tight circle around Kelleren.

"You went off on your own, again," Miala chided.

Leon looked into her eyes, "I had to protect you all. Turns out it was the only–"

"I'm not mad, I just don't like it when you leave." She clarified.

"Woof!" Kelleren opined, just before Miala scratched behind his ears.

"There's no way I coulda kept up with ya down there anyway." Duamé commented, before he peeked around Leon's shoulder to look behind him. "Ya alright lad? Whatcha had ta do… facin' yer ol' da and all…"

Leon took the chance that presented itself to begin explaining Lucien's possession to them. The crowd around them grew as more people walked and hobbled from the *Esperella*, and he continued on to describe Adonai's intervention. With each face he saw, Leon's gratitude increased. Schalae, Princess Giselle and King Garinth, Kérik and Ophelia, Gérda and the children… More and more people streamed from the grounded aircraft, looking around in obvious wonder at the battle's aftermath. Some dropped to their knees and wept, while others let out celebratory shouts or listened to Leon's account of facing Xhormas.

With the ziggurat and its bridge in ruins, Leon thought there would be no way for the people from the city to ascend the plateau. Just as that thought registered in his mind, the sleek shape of the *Golem* rose from the depths of the chasm. It alone was the only airship still capable of flying. The rest of the fleet's ruined vessels were dotted throughout the city and lands beyond. Leon's eyes anxiously scanned the transport for the two small figures who stood at the nearest railing. A loud, piercing voice, from the figure with shaking purple pigtails, cried out in a frenzy:

"WHAT IN THE BLAZES DID YOU DO TO MY SHIP, PUFFBALL?"

Gionna and Magnus, along with a few soldiers, disembarked from the *Golem* as soon as it landed. While everyone began recounting their experiences, Gionna and Kérik surveyed the *Esperella's* damage. The soldiers who had been on board immediately beelined for King Garinth after spotting him. According to their reports, which Leon overheard when he joined them, the undead forces had indeed turned to salt, and not one undead enemy remained to be found. They also confirmed that the walls had been fully breached and the city invaded, which had led to substantial loss of life. Approximately a quarter of their ground forces were gone, and with the exception of the *Golem*, the entirety of their naval air forces had been annihilated. Almost the entirety of Xaelon's higher-level military command structure had been wiped out within the ziggurat, which left a significant hole that needed to be filled in their leadership.

That thought reminded Leon of King Garinth's plan to crown him as the new king once they won the war. His real father must have had similar thoughts running through his mind, because at that exact moment King Garinth turned toward Leon and said, "You have exemplified real leadership skill here today. More than I could have dreamed possible. I would be honored to retire and pass the crown to you, despite Master Onyxwill's claims about your shortcomings. Those things can be learned."

Leon mentally cringed, though he was too tired from the battle to put up an argument at the moment. A quick glance cast at Princess Giselle confirmed that she was also not very happy about the king's statement. She had previously called both Leon and herself pawns of the king's will, and told him that his being used as a replacement for Prince Gelan would make him an even more vulnerable target.

Gionna returned from surveying the damage inflicted upon the *Esperella*, habitually tapping a finger against her mechanical glasses. "Your Majesty," she began, "far be it for me to countermand your wishes, but as I have firsthand knowledge of Leon's shortcomings with regard to economics, I would caution you that crowning him would prove disastrous."

"Disastrous?" Leon protested.

"Absolutely, dearie. The surviving lords and ladies would soon begin taking advantage of your lack of business sense. The royal treasury would likely be bankrupt within weeks."

"Weeks?" The king's face blanched as he stared at Leon with a horrified expression.

"May I propose an alternate solution?" Gionna queried.

The rebuilding process had begun quickly after their final battle. All of their dead needed to be buried, and the repairs to Last Bastion city were determined to be of paramount importance. The *Golem* had been dispatched to retrieve help from Masterwork Halls, and within a matter of days a delegation returned to assist Last Bastion in their recovery efforts. Thanks to the coordinated help of the few remaining dwarven geomancers, and others who were skilled at such things, the ziggurat at Last Bastion began its transformation into a castle. The former structure gave Leon, and many others, uncomfortable reminders of everyone who had been lost during their fight for survival. By creating a new structure from the rubble, it was as if the kingdom was proclaiming its rebirth. Xaelon would endure; beauty would be brought forth from the ashes, even if it meant starting from scratch.

Relationships had also budded and grown after the war ended. Regardless of the task, whether it was harvesting crops, completing repairs to homes or to the *Esperella*, or helping to build Last Bastion's castle, Miala remained by Leon's side. She didn't depart from him even when his presence was required during numerous planning sessions and council meetings. Leon never tired of her companionship. After all, he always found her warm smile far more captivating than any of the progress reports and figures being discussed.

It also became impossible to ignore King Garinth's feelings towards Leon's mother. It seemed that the only barrier preventing them from pursuing one another was propriety. Lucien Rhise had had his faults, but he was still given a proper burial next to Laric's recovered body. While it was blatantly apparent to Leon that his mother and the King wanted a relationship, he understood that it was definitely too soon. But, as the months passed, and a mild winter gave way to a welcome spring, it was announced that the last stone had been set on the castle, and that King Garinth Galcyon would wed Lady Erika. It proved to be just the type of exciting event for the entire kingdom to rally around, lending hope to the masses.

More weeks flew past, swallowed in the whirlwind of grand wedding plans. When the much anticipated day finally arrived, Leon found himself glad to be out of the limelight, and relegated to guard duty.

"Leon, I realize that you have an uncanny ability to crash engagement parties and weddings, but please do try to just be nice and sociable today." His mother called out from inside her dressing room.

"Yes, Mother." Leon replied, while he fidgeted and tugged at the uncomfortable formal wear that he was quite unaccustomed to. While grateful that puffy sleeves and voluminous color-coordinated gowns were only required for the ladies, and that he had only been forced to wear a dress shirt and jacket, the garb still left him feeling incredibly unprotected. Being assigned to guard the womenfolk while they arranged their hair and fussed over their gowns was something Leon took seriously. Plenty of courtiers and passerbys attempted to gain entry into their room under the pretense of discussing event details, but Leon would have none of it. A scowl, paired with a recommendation to seek out the event's organizer, Countess Serina, successfully turned away most. Lorog, who also stood guard at the room, had to occasionally growl at a few of the most persistent people. Those obnoxious courtiers were usually quick to scamper away after that.

Leon looked over to the orc who was currently leaning against the stone wall. Dressed in actual armor instead of formal wear, Lorog shifted uncomfortably on his new wooden foot. Gionna had specially made it for him after the orc had defended the Archives during the final battle. His defense efforts had left him maimed, but the grateful inventor ensured that he hadn't stayed incapacitated for long. Lorog's family had also survived the battle, and Leon had helped the steadfast orc continue to provide for his family by promoting him to Captain, and filling one of the voids within their military's leadership. Though his prosthetic foot had been an adjustment, Lorog had adapted quickly, and then made sure that everyone knew it did not slow him down.

"What is it, Sir?" Lorog asked after he caught Leon staring.

"If you need to sit or take a walk, Captain…" Leon began.

"I'll be fine, Sir. Just grateful to still be alive." Lorog intoned, as he had numerous times before.

"Is he here yet?" Miala called from within the room.

"No… Wait, there he is!" Leon replied.

Duamé had just rounded a corner down the hall, dressed in finery that could only have been rivaled by royalty. A maroon silk shirt and black pants replaced the toolbelt and stained work shirt the dwarf normally wore. Since becoming the official liaison between Masterwork Halls and Last Bastion, and cashing in on his portion of the fortune from the Strongarm Smithy chain, Duamé had become quite well off. It had been a couple of months since Leon had last seen Duamé, but he knew the dwarf had been busy settling into his newly appointed role while also courting Gérda. The two dwarves had hit it off after the battle, and they had taken two of the mancer children back to Masterwork Halls with them. Gérda had shown herself to be fiercely protective of Tyne, Sam, and their thrown-together family unit. Duamé hadn't batted an eye when she told him the children were to live in Masterwork Halls with her, as she had all but adopted the orphaned orc and gnome mancers.

Duamé let out a joyous shout and shook Lorog's hand before gripping Leon in a bearhug. "How've ya been boyo? Ya look great!"

"And you as well, Duamé. How is–"

The cries of joy continued when Miala crept out of the dressing room. She was breathtaking in her pale green bridesmaid dress, and the way her red hair was pinned back begged Leon to run his hand through it. "Where's Kelleren?" Duamé asked.

Miala closed her eyes and concentrated before a broad smile lit her face. "He's practicing in the main hall. It took a while to explain the concept to him, but now he's excited to carry the rings up the aisle. Where are Gérda and the boys?"

"Gettin' seated with tha elven royalty. Gérda was askin' about Brigid on tha way here. Speakin' of–"

Brigid shyly poked her head out from the dressing room. Her pale green gown was simpler than Miala's, but satisfactory to her. Ever since the end of the war, the young girl had been stuck to Miala like glue. After much discussion, Miala and Leon agreed that they would both look after her, much like Duamé and Gérda looked after Sam and Tyne. Leon had re-read the letter from Calvin prior to making any decisions about it, just to make sure they were doing the right thing. The chronomancer told him that the kids were important to the future, but he hadn't said how. Leon could see the usefulness of Sam's supernatural strength, Brigid's icy aquamancy, and Tyne's own chronomancy, but he hoped they wouldn't have to use their powers much since there had been no undead sightings over the last half a year.

Brigid looked all around the hallway behind Duamé before she asked, "Tyne? Sam?"

Duamé reiterated, "They're finding seats fer tha weddin' little miss."

Her pleading gaze landed on Miala, which elicited a rich laugh as the pyromancer chortled, "Of course you can go join them. Just be on the lookout for the procession."

Brigid smiled and nodded enthusiastically. Then, after giving Leon, Duamé, and Lorog silent hugs, she all but ran down the hallway to look for her friends. Duamé waited until she was gone before he turned to Miala and asked, "Still tha quiet type?"

"We're working on it." Miala answered. From what she and Leon had been able to ascertain from Brigid, she had been captive in the Dark Room for years. The pain and suffering of that place was practically all she had ever known. Which, Miala had explained, was why Brigid's power was so incredible. The trauma mancers suffered is what sparked their unnatural abilities, so it was no wonder that her powers rivaled Miala's at such a young age. Still, Miala made every attempt to not only help the girl heal emotionally, but to also harness and control her powers for good.

The familiar tap of a metallic cane against the ground preceded Gionna Gærheart as she exited the dressing room. She wore a pale green shirt, which clashed with her purple pigtails. More functional, her clothes were accompanied by a few pouches and various trinkets slung around her tiny frame. The inventor was set in her ways, and not even a formal occasion would change her. "What is going on out he… Oh, hello, dearie! It's been a bit."

Another round of pleasantries were exchanged, then Duamé said, "I talked ta Magnus out there before I came back here. Looks like married life agrees with him."

"Third time's the charm. For Mags and I at least." Gionna clarified. "I think with our newfound respect for each other, and our acceptance of who we are in Adonai, we can make it stick this time. When I think of all the time we wasted…" Gionna trailed off and shook her head, "What's done is done though, and we are moving forward, dearies. Between Magnus heading the Archives, and my new position at the Innovation Institute, we are quite busy but enjoying our time."

"Okay everyone, it's time!" Leon's mother exclaimed as she joined everyone in the hall. Rows of pearls and peridots were woven and criss-crossed throughout her intricately designed dress, all cascading down into a long train that a beaming Liara currently held. Everyone oohed and aahed their approval, and Lady Erika graciously curtsied to each of them as she spoke. "Thank you all so much for your support. Really though, it's just a dress. What's important is the ceremony."

"Mother, you look radiant." Leon commented.

"Thank you, but the true thanks goes to your friend here." Erika replied as she gestured to Gionna. The gnome's mischievous eyes were magnified in her clockwork spectacles as she waved her cane about dismissively. "It was nothing I did. You had to decide to rekindle whatever spark you had with his majesty in the first place. Now you two can go off and enjoy yourselves while Princess Giselle manages the kingdom and a legitimized Leon helps to oversee the military. When I stirred that pot it just seemed… prudent."

"I am not complaining, Gionna. I simply have you to thank for playing matchmaker. This was what you envisioned, correct?"

"More or less, dearie. More or less."

As they all walked and talked down the hall, Leon saw Duamé covertly trying to get his attention. They slowed their gaits to trail slightly behind the rest of their group, and Duamé hissed, "Oi. Meat shield."

"What?"

"Check yer pocket." Duamé whispered.

Leon patted at his dress pants pockets and felt a small lump that hadn't been there a few minutes before. *Duamé must have slipped it there when we hugged.* Leon reached in, felt what it was, and grew wide eyed as he whispered back, "It's done?"

"Whaddaya think, genius?"

Leon risked slowing his pace even further, letting the ladies travel ahead, then turned his back to them and pulled out the item to examine it. Loose braids of white gold and aeonyte were woven together in an intricate lattice pattern. It continued all the way around the ring until the gossamer metal strands twisted and swirled into prongs where a circular cut diamond was securely seated. Leon had given the basic idea, ring size, and instructions to Duamé months earlier, but hadn't expected it to be done so quickly. After all, they both had a lot on their plates these days. Still, just holding the ring in his hands caused a shiver of excitement to race through his body.

"It's perfect, Duamé!" Leon whispered.

"Course it is! Had ta use me new tools an' everything."

"What's perfect?" A suspicious voice asked from behind them.

Leon palmed the ring as he and Duamé turned back around to see Miala's suspicious expression. The rest of the ladies were close behind her, and they all looked at Leon and Duamé expectantly. Lorog was near the front of the group, and took the opportunity to learn against the stone corridor as he waited for everyone. The captain's tusked grin was telling, since he knew of Leon's plans to propose to Miala.

Amidst the excitement of actually getting the ring, Leon realized his error of stopping to examine it. Miala's keen scrutiny now demanded an answer he hadn't planned on providing yet. Gionna started to chortle as she used her special glasses lenses to peer at Leon and the ring.

"Leon? What is it?" Miala asked again, a smile trying to tug at her lips.

Left with everyone in the hallway staring at him, Leon could think of nothing else to do but get on one knee in front of Miala. Last Bastion's cold stone floor was unforgiving on his knee, but he pointedly tried to ignore it. Miala's hands shot up to hide her grin as he began to fumble his way through an impromptu proposal.

"Well, um… Miala, I wanted to ask, uh–"

"Yes." She said, slightly muffled by her hand.

Why is it so confoundingly hard to talk to her sometimes?

"Would you do me the-the honor of, well that is, I would be honored if-if you would… Oh!"

Leon's shaking hands almost dropped the ring. He juggled it a few times as it bounced from his sweaty palms. Finally catching it, Leon held it up to her as the onlookers who had crept closer gasped and crooned over its intricacy.

"Yes." Miala repeated, just as Leon blurted out, "Miala, will you marry me?"

"Leon!" Miala exclaimed.

"Wh-what?" Leon asked.

Miala gently clasped Leon's face and tugged him up off his knee. He stood in front of her, and slowly realized that she had been answering him the whole time. Miala enunciated her response once more, and everything in Leon rejoiced.

"Yes!"

After the royal wedding between King Garinth and Leon's mother, another ceremony was held to announce Princess Giselle as the new Queen. While the royal wedding had been a fairly simple affair, Giselle's crowning was filled with as much pomp and celebration as possible. She represented a new direction and future for Xaelon; a future that many had thought impossible. The joy that stemmed from the populace was overwhelming, and it seemed as if every citizen of Xaelon made sure to be present for both events. Thousands lined Last Bastion's rebuilt stone bridge and filled the streets beyond, all desiring to witness the crown being placed on Giselle's head.

She maintained her demure composure throughout the entire ceremony, but Leon knew Giselle was overjoyed by the day that she had thought would never come.

Her first act as queen of Xaelon was to announce Leon as Lord Protector of the kingdom. It was a new title, and it essentially gave him command of Xaelon's military. With the undead defeated, and any who died remaining dead, the armies of the kingdom suddenly found themselves without an adversary to fight. They still needed structure and organization though, and without any generals to replace Xiphos and Ciaye, it was decided that Leon would lead them. He would work with his half-sister to guide and protect the kingdom as they rebuilt.

After her coronation and his promotion, while the onlookers were dispersing back to their homes, Leon announced his and Miala's engagement to his family and friends. Miala gushed over her engagement ring with Liara and Giselle, and Leon received so many congratulatory pats on the back that he wished he still had on his armor. So much had happened in such a short time that the day seemed like a blur to Leon.

Successfully navigating all of the events of the day left Leon exhausted. Finding it hard to sleep in the soft, oversized bed that was in his new room, Leon stripped the blankets from it and laid them on the floor. Being used to hard surfaces and hammocks, Leon quickly drifted off to sleep and was surprised to find the grey expanse waiting for him. He had not had one of these dreams since before the climactic battle against Xhormas.

The dreamscape wasn't as dreary as before though. Along with the gigantic ball of light in the sky, ribbons of color would occasionally burst forth around Leon. There was so much more vibrancy in the dream now, and Leon looked all around in wonder.

"Congratulations on your engagement."

Rohiel and Lochemetel both spoke as they stepped forward, appearing in front of Leon. They were still in their aeonyte armor, and Leon felt underdressed in his pajamas. Nevertheless, the two advisors both approached, stopping just a few steps away. Leon was used to averting his eyes from Rohiel's shining head, but now it blazed brighter than it ever had before and he had trouble even looking in that general direction. "Thank you both, but what happened? Why haven't I seen either of you for a while?"

"As you have been busy, so have we. The adversary is imprisoned, but there are still others who rebel. Others who reject Adonai and his unfailing love." Lochemetel replied.

Leon almost missed the meaning in their cryptic response. Almost. But based on the warrior angel's words several questions and concerns burst from him. "Wait, Xhormas is imprisoned? I thought he was destroyed! I thought the war was over!"

"Xhormas and his spawn were bound by your efforts, Judge. They are imprisoned in Tartaroo, where they await their final judgement. It is a prison meant for their kind, one from which they cannot escape. Your Dead Wars are over, and Xhormas will influence your world no more. But there are other powers and principalities out there. Other b'nei ha'elohim and Nephilim that defy the one true God. Others who would seek to supplant him, and taint creation to suit their will. It is a futile effort, but they have chosen their fates." Rohiel responded.

Crushing disappointment filled Leon. He felt as though his efforts hadn't been enough, that he would somehow have to keep fighting these entities over and over again until it was time for him to die. "Can we tell them to back off for a while? Maybe let us enjoy some peace and quiet?"

An ethereal chuckle filled the air. It was a sound that brought a warmth inside of Leon as Lochemetel replied, ***"There is a time for peace, and a time for war. Enjoy the peace while you can."***

I could certainly use some peace. Leon thought. There was still a lot to do to rebuild the kingdom. Leon had already assigned the remnants of Xaelon's military to reclaim towns and cities, as well as to rebuild the airship navy. He enjoyed the kingdom's rebuilding process far more than any fighting. Being the Lord Protector was all well and good, but Leon inwardly hoped that he wouldn't have to do much protecting for a while. Even though he had gained new titles of 'Prince' and 'Lord Protector', Leon couldn't help feeling that he was also losing one.

"Does…does this mean I am no longer a Judge?" Leon asked sheepishly.

"All the days of your life you will be Judge Leon. How effective you will be as a Judge is entirely up to you. Adonai will raise up other Judges after you, just like there were Judges before you. Your world still needs leaders. People who can show the love of Adonai, and keep his tenets. Know them. Live them."

"I will." Leon nodded, relief flooding through him as a wave of light pulsed from above. It washed over and through him, leaving an indescribable warmth and feeling of joy. An understanding of what he could continue to do filled him. He would live each day for Adonai. Adonai's tenets of love, joy, peace, patience, kindness, goodness, faithfulness, gentleness, and self-control would continue to be what he showed the world around him.

"Good. Then this is where we must part, Leon." Rohiel said.

The comfort of the light that washed through him became bittersweet as Leon asked, "Will I ever see you two again?"

"When you pass from your world to the next, we will be there to greet you as friends." Lochemetel replied. ***"Until then, you must keep the faith."***

"Thank you. For… everything."

"You are quite welcome, my friend. Until we meet again." Rohiel responded.

Another wave of light burst from overhead, and as it hit Leon, he disappeared from the dream and passed back into a restful sleep.

Rohiel sighed contentedly before he turned to Lochemetel. ***"Continue to protect him and his family in the time ahead. You are, as always, a wonderful and skilled guardian."***

"As you command." Lochemetel replied, before walking a short distance away and disappearing as well.

For a few moments, Rohiel stood by himself, patiently waiting and enjoying the dreamworld's scenery. Creation, in its complexity, was quite beautiful when one could stop to enjoy it. The light above radiated warmth, and when it pulsed again another figure materialized nearby in its wake. The young person looked about in panic and confusion, wrapping their arms around their stomach as concern welled up inside them.

Rohiel stepped forward to address the next Judge Adonai had chosen, and as he did so, he spoke words of reassurance. Words that Adonai wished all to know in the midst of the great war that raged across creation. Words that were a foundation for faith in Adonai to be built upon. Words that should infuse and dwell inside the heart of every believer.

"Have no fear."

Author's Note

When I started writing this series, I had a mission that resonated within me: entertain, educate, and evangelize.

I hope and pray that you have been entertained as you have fought alongside Leon and his friends. I hope that some of the things you saw along his journey educated you to the spiritual war that is being waged all around us. Finally, I hope this story evangelized to you and resonated with your own spiritual journey. Whether you have yet to come to faith, are a newfound Christian, or have been a believer for many years, this story is for you.

This part of Leon's journey as a Judge is over, but I would dare say that this may not be the last you see of him and his companions.

What is next in this world? Well, that is in part, up to you, the reader. You can spread the word about this book series to everyone you know, create inspired art to be posted on the website, or even email to say who you want to see more of in future works. I would greatly appreciate it though, if you would take a few minutes to rate or review the books and the series wherever you can. Until next time, let your light shine!

Acknowledgements

Thank you to all of those who believed in me from the beginning. Without you, and your persistent, incessant needling to get this series done, I never would have in such a time.

A special shout-out goes to Pastor Derrick Rawlings and the people at Freedom Worship Center.

Mack, your friendship is a treasure.

Thank you to my writer's group for the inspiration and accountability through this process.

Thank you to those who have done the research. Everyone at SkywatchTV, as well as Dr. Michael Heiser, Derek and Sharon Gilbert, Tyler Gilreath, and Mike Stibs.

Kenny Seay, you are a fantastic man of God, and I truly cherish our growing friendship.

Thank you to my family for believing in me, even when I didn't.

Finally, thank you again to Jesus Christ of Nazareth, for everything you have done and will do. I will continue to work for you as long as I live.

Bible Verses

He reveals the deep things of darkness and brings utter darkness into the light. - Job 12:22 (NIV)

"The people living in darkness have seen a great light; on those living in the land of the shadow of death a light has dawned." -Matthew 4:12 (NIV)

"My people are destroyed for lack of knowledge: because thou hast rejected knowledge, I will also reject thee, that thou shalt be no priest to me: seeing thou hast forgotten the law of thy God, I will also forget thy children." - Hosea 4:6 (ESV)

The thief comes only to steal and kill and destroy. I came that they may have life and have it abundantly. - John 10:10 (ESV)

"Rejoice with him, O heavens; bow down to him, all gods, for he avenges the blood of his children and takes vengeance on his adversaries. He repays those who hate him and cleanses his people's land." - Deuteronomy 32:43 (ESV)

And we know that in all things God works for the good of those who love him, who[a] have been called according to his purpose. -Romans 8:28 (NIV)

For if you remain silent at this time, relief and deliverance for the Jews will arise from another place, but you and your father's family will perish. And who knows but that you have come to your royal position for such a time as this?" - Esther 4:14 (NIV)

"You are the salt of the earth. But if the salt loses its saltiness, how can it be made salty again? It is no longer good for anything, except to be thrown out

and trampled underfoot. You are the light of the world. A town built on a hill cannot be hidden. 15 Neither do people light a lamp and put it under a bowl. Instead they put it on its stand, and it gives light to everyone in the house. 16 In the same way, let your light shine before others, that they may see your good deeds and glorify your Father in heaven." - Matthew 5:13-16 (NIV)

"And then I saw four wheels beside the cherubim, one beside each cherub. The wheels radiating were sparkling like diamonds in the sun. All four wheels looked alike, each like a wheel within a wheel. When they moved, they went in any of the four directions but in a perfectly straight line. Where the cherubim went, the wheels went straight ahead. The cherubim were full of eyes in their backs, hands, and wings. The wheels likewise were full of eyes. I heard the wheels called 'wheels within wheels.'" - Ezekiel 10:9–13 (ESV)

There are six things the Lord hates, seven that are detestable to him: haughty eyes, a lying tongue, hands that shed innocent blood, a heart that devises wicked schemes, feet that are quick to rush into evil, a false witness who pours out lies, and a person who stirs up conflict in the community. - Proverbs 6:16-19 (NIV)

Then he said to the man, "Stretch out your hand." And the man stretched it out, and it was restored, healthy like the other. - Matthew 12:13 (ESV)

Heal me, O LORD, and I shall be healed; Save me, and I shall be saved, For You are my praise. - Jeremiah 17:14 (ESV)

The light shines in the darkness, and the darkness has not overcome it. - John 1:5 (ESV)

A time to love, and a time to hate; a time for war, and a time for peace. - Ecclesiastes 3:8 (ESV)

Greater love has no one than this, that one should lay down his life for his friends. - John 15:13 (BLB)

Therefore, if anyone is in Christ, he is a new creation. The old has passed away; behold, the new has come. - 2 Corinthians 5:17 ESV

www.ingramcontent.com/pod-product-compliance
Lightning Source LLC
Chambersburg PA
CBHW030422310726
48979CB00009B/1581/J

9781736998984